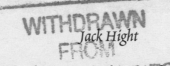

Jack Hight

Jack Hight has a doctorate in history from the University of Chicago. He lives with his wife, children and dog in Washington, DC. Hight is the author of three acclaimed previous novels: *Siege*, and the first two parts of his Saladin Trilogy, *Eagle* and *Kingdom*. All are available from John Murray.

Praise for Jack Hight

'This is an ambitious book, written on an ambitious scale, offering a fascinating picture of momentous events' *Daily Mail*

'Action, politics and drama are the hallmarks of this excellent series which gives a fascinating and balanced insight into one of the most turbulent periods in world history' *Lancashire Evening Post*

'Excellent . . . a trip to a distant and dangerous era' Barry Forshaw

'An interesting look at a fascinating historical figure, and time and place are conveyed powerfully throughout . . . Recommended' *Historical Novels Review*

'There are times when you come across a book that piques your interest, especially when its subject is one you are very interested in learning about. You know there will be some artistic licence, but you want the story to be as factual as it possibly can and also entertain you. Jack Hight has done all of that with a truly majestic account' *sir-readalot.blogspot.co.uk*

'Well researched, the characters are all strong and believable, while the action sequences are exciting and believable . . . Fans of this ge   *Novels Review*

Also by Jack Hight

Siege
Eagle
Kingdom

Holy War

Book Three of the Saladin Trilogy

JACK HIGHT

JOHN MURRAY

First published in Great Britain in 2013 by John Murray (Publishers)
An Hachette UK Company

First published in paperback in 2013

1

© Jack Hight 2013

Maps drawn by Rosie Collins

A CIP catalogue record for this title is available from the British Library

ISBN 978-1-84854-537-3
Ebook ISBN 978-1-84854-536-6

Typeset in Monotype Bembo by Servis Filmsetting Ltd, Stockport, Cheshire

Printed and bound by Clays Ltd, St Ives plc

John Murray policy is to use papers that are natural, renewable and recyclable products and made from wood grown in sustainable forests. The logging and manufacturing processes are expected to conform to the environmental regulations of the country of origin.

John Murray (Publishers)
338 Euston Road
London NW1 3BH

www.johnmurray.co.uk

For Cora

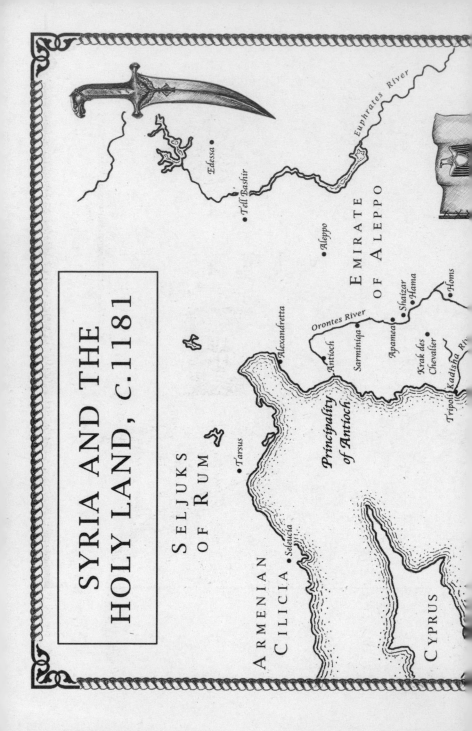

SYRIA AND THE
HOLY LAND, c.1181

SELJUKS
OF RUM

ARMENIAN
CILICIA · Seleucia

· Tarsus

· Edessa

· Tell Bashir

Euphrates River

· Aleppo

EMIRATE

OF ALEPPO

· Hama

· Shaizar

Orontes River

· Sarminija

Apamea ·

· Homs

Krak des
Chevalier ·

Alexandretta ·

· Antioch

Principality
of Antioch

Tripoli · Kadisha Ri

CYPRUS

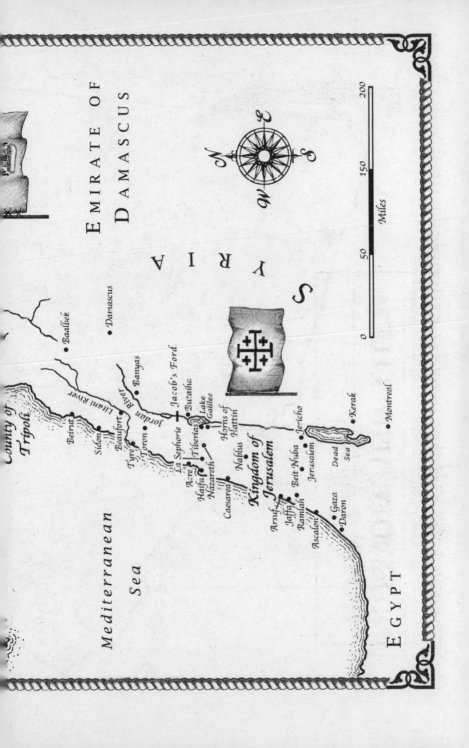

CRUSADER JERUSALEM

St Anne

Gate of Jehoshaphat

Golden Gate

Templum Domini

Jehoshaphat Street

Gates of Grief

Street of the Turners

Syrian Quarter

Spanish Street

St Stephen's Street

Syrian Exchange

Malquisinat

of Herbs

St Stephen's Gate

Church of the Holy Sepulchre

Patriarch's Palace

Patriarch Street

Patriarch's Quarter

Postern of Lazarus

Lepers' Quarter

Tancred's Tower

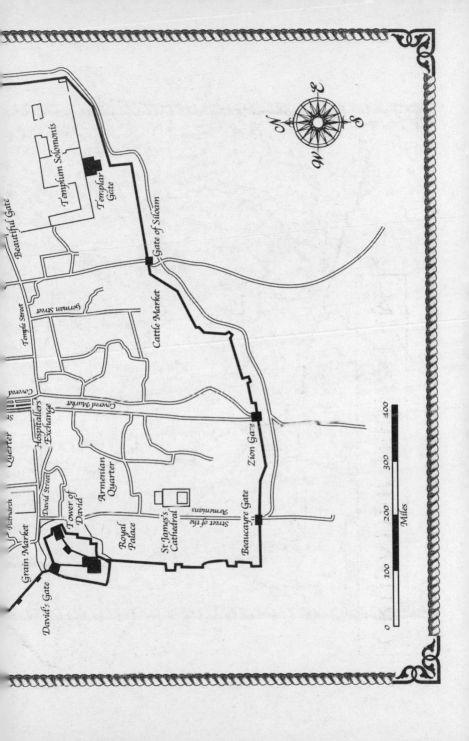

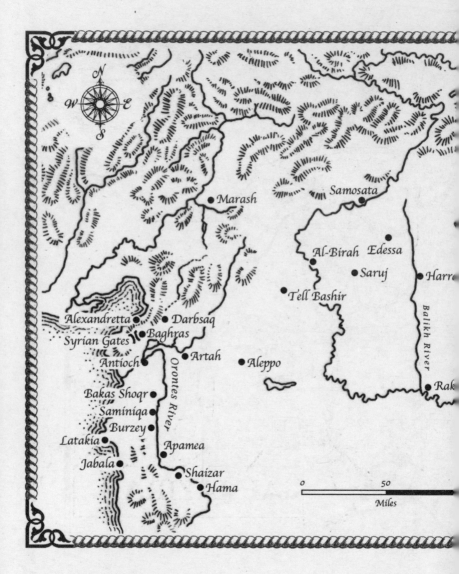

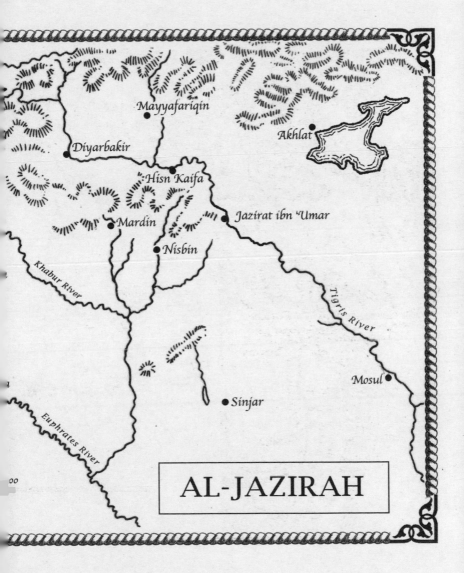

AL-JAZIRAH

Part I
Jerusalem

I was not with Saladin in the years following Montgisard, and I thank God for that. I had known him since he was a boy, but the man he became after his defeat was strange to me. He had vowed to take Jerusalem, and he set about his task with a ruthless energy that was frightful to behold, even at a distance. He unified his people as never before, forging competing emirs and enemy tribes into a single, dangerous weapon.

In Jerusalem, the king and his courtiers knew little enough of this. All they knew was that Saladin had turned his attention elsewhere, and that for the first time in many years there was peace. But they wasted it in vain squabbling for the throne, and when finally they saw the approaching danger, it was too late . . .

The Chronicle of Yahya al-Dimashqi

Chapter 1

Yusuf tugged his panther-skin cloak more tightly about him. The chill wind from the north brought with it a stinging rain and the sound of distant masons' hammers. The winter weather had not stopped construction on the citadel rising on the hills south of Cairo; nor would it prevent Yusuf's monthly inspection of his troops. The pennants that rose above the ranks of the army hung wet and limp, but the men beneath them sat straight in their saddles, despite the rain that soaked their caftans and beaded on their burnished mail.

'You have done well,' Yusuf told his younger brother. It had been Selim's task to rebuild the army after the disaster at Montgisard. Four years ago, Yusuf's army had marched to within a few miles of Jerusalem before being surprised and routed by the Christians. Yusuf had lost thousands of men. Afterwards, he had given his brother five years to rebuild the army. Selim had done it in four. The army before them was fifteen thousand men strong, larger than it had been before Montgisard. 'You have earned yourself a new name, brother: Saif ad-Din.'

'Shukran Allah.' Selim bowed in the saddle. 'Sword of Islam. It is a good name.'

Yusuf spurred forward to inspect the ranks. He rode past the mushtarawat: four thousand mounted men, all wearing saffron-yellow caftans over their mail to distinguish them as his personal troops. Each man carried a light bamboo spear in one hand and a small round shield in the other. Curved bows were tucked into their saddles and swords hung from their sides. The rain pinged off their steel helmets. They were Yusuf's most skilled warriors, and among them were some of his oldest friends. He nodded as he passed Husam, with his gold tooth, and Nazam, a bald-headed, lean man, quick as a snake. Yusuf acknowledged several other men, but it was the absences that struck him. The peerless archers Liaqat and Uwais and the giant Qadir had all fallen at Montgisard.

Beyond his yellow-clad warriors were his brother's mamluks and those of the emir Qaraqush. Some of them wore jawshan vests composed of hundreds of tiny steel plates sewn together. Others wore mail or padded cotton lined with steel plates. Next came the five thousand men of the light cavalry, all in padded vests and with only bows and light spears for arms. Last of all, Yusuf rode through the ranks of the infantry. The five thousand men carried tall shields and long spears, which would allow them to turn aside a cavalry charge.

When he had ridden past the final row, Yusuf turned his horse and cantered back to the front of the army. 'Are there any cases for me to hear?' he asked Qaraqush.

The stout emir with the grizzled beard nodded. 'Prisoners!' he shouted, and the guards herded forward three men. Yusuf was disappointed to see that one of them was his cousin, Nasir ad-Din. It was not the first time that the young man been brought before him. Nasir ad-Din had been a boy of only seven when his father Shirkuh died. He had been raised at the palace in Cairo, and had become fast friends with Yusuf's nephew, Ubadah. Yusuf had given his cousin Homs to rule, hoping that commanding others might teach him discipline, but Nasir ad-Din had not yet set foot in his lands. He preferred to stay in Cairo while he enjoyed the revenues from Homs. Qaraqush pointed to him. 'Nasir ad-Din was found drunk in the barracks with two women. One of them was married.'

Nasir ad-Din was thin as a stalk of wheat, and like a stalk of wheat he was trembling, though more likely from fear or shame than the cold wind. His eyes were fixed on the ground at Yusuf's feet.

'Look at me, Cousin,' Yusuf commanded. 'Explain yourself.'

'I – I meant no harm,' Nasir ad-Din began. He spoke haltingly at first, and then the words came out in a rush. 'Three of my men reached their eighteenth year this last month. They were freed and became full mamluks. A leader must share his men's joys as well as their pains. My father taught me that. I took them to Chandra's to celebrate. I fear I became quite drunk.'

'And the married woman? Who was she?'

'She never told me her name, Malik. She never told me she was married, either. I swear it! I—'

'Enough.' There was a time when Yusuf might have forgiven his cousin's indiscretions. After all, he too had once slept with another man's wife. But Yusuf had been a different man then, before Montgisard, before the desert. 'You have disgraced yourself and our family with your drunkenness and lewd actions,' he said sternly. 'There are few crimes more heinous than to sleep with another man's wife, and to do so in public, in the barracks amongst your men . . .' Yusuf shook his head. 'You will suffer ten blows from the lash, and you will pay a hundred dinars to the man you have wronged. As of tomorrow, you are banished from Cairo. Go to your lands in Homs and learn to rule justly and wisely. I pray for your sake that I do not hear further ill tidings of you.'

Nasir ad-Din opened his mouth to protest, then thought better of it. 'Yes, Malik.'

The next man to be brought forward was bald, with a fat face. His sodden caftan was plastered over a round belly 'Shaad is a cook,' Qaraqush declared. 'He has been found guilty of thievery.'

'Malik, I never! I have been a cook for twenty years and more. I served your uncle, Shirkuh. I—'

Yusuf drew his sword and the cook fell silent. 'What did he steal?'

'Each month, he kept some of the money intended to buy food for the troops.'

Shaad fell to his knees on the muddy ground. 'It was only the once, Malik. I swear it. Have mercy!'

Yusuf dismounted. 'You have grown fat on food that was intended for your fellow soldiers. You shall lose your post and suffer a thief's punishment.' He gestured to the guards, who grabbed the cook from behind. One of them stretched out his right arm. Another took a strip of cloth and tied it tightly just below the elbow, to staunch the flow of the blood that was to come. As Yusuf raised his sword, the cook thrashed and squirmed. 'I will have your hand,' Yusuf told him. 'Hold still if you want a clean cut.' Shaad ceased resisting, and Yusuf brought his sword down. The cook fainted, and the guards dragged him away, leaving his severed hand on the parade ground. Yusuf's gut burned, but he hardly noticed. It was always burning of late.

He returned to the saddle as the final prisoner was brought forward. The man was very handsome, with a trimmed black beard and golden eyes. 'What did this one do?'

'Rape, Malik. A glass merchant's daughter.'

'There are witnesses?'

Qaraqush gestured to four men in silk caftans. With them was a woman wearing a niqab that hid all but her eyes. 'Four men, as required by law, Malik.'

The prisoner met Yusuf's eye without flinching. 'It was no rape. She wanted it, Malik.'

'He lies!' one of the men in silk shouted. 'Look what he did to my daughter, Malik.' The woman removed her niqab. Her cheek was bruised, her lip split and bloodied. 'He has disgraced her. What sort of bride price will I find for her now?'

'The mamluk will be stoned to death as decreed by law,'

Yusuf declared. 'You shall be compensated for your loss. A hundred dinars.'

The father was bowing his thanks as Yusuf turned his horse and rode for Cairo with his guard trailing behind. He was cold and wet and in a black mood, as he often was after dispensing justice. He wanted nothing more than a hot bath and a warm meal, but that was not to be. No sooner had he shed his cloak in the palace entrance hall than Al-Fadil limped towards him. The tiny, hunchbacked secretary was suffering from gout.

'The birds have brought news,' Al-Fadil said. Yusuf frowned. 'It is important, Malik.'

'Walk with me,' Yusuf told him and continued on to his chambers.

'I have a letter from the Barka. The Almohad sultan is said to be preparing his fleet to move on Tripoli, on the African coast.'

Yusuf's forehead creased. He had sent Ubadah to conquer the coast west of Egypt over a year ago, but his nephew's victories had brought nothing but trouble. 'Reduce the size of the garrison. Inshallah, the sultan will take Tripoli from us. It has cost me more to keep the city than it pays in tribute.'

'Very good, Malik.' Al-Fadil took another message from one of the pockets that lined his silk robes. 'News from Alexandria. Two more ships have launched to join your new fleet.' Yusuf could only nod. He stopped for a moment and clutched at the wall, sweat beading on his brow as the pain twisted like a knife in his gut. 'Are you well, Malik?'

'A passing indisposition . . .' Yusuf straightened and continued down the hall. He could not think of Alexandria without thinking of Turan. Yusuf had sent his older brother to govern the city after his failure during the Montgisard campaign. In a few short months, Turan had run up debts of more than two hundred thousand gold dinars before he died of what was officially declared an excessive use of hashish. Yusuf knew better. It had been justice, but the memory of his brother's death still pained him.

When they reached Yusuf's study, Al-Fadil handed him a scrap of paper. 'I thought it best that you read this in private.'

Yusuf scanned the message, which was written in the minuscule script used for the pigeon post. Al-Salih was dead. The young man had been the ruler of Aleppo, and he was Yusuf's son, the product of his affair with Asimat when she was still the wife of his lord, Nur ad-Din. Yusuf dropped the message and went to stand at the window. His knuckles whitened as he gripped the ledge. 'It does not say how he died.'

'It appears he was murdered, Malik.'

'And who rules in Aleppo now?'

'The boy's cousin, Imad ad-Din. He was given the city by his brother, Izz ad-Din, who rules in Mosul.'

Yusuf turned to face Al-Fadil. 'That cannot be allowed to stand. You will begin setting aside coin for a campaign.'

'To Aleppo?'

'Mosul. Izz ad-Din is the true threat.' As ruler of Al-Jazirah, the fertile lands between the Tigris and the Euphrates, Izz ad-Din was rich in both money and men. Yusuf had met him when they were both young men at Nur ad-Din's court. Even then, Izz ad-Din had been ambitious. 'I cannot take Jerusalem if I must also defend Damascus from Izz ad-Din and his brother. We will march in the spring, when the winter rains have ended. Go now and tell my brother Saif ad-Din to begin gathering arms and provisions.'

'Very good, Malik.' Al-Fadil moved to the door, where he paused. 'One more thing. I have received news that your wife Asimat is on her way here from Aleppo.'

Yusuf had not seen Asimat in years. After their marriage, she had stayed in Aleppo with their son. He did not wish to face her now, but he could hardly refuse. 'You will make her comfortable when she arrives.'

Al-Fadil bowed and left. Yusuf returned to the window. He thought of those nights long ago in Aleppo, when he had snuck through the window of Asimat's chambers to be with her. They

8

had risked everything. They had made a child together. And now that child was dead.

The door behind Yusuf creaked open, and he turned to see Shamsa enter. His first wife was no longer the beauty she had been when he met her. Age had left fine wrinkles at the corners of her eyes and mouth, and had sharpened her features, making her cheekbones more prominent. But he still saw that enticing mixture of challenge and invitation in her dark eyes. She smiled, showing straight white teeth. Then, her smile faded. 'You are not well, habibi.'

'I am fine.'

She came to him and wrapped her arms around his waist. 'You work yourself too hard. Come. We must get you out of these wet clothes.' She began to untie the lacing that secured his vest of golden jawshan armour.

Yusuf gently pushed her away. 'There is work to be done, Wife. We will have war in the north.' He sat and placed a portable desk on his lap. He reached for a quill, but Shamsa plucked it from his hand.

'Surely that can wait until after you have had a bath. The roads will not be passable for some months.'

Yusuf picked up another quill. He did not want to bathe. He wanted to lose himself in work, to drive away his thoughts of Turan and Al-Salih and the man he had ordered stoned today. 'And we must be ready to ride when they are. I cannot allow Imad ad-Din time to build his strength in Aleppo.' Yusuf picked up a sheet of paper. His brow furrowed in concentration as he began composing a message to Al-Muqaddam, his governor in Damascus.

Shamsa watched him for a moment. 'You are not alone, habibi,' she said softly. 'You should share your burdens with me.'

'No.' Yusuf feared she would not call him her beloved if she knew all he had done. 'I am the king, Shamsa. They are not your burdens to bear.'

Yusuf's face was an expressionless mask as he waited in the entrance hall of the palace. Asimat would arrive any moment, and despite his calm demeanour, Yusuf could feel sweat trickling down his spine. He had dressed in his kingly garb: robes of heavy gold thread, a tall white turban, and a jewelled sword at his side. Selim and Shamsa stood just behind him, along with his children. Al-Afdal and his brother Al-Aziz were ten and nine now, almost old enough to be given lands of their own. They both fidgeted, unable to contain their boyish energy. Az-Zahir, who was Al-Aziz's junior by two years, stood motionless, a mirror image of his father. The younger children – Ishaq, Mas'ud, Yaqub and Da'ud – were off to the side with their nurses and Yusuf's six daughters. Yusuf noticed the budding breasts on his oldest daughter, Halima, the child of a slave girl. He would have to find her a husband soon.

The doors to the hall opened, and Yusuf squinted against the bright sunshine. Asimat strode forward out of the light, followed by an entourage of guards and courtiers. They knelt while Asimat continued towards Yusuf. She seemed to have aged immensely in the five years since he had last seen her. Her skin was still milky white and smooth, but now her cheeks were hollow and there were dark circles under her eyes. Her long black hair was touched with grey.

'Wife,' Yusuf greeted her.

'Husband.' She bowed. Her gaze moved from him to Shamsa, and then to the children. She blinked away tears. 'I wish to speak with you alone.'

'Of course. I will show you to your quarters. Selim, see that her retinue is made comfortable.'

They did not speak as Yusuf led her across the palace to the harem. 'These will be your quarters,' Yusuf said as they entered a comfortable suite of rooms, the floors covered with thick goat-hair carpets and the walls decorated with silks. The windows looked out on a courtyard filled with fragrant rose bushes.

Asimat hardly spared a glance for her new home. 'It will do.' She met his eyes. 'You do not seem happy to see me, Husband.'

'Why have you come? You could have stayed in Aleppo.'

'With the men who murdered my son? He did not die a natural death. He was poisoned.'

'I know.'

Her eyes widened. 'You know?' She seized his arm. 'Who did it? Tell me.'

'Izz ad-Din.'

'But he is Al-Salih's cousin.'

'He is an ambitious man. Now he rules from Mosul and his brother sits on the throne of Aleppo. With Al-Salih dead, they are the heirs to Nur ad-Din's kingdom. They will look to Damascus next.'

'Izz ad-Din,' Asimat murmured. 'I should have known.' All strength seemed to suddenly go from her, and she sank into a pile of cushions on the floor. She sat with her head cradled in her hands for a moment; then she met Yusuf's eyes. 'I am the one who found him. He was alone in his chamber when he died. His cup of wine had fallen from his hand. His face was blue as if he had been strangled, but there was no sign of a struggle. I should have been there. I should have protected him.'

Yusuf knelt beside her and took her hands in his. 'You did all you could.'

'No. There is one last thing I must do for my son. I must give him vengeance.' She clutched his hands. 'If you ever loved me, Yusuf, then avenge me. Avenge our son. March on Mosul. Kill those who took my child from me. Kill that bastard Izz ad-Din.'

Yusuf looked away, unable to bear the sight of her grief. His stomach was burning and he tasted bile in the back of his throat. 'Those who killed Al-Salih will suffer,' he told her. 'You have my word.'

A long stretch of the imposing sandstone wall of Mosul was sheathed in flames that licked up from the battlements towards a sky that threatened rain. The fires were the last trace of the burning naphtha that the defenders had poured down on Yusuf's men, leading him to call off the attack. The breeze had brought Yusuf the stench of burning flesh. Now, it carried him the cat-calls of the city's defenders, who mocked his men as they limped back to camp, carrying their dead and wounded. Stones and other objects hurled from catapults soon joined the insults. Yusuf's fists clenched so tightly that his nails dug into the palms of his hands.

His army had arrived a week ago. Yusuf had deployed his troops around the city and begun a bombardment, but with winter coming, he did not have time for a long siege. He had hoped that a show of force would hurry the decision of the caliph in Baghdad. Yusuf had written to him to request that he be given rule of Mosul. After today, he feared the reply he would receive. Yusuf was still watching his army limp back into camp when Qaraqush galloped up and dismounted. His face was spattered with blood, and part of his caftan had been burned away. He gingerly held a boot in his calloused hands.

'Casualties?' Yusuf asked him.

'A hundred men, give or take. Ubadah's men took the worst of it. They were the ones hit by the fire.' Qaraqush shook his head. 'It's no use, Malik. Izz ad-Din has too many men for us to storm the city. They fight like devils. Look at this.' He held out the boot.

Yusuf took it carefully. It was filled with nails, some of which protruded from the sides. They were wet with blood.

'They are hurling buckets full of them with their cursed cata-pults,' Qaraqush explained, shaking his head. 'This one hit the man beside me in the face.'

Yusuf studied the boot for a moment before tossing it

aside. 'They will stop soon enough, else they will run out of shoes.'

'It is no laughing matter. I shudder to think what they will send us next.' Qaraqush scratched his beard. 'Our catapults have hardly put a dent in their walls, Malik, and the wet weather makes mining impossible. Forgive my bluntness, but we are wasting our time here.'

Yusuf knew Qaraqush spoke for the rest of his men, and he was no doubt sparing him the worst. He forced himself to smile. 'We will sit before the fires in the palace of Mosul soon enough, old friend. I expect the Caliph's messenger any day. Once Al-Nasir grants me lordship over Mosul, Izz ad-Din will be forced to admit my lordship and welcome us into the city.'

'And if the Caliph does not do as you hope?'

'He will. I sent him gifts worth many thousands of dinars: a valuable Koran, musk, amber necklaces, aloe, balm of Judea, a hundred bows, seven hundred arrows of the best quality, and twenty horses with fine saddles.'

'Izz ad-Din no doubt sent him gifts as well.'

Yusuf frowned. 'I cannot take Jerusalem while the men of Mosul sit poised like a dagger at my back. Even the Caliph must see that.'

'Inshallah.'

'I must see to the wounded. Speak to the emirs, Qaraqush. Tell them what I have told you.'

A light rain began to fall as Yusuf made his way down the hill with Saqr at his heels. Yusuf had made the young man the head of his private guard years ago, after Saqr saved his life during the siege of Alexandria, and he had never had cause to regret the decision. The men called Saqr 'Saladin's Shadow', because he was always at Yusuf's side. They walked past the ordered tents of the mamluks to where a sprawling tent had been set up at the centre of the camp. Inside, shaded lanterns hung from the ceiling, casting a dim light on dozens of injured men. This was the dark side of glory, the side the poets never spoke of. The wounded sat close together, some moaning in pain, others staring forward in grim-faced silence. Most of these men would live. They had suffered minor cuts or small burns. Those who were worse off were kept at the centre of the tent, in a section screened off from the rest. Yusuf headed there first.

As he entered, he stepped past a man who clutched an arm that was missing a hand. Beside him a man lay on his side trying to hold in his guts, which protruded from a ragged gash in his stomach. His eyes were glazed and he was mumbling something under his breath.

'You fought well,' Yusuf told the men. 'Allah will reward you.'

The man with the missing hand nodded. The other man showed no sign of having heard. Yusuf continued into the room, past dozens of men who had suffered terrible burns. Some clutched their bloody, blistered flesh and moaned in pain. Others had skin that was black and charred. They made no sound at all. Yusuf said what words of comfort he could. He paused when he came to a man whose face was one raw, bleeding wound. Ibn Jumay knelt beside him. The doctor noticed Yusuf's pained expression.

'His face is not the worst of it,' Ibn Jumay said. 'His lungs have been burned. There is no hope for him. I have given him extract of poppy for the pain.'

The man moved, and his eyes blinked open. The fire had blinded him, and he stared straight ahead without seeing. He whispered something in a rasping voice. Yusuf knelt beside him. He had to bring his ear close to the man's mouth to hear. 'Malik.'

'Yes, soldier.'

'Remember – when –' Each word was a gasp that caused the man's face to contort in pain. '– we – fought.' Yusuf frowned. He looked again at the man's face, but his features had been burned away. 'Tell Bashir.'

'Nazam.' The man nodded. Yusuf took his hand. 'I remember, friend.'

'Wife.' Nazam took a long, shuddering breath. 'My wife!'

'She will be provided for.'

Nazam sank back, a smile on his ruined lips. Ibn Jumay gave him another spoonful of poppy extract, and Nazam's eyes closed. After a moment, his rasping breathing stopped.

'Malik!'

Yusuf turned to see Ubadah and Nasir ad-Din enter the screened-off portion of the tent. His nephew's mail was red with blood and his hair was singed. At twenty-four, lean and strong, Ubadah looked more like his father, John, than ever. Nasir ad-Din's tunic was also red, but it looked to be from spilled wine, not blood. Yusuf's jaw set. He pointed to Nasir ad-Din's tunic. 'You dare come before me in this state? I had hoped you would learn discipline in Homs, but I can see my hopes were ill founded. Were it not for the love I bore for your uncle, Shirkuh, I would have your tongue cut out as an example. Instead, I shall have your lands. You are emir of Homs no longer.'

Nasir ad-Din's cheeks had flushed scarlet. 'But Malik—'

'Go, or I will have your tongue after all!'

The young man bowed and backed from the room.

Yusuf turned to Ubadah. 'And you! Where have you been? Your place is here. These men fought for you. They are dying for you.'

Ubadah's nose wrinkled in disgust as he took in the wounded men. 'What of it? They are mamluks, bought and raised as slaves. It is their duty to die.'

Yusuf slapped him. 'I was like you once, Nephew,' he said, his voice as sharp as a sword's edge. 'When I was given my first command, I thought that I could force the men to obey me with threats and beatings. I was lucky they did not wring my neck. My uncle Shirkuh taught me what I now tell you: each time you go into battle, you put your life into your men's hands.

Men who despise you will let you die; men who respect you, love you even, will give up their lives to protect you. But you cannot win your men's respect by keeping apart from them. You must share their joys, and their pains, too.'

'Yes, Uncle,' Ubadah murmured as he stared at his feet. He cleared his throat. 'I came to tell you that there are messengers from the Caliph. They have been shown to your tent.'

'You stay here. Talk to the men. Comfort them as you are able. I will speak with the Caliph's emissaries.'

Outside, the rain was now coming down in sheets. Yusuf was cold and splattered with mud by the time he reached his tent. He stepped inside to find three bearded men in robes of black silk enjoying food and drink with Qaraqush and Yusuf's secretary, the grey-haired scholar Imad ad-Din. Yusuf walked to his camp-stool. He sat and gestured for the messengers to approach. 'The servants of Caliph Al-Nasir are always welcome in my tent. What message do you bring?'

The shortest of the messengers stepped forward and gave a small bow. 'The Caliph prays for your success and the prosperity of your kingdom. And he sends this . . .' The man produced a scroll from his robes.

Yusuf took it and broke the seal. It was all he could do to keep his face impassive as he scanned the text. This was not the diploma of investiture for which he had hoped. *I confirm you as king of Syria and Egypt*, the caliph wrote, *but I cannot turn my back on my loyal servant Izz ad-Din. It pains me to see conflict between two great men of the faith. I urge you to make peace and to turn your attentions to the Franks in the west*. He stopped reading. The rest was compliments and false piety: empty words.

Yusuf set the scroll aside. The three messengers were shifting nervously. No doubt they knew the contents of the message and feared his wrath. Yusuf smiled at them. The caliph had failed him this time, but Yusuf might have need of him again. Sweet words would help his cause more than threats and curses. 'My thanks for bringing this message,' Yusuf told them.

'My servants will show you to a tent while I prepare my response.'

When they had gone, Yusuf rose and tossed the letter on the brazier. It smoked for a moment and burst into flames. 'The blind fool!' he growled. 'He takes my gifts and spits in my face. He tells me to make peace with Izz ad-Din.'

'Perhaps you should,' Imad ad-Din ventured. 'Mosul— '

'Must be mine if I am to take Jerusalem. I cannot turn west while Izz ad-Din sits on my borders, waiting to pounce.'

'The walls of Mosul are thick and its defenders many,' Qaraqush cautioned. 'Today's defeat was just a taste of what lies in store, Malik. You will lose thousands if you attempt to take the city by storm.'

'And I will gain as many men when the city falls.'

'Men who were once your enemies; men you cannot trust.'

'We could starve them into submission,' Imad ad-Din suggested.

'We are not prepared for a long siege,' Qaraqush countered. 'Who will feed us while we wait for them to starve? Mosul is a prize for another day, Malik. First isolate Izz ad-Din. Take his lands in the west. Aleppo is the prize you should seek now.'

Yusuf frowned as he gazed at the smouldering coals in the brazier. It pained him to retreat, but Qaraqush was right. 'Izz ad-Din can keep Mosul. We will take everything else from him. Once Aleppo is ours, he will surrender, or he will die.'

Chapter 2

A snowflake stung the tip of John's nose before melting. He looked up at the narrow strip of slate-grey sky that was visible between the buildings crowding the street on either side and saw more flakes drifting down. John normally preferred a coat of mail to his priest's vestments, but for once he was grateful for the warmth of his tentlike chasuble. It was made of thick white silk and was heavily embroidered with silver to reflect his new station. After saving the king's life at the battle of Montgisard, he had been appointed Archdeacon of the Church of the Holy Sepulchre, second only to the patriarch in Jerusalem.

John glanced to the king. Despite his silk robes and heavy cloak lined with ermine, Baldwin was shivering, making the crown of the Kingdom of Jerusalem dance atop his head. Baldwin spent most of his days huddled before the fire in his chambers, but he had insisted on walking in the Christmas procession. It had been five years since Montgisard, and memories of his victory were fading, replaced by rumours of his failing health. The king had suffered from leprosy since he was a child. He had lost his eyebrows and the skin on his brow had thickened, making him look much older than his twenty-one years. The lesions on his face were only partly covered by his blond beard. He wanted to show the barons that he was strong and capable, but the long trip across the city from the palace to the Templum Domini and then back to the Church of the Holy

Sepulchre had taken its toll. Baldwin's legs were shaking with fatigue. It would not do to have him fall. John stepped forward and took the king's arm.

'I do not need your help,' Baldwin snapped.

'Of course, Your Grace. It is only that the way is long, and I have grown faint. I would be grateful for your support.'

Baldwin gave John a nod of thanks and allowed himself to be supported.

His sister Sibylla smirked. 'Thank the Lord my *strong* brother is here to lend you his arm, priest. We would not want you to fall on your face before our beloved people.' A year Baldwin's senior, Sibylla was everything he was not. Her long auburn hair framed a fine-boned face with large blue eyes and skin that glowed with health. She walked with her head held high and her shoulders thrown back. And where her brother was reflective and patient, Sibylla was all fiery passion. Two years ago, on the eve of her betrothal to Balian of Ibelin, she had been found in bed with the French crusader Guy of Lusignan. Baldwin had been furious, but when a week later she was found to be with child, there was nothing to be done but for Guy and Sibylla to marry. John suspected that the king's mother Agnes was behind the whole affair. She was the one with the key to Sibylla's chastity belt, and Guy was one of her creatures.

Agnes was walking beside Sibylla's son from her first marriage. With his uncle rendered impotent by leprosy, the younger Baldwin would inherit the throne. The sickly child rode in a shaded chair carried by four servants. He was pale as milk and painfully thin. Sibylla had not wanted him to take part in the procession, but Agnes had insisted. The entire populace of Jerusalem would turn out for the Christmas Mass, and Agnes thought it important that they see their future king.

The towering dome of the church was just ahead. The Templars carrying the True Cross led the procession into the church courtyard, and then stepped aside. Patriarch Heraclius paused just inside the Gate of the Crucifixion, which led into the church. 'What now?' Baldwin grumbled. His lips had taken on a bluish tint.

Heraclius raised his arms and began to pray in his high, piercing voice. John hated the sound of it. He had painful memories of Heraclius purring in his ear while the priest tortured John after he had been captured fighting for the Saracens at Butaiah. John might now serve as Heraclius's deputy, but the two men still hated one another.

'Will he ever stop talking?' William muttered as he stamped his feet. The Archbishop of Tyre's dislike for Heraclius was no secret. 'It is damnably cold, and his Latin is so poor no one can understand him anyway. Did he just call the faithful the erect of God?'

The constable Amalric snorted in amusement and was joined by his brother, Sibylla's husband Guy. Guy was clean-shaven, with long blond hair and emerald-green eyes. He would have been handsome were it not for his snub nose, an unfortunate feature that he shared with his brother. Neither man knew any Latin, but they both had a crude sense of humour.

'And I am delighted to learn that Jerusalem is the bookmark of cities,' William continued. 'How can anyone confuse *regestum* and *regina*? What does that make Acre, I wonder? The inkpot? You should never have made him patriarch, Your Grace.'

'Don't you start,' Baldwin snapped. 'I had to do something to heal the rift in my court. I cannot defend my kingdom against the Saracens while my own subjects are at one another's throats.'

After his great victory at Montgisard, Baldwin had sought to reconcile the two factions that split his court: on the one side his mother, Agnes, with her brother, Joscelin, Guy and Amalric of Lusignan and Reynald of Chatillon, lord of Oultrejourdain; and on the other the old families represented by Raymond of Tripoli, Reginald of Sidon, the Balians and William. When old Humphrey of Toron died in battle, the king had appointed Amalric constable to replace him. Baldwin had betrothed his half-sister Isabella to young Humphrey of Toron, heir of one of the old families but also Reynald's stepson. And after the patriarch died, he had allowed his mother to choose his successor. Agnes had surprised no one by selecting her pet, Heraclius. Baldwin had been pleased. His mother was happy, and her choice meant that he could keep William as chancellor.

Heraclius finally finished his prayer, and the procession continued into the church. They made a tour around the sepulchre – a stone structure topped with a cupola on which stood a larger-than-life silver statue of Christ – and were then led through the colonnade that separated the sanctuary from the rest of the church. John went to the altar to help Heraclius perform the Mass, while Baldwin took a grateful seat on his throne and the canons went to their benches. The rest of the procession remained just outside the sanctuary. The populace flooded through the doors to join them. Men-at-arms held them back from the lords and the king's family, forcing them to the back of the church.

John held the large prayer book while Heraclius read. But even as John assisted with the service, his focus was on the king. Baldwin sat rigidly straight on his throne, in a pose intended to convey authority. And perhaps it did so to the people outside the sanctuary. John was closer, though, and he could see the veins standing out in the king's neck and the crown trembling on his brow. When the service ended, he went to the throne, but Baldwin waved him away and stood. John stayed close as the king strode from the sanctuary and through the crowd, allowing the people to touch him. The touch of the king was said to cure disease, but John did not understand how the people could believe that when Baldwin could not even cure himself. Outside, horses were waiting. John helped the king into the saddle and they trotted to the palace, the new-fallen snow swallowing up the sound of the horses' hooves. John helped Baldwin from the saddle and followed him inside. The moment he passed through the door, the strength that had seemed to animate Baldwin vanished. His legs failed, and John had to catch him to keep him from falling.

'Carry me, John,' Baldwin whispered, his voice weak.

John lifted him with ease. The king was all skin and bones. John carried him to his chamber and deposited him in a chair before the fire. He tucked a blanket around the shaking man.

William had followed them in. He shrugged off his cloak and moved to the fire to warm his hands. 'Bring warm wine for the King!' the priest called.

'The wine can wait,' Baldwin countered. 'Bring me Amalric and Jos.'

William exchanged a glance with John and then nodded. 'Of course, Your Grace.' He left to retrieve the constable and seneschal, while John went to fetch the wine himself. He was pouring a glass when William returned with Amalric.

'Your Grace,' the constable murmured.

The seneschal, Joscelin of Courtenay, entered a moment later. He was a short man, with the same slim build, wavy blond hair and blue eyes as his sister Agnes. He bowed gracefully. 'Your Grace, I apologize for my absence at Mass. I was occupied with—'

'That is not why I have asked you here, Uncle. The whores you fuck may trouble your wife, but they are no concern of mine.' Baldwin paused to look at each of the men gathered around him. 'I have brought you here to discuss war.'

'War, Your Grace?' Amalric's forehead wrinkled in confusion. 'The last I heard, Saladin's army was far off in Al-Jazirah.'

'Yes, and his absence is a chance not to be missed. As soon as the army is gathered, we will march on Damascus.'

John glanced at the men around him. Their stunned expressions mirrored his own surprise. Joscelin was the first to recover. 'Forgive me, Your Grace, but is that wise? Perhaps we can attack later, when you have recovered your strength.'

'I am a leper, Jos! Rest will not cure what ails me. Last year, I walked in the procession with hardly an ache. This year, it was all I could do not to collapse before I reached the palace. My days are numbered, and my heir is only a child. I must make the Kingdom secure before I die, or I fear it will not stand.'

'The King is right,' John agreed. 'Once Saladin has Aleppo and Mosul in hand, he will turn on us. If we wait, we will fall.'

'What of peace, John?' William asked. 'You once told me that Saladin was a reasonable man.'

'He was. Since Montgisard, I am not so sure . . .' John had heard disturbing rumours coming from Egypt, where Turan had died a suspicious death, and from Aleppo, where the young emir had been poisoned.

Baldwin nodded. 'John knows Saladin better than any of us.'

'I too spent many years amongst the Saracens, Nephew,' Jos said. As a young man, he had been a prisoner of Nur ad-Din for twelve years after being captured at the Battle of Harim. 'I spent much of that time in Damascus, and I tell you it is no easy prize. Your father failed to take it, as did your uncle before him.'

Baldwin straightened in his chair. 'I am not my father. Gather the army, Amalric. Damascus will fall.'

DECEMBER 1182: DAMASCUS

John's horse splashed through a muddy stream that ran along the floor of the narrow ravine, or wadi. He had made this trip many times: in 1148 as part of the doomed Second Crusade; in the opposite direction while serving as the commander of Yusuf's private guard; and most recently in 1174, with Baldwin's father. He did not remember crossing any streams, but then again, much of this trip had been unfamiliar. Steady rain had transformed the landscape. Where once there had been only dusty hills and dry ravines, now there were rivulets and desert flowers blooming in the rain. John's horse was caked in mud, and he found it impossible to stay dry, no matter how tightly he wrapped his cloak about himself. He hunched forward in the saddle, shivering in the cold wind that blew from the sea.

The foot-soldiers were worse off. All around John, men wearing heavy packs and with spears over their shoulders slogged through mud that came up to their calves. Just ahead, a soldier stumbled and fell. His fellows helped him up, and as the poor man wiped mud from his eyes, he gave John a resentful look.

'Spare your horse for a poor soldier, father?'

John made the sign of the cross. 'God will give you strength.'

The soldier spat. John could not blame him. He continued past him and on down the long line of men. Baldwin had gathered five thousand infantry, but only two hundred knights had joined him. Guy and Reynald were keeping their men in the south, claiming they were needed to prevent Saracen incursions from Egypt.

'John!' Baldwin called brightly as he trotted up alongside. The king, at least, was in good spirits. He always seemed younger when in the field, and healthier, too, thanks to the gloves that hid his scarred hands and the helmet whose nasal and broad cheekpieces disguised his face. 'How much farther?'

'Damascus should come into view once we are atop that hill.' As Baldwin gazed at the distant slope, whose crest disappeared in the driving rain, John took a closer look at the king. Baldwin's face was flushed, his eyes bright and feverish. 'Perhaps we should camp here, Your Grace, until the worst of the storm has passed.'

'Camp? When we are so close?'

'You look unwell, Your Grace.'

Baldwin's mouth set in a thin line, and he spurred ahead. John should have known better. The king was stubborn when it came to his illness. He hated nothing more than when people made allowances for him.

John reached the hill, and his horse struggled up the muddy slope. At the top, he was surprised that he could not see Damascus. Instead of green orchards stretching towards mud-brown walls, he saw only driving rain.

'John! Are you certain we are close?' Baldwin called from near by.

'I have marched up that hill more than once, Your Grace. I will not soon forget it. Damascus is there.'

Baldwin raised his voice. 'Constable!'

Amalric rode over. He was huddled under so many furs that only his dull eyes were visible. They betrayed an oxlike stupidity, but the constable was undeniably brave and a fierce warrior. 'Yes, Your Grace?' he said, and blew snot from his nose.

'Have the men form a column with the knights in the centre. We will march in formation until we reach the city. We will make camp south of Damascus, on the banks of the Barada. Have the sergeants build an earthen rampart and keep a careful watch. I want no surprises during the night.'

'Yes, my lord.'

'Your Grace,' John said when Amalric had cantered away. 'The orchards to the west of the city—'

'I know, John. I must take them if I wish to starve out Damascus. But I do not plan to starve them; nor do I intend to waste our men's lives fighting in those orchards. You have told me what a death-trap they are. We do not need them. I have brought enough food for a month in the field. By that time, Damascus will be ours. We will take the city by storm.'

The next morning John rose before dawn. It was an old habit from when he had been a slave and would be whipped were he not at his post by sunrise. He was stiff after a night spent on the hard ground. He had turned fifty earlier that year, and nights in the field were not so easy as they once were. He slowly worked out the aches left by a half-dozen old injuries. His right shoulder had been badly injured outside Damascus during the Second Crusade, the day he was captured by the Saracens. He rolled it until it loosened, and began on his left shoulder, which had been dislocated on the rack after the Christians captured him at the Battle of Butaiah. His sword hand was always stiff in the morning. He flexed it and massaged his forearm, which was scarred where he had received a nasty gash a few years back while fighting Reynald of Chatillon's men. After stretching, John pulled on his padded vest, then lifted his suit of mail over his head and wriggled into it. He buckled the strap that tightened the collar, placed a steel cap on his head and grabbed his mace. It had a three-foot handle that led to a heavy, grooved head. As a priest, he was forbidden to shed blood, but that did not mean he could not bash in his enemies' heads.

John stepped from his tent to find that the rain had stopped. The tents of the army dotted the plain south of Damascus. He walked through them and away from camp to the latrine. It had been poorly dug due to the muddy ground and was filled with rainwater. As he pissed, John looked towards the orchards east of the city. Even in the dim light of early dawn, he could make out trees heavy with oranges. The city was nothing more than a dim shape, a greater darkness crouching in the morning gloom.

When he had finished at the latrine, John went to the river and splashed water on his face. It stung it was so cold. He scooped up more to wet his short hair. The men were starting to stir when John returned to camp. He heard the rasp of swords being sharpened and the jangle of mail as men dressed. He went to the cooking fires at the rear of the camp. One of the cooks – a fleshy man with a prominent mole on his cheek – offered John a piece of hot flatbread and ladled boiled wheat into his upturned helmet.

'Does God favour us, father?'

John had seen enough of battle to know that God did not concern himself with the wars of men, but that was not what this cook wanted to hear. The man was fiddling with the medallion of the Church of the Holy Sepulchre about his neck. 'God favours the virtuous,' John told him.

The cook grinned. 'Have another piece of bread, father.'

John took it with a nod of thanks. He ate as he made his way to the king's tent. He was using the bread to scrape up the last of the boiled wheat as he stepped inside. Though it was early, Baldwin already wore his hauberk, a tunic of mail that covered him from neck to mid thigh. He stood leaning over a table covered with papers. The king's face was flushed; he was sweating despite the morning cool. John knew better than to mention Baldwin's health. He knelt. 'God grant you good day, Your Grace.'

'John.'

'Have you broken your fast, my lord? I can have food brought.'

'Later. Come, have a look at this.' A map had been laid out at the centre of the table. It showed the city of Damascus with hills to the west, plains to the east and the Barada River running from north to south through the city. 'I will send a thousand men against the southern wall to draw their defences. The bulk of the army will attack here.' Baldwin pointed to a stretch of the eastern wall.

John nodded. 'The walls are weakest in the east.' He met Baldwin's eyes. 'But they would be weaker after a week's bombardment.'

'And we will be weaker, too. I have read the histories, John. The Second Crusade failed because they waited too long. We will attack today, while the men are strong and eager.'

'As you say, Your Grace.'

Either Baldwin did not notice the reluctance in John's voice, or he affected not to. 'I will focus the attack at the Gate of Saint Thomas,' he continued. 'Our men have only to scale the walls and open the gate. The knights will be waiting to charge through. Most of Damascus's warriors are in the north with Saladin. They will not be able to stop us once we are inside the city.'

John's forehead creased. The last time the Franks had conquered a Saracen city, the streets had run with the blood of men and children, and hundreds of women had been raped. He might be a servant of the king, but he still had friends in

Damascus. He did not want to see Al-Muqaddam gutted or Faridah raped. 'If you pillage the city, you will stir up resentment amongst the populace, Your Grace. You will make Damascus that much harder to hold.'

'I will think on it.' Baldwin stepped away from the table. 'Pray with me, John.' They knelt. The ground had been covered in carpets, but they were wet, water having seeped through from the muddy ground beneath.

'*De profundis clamavi ad te domine,*' John began. '*Domine, exuadi vocem meam.*' When he had finished the *De profundis*, he added, 'Lord God, strengthen the arm of your servant Baldwin, that he might win victory in your name. Grant him the wisdom to lead his men wisely, and the grace to treat his enemy with compassion.'

Baldwin took his helmet from the table and started for the tent flap, but stopped. He drew his sword and turned to John. 'Bless my blade.'

John made the sign of the cross over the sword. 'I beseech thee, O Lord, to hear our prayers and to bless with your majesty the sword of your servant Baldwin. May it be the scourge and terror of your enemies and the salvation of the people of God.'

'*Amen!*'

John followed Baldwin outside. The thousand sergeants who would attack the southern wall had already formed a column bristling with spears. Some of them carried scaling ladders; others held ropes with grappling hooks or heavy crossbows to pick defenders off the wall. The rest of the sergeants were just beginning to form ranks. The knights were mounting their horses and being handed lances and kite-shaped shields by their squires.

'My horse!' Baldwin shouted. One of the king's squires led forth a chestnut destrier. It pranced as it came, showing off a thickly muscled chest and hindquarters. The seat of the saddle was higher than Baldwin's head, and it took two squires to help him mount in his heavy armour. Another squire handed

Baldwin his shield. He urged the horse towards where the knights were gathering, but it had only taken a few steps when the king swayed, then fell from the saddle.

John was the first to reach him. 'My lord!' he cried, but there was no response. As the squires and knights gathered around, John gently removed Baldwin's helmet. There was a swelling bump on the king's temple where he had struck his head during the fall. 'My lord!' John repeated, this time shouting.

Baldwin's eyes fluttered open. He stared straight at John, but did not seem to see him. 'It's poisoned . . .' he murmured. 'Father! Father!' His eyes closed as he lost consciousness.

John looked to one of Baldwin's squires. 'A doctor. Fetch a doctor!' The boy raced off. 'Carry the King to his tent,' John ordered the onlooking knights.

Four men took hold of the king. John was following them to Baldwin's tent when Amalric grabbed his arm and pulled him aside. 'What of the men?' he asked in a low voice. 'The battle?'

'Are you mad? The King is ill. We cannot fight.'

'But the men stand ready,' Amalric protested. 'We may not have another chance to take Damascus. It would be a great victory.'

'A great victory for you.' Amalric opened his mouth to protest, but John continued before he could speak. 'And a bitter defeat if you should lose. With the King ill, you would bear all the blame.'

'Yes,' Amalric murmured, his brow furrowed. 'Yes. I will tell the men to return to their tents.'

Amalric began shouting orders. John hurried inside. The knights had laid Baldwin on his bed and removed his mail shirt. The padded vest beneath was soaked with sweat. The king's fingers began to tremble, and soon his whole body was shaking. The knights stepped back.

'He is cursed,' one of them muttered.

'It is a fever, nothing more.' John drew a blanket over the king, and the shaking soon ceased.

A moment later, the doctor entered. He was a clean-shaven man in a monk's brown robes. He looked young enough to be John's son. The doctor carried a trunk, which he set down at the foot of the king's bed. 'Off with you,' he instructed the knights. 'You, too, father. Leave me to my work.'

The knights trooped out of the tent, but John stopped at the flap. The doctor placed the back of his hand on the king's forehead. 'He burns,' he murmured. He began to chant the Pater Noster as he went about his work. He lit a brass brazier and placed a small pot on it. Into the pot he poured water and a splash of vinegar and added some white crystal, a handful of tiny seeds and some shavings that he peeled off a long root with his knife.

'What is that?' John asked.

The doctor looked up, startled. 'I told you to leave.'

'What is it?'

'Horseradish, along with salt and caraway seeds. Together, they are an infallible cure for fever.'

The doctor continued to chant the Pater Noster until the water boiled. He put his face in the steam. 'Good, good.' He used the hem of his tunic to grip the pot and move it to the floor. 'We must let it cool. Now I will restore his humours to balance.'

He opened his case and removed a small lancet and a bowl to collect blood. John crossed the tent and grabbed the doctor's arm. 'Do not bleed him.'

The doctor shook free. 'Do not tell me my business. The King burns. I must reduce his blood to bring the fever down.' He found a vein and took the blade of the lancet between his thumb and forefinger. Before the doctor could make the incision, John grabbed his arm and twisted it behind his back. The doctor gasped in pain. 'Are you mad? Stop! I—' He fell silent as John took the lancet from him and held the blade to the doctor's throat.

'If you bleed the King, you will bleed. Do you understand?'

'Y-yes, father.'

'John!' Amalric cried as he entered the tent. 'What are you doing? Unhand Brother Jaquemon.'

John released the doctor but kept the lancet.

'Come,' Amalric called. 'This is no place for us. Let the man do his work in peace.'

Before John stepped out, he turned back to Jaquemon. 'No bleeding.'

John spent the remainder of the day pacing before Baldwin's tent. At first, several dozen anxious knights kept vigil with him, but when the rains returned, shortly after midday, they left one by one. Darkness was falling when Jaquemon finally emerged. He stopped short when he saw John. 'I did not bleed him. I swear it!'

'How is he?'

Jaquemon shook his head. 'The fever is very bad. The King has not woken. Go to your tent. I will send for you if his condition changes.'

John spent a restless night tossing and turning on the damp ground as the rain beat down on the fabric of his tent. Over the next two days, while the men huddled in their tents attempting to stay dry, John stood in the rain outside Baldwin's tent. He did not know what else to do. On the third night, John was standing by the tent flap, nodding off as he hunched beneath his cloak, when he felt a hand on his shoulder. It was the doctor.

'He is awake,' Jaquemon said. 'He asked for you.'

The interior of the tent was dark. John felt his way to the king's bedside and knelt. He could just make out Baldwin's face. A wet cloth lay across the king's forehead. His eyes fluttered open.

'John? Is that you?'

'I am here, Your Grace.'

'I – I cannot see, John.'

'I will light the lamp, Your Grace.'

John started to rise. 'No! It is not that. I *cannot* see. I am blind.'

John felt a pain in his chest. 'You will recover,' he told Baldwin, trying to convince himself as much as the king. 'Once the fever has passed.'

'I cannot move my arms, John.' Baldwin's voice trembled. 'I am afraid.'

John gripped the king's hand, unsure of what else to do. 'You must drink something,' he said at last. 'You will feel better afterwards.' John went to the pot the doctor had prepared and scooped out a cup of the potion. But when he returned to the king's side, Baldwin was asleep. John set the cup down and sat beside the king. He gently pushed the hair back from Baldwin's forehead. He looked up as Amalric entered the tent.

'The doctor tells me he may not survive,' the constable said.

'He will live. He is too stubborn to die.'

'He also said the King is blind and crippled.'

'Perhaps when the fever leaves him—'

'A crippled king cannot rule,' Amalric said with certainty. 'We must return to Jerusalem and choose a regent.'

JANUARY 1183: JERUSALEM

Smoke from the bakeries and kitchens of Jerusalem hung in the clear blue sky, showing John where the city lay long before the walls came into view. The sunshine and unseasonably warm January weather were at odds with the sombre mood of the army as it trudged the last miles to the city. Amalric had sent messengers galloping ahead to call for a meeting of the Haute Cour. They would have reached the city in only two days. The main body of the army had taken six days to make the journey from Damascus; they had been slowed by the king, who was carried in a covered litter to spare him the bumps and jolts of the road. Baldwin had awoken twice to murmur incoherently.

At least the doctor had managed to feed him a little broth before the king lapsed back into unconsciousness.

The litter-bearers were now struggling up the hill past rows of grapevines. John spurred ahead. From the top, he could see the north wall of Jerusalem, the domes of the Church of the Holy Sepulchre and the Templum Domini rising behind it. Two dozen knights had set out from Saint Stephen's Gate and were making their way towards the army. The flag of Jerusalem flew over them. Next to it was another banner: on the left a field of blue topped with a band of gold; on the right three red disks on a field of gold. They were the arms of Agnes of Courtenay.

John urged his horse down the far side of the hill at a canter. He slowed to a walk as he approached Agnes. Her face was drawn, and there were dark circles under her eyes. The king's mother had aged gracefully, but now she looked every one of her forty-nine years. 'John,' she greeted him. 'How is he?'

Agnes had been his lover once, but she had betrayed him for power. She had bedded the constable Amalric – and likely other men besides – to establish her influence at court. And she had masterminded the plot that led to the death of the previous king. John despised her even as he desired her, but today, in the face of her grief, he could not summon his usual resentment. 'He is rarely conscious,' he told her. 'He has lost his sight and the use of his arms and legs.'

Agnes blinked back tears. 'Where is he?'

'I will take you to him.'

John headed back up the hill with Agnes riding beside him. 'You must be on your guard in Jerusalem,' she said.

'What do you mean?'

'There are those who mean harm to my son, and to those who would protect him.'

'Who? And why tell me this? Do not pretend that you care for me.'

'I do not need to pretend, John. But if you will not believe that, then perhaps you will believe this. My daughter Sibylla wants Baldwin dead. If he dies, then she becomes queen, and her husband Guy will take power, along with his friends Reynald and Heraclius. You would do anything to protect Baldwin, and so would I. That makes us allies, and puts us both in danger.'

They had reached the litter, and Agnes dismounted and entered to ride with her son. Her men fell in around the carriage. John followed them. As he approached the gate, he took his mace from his saddlebag and hung it from his belt. He did not trust Agnes, but it would not hurt to be cautious.

At the palace, the courtyard was filled with anxious guards and servants. They watched silently as Agnes stepped out of the litter and began to issue orders. 'You men,' she snapped, waving at some of the guards near the door. 'Bring a stretcher for the King.' The men returned a moment later, and Baldwin was transferred to the stretcher. 'Take him to my quarters,' Agnes instructed. 'I will care for him myself.' Four men lifted the stretcher, and she accompanied them into the palace.

John started to follow, but the guards framing the door crossed their spears to bar his way. 'What is the meaning of this?' John demanded. 'I am the King's councillor.' He was about to call out to Agnes when two more guards grabbed his arms from behind.

'Come quietly now,' one of them whispered in his ear, 'and we'll do you no harm, father.' He reached for John's mace, but John managed to pull away. He elbowed the man in the throat, then took his mace and swung for the guard holding his left arm. His mace clanged off the man's helmet, dropping him. Next moment, John felt a blow to the back of his head. He slumped to the ground, and the world went black.

He jerked awake only a moment later. He felt the back of his head and winced. His hair was wet with blood. The four guards were standing around him. John started to rise when one of them punched him in the gut, doubling him over.

'Leave that man be!'

John looked up to see Agnes's brother Joscelin of Courtenay standing in the doorway to the palace.

The guards stepped away from John. 'The regent said—' one of them began.

'I am the seneschal, and I tell you I will see to him.'

'Yes, my lord.'

The guards moved away. Joscelin helped John to rise and kept hold of his arm as he guided him inside the palace.

'Thank you, Jos. What was that about?' Joscelin led them down a staircase, away from Agnes's quarters. 'Where are we going?'

'The dungeons.' John stopped and pulled his arm free. Joscelin met his eyes. 'You can follow me willingly, John, or I can have the guards take you.'

John's gaze went to the dagger at Joscelin's belt. The seneschal was a small man. He could overpower him. With his dagger, he might get past the guards outside and to a horse. But even if he managed to get away, where would he go? John still remembered the look of hatred that Yusuf had given him before he limped off the field at Montgisard. His friend would not take him in. 'Lead on,' he said and fell in behind the seneschal. The stairs ended in a long hallway. The air was chill and damp. Their footsteps echoed loudly. 'Why?'

'Regent's orders.'

'The regent?'

'Guy.'

'The Council chose Guy?' Sibylla's husband was brave enough, but John was surprised that the native lords had not selected one of their own.

'The Council has not yet met,' Joscelin said as he led John down another, narrower staircase. 'Sibylla came up from Ascalon three days ago at the head of two hundred knights led by Reynald of Chatillon. She named her husband regent, and with the army gone to Damascus, there was no one to stop her.'

Joscelin frowned. 'We had best get used to it. She will be queen when her brother dies.'

'Baldwin will live.'

'You had best hope so. Heraclius has the ear of the queen, and he has sworn you will rot to death before you see the light of day. You made a mistake when you made an enemy of that one.'

They reached the bottom of the stairs and stopped before a thick wooden door. Joscelin knocked, and the grille in the centre of the door slid open to reveal a man's face. He was bald, with sallow skin that hung from his cheeks in folds.

'I bring a prisoner,' Joscelin told the gaoler. 'The priest, John of Tatewic.'

The gaoler grunted and slid the grille shut. There was the clank of a key in the lock, and the door swung open. The gaoler proved to be a block of a man, dressed entirely in boiled leather. He raised a wicked-looking mace with a head of grooved steel. 'If you make any trouble, I'll spill your brains on the floor, priest.' He returned the mace to his belt and began to pat at John's robes, looking for weapons or coin. After finding neither, he moved to close the door.

'I will do what I can for you, John,' Joscelin said just before the dungeon door slammed shut.

MARCH 1183: JERUSALEM

John started awake. His cell was dark; he could barely see his hand in front of his face. He groaned as he sat up. He was sore all over from weeks spent sleeping on the stone floor with only his cloak for covering. He cocked his head at the sound of approaching footsteps. Breakfast already? His stomach turned at the thought. Breakfast was rancid boiled wheat with dead weevils in it. At first, John had picked the weevils out. Now, he ate them first. At least they weren't spoiled.

The footsteps stopped, and torchlight filtered in through the grille in the cell door. John was rising as the door swung open. He blinked against the light.

'You smell awful, John.' It was William, torch in hand.

John embraced him. 'And you smell sweet as a rose. Thank God you have come.'

William's brow furrowed. The cell door shut behind him. 'I am sorry, John. I have not come to free you.'

It was as if John were a marionette, and the string holding him up had been cut. He started to fall, but William caught him and helped him to the wall to sit. 'I have no influence in Jerusalem now. Sibylla and Reynald rule; Guy is their stooge. I have come to say farewell.'

'Farewell? Where are you going?'

'To Rome.' William sighed. 'Guy removed me from my post as chancellor, and Heraclius has excommunicated me. I am travelling to Rome to ask the Pope that I be reinstated as Archbishop of Tyre.'

'No. You must stay here. Fight them! When Baldwin recovers—'

'It has been two months now, John. Baldwin is only rarely lucid. The doctors say he will not recover.'

'So you will leave me here to rot?'

'I have done all I could, but I fear any further efforts on my part will only make matters worse for you. And if I do not leave soon, I may be joining you in the dungeons. I am sorry, friend.'

John's head fell. William bent down and put a hand on his shoulder. 'You do have friends in the Kingdom. Raymond and Reginald have demanded your release. Agnes, too.' John's head jerked up. 'I do not know what game she plays, but she can be a powerful ally. Be patient. You are a noble and a man of the cloth. They cannot hold you here forever without a trial.'

The cell door creaked open. The gaoler stood there with mace in hand. 'Your time is up, priest. You must go, unless you have more coin.'

William stood. John rose and embraced him again. 'I will pray for your success in Rome.'

William stepped from the cell and handed the gaoler a heavy pouch of coins. 'This is for my friend. See that he is treated well.'

The gaoler grunted affirmatively.

William looked back to John. 'God save you, friend.'

Chapter 3

'I bear witness that there is none worthy of worship except Allah, and I bear witness that Muhammad is His servant and messenger.' Yusuf looked to his right and murmured, 'Peace be upon you.' He looked left and repeated the phrase. He rose, his morning prayers completed, and stepped outside his tent. The hundreds of tiny plates of his golden jawshan armour flashed in the light of the newly risen sun. Before him, the Tigris River valley was covered in a low mist pierced by the roofs of hundreds of tents. Beyond them, his men had drawn up ranks on the plain. The thousand closest to Yusuf were mounted, but the rest were on foot and the mist came up to their chests. Spears as numerous as blades of grass poked up from the ranks.

Beyond the army rose the black walls of Diyarbakir. They were fifteen feet thick and reached a height of forty feet. Massive towers studded the wall and framed each of the city's four gates. They were the most impressive fortifications Yusuf had ever seen, and they had made the emir of Diyarbakir bold. Yusuf had spent the last months isolating Aleppo by subduing the towns and fortresses between it and Mosul. The cities of Edessa, Saruj, Rakka and Nisbin had surrendered with hardly a fight. But Ishfaq of Diyarbakir had decided to resist. Yusuf would make an example of him. After today, none of the other minor emirs would dare oppose Yusuf.

'As-salaamu 'alaykum, Malik,' Qaraqush called as he

39

approached along the spine of the hill with Ubadah at his side. Behind them came Muhammad. The carefully groomed emir of Hisn Kaifa had soft hands, an immaculately trimmed beard and a tongue of silver. He looked uncomfortable in a coat of heavy mail. He was one of three emirs of Al-Jazirah who had joined Yusuf in return for new lands. Muhammad had been promised Diyarbakir.

Saruj had gone to Gökböri, the governor of Harran, who was huffing along after Muhammad. He was as fat as Muhammad was thin, with red cheeks and a curly black beard that hung down to his ample belly. 'A beautiful day for a battle!' he declared with a grin as he tucked his beard inside his suit mail. 'Been growing this since I was a boy. Don't want it to get cut off, Malik.'

'You know what they say about men with long beards,' muttered Nu'man. The emir of Al-Birah was short, almost a dwarf, with pinched features and a scowl that never seemed to leave his face. He wore a suit of oft-repaired mail that looked to have seen a dozen battles, and strapped to his back a massive battle-axe. Yusuf had given Nu'man the rich city of Edessa, and he had not regretted it. He would not have wanted the man as a foe.

'And what would you know about the size of my cock?' Gökböri asked the short man. 'Did your mother give you a full report? *Hah!*'

Nu'man's scowl deepened. Qaraqush guffawed but then grew serious as he turned to Yusuf. 'The men await your command.'

Yusuf kept his instructions simple, so there would be no mis-understandings. 'When the horn sounds, Ubadah will lead the first wave. His men will strike the western wall, forcing the defenders to spread themselves thin. The torchbearers will strike there.' Yusuf pointed to where three weeks of tunnelling and bombardment had opened a ten-foot gap in the wall. The city's defenders had built a wooden wall atop the rubble. 'Once that wall begins to burn, the drums will signal for the second wave to attack. Qaraqush and Gökböri, you will lead five hundred men through the gap and open the gate.'

Muhammad stepped forward. 'As Diyarbakir has been promised to me, I request the honour of leading the—'

'I will lead the cavalry charge myself,' Yusuf said. 'Once we have taken control of the central square, Muhammad will move on to secure the north gate and Nu'man the south. I will take the east gate. You all understand your roles?' The men nodded. 'Good. Take your positions, and Allah yasalmak.'

As his emirs departed, Yusuf went to his horse and swung into the saddle. He checked to see that his shield, light spear, bow and quiver were all in place, and looked up to Diyarbakir. The sun had risen clear of the horizon and was gilding the city's tallest minaret with golden light. On the plain before the city, Ubadah was galloping towards the front ranks of the army. His red standard dipped when he was in position.

Yusuf nodded to Saqr. 'Signal the attack.'

Haa-room! Saqr blew a piercing blast on a curved ram's horn. Before the sound had faded, the front ranks of Yusuf's army were already surging forward, spreading out across the golden plain like ink spilling over parchment. A cloud of arrows flew from the wall. Most fell harmlessly to the ground or thumped into the shields that the foot-soldiers had raised over their heads. The stones hurled by catapults mounted on the towers struck with more devastating effect. They splintered shields, crushed helmets and ripped off limbs. But the catapults were too few to slow the charge. Yusuf's men reached the wall and began to throw up ladders. Other men hurled grappling hooks and climbed up the ropes. A soft breeze from the east brought Yusuf the din of battle – screams of pain and rage mixed with the clang of steel upon steel.

The torchbearers had reached the breach and were hurling torches at the foot of the temporary wall. The wood began to smoke, but then the defenders tipped several cauldrons of water over the wall and extinguished the flames. Yusuf's face remained impassive, but inside he was cursing. The emir of Diyarbakir was a clever man. He had been prepared.

'Shall I signal the retreat, Malik?' Saqr asked.

'No. We will give Ubadah more time.'

Yusuf had spotted his nephew. He thought the red cloth that Ubadah tied about his helmet was a foolish affectation, but Ubadah claimed it helped his troops to rally to him in battle, much like Yusuf's golden armour. It seemed to be working now. Ubadah was on horseback only a dozen yards from the breach. He waved his sword, gathering several dozen men around him, and then pointed his sword to the wall. Some of the men began shooting arrows at the defenders while the rest ran forward and threw grappling hooks over the wooden barrier. But instead of climbing, they began to pull on the ropes. The wooden wall shook, then tilted outwards and collapsed.

'Saqr, signal Qaraqush and Gökböri.'

'Drums!' The command was relayed to the drummers at the base of the hill. *Boom, boom, boom.* They beat their large goat-skin drums, and five hundred mamluks surged forward with Qaraqush and Gökböri at their head. *Boom, boom, boom.* The beat increased, and the men began to run, driving like a spearhead towards the gap in the wall.

Yusuf turned to Saqr. 'Sound the horn when the gate opens.'

The hundred men of Yusuf's khaskiya fell in around him as he rode down the hill. The ranks of the cavalry waiting below parted to allow him and his private bodyguard to ride to the front, where he joined Nu'man and Muhammad. From the plain, the walls of the city looked even taller. He could see men swarming around the breach, but it was difficult to make out what was happening. He busied himself stringing his bow. To his left, Muhammad was readying a large shield. His free hand drummed nervously on the hilt of his sword. Beyond him, Nu'man held his double-bladed war-axe in both hands. Yusuf located Nasir ad-Din in the ranks of cavalry. He hoped his cousin was sober for a change.

Yusuf raised his voice. 'The men of Diyarbakir have defied us, and now they will suffer for their arrogance. Spare the women and children, but grant no quarter to any warrior. And bring me the head of Ishfaq!'

Yusuf's last words were lost in the blast of the horn sounding behind them. He readied his small shield and took his light bamboo spear from his saddle. 'It is time, men. For Allah!'

'For Saladin!' the men roared back.

Yusuf spurred his horse to a gallop. He passed fallen men, some dead, some moaning in pain. He weaved around a man whose chest had been crushed by a rock from a catapult. Ahead, the Urfa gate was open. As Yusuf neared it, arrows began to fall around him. One struck him in the chest, but did not penetrate his mail. He spurred his horse still faster. He sped through the gate but then pulled back on the reins; the road ahead was blocked by several hundred enemy foot-soldiers with spears bristling from their ranks.

Nu'man galloped past, his axe raised high. 'Kill the bastards!' he roared. 'Kill them all!' He rode straight for the enemy, turned at the last second and swung down, cleaving a man's skull in two. He urged his horse into the gap, hacking at the men to his left and right.

Yusuf followed. He jabbed his spear, catching one of the enemy soldiers in the throat. The next man caught the spear on his shield, and the bamboo shaft shattered. Yusuf drew his sword and spurred on into the enemy ranks. A warrior jabbed at him, and Yusuf twisted out of the way as he slashed across the man's face, spraying the cobblestones with blood. A spear glanced off Yusuf's side, tearing away several scales of his gold armour. He hacked down at his attacker, and the man cried out in pain as the sword cut through his mail and into his shoulder. As Yusuf wrenched the blade free, another man plunged a spear into the neck of his horse. The beast collapsed, and Yusuf rolled free before it pinned him beneath it. He sprang to his feet just in time to sidestep another spear thrust. Yusuf cut across his attacker's thigh, dropping him. He heard a shout from behind and was turning when an enemy soldier slammed into him, knocking away Yusuf's sword and sending the two of them skidding across the bloody cobblestones. The man who ended up on top of Yusuf had a bushy black beard and wild eyes. His hands closed around Yusuf's throat. Yusuf tugged at the man's arms, but it was no use. His foe had the heavily muscled fore-arms and thick fingers of a smith. Lights began to swim before Yusuf's eyes. His gasped in vain for breath.

'Die!' the bearded man growled, showing rotting brown teeth. 'Die!'

Suddenly, the pressure on Yusuf's throat lessened as someone grabbed a handful of the man's beard from behind and yanked his head back. His throat was slit, spattering Yusuf's face with hot blood. The bearded man slumped to the side. In his place stood Nasir ad-Din. He extended his hand and helped Yusuf to his feet.

'Shukran, cousin,' Yusuf managed. His throat was bruising already, and it hurt to speak. Yusuf looked about for someone to fight, but the enemy had begun to fall back, retreating towards the square at the centre of the town. Yusuf's men spurred after them, and the retreat became a rout.

'Congratulations, Malik,' Muhammad said as he gingerly picked his way towards Yusuf over dead bodies. There was not a drop of blood on the emir's armour or on the blade of his sword. 'A great victory. I—'

'Malik!' Nu'man was cantering towards them. A cut above the dwarf's eye had left his face masked in blood. He held a decapitated head in his hands. Nu'man slid from the saddle and held it towards Yusuf. 'The head of Ishfaq of Diyarbakir.'

Ishfaq had been a thin man with hollow cheeks and steel-grey hair. His bloodless face looked strangely peaceful. Yusuf tossed it aside. 'Thank you, Nu'man.'

Muhammad looked as if he were going to be sick. 'Excuse me, Malik.' He gestured to the walls. 'Diyarbakir is mine now.

Its soldiers are laying down their arms. Perhaps it would be best to spare them?'

Yusuf shook his head. Killing defenceless men did not sit well with him, but it had to be done. 'I know Imad ad-Din, the ruler of Aleppo. After he learns what happened here today, he will not stand against us.'

JUNE 1183: ALEPPO

The sound of the muezzins calling the faithful of Aleppo to evening prayer reached Yusuf as little more than a faint murmur as he completed his circuit outside the city walls. He would make up the prayers he missed that night. For now, seeing to his men was more important. It had been more than a year since Yusuf and his men had left Cairo, and he knew they were weary of war. The emirs wished to return to their lands, and the mamluks grumbled of arrears in pay. It was only Yusuf's force of will that kept the army together. So each evening and morning, with only Saqr at his side, he walked around the city, stopping to encourage and commiserate with the men that he had stationed before each of Aleppo's six gates. As he approached the next watch, some of the men rubbed their fingers together in the universal sign for coin.

Yusuf greeted them with a smile. 'You shall have your pay soon enough, men, when Aleppo falls.'

A thin, grizzled warrior stepped forward. Husam had already fought for Shirkuh for many years when Yusuf met him. He removed a piece of straw from between his teeth before he spoke. 'And when might that be, Malik?'

Yusuf knew Husam spoke for the other mamluks. The old warrior's long service had earned him the right to be more direct. 'Soon enough,' Yusuf promised.

Husam smiled, and his gold tooth glinted. 'That's what you said yesterday.'

'And it is just as true today. The siege is twenty days old. Food will be running short in the city. But worse than the lack of food is the absence of hope. We have conquered all of the fortresses between Aleppo and Mosul. No one will come to save Aleppo, and the people of the city know it. They also know what will happen if we take the city by force. It is this knowledge that will open the gates to us.'

A young mamluk with a patchy beard stepped up beside Husam. 'Talk of hope is all well and good, but I want money. We are not slaves, but soldiers. I expect to be—'

Husam slapped him, jerking the man's head to the side. The old mamluk grabbed his young companion by the chin. 'I have served Saladin for over thirty years, and in all that time, I have never known his word to prove false. If he says the city will soon fall, then it will fall.'

The man rubbed his cheek, then turned to Yusuf and bowed. 'My apologies, Malik.'

Yusuf nodded and continued on his way. So long as he had men like Husam, he knew he could count on his army. He strode through a field of spring wheat towards the final watch, which guarded the Gate of Gardens. The men were lounging in the green grass that grew near the Quweq River. They rose at his approach. Az-Zahir stepped forward. Yusuf had given each of his sons command of one of the watches. Al-Afdal, Al-Aziz and Az-Zahir had joined the army two weeks ago. In letters, Shamsa insisted that the boys were too young to go to war, but Yusuf wanted them by his side when he took Aleppo. Looking at Az-Zahir, however, made him think that perhaps Shamsa had the right of it. The nine-year-old boy's mail armour hung in folds from his skinny frame. He stood straight, though, and met his father's gaze without blinking. He reminded Yusuf of himself at that age.

'Malik,' Az-Zahir greeted him formally.

'All is well?'

'No sign of movement in the city.'

'At the first sign of a sortie, sound your horn. Keep your men around you at all times. Your first duty—'

'Is to stay alive. I know, Father.'

'Good. Carry on.'

Yusuf turned towards the camp. It had been set up amidst the gardens on the far side of the Quweq River, which would provide a line of defence against any sorties from the city. The dusty path that Yusuf and Saqr followed led them between orchards of pistachio and olive trees and over a wooden bridge. The light was fading from the sky by the time he reached his red tent, perched on a hill at the centre of the camp. He entered and turned to Saqr.

'Inform Taqi ad-Din, Qaraqush and my sons that they are invited to dine in my tent. Nasir ad-Din is to come as well.' Yusuf had yet to properly thank his cousin for saving his life at Diyarbakir. He would reinstate him as emir of Homs. Inshallah, the boy would rule more wisely this time.

While Saqr relayed the message to the runners outside, Yusuf stepped into the screened-off portion of his tent and removed his armour. He donned a padded vest lined with steel plates – a precaution against assassins – and over it, a caftan. He poured a glass of water and took a long drink, then stepped back into the main room. Servants had spread down-filled cushions around a low round table set with bowls of creamy hummus and a basket of flatbread. Yusuf sat while he waited for his guests.

Qaraqush arrived first, looking uncomfortable in robes of indigo blue silk. He was followed shortly afterwards by Ubadah. Yusuf's sons entered together. Al-Afdal, almost twelve, was tall and well muscled. He reminded Yusuf of his brother Turan. Al-Aziz was just as tall but thin as a reed. He was a fearless child, who was determined to do anything his older brother did. Az-Zahir came last. The boys remained silent during supper, while Yusuf and his advisors discussed the siege. They were finishing the last course when Saqr entered. 'Malik, a visitor.'

Yusuf scowled. 'I am dining, Saqr.'

'You will want to meet with him, Malik.' Saqr stepped aside and a man entered. He wore a black cloak with a hood that cast his face in dark shadows. He pushed the hood back.

Yusuf managed to keep his face impassive, even as the eyes of his men widened. 'Imad ad-Din.' The emir of Aleppo was fifteen years Yusuf's junior. He was a thin man with narrow shoulders and soft hands. His short beard was flecked with grey despite his relative youth. 'You are welcome in my tent.'

'Shukran, Malik. I wish to speak with you. Alone.'

'These are my sons and most trusted councillors. I have no secrets from them.'

Imad ad-Din licked his lips nervously but nodded. 'Very well.'

'Sit.' Yusuf gestured to the table. 'Eat. Drink.'

Imad ad-Din took a place across from Yusuf. He took a bite of bread and washed it down with a long drink of water. His shoulders relaxed. Now that he had eaten in Yusuf's tent, he had guest rights. It would dishonour Yusuf to harm him. Imad ad-Din licked his lips and began. 'The situation in Aleppo is not good.'

Yusuf raised his eyebrows but did not speak.

'The treasury is empty. Tomorrow, my troops are due their pay. I fear a mutiny.'

'That is unfortunate for you.'

'And for you as well, Saladin. I am not an unreasonable man, but those who would rule the city in my place will fight until the last man to defend Aleppo.' Imad ad-Din shook his head. 'A foolish gesture. The city will fall. They know it as well as you and I. Their stubborn pride will only drown us all in blood, as at Diyarbakir.'

'I wish to avoid bloodshed as much as you do. What do you propose?'

Imad ad-Din's tongue again flickered over his lips. 'I can offer the city to you, for a price. But you must decide now. After tomorrow, it will be too late.'

'And what is this price?'

48

'Sinjar, Saruj, Rakka and Edessa.'

Yusuf sipped at his water as he considered the offer. He would accept, of course, but there was no sense showing Imad ad-Din how delighted he was. He could see beads of sweat forming on the emir's forehead. 'I will not give you Edessa,' Yusuf said at last.

Imad ad-Din nodded. 'And the others?'

'Yours.'

'But Uncle!' Ubadah protested. 'Those are—'

Yusuf silenced him with a glance. He turned back to Imad ad-Din. 'And you shall have precious silks, horses and camels, as befits your station.'

'You are too generous, Malik.'

'You will find that I treat my subjects well. You may rule your new lands as you see fit, but you must swear to serve me loyally, to pay tribute, and to provide men for my wars with the Franks.'

'I swear it.'

'Then we are brothers.' Yusuf rose, and the others did likewise. He embraced Imad ad-Din and kissed him on the cheeks. 'You brought men with you?'

'Of course. Four guards.'

'Saqr, see that his men are given a dozen of our yellow banners. Imad ad-Din, your men will unfurl them atop the walls at first light tomorrow as a sign that the city is ours.'

'It shall be as you say, Malik.'

'Good.' Yusuf embraced him again. 'Ma'a as-salaama.'

As soon as Imad ad-Din stepped outside, Ubadah stepped forward. 'Sinjar was mine, Uncle!'

'We lost good men to take the city,' Qaraqush agreed. 'And Saruj belongs to Gökböri. He has been a faithful ally.'

'When Mosul is ours, you shall all have something better. Saruj and Sinjar are nothing, friends. We have exchanged dirhams for dinars.'

★

Yusuf sat in the saddle and peered towards the walls of Aleppo, which were lost in the pre-dawn gloom. A horse nickered behind him, and he could hear his son Az-Zahir murmuring calming words to his mount. Yusuf drew his dagger and began to sharpen it, the long rasping strokes calming him. The world around him slowly brightened. The grey shapes lining the road to Aleppo resolved into pistachio trees. A bird tweeted from one of the branches. Another joined it, and another, and soon the air was alive with their song. Yusuf could now make out the distant walls. Yellow banners were being unfurled atop them. Yusuf sheathed his dagger.

'It is time.' He urged his horse forward over the Quweq River. His men followed, the hooves of their mounts clattering on the wooden bridge. The walls loomed ever higher as Yusuf approached. The gate began to swing open, and Yusuf urged his horse to a trot. He reached the gate to find Imad ad-Din backed by a hundred of his men.

'Wa 'alaykum as-salaam, Malik,' Imad ad-Din called. 'The city is yours.'

'Will you come to the citadel with me to feast my arrival?'

'I am honoured by the invitation, Malik, but I must refuse. I am not well loved in Aleppo, and I fear I shall be less so after today. I will leave for Sinjar, if it please you.'

'Very well. God protect you, Imad ad-Din.' The emir nodded and led his men from the city. Yusuf turned to Qaraqush. 'Take charge of the city gates. Take the defenders' weapons, but do them no harm.'

Yusuf continued into the city, followed by Ubadah, his sons and a guard of five hundred men. The only sound was the clip-clop of hooves on the cobblestones. The streets were empty, but Yusuf saw the faces of men in the windows that they passed. The main square, too, was deserted. He crossed it to the bridge that led across the citadel's moat. A dozen guards with lowered spears stood on the bridge. Yusuf rode forward to address them.

'I am Saladin, al-Malik al-nasir. I have come to take charge of

Aleppo. Let me pass.' Several of the guards stepped aside, but the rest held their ground. Yusuf's hand went to the hilt of his sword. 'Stand aside,' he barked in his most commanding tone, 'or you will die.' Behind him, he could hear the creak of his men's bows as they were drawn taut.

After a moment's hesitation, the men stepped aside. Yusuf cantered across the bridge and up the causeway. The guards at the gate parted as he rode through and on to the grassy pitch at the centre of the citadel. Yusuf headed for the palace at the east end of the grounds. A dozen men came out to greet him. When they saw his golden armour, some knelt. Others simply stood wide-eyed. The rest looked to an older man in mail. He stepped forward, his hand on his sword hilt.

'Saladin? What is the meaning of this?'

'Imad ad-Din has turned the city over to me.'

'Damn his seventh grandfather! The man had no right!' He turned to the men behind him. 'I told you we couldn't trust the bastard.'

'What is your name, emir?'

'Salamat,' the man said as he turned back to Yusuf. 'My family has served the Zengis for generations.' He drew his sword. 'We will not stand idly by while Aleppo is turned over to an usurper.'

'Put your sword away, Salamat. I am no enemy of yours.' Yusuf raised his voice to address all of them. 'Imad ad-Din is the grandson of Zengi, the founder of the line. He entrusted me with the rule of Aleppo. If you swear loyalty to me, then you will keep your property and your posts. As for me, I swear that I shall make Aleppo a great city, a holy city. As a sign of my intentions, I hereby abolish all taxes not permitted in the Koran.'

The men before Yusuf began to murmur amongst themselves. Yusuf looked to Salamat. 'Will you help me to dismount, emir?'

Salamat hesitated. To hold another man's stirrup was a sign of fealty. Finally, he sheathed his sword and took hold of the stirrup. Yusuf swung from the saddle and kissed Salamat on the cheeks.

'You have chosen wisely,' he told the emir, then raised his voice. 'There shall be a feast today to celebrate my return to Aleppo after so many years. You are all invited.' Yusuf strode past them and entered the place, Saqr, Ubadah and his sons at his heels.

Ubadah was scowling. 'The taxes, Uncle – we could have used that money in our campaign against Mosul.'

Yusuf looked to his three sons. 'Al-Afdal, tell Imad ad-Din why I did it.'

The boy's forehead creased in concentration. 'It was the righteous thing to do,' he said at last. His brother Al-Aziz nodded in agreement.

'It was righteous, yes, but that is not why I did it. Az-Zahir? Can you enlighten your brothers?'

'It was necessary,' the skinny boy said quietly. 'By removing taxes, you will win the people to your side. The emirs who still oppose you will find they have no support.'

Yusuf nodded in satisfaction. 'You are wise beyond your years, my son. When I leave Aleppo, you shall have the rule of it.'

Yusuf took a bite of roast lamb spiced with coriander and closed his eyes to savour the rich taste. The tender lamb melted in his mouth. He made a mental note to find the cook responsible for the dish and to take him when he left Aleppo. Despite the delicious food, though, his celebratory feast was a sombre affair. Yusuf had taken careful note of the dozen emirs of Aleppo who had not come. It was an act of rebellion. They were no doubt fleeing for Mosul even now. Their lands would be forfeit, and their lives, if Yusuf captured them. Salamat and the other Aleppan emirs knew as much. They had lost their city and now their friends, and that had cast a cloud over the feast.

Yusuf turned to Salamat, who had been given the seat of

honour to his right. If he could win this man's loyalty, then Yusuf was sure the other emirs would fall in line. 'The last time I dined in this hall, it was in the presence of Nur ad-Din. He gave me my first lands: Tell Bashir.'

'I know it, Malik.'

'Nur ad-Din was a great man. He united Aleppo, Damascus and Mosul against the Franks, but he died before he could strike the finishing blow. I will complete his work. Once Mosul has joined me, I will turn on Jerusalem. When that day comes, I hope you will ride with me.'

The other conversations had ceased and all eyes were on Salamat. He nodded. 'I have always dreamed of seeing the Noble City.'

'And you shall, inshallah.' Yusuf noticed that Imad ad-Din had entered the hall with a letter in his hand. His secretary would not disturb him were it not important. 'Excuse me,' Yusuf told Salamat. 'I will return shortly.'

He joined Imad ad-Din in a side room off the hall. 'A letter from your brother Selim,' the secretary told him. 'The Lord of Kerak, the one called the Wolf, has raided the Hijaz.'

Reynald. He was an old enemy. Yusuf knew him to be an oath-breaker and unspeakably cruel, but to raid the Hijaz – the stretch along the east coast of the Red Sea that included the holy cities of Mecca and Medina – was brazen, even by Reynald's standards.

Yusuf took the letter and scanned the contents. Reynald's men had built boats that they disassembled and carried across the desert to the Red Sea, where they reassembled them. They had burned the ports that served Medina and sacked the Nubian port of Ajidib, across the sea from Mecca. Yusuf flipped another page. Selim had sent a fleet to deal with them. They had met the Frankish ships off Al-Hawra and destroyed them. The captives had been sent to Cairo. Reynald had escaped and returned to Kerak.

Yusuf crumpled the paper in his fist. His authority rested on

his claim to defend Islam against the infidels. That was his justi-
fication for unifying Syria, for moving against Aleppo and
Mosul. He could not let Reynald's raid go unpunished; to do so
would make him look weak in the eyes of the Caliph and his
people. 'Send word to my brother in Cairo that the captured
Franks are to be beheaded. Send four of them to Mecca to be
killed at the Place of Sacrifice during the next hajj. Their deaths
will be a lesson to the Franks and a message to the faithful that
I will protect our holy sites. As for the Wolf, it is time he be
brought to bay. Mosul can wait. As soon as Aleppo is secure, we
march for the Kingdom.'

Chapter 4

'Come, Reynald. Let us finish this.' John dropped into a crouch and raised his imaginary sword. He skipped back a few steps and his back came up against the wall of the cell. John brought his sword up to parry, then spun away from another blow. He knocked aside a thrust and sprang forward to counter, lunging at the shadows on the wall before giving ground. He parried a dozen imagined blows. He could almost see Reynald grinning fiercely as he hacked down again and again. John's back pressed up against the wall, and he lashed out before again spinning away. He slipped on some straw and stumbled, but it was only a feint. He sidestepped a clumsy blow and finished Reynald with a slashing blow to the neck. In his mind's eye, he watched Reynald grasp his throat, the red blood welling up between his thick fingers. Then he fell to the ground, dead.

John's chest was heaving. He wiped the sweat from his brow and sank down on his straw mattress. He was weaker than he would have liked. He got up again and began to pace his cell. *Five paces. Turn. Five paces. Turn. Five paces. Turn.* He did the circuit one hundred times after both his morning and evening meal. He would add another session in the afternoon, and another session of practice swordplay. If he was ever freed from this dungeon, he would be ready to make his enemies pay.

He had been in prison for something like eight months. It

55

was hard to be exact when there was no sunlight, and the torches in the hallway outside his cell burned night and day. Only the food, which came twice a day, let him know when one day ended and the next began. Sometimes, though, he lost track of which meal was breakfast and which supper. After William's visit, the food had improved, but it was always the same: a thick slice of black bread and a cup of thin vegetable broth. On good days, there would be a small piece of onion or carrot in the broth. Between meals, when not exercising, John thought of those who had put him in his cell – of Heraclius, Guy and Sibylla. He thought of Baldwin, of Yusuf, of his son Ubadah and of Zimat. He thought again of Reynald and rubbed the scar on his forearm.

John finished pacing and lay down. He could hear the distant drip of water. Until recently, he would have also heard the Weeper, as John had dubbed the man in the cell across from him. He had cried quietly for hours on end. Sometimes, he had sobbed loudly and banged on his door. Until the day the gaoler came to his cell. John had not thought it possible for anyone to scream so loud. After that, John had not heard from the Weeper again. One-Eye was gone, too. He had not lasted long after the gaoler put his eye out.

Scratchy occupied the cell to John's left. Each night – or what he thought was night – John heard a faint scratching sound coming from his cell. He had thought the man might be trying to communicate. He had found a small pebble and scratched on the wall of his own cell. The sound from Scratchy had ceased at once and not returned until the following night. John had not tried again. If the man was trying to tunnel out through the thick walls, then he was mad, and John would not waste his time on a madman. It was hard enough keeping himself sane.

John called his neighbour to the right le Père. Every time food was brought, the man asked after the health of his son. Other than that, he made no sound. John kept his silence, too. He had asked after Baldwin for the first few weeks, but had received nothing more than sullen grunts and the occasional cuff to the head.

John heard the creak of rusty hinges as the door to the dungeon swung open. It was too early to be supper. It must be a visitor, or a new prisoner. John went to the grille in his cell door. He heard voices. He could not make out what they were saying, but one of them sounded like a woman. A visitor, then. John peered through the metal grate. Any change in the monotony of his days was welcome. He heard footsteps approaching along the hall. When he saw the gaoler, he stepped back. John knew better than to peer through the grate at him. That was how One-Eye had lost his eye. The gaoler had put a dagger in it.

The footsteps stopped before John's cell. He heard the gaoler fumble with his keys, and a moment later the door creaked open. The gaoler stepped aside to reveal Agnes. She was dressed in robes of buttery silk and had a fur around her neck. She winced when she saw John.

'Leave us,' she told the gaoler.

'Wha—' John croaked, his voice rusty after weeks of disuse. 'What do you want?'

'I am freeing you. Come with me.'

John did not move. 'Why now? It has been months.'

'The regent Guy forbid me to come. He had me watched. I dared not even visit so long as he was in the city.'

'Where is he now?'

'La Sephorie. He has called on the barons to join him there. Reynald attacked the ports of Medina and Mecca, breaking the treaty with Saladin. The Saracens are invading, John. The Kingdom is going to war.'

'I understand. You made Reynald a great lord, and now that he has damned us all, you have come to ask for my sword.' John went and sat on his mattress. 'You will not have it.'

Agnes stepped into the cell. 'I have made mistakes, John. I will not deny it. But now I am trying to set things right.'

'You are wasting your breath, Agnes. I will not fight for Guy.'

'I am not asking you to. I want you to fight for Baldwin.'

John's head jerked up. 'He lives?'

'I will take you to him.' As Agnes was leaving the cell, she paused and looked back. John still had not moved. 'You can stay here if you wish, John, but I will not come again.'

This time, John followed. Agnes led him out of the dungeon and up a pair of staircases. The second opened into a hallway filled with sunshine spilling in through arched windows. John blinked in the bright light. He went to stand at a window, closed his eyes and let the sunshine spill over him.

'John,' Agnes called. 'Are you coming?'

She led him up another, broader staircase to her private quarters. A table had been set with food: roast lamb in a thick gravy, fresh bread and wine. John's mouth began to water.

'Eat,' Agnes told him.

'The King—'

'Eat first.' Agnes's tone brooked no debate.

Food had never tasted so good. Agnes watched him from beside a door on the far side of the room. She wrinkled her nose. 'You look horrible, John. And you smell like a latrine.'

'They do not offer baths in the dungeons.'

'No. I suppose not.'

John finished the roast and sopped up the last of the gravy with the bread. He drained the cup of wine and stood, a little unsteadily. The alcohol had gone straight to his head. 'Take me to Baldwin.'

Agnes produced a key and unlocked the door she stood next to. John followed her into a waiting room, where a guard stood. Agnes nodded to him, and the guard pulled another door open. She gestured for John to go first. The room he entered was dim. Heavy curtains had been hung over the windows. On the far side of the room, he made out a large bed. He crossed the room. Baldwin lay beneath thick covers. The king's face was skeletal, his cheeks sunken and his skin impossibly pale. His breathing was shallow.

'He has been this way for months,' Agnes said. 'It is all the doctors can do to keep him fed. He wakes sometimes, but he speaks no sense and soon relapses.' She crossed the room and took a cloth from a bowl of water at the bedside. She carefully wrung the cloth so that water dripped into the king's mouth. 'Heraclius has helped Sibylla draw up a letter of abdication. They will sign it for him, and then Sibylla will make her husband Guy king.' She met John's eyes. 'We must stop them.'

'Why would you want to do that? Guy and Heraclius are your creatures.'

Her mouth tightened. 'Baldwin is my son, John. I had no part in these plots. With my brother's help, I have taken control of the citadel and placed Sibylla in my custody. I can prevent the letter of abdication from being signed, but only until Guy returns. That is why I need you.'

'And what would you have me do? I have been stripped of my position in the church. I am nothing.'

'No longer. The abbot of Mount Sion has died. I have arranged for you to replace him.'

'Under whose authority?'

'The King's.' She took a scroll from the sleeve of her robe and handed it to John. He unrolled it and squinted to read in the darkness. It requested that John be made abbot of the abbey of Our Lady of Mount Sion in return for a gift of five thousand gold bezants. At the bottom, it bore Baldwin's seal. 'I, too, can forge documents,' Agnes said. 'The monastery has one hundred and fifty sergeants at its command. Take them to La Sephorie.'

John shook his head. 'I have no wish to return to my cell. Guy will have me cast in irons the moment he sees me.'

'I think not. When you arrive, seek out Raymond, the Count of Tripoli. He will support you. And you will have your men. Guy needs every sword he can get, even yours. He will grant you your freedom, if only so long as Saladin's men threaten the Kingdom.'

'So I go to La Sephorie. What then?'

'You must see to it that Guy does not return.'

John met her emerald green eyes. They had no warmth in them. 'I am not you, Agnes. I am no murderer.'

'I am not asking, John. You can help me, or you can return to your cell.'

'I thought you knew me better than that.' John headed for the door.

'I know you love my son! I have kept Baldwin safe until now, but once Guy is king, I will not be able to protect him. How long do you think he will live then?'

John paused in the doorway and looked to Baldwin. He had known the young man since he was a child. He had tutored him and taught him to fight. The king was more of a son to him than Ubadah. 'This Guy, does he truly deserve to die?'

'Does Baldwin?'

'Very well; I will do it.'

OCTOBER 1183: LA SEPHORIE

John rode hunched forward in the saddle. His exercises in prison had not prepared him for the weight of his mail hauberk or for days spent on horseback. He felt as if a dagger had been plunged into the small of his back. He would have liked to call a halt, but La Sephorie was not far off.

He and his men had left Mount Sion three days ago. The abbey was located just outside the wall of Jerusalem, and when John first arrived after meeting with Agnes, the brothers had received him with indignation. A stranger, straight from the palace dungeons, would not rule over them; it was an outrage! In the end, the gold had won them over. John had been elected abbot the next day. His first act had been to call the sergeants who owed service to the abbey. They had set out the next morning, riding up the west bank of the Jordan. The previous night they had reached Beisan. Both the fortress and the town huddled at its base had been sacked and burned. He and his men had passed an anxious night amongst the blackened stones of the castle. Today, John rode with his hand on his mace.

A breeze stirred his hair, and John's nose wrinkled. He could smell the stench of unwashed men, horses and full latrines. The camp was close. He spurred ahead, leaving behind the sergeants, who marched on foot. He rode to the top of a low hill, and there was the camp. Dozens of large barracks tents and hundreds of smaller ones sat on a broad plain amidst fields of golden wheat and groves of olive and pomegranate trees. At the centre of the camp, two dozen homes of stone and mud were huddled at the base of a hill topped by a squat square keep with one tower. Above the keep flew the flag of Jerusalem, and beside it, Guy's flag – two silver crosses on fields of azure, quartered with red lions rampant on silver and blue. John scanned the camp until he spotted Raymond's standard flying over his tent. He turned and signalled for the captain of his men to join him.

John had first met Aestan years ago, shortly after the Englishman had arrived in the Holy Land to seek his fortune as a soldier. Aestan's dark hair had now gone white, and his once fair skin was tanned and wrinkled like worn leather. But his green eyes still twinkled when he laughed, and he was still well muscled and flat-bellied. John had been delighted to find him serving amongst the sergeants of Mount Sion.

'Domne,' Aestan greeted John, using the Saxon for lord.

'I must speak to Raymond. Find a place for the men to camp. Keep well away from Reynald's men.'

'You don't have to tell me. I served under the bastard before the Saracens captured him.'

John dismounted and handed the reins to Aestan. 'See to my horse.'

Guards had been posted at the edge of the camp, but they

were chatting as they leaned on their spears and hardly spared John a glance. He wove between tents, passing sergeants in boiled leather and knights in mail, blond Franks and Syrian Christians with the same olive skin and dark hair as the Saracens. He reached Raymond's tent, which was topped by a flag bearing the outline of a gold cross on a field of scarlet. Two men in mail stood guard at the tent flap.

'I must speak with your lord,' John told them.

'Raymond is at council in the keep.' The guard nodded towards the hill, which began only a dozen paces away.

'My thanks.'

John examined the keep as he climbed the hill. The walls were uneven, incorporating stones in a variety of shapes and sizes, some decorated with inscriptions in Latin or carvings of animals. They had no doubt been taken from the ancient Roman town that had once stood on the site. On the upper floor there were a few windows, each too narrow for a man to crawl through. The single tower stood at the north-west corner of the keep. A privy extended from the tower, a tall pile of shit buzzing with flies on the ground beneath.

The door to the keep was guarded by a dozen men. Their captain, a handsome man with only one hand, stepped forward to confront John. 'Where do you think you're going?'

'To the council meeting.'

The captain's eyebrows rose. 'You a lord?'

John could understand the man's doubts. He was thin and ghostly pale – no man's idea of a great lord. He gestured to the gold cross with split ends that adorned his surcoat. 'I am the Abbot of Mount Sion. I bring one hundred and fifty men.'

The captain studied him a moment longer, then pointed to John's mace. 'Leave your weapon here.' John handed the mace over, and the guard stepped aside. 'You're late, abbot. You had best hurry. First door on your left.'

John went inside and paused beside the door to the council chamber. He could hear raised voices. Despite the pain in his back, he straightened and walked in with a determined stride. A dozen men were gathered around a table. John recognized most of them: Guy and his brother Amalric, the constable; Reynald and his son-in-law Humphrey of Toron, a fat-cheeked young man with an unfortunate overbite and weak chin; Raymond of Tripoli, a slender, straight-backed man with dark hair and a swarthy complexion; and beside him taciturn, balding Reginald of Sidon and Balian of Ibelin, a handsome man with a thin nose and wide, dark eyes. The men fell silent as John entered the room.

'Saxon?' Reynald asked. 'What are you doing here?'

Guy frowned. 'That man should be in prison. Guards!'

Two men in mail entered the room, but Raymond and Balian stepped between them and John. 'Let him be,' Raymond said. 'We need every sword we can muster.'

'I have brought one hundred and fifty sergeants,' John said.

Reynald's eyebrows shot up. 'And whose men are these?'

'Mine. I have been elected abbot of Mount Sion.'

'On whose authority?' Guy demanded.

'The King.'

Reynald snorted. 'The King is too ill even to feed himself.'

'Then John's election is nothing short of a miracle,' Balian declared in a soft voice that matched his delicate features. 'All the more reason to welcome him.' He looked to Guy. 'Unless you wish to lose his men.'

Guy's forehead creased. He rubbed the hilt of his dagger with his thumb as he tried to come to a decision.

John met his eyes. Perhaps this was his opportunity to eliminate the regent, and to do so in a way that would not stain his own honour. 'I have been found guilty of no crimes, my lord. If you wish, I will undergo trial by combat against my accusers to prove my innocence. I believe that means I would fight you.'

'That will not be necessary. You may stay.'

'But he is a traitor!' Reynald protested. 'He—'

'My brother said he may stay!' Amalric roared. 'He rules here, not you!'

John could feel the tension in the room. Balian cleared his throat and turned to John. 'We were discussing strategy. Six days ago, Saladin's army crossed the Jordan and sacked Beisan. They made camp here —' he pointed to the map on the table — 'at the Spring of Goliath. We marched to the spring and forced him to withdraw to Mount Tabor.'

'Where he sacked the monastery and surrounding villages,' Guy noted.

'An outrage that must not go unpunished!' Reynald declared. 'We must march to meet him.'

'We would be fools to do so,' Raymond countered.

'And cowards to stay here.'

Raymond's voice was quietly threatening. 'I am no coward, Reynald. If you wish to test that truth, please step outside.'

'Peace!' Guy shouted. 'We are not here to fight amongst ourselves. Reynald, you have had your say. Raymond, tell me what you propose.'

'So long as we stay at La Sephorie, we can choose the time and place of our next battle. Saladin must pass this way if he wishes to attack Acre. If he marches on Jerusalem, we can follow and crush him against the walls of the city. If we attack now, then we leave behind a sure source of water and put ourselves at risk.'

'Hmph. We marched once already, and Saladin fled before us,' Reynald pointed out.

'And the result of our efforts was a hundred sergeants with arrow wounds. Next time, we might not be so lucky. Tell them, John. You know Saladin better than any of us.'

All eyes turned to John. 'Raymond is right,' he said. 'Saladin seeks to draw us out. He will march to meet us, only to retreat and draw us into a trap. It is the Saracen way.'

'I, too, spent years amongst the Saracens,' Reynald countered. 'I know them as well as you, Saxon. When they spring their trap, we will be ready, and we will crush them.' He looked to Guy. 'Remember Montgisard!'

'And Jacob's Ford,' Raymond retorted. 'Just last week, Humphrey lost over half his men while marching up from Kerak.'

'Do not listen to him, lord regent,' Reynald insisted. 'You know that he resents your rule. Raymond only seeks to deny you a chance at glory.'

'You are regent, Guy,' Raymond said. 'Your purpose is not to win glory; it is to protect the Kingdom. The monastery at Mount Tabor can be rebuilt. Beisan can be rebuilt. But if we lose in the field, you will lose us the Kingdom.'

All eyes turned to Guy, but the regent hesitated still, rubbing at his dagger. He was waiting for someone to make the decision for him. No one spoke. Finally, Guy cleared his throat. 'We will send out scouts. Once we know the enemy's exact disposition, we will decide whether to march.' Reynald shook his head and stormed from the room. 'You are dismissed,' Guy told the rest of the men.

Raymond fell in beside John as they left the keep. 'Thank God you came,' the count said. 'I had feared Reynald would win the day. Guy is a weak man, irresolute. Without his wife to lead him by the nose, he is as lost as a newborn puppy.'

'He would make a poor king, then?'

Raymond snorted. 'I would sooner Reynald rule. At least that bastard knows what he wants.'

Rasp. Rasp. Rasp. John sat outside his tent and drew the blade of his dagger over his whetstone. The moon had not yet risen and the night was dark, which suited his purposes. He could not see the keep, only a black space where there hung a single light. It was a candle, glowing in the chamber where Raymond had told him Guy slept. Abruptly, the light winked out. John returned the whetstone to the pouch at his belt, sheathed his blade, and rose. He raised the hood of the black cloak he wore and set out for the keep.

The camp was quiet. John kept well clear of the few men who were awake. He circled around to the north-west of the keep and, crawling on all fours, crept up the hill. There were no guards; they were kept away by the stench of piss and shit below the privy. That was where John headed. He reached the wall of the keep and edged along it until his boots sank in the filth. Above him, he could just make out where the privy jutted out from the tower. The wall before him was coated with piss and shit.

'God help me,' he muttered and crossed himself. He reached up and managed to squeeze his fingers into a narrow crack between two stones. His nose wrinkled as he pressed his body against the wall. For a moment, he thought he might retch. Then, gritting his teeth, he hauled himself upwards. He found a toehold and felt with his left hand for another point of purchase. He found it and pulled himself up further.

He made his way up the wall handhold by handhold and inch by inch. The smell had grown less rank by the time he reached the point where the bottom of the small stone enclosure that held the privy jutted out from the wall just above his head. The privy hole itself was behind him, some three feet away from the wall. To get to it, John would have to lean backwards, kick off the wall, and wedge his hands in the hole, all in one fluid movement. He could then wriggle his way upwards. If the lunge missed, however, then he would fall more than twenty feet. With any luck, the shit would cushion him.

He counted to three and then kicked off from the wall, thrusting his hands upwards and into the hole. The sides of the hole were wet with what he did not care to ponder, and John slipped a few inches before he caught himself. He hung there for a second and then began to inch his way upwards. He had just begun when someone stepped into the privy and urinated on him. John squeezed his eyes and mouth shut and held his breath. After a few seconds, the person finished, and a moment later, John heard the privy door open and close. He quickly wiggled the rest of the way through the hole, emerging into a small space with a door on the far side. He pulled off his filthy cloak and cleaned himself as best he could, then cracked open the door and looked out into an empty hallway. Guy's room would be to the right. John tiptoed to his door. He turned the handle and pushed gently. It was unlocked. John drew his dagger and slipped inside.

He had hoped to find Guy asleep, but the regent was standing at the window in only a thin cotton shift. He turned. 'John?'

John froze. If Guy called for the guards, he was as good as dead. The room was dark, and Guy seemed to have not seen the dagger. John turned slightly so that the blade was hidden by his profile. He bowed. 'Lord regent.'

'You have news of the scouts?'

'The scouts?' John's mind was racing. He nodded. 'Yes, they are—'

'It can wait. Sit.' Guy gestured to the bed. John managed to hide the dagger blade beneath his leg as he sat. The regent stayed at the window. 'I am glad you came. I wish to apologize, John.'

John blinked. 'My lord?'

'For imprisoning you. Heraclius and Reynald urged me to. Why do they hate you so?'

'Old disagreements, my lord.'

Guy nodded. 'I was driven from France by men who hated me. And now I am to be king. I never wished it, John. But Sibylla dreams of the throne. She says I will be a great king.' He sighed as he turned to look out of the window. John stood, the dagger in his hand. 'I love her, but I sometimes feel I am only a pawn in some game she is playing. I have so many advisors telling me what to do. Sibylla. Heraclius. Reynald. I sometimes do not know who to trust.'

John lowered the dagger. This man was not worth killing. Heraclius and Reynald, they were the true danger. He was slipping the blade back into its sheath when there was a knock on the door.

'Enter!' Guy called.

Reynald stepped into the room. His eyes widened when he saw John. He sniffed the air. 'You smell like shit, Saxon.' He looked back to Guy. 'The scouts have returned, lord regent. Saladin is no longer at Mount Tabor. His army's tracks head south.'

'Jerusalem,' John said.

'There are other targets in the south, lord regent. Kerak, Shawbak and Ascalon.'

The regent nodded. 'You are right. Our southern border must be protected. You go to Kerak. I will ride for my lands in Ascalon. John, you are the abbot of Mount Sion. Your place is in Jerusalem. You will go there with Raymond to defend the city.'

Chapter 5

Yusuf pulled up the hood of his cloak as a light rain began to fall, rippling the waters of the Dead Sea. It was the first rain of the year. Yusuf would see to it that a few sheep were slaughtered that night so the men could celebrate properly. Some had begun to pray in thanks. Others stood beside their horses, which were drinking from a stream that flowed into the sea. More men huddled under their cloaks and chewed on hard bread. Yusuf bit into his own piece and looked south towards Kerak.

His army had left Mount Tabor two weeks before. The feint north had served its purpose. Yusuf had drawn the Frankish army to Saffuriya, and while they sat there, Selim had led Egyptian troops up from the south. Today, Yusuf would join them at Kerak.

Yusuf turned at a sudden burst of merriment. Nu'man was emerging naked from the Dead Sea, and Gökböri was roaring with laughter, his belly shaking. 'Never seen a real man before?' Nu'man grumbled as he strode to his horse. He noticed Yusuf watching. 'I wanted to see for myself, Malik.'

'See what?'

'Gökböri says the waters have healing properties.'

'I've been drinking a spoonful a day for years,' Gökböri declared. 'Costs more than a few fals to have it shipped north, but it's worth it. Look at me.' He slapped his belly. 'Strong as a mule.'

Yusuf could not help but smile. 'Well, how do you feel, Nu'man?'

Nu'man shrugged as he pulled on his tunic. 'Still too short.' He pulled on a boot, then stopped and pointed to the north. 'A scout is returning.'

Yusuf spotted the rider cantering along the shore of the lake. He had left a few men behind to keep track of the Frankish army.

The scout's horse spattered Yusuf with mud as it was reined in before him. The scout swung from the saddle and prostrated himself. 'My apologies, Malik!'

'Get up. What news do you bring?'

'The Frankish army has broken up. Most went to Jerusalem.'

'And Reynald?'

'He headed down the west side of the Dead Sea. At the pace he and his men were riding, they should have reached Kerak some time last week.'

'Good. The bird has come home to roost.' Yusuf looked to Nu'man. 'Get dressed. I wish to reach Kerak before nightfall.'

They continued south along the shore. The rain stopped, and the sun broke through the clouds, transforming the sea from flint grey to a brilliant turquoise. Their Bedouin guides led them into a green valley that wound its way through the hills east of the sea. Yusuf saw the tall white walls of Kerak from more than a mile off. The castle sat on a spur of land that thrust out on to a barren stretch of white sand and dusty soil. Steep hills faced in stone dropped away from either side of the spur. There was no way up those hills. The attack would have to come along the neck of the spur.

Yusuf rode out from the hills and on to the arid plain. Nothing grew there, but Kerak's wealth did not come from the land. It came from preying on the caravan route that ran from Damascus to Ayla, and from there across the Sinai to Cairo. To the north, hundreds of tents sat in the shadow cast by the castle above. A group of men rode out from the tents to meet the army. Yusuf recognized his brother Selim at the head. He had Yusuf's sharp features and thin build, but he was half a head taller than his older brother.

'As-salaamu 'alaykum, Brother,' Selim declared as he drew alongside Yusuf and leaned over to exchange the ritual kisses.

'Wa 'alaykum as-salaam,' Yusuf replied. He reached out to touch his brother's beard, which showed traces of grey. It still seemed only yesterday that Selim had been a fat-cheeked boy. 'You grow old, Brother.'

Selim let out a short bark of laughter. 'The camel calls the mule stubborn. Tell me, was it snowing in the hills, Brother? I see more white than black in your hair.'

'A mark of wisdom,' Yusuf replied with a smile. He looked to Kerak and grew serious. 'How goes the siege?'

'We arrived three days ago. We took the town easily enough, but the castle is another matter. The walls—'

A gust of wind brought with it the sound of music. Yusuf looked to Selim's camp and frowned. 'What is this?'

'Not my men, I assure you, Brother. The Wolf is celebrating a wedding. His son-in-law Humphrey of Toron is marrying King Baldwin's half-sister, Isabella.' Selim spat in the dust. 'The girl is only eleven. It is an abomination.'

Yusuf shrugged. Frankish marriage customs were no business of his. But if the girl were the king's sister, that might create problems. 'We must take the castle quickly. Tell me of the walls.'

'I will show you, Brother.'

Yusuf followed Selim through the camp and on to a trail that zigzagged up to the plateau on which Kerak sat. A dozen men from Yusuf's khaskiya followed them to the top. The light was brighter up here, where the sun had not yet set. They rode through the town and out on to the narrow spur of land that led to the castle. A line of four catapults stretched across the spur. As Yusuf watched, Selim's men loaded a heavy stone into one of them. The catapult sprang into action, hurling the rock towards the castle. Yusuf lost track of it, then spotted it again just before it slammed into the wall with a loud crack. Tiny flakes of rock flew from the wall, but nothing more.

'Rest for a moment,' Selim told the men at the catapults as he rode past. Beyond the siege engines, an earthen barricade topped with spikes had been erected across the face of the spur. Three hundred mamluks stood watch behind it, ready in case of a sortie from the castle.

'It is best if we continue on foot,' Selim said. He dismounted and took hold of Yusuf's stirrup.

'Saqr, come with us,' Yusuf said as he dismounted. He followed his brother through a narrow opening in the barricade. Ahead, the land of the spur had been cut away by the Franks to create a gap twenty feet across and ten feet deep. A bridge lay across the gap. As Yusuf crossed, he looked down and saw burnt timbers on the ground below.

'They burned the bridge,' Selim explained. 'We had to build a new one.'

'Be sure to post guards at night, in case they seek to burn this one.'

They stopped at the far side, only fifty yards from the castle wall. The music had become much louder – flutes were playing a cheerful melody over the strumming of a lute.

'We should go no closer,' Selim cautioned. 'They have cross-bowmen on the wall.'

The wall was higher on the right, where it protected the upper court of the castle. Here and there, the facade was rough where bits of stone had fallen away, and Yusuf saw a few cracks near the top of the lower wall. That was the extent of the damage from the catapults. 'Concentrate the bombardment on the walls of the lower court,' he said. 'When last I besieged Kerak, those walls fell first. Once we take the lower court, we can storm the upper.' He put a hand on Selim's shoulder. 'You have done well, Brother.'

'I am glad you are pleased. Perhaps you would grant me a request?'

'Name it.'

'I am wasted counting coins in Cairo, Brother. The battle is in the north, with Mosul and the Franks. When we are done here, give me Aleppo.'

Yusuf's lips pressed into a thin line. 'My son Az-Zahir rules in Aleppo.'

'He is clever, Brother, but he is only a boy. I will teach him how to govern.'

'And who would govern Egypt for me with you gone?'

'Ubadah.'

'Our nephew is too impulsive.'

'A few years counting coins might help cool his temper.'

Yusuf rubbed his beard. 'I will think on it.'

'Shukran Allah. Now come, Brother. I am staying in the town. I have prepared refreshments in my home.'

When they had crossed the bridge there were shouts of alarm from amongst Selim's men, who began to pour forth from behind the barricade. Yusuf turned to see the gates of Kerak swing open. His hand fell to his sword hilt. But this was no attack. Two stooped old men in tunics came out. Each carried a platter heaped with food. Yusuf motioned for the troops to stay back. 'Saqr, search them.'

Saqr met the men on the far side of the bridge, and they submitted to his search. 'They bear no weapons, Malik.'

Yusuf waved them forward. One man carried a platter with a whole roast suckling pig. Selim paled at the sight of it. The other carried a pitcher of wine and a haunch of lamb, dripping with bloody juices. It was clearly not halal.

Yusuf gestured to the food. 'What is this?' he asked in Frankish.

'From our lord,' the man with the pig said. He pointed back to the wall. Squinting, Yusuf could just make out Reynald.

'Saladin!' the lord of Kerak shouted. 'You honour me by

your presence at the marriage of my son. I have sent you these dishes so that you may take part in the feast!'

'The insolent dog,' Selim spat. He knocked the platters to the ground. The wine from the pitcher soaked quickly into the sandy soil.

'Your master has our answer,' Yusuf told the old men. He turned his back to them and strode through the barricade to where the catapults stood. 'Resume your work,' he told the men. 'Chase that faithless dog from the wall.'

Rain pitter-pattered off the hood of Yusuf's cloak, and the muddy ground sucked at his boots as he and Saqr trudged towards the walls of Kerak for Yusuf's daily inspection. At this distance, the walls appeared as only a vague shape looming through the curtain of rain. Frequent showers had plagued them throughout the first month of the siege, leaving the bowstrings of his men slack and making it impossible to roll a ram through the mud to the citadel gate. Yusuf had never known such a wet autumn. As he passed the catapults, one of them swung into action. Its basket had filled with rain, and it hurled a shower of water along with its stone. Yusuf lost track of the projectile against the cloudy sky, but he heard the loud crack as it struck the walls. At the barricade, the mamluks were huddled under their cloaks. They straightened as Yusuf approached.

'What did he send today?' Every day, Reynald sent Yusuf a new dish. None was halal. They were both an insult and a message: the citadel had plenty of food and could hold out for weeks to come.

'Some foul thing,' one of the guards replied. 'I have never seen the like.' He signalled to another man, who brought forth a basket. It held sausages that were almost black, with just a faint reddish sheen. 'They smell of blood.'

'Put them with the rest.' After that first day, Yusuf had begun setting the dishes aside. When Kerak fell, he planned to shove them down Reynald's throat. He stepped through the barricade and strode across the bridge. The rain was heavy, and he had to get close to clearly see the walls. The ground before them was a sea of churned-up mud littered with the debris left by half a dozen assaults. Yusuf had to pick his way carefully in order to avoid the broken arrow shafts and the occasional blade buried in the mud. He stopped within thirty yards of the castle – well within crossbow range on a dry day, but the rain would have played havoc with the crossbow strings, as with his men's bows. Besides, the wall was empty save for the impaled heads of a dozen of Yusuf's men, who had fallen in battle, and two guards, who were hunched under their cloaks, paying him little mind. He turned his attention to the lower wall. A network of cracks ran across its face and pieces of the battlement had been knocked away, but the wall looked no closer to falling than it had a week before. Yusuf frowned. He was running out of time. The Frankish army was on its way. And his scouts told him that it was not Raymond or Guy who led it, but King Baldwin himself and a priest: John.

Yusuf heard squelching footsteps approach from behind. It was Selim. 'The scouts have returned,' Yusuf's brother said as he splashed to his side. 'The Franks are only two days off, less if the rain stops.'

Yusuf nodded. He continued to examine the wall. He looked again to the guards huddled under their cloaks. A week ago, Yusuf had sent a dozen men under cover of darkness to scale the wall and open the gates. They had failed, but perhaps if he tried again, during heavy rain . . .

Selim guessed what he was thinking. 'We have done what we can here, Brother. Another attack will only waste lives.'

'We need Reynald dead.'

'The Franks march with a thousand knights and nearly ten thousand sergeants. If we are caught between their army and Kerak, they will grind us to dust against its walls. Even if we take Kerak, we will only find ourselves besieged in turn.'

It was all true. And yet . . . 'Our family comes from nothing,

Selim. We are Kurds, son of a provincial governor in Tikrit. My authority rests on one thing and one thing alone: the defence of Islam against the Franks. Reynald raided to the very doorstep of Mecca and Medina. He must be brought to account.'

'You wrong yourself, Brother. Your people love you. Your men love you. Where you lead, they will follow.' Selim put his hand on Yusuf's shoulder. 'We will be back, Yusuf. Once we have Mosul, the Franks will not have enough men to resist us. Reynald will then be punished. Let me go to Aleppo and prepare the attack on Mosul.'

Yusuf's gut was burning again. Defeat was a bitter draught to swallow. But he did miss Shamsa and his children. He had been too long gone from them. He was sure his men missed their homes as well. 'Very well, Brother. Go north and gather gold and supplies for a campaign. Inform Ubadah that he is to rule in Cairo.'

'Yes, Brother.'

Yusuf remained before the walls while the tents were taken down and stowed and the baggage packed. The catapults were too heavy to carry along the muddy roads to Damascus and Cairo, so they were broken down and the wood hacked to pieces. The stones that had been collected as ammunition were rolled off the spur to fall to the plain below. The rain had stopped when Yusuf saw a new figure emerge on the wall. Reynald.

'Saladin!' the Frankish lord shouted. 'I am sad to see you go. I enjoyed watching your men die before my walls.' He gestured to the impaled heads. 'I was hoping to add you to my little collection.'

Yusuf made no reply.

'Allow me to make you one last gift before you go.' Reynald signalled and two men-at-arms dragged forth a man to stand beside him. The man was clearly a Muslim, with olive skin and a long black beard. He must have been captured during one of the assaults on the wall. He was naked and shivering in the cold.

Reynald produced a knife. 'I know how dearly you love cock, Saladin. Here—' The mamluk cried out in pain as Reynald sliced off his member. He threw it from the wall towards Yusuf. The mamluk was sobbing. 'He sounds like a woman, does he not?' Reynald demanded. 'Pitiful. I will shut him up.' The mamluk shrieked in pain as Reynald carved out his tongue.

Yusuf turned away, his jaw clenched. 'Saqr, have the village set on fire. Tear down what will not burn. And send raiders to ravage Reynald's lands. Leave no crops in the valleys. Leave him nothing.'

'Yes, Malik.'

Yusuf strode away from the wall. He would return once Mosul was his. Reynald would pay, and the Kingdom with him.

'What is happening, John?' Baldwin asked. The king wore mail, but he would not be riding into battle. He could not see, nor could he walk. He sat in a chair mounted on poles and carried by four men. Leprosy had ravaged his face during his long illness, and he now wore a mask of silver in which only his sightless eyes moved. It created an unnerving impression.

'The Saracen army is gone,' John reported from where he sat on horseback beside the king. The rain had stopped the day before, but the ground was still soft, and the Saracen retreat had turned the plain below Kerak into a muddy expanse dotted with the remains of cooking fires.

'Good.' Baldwin's voice took on a hard edge. 'Now we will deal with Reynald. John—'

The king was interrupted by a fit of coughing. His health was still fragile. Within a week of regaining consciousness, he had named John commander of the army and set out for Kerak. They had left the constable Amalric confined in the palace under Joscelin's guard. Raymond had been sent to Ascalon to fetch Guy and Sibylla back to Jerusalem.

Baldwin wiped his mouth with a silk handkerchief as the

coughing fit passed. The king quickly tucked the handkerchief back into his robes, but not before John noticed that it was spotted with blood. When Baldwin spoke again, his voice was raspy. 'Take control of the citadel. Disarm Reynald's men, but do them no harm. When the citadel is in hand, I will come for Reynald. I want him brought before me in chains. Alive.'

John frowned. Chains were not what he had in mind. He had come to Kerak to kill Reynald. Now that Baldwin had recovered, Guy did not matter. The regent was only a fool. Reynald was dangerous; too dangerous to live. 'If he resists, Your Grace, I may have to use force.'

Baldwin turned his blind eyes towards John. 'We are not here for vengeance, John.'

'Yes, Your Grace.'

John rode a short distance to where Balian of Ibelin sat astride a magnificent roan of easily sixteen hands. Balian wore a new coat of mail, and over it a shining steel breastplate emblazoned with his arms, a red cross on a field of gold. With his long dark hair and handsome features, he looked the part of a king more than Baldwin ever would.

'We are to seize control of the citadel,' John told him. 'A thousand sergeants should be more than sufficient. When we enter, you will take charge of the gates and lower court. I will take the upper court and the keep. Tell the sergeants I want three spearmen beside every one of Reynald's men.'

'And what of Reynald?' Balian asked.

'Leave him to me. Aestan!' The Saxon was at his side at once. 'Fetch a pair of shackles. Be certain they are heavy.'

While Balian gathered the men, John checked his armour. He wore a mail hauberk with long sleeves under a surcoat blazoned with the cross of Mount Sion. He took leather mittens backed with mail from his saddlebag and pulled them on, and then took his buckler from where it hung on his saddle. The buckler was a circular shield that John gripped in his fist. It was much smaller than the kite-shaped shields knights usually carried, but John would be facing no arrows or lances. He preferred the buckler for hand-to-hand combat.

Balian had formed the men into a column ten wide. John rode to their head and raised his voice. 'The King has declared Reynald a prisoner of the Crown. We are here to take him, not to fight his men! Keep your swords sheathed and your spears on your shoulder unless you are told otherwise. If so much as one of Reynald's men is injured or killed without provocation, I will see the man who did it hang.'

'A stirring speech,' Balian said with a wry smile.

'I do not want them stirred.'

John turned his horse and urged it to a walk. Balian fell in beside him. Aestan took his place in the front row of the column, beside the man carrying the standard of the Kingdom of Jerusalem. They crossed muddy ground dotted with puddles and the charred remains of campfires. At the foot of the plateau, they took a zigzagging trail up to the town of Kerak. A few of the inhabitants had already left the fortress to return to their homes, but there was nothing to return to. The village of Kerak had been reduced to tumbled stone and broken timber. Some stood dejected, staring glassy-eyed at the remains of their homes. Others wept quietly. One old man ran to Balian and bowed.

'My lord!' he cried, mistaking him for the king. 'Help us, Your Grace! The sand devils took everything. Everything!'

John could not help the man. He rode on through the town and out on to the spur. The Saracens had built a barricade across it. John passed through and could now see men lining the walls ahead. They began to cheer as John crossed the bridge leading to the castle. The gates swung open, and a fleshy, sunburnt man in mail hurried forward to meet them.

'Thank God you have come, Your Grace!' He knelt before Balian.

'Stand up,' John told him as he dismounted. 'He is not the King. Where is your lord?'

'He awaits you in the upper court,' the sunburnt man said.

John turned to Balian. 'You know what to do.'

Balian's men spread out around the lower court. John headed up the ramp to the upper court, his sergeants trooping after him. Around a hundred of Reynald's men lined the walls. John paused once he was through the gate in order to allow his own men to spread out. His grip tightened around the handle of his mace. On the far side of the courtyard, Reynald stood near the entrance to the keep. He was dressed in mail, a sword at his side. Beside him stood his wife, his son-in-law Humphrey, and the boy's new wife Isabella. She was no more than a girl, still flat-chested and narrow-hipped. She gripped the hand of Reynald's wife Stephanie as if it were a lifeline.

When John's men were in place, he strode forward. Reynald's expression darkened when he recognized John. 'Where is Guy?' he demanded.

'In Ascalon. It is Baldwin who leads the army. He has sent me to take charge of the castle.'

'Take charge? Kerak is mine.' Reynald's hand dropped to his sword.

Good. Draw that sword, and I will kill you. John raised his voice so that Reynald's men could hear. 'The King has declared Reynald of Chatillon a prisoner of the Crown. Throw down your arms, and there will be no bloodshed.'

Each of Reynald's men found himself confronted with three spear tips. One man drew his sword and was impaled through the chest. The others began to drop their weapons.

Reynald's face purpled with rage. 'How dare you! I held Kerak against the Saracens for over a month. The King should be thanking me.'

John gestured to Aestan, who held a pair of heavy iron manacles. 'Step inside, Reynald,' John said quietly, 'unless you wish to be manacled before your family and your men.'

'Deceitful bastard,' Reynald growled. 'I should have killed

you when I had the chance.' He spat at John's feet, then turned and strode towards the keep. Aestan and three other sergeants fell in around him.

John followed them inside. 'This way.' He turned into a long hall dimly lit by light filtering in through the loopholes on the right-hand wall. 'Leave us,' John told his men.

'But domne!' Aestan protested.

'Go! And see that we are not disturbed.' The men trooped out and Aestan closed the door behind him. John took his mace from his belt as he turned to Reynald. 'You wish to kill me, Reynald? Now is your chance.'

Reynald's eyes narrowed. 'What trick is this, Saxon?'

'No trick.' John adopted a fighting stance: legs wide, mace raised, his body turned so that his buckler was towards his foe. Reynald drew his sword and held it with both hands. John met his eyes. 'I have waited a long time for this. You betrayed me when I first came to the Holy Land. You sent men to kill me. You—'

'Enough talk.' Reynald stepped forward and took a two-handed cut at John's throat. John blocked with his buckler, and Reynald brought his blade slicing back towards John's gut. John jumped back out of the way and swung his mace for his opponent's head. Reynald knocked the mace aside and charged. He planted his shoulder in John's gut, lifting him from the ground and slamming him down. The two men skidded a few feet on the stone floor. John dropped his shield and managed to push Reynald off him. He rolled away just before Reynald's sword struck where his head had been.

John was breathing hard as he scrambled to his feet. He was still not fully recovered from his time in prison, and Reynald was bigger and stronger. He backed away and circled to Reynald's left. John saw Reynald's knuckles whiten around his sword hilt a moment before he charged. John was already moving. He sprang to the right, avoiding the thrust, and brought his mace down on Reynald's shoulder.

Reynald roared with pain as he spun to face John. His left arm now hung limp at his side. 'I'll gut you, Saxon!'

'Come and try.'

Reynald advanced more cautiously this time. He lunged, and John skipped back out of the way. Reynald followed with a backhanded slash towards John's face. John knelt, and the sword flashed over his head. He slammed his mace into the side of Reynald's knee. Reynald dropped his sword and collapsed, clutching his leg. John knelt on his chest and raised his mace.

Reynald spat in his face. 'Come on, you faithless dog. Do it!'

John's grip tightened on the mace.

'John! Stop!'

John looked up to see the king. Baldwin's chair had been set down just inside the door. Reynald's wife Stephanie was beside the chair, whispering urgently to the king. Baldwin raised a hand to silence her. 'I have not come for Reynald's life,' he declared. 'I have come to dispense justice.'

John moved aside and Reynald pushed himself to his feet. He leaned heavily on his sword. 'Justice, Your Grace? What sort of justice is it that strikes a loyal servant of the King? I have fought at the head of your armies. I have fought when others cowered behind unholy treaties with the infidel. Now, you send this Saxon dog to my castle with orders to put me in chains? I am a lord. I demand to be judged by my peers.'

'You will be judged, Reynald. Never fear. Chain him and bring him before me.'

A dozen sergeants with spears surrounded Reynald. Aestan came forward with the manacles. John took Reynald's sword and closed one of the manacles around his left hand.

'You are enjoying this, aren't you, Saxon?' Reynald snarled.

John ignored him as he manacled the other hand. He tugged

on the chain lead, and Reynald limped forward to stand before the king. Baldwin's silver mask glinted in the light streaming through the loopholes.

Reynald bowed with some difficulty. 'Tell me my so-called crimes, Your Grace. I am ready to answer for them.'

'You conspired with Guy to remove me from the throne. A dozen men attest that you called him king. I am not dead yet, Reynald.'

'Of course not, Your Grace. My apologies if I misspoke when addressing the Regent.'

Baldwin waved aside the apology. He leaned forward. 'How do you answer to the charge that you sought to remove me and place Guy on the throne?'

Reynald straightened, his shoulders back and his head held high. 'I do not deny it.' Baldwin's knuckles whitened where he gripped the arms of his chair, but Reynald went on. 'The Kingdom needs a king. You were incapacitated, and the doctors feared the worse. We could not wait forever for a recovery that seemed doubtful.'

'You swore fealty to me. It was your duty to wait.'

'It is my duty to defend the Kingdom.'

'If you wish to defend the Kingdom, then what possessed you to attack the ports of Medina and Mecca? You might have doomed us all with your mad raid. I have a mind to take your head for it.'

The colour drained from Reynald's face as he realized the severity of his situation. He licked his lips. 'It was Guy, Your Grace. He ordered me to do it. He said he wanted to start his reign with a great gesture, to show the infidels that they were not safe anywhere.'

'He lies to save his life, Your Grace,' John interrupted.

Baldwin raised a hand for silence. 'If what you say is true, Reynald, then Guy is an even greater fool than you.'

'Yes, Your Grace.'

Baldwin sat back and slumped in his chair. He was clearly

exhausted. John had forgotten how ill he was. 'You will swear loyalty to the throne,' he said in a tired voice.

'I swear it, Your Grace.' Reynald knelt. 'My sword is yours until the day I die.'

'You will lead your men when and where I command. Until then, see that you stay in your castle. You may go.'

Reynald rose and bowed. 'Thank you, my lord.' He limped from the room.

'But, Your Grace!' John declared when he had gone. 'You cannot mean to let him keep Kerak?'

Baldwin sighed. 'He is a fool, but a brave fool, John. We have precious few knights his equal. The Saracens fear him. If properly muzzled, Reynald can be useful.' The king raised his voice. 'Porters! Take me to my bed. I must rest. Tomorrow, we start for Jerusalem. It is time I dealt with Guy, my sister, and that snake Heraclius.'

DECEMBER 1183: JERUSALEM

The bells were tolling as John walked through the small cloister of the Church of the Holy Sepulchre. Baldwin had restored him to his post as archdeacon of the church, but John was not headed to prayers. He had another task to perform. He wore mail and a mace hung from his belt. Ten sergeants marched behind him, Aestan at their head.

From the cloister, they passed through a hall and on to the entryway that gave access to the palace of the patriarch. The door was guarded by four knights of the Holy Sepulchre, the Jerusalem cross blazoned on their surcoats.

'I have come to see the Patriarch,' John told them. He held up a parchment with the royal seal at the bottom. 'King's business.'

The guards eyed the document and the men behind John. They stepped aside and pulled the doors open. The floor of the patriarch's palace was covered with thick carpets that swallowed up the sound of John's boots. Gold and silver thread glittered in the rich tapestries that hung on the walls. The air smelt of incense. John took the stairs to Heraclius's private suites. Two more guards stood at the door.

John presented the parchment. 'Stand aside. I come on King's business.'

'The King has no authority here.'

John's hand went to his mace. 'Step aside.' This time, it was a threat. The guards hesitated a moment longer, then moved aside. John entered to find Heraclius at table. He wore his robes of silk open at the front. A buxom young blonde in a translucent cotton shift sat on his lap. Her braying laughter stopped short at the sight of John.

'What is the meaning of this?' Heraclius demanded.

'The King has requested your presence.'

'I am the Patriarch, not some servant to be—'

John pushed the woman off his lap and grabbed Heraclius by the arm, hauling him from the table.

'Unhand me!' Heraclius squealed as he struggled in vain to pull free of John's grip. 'I am your superior!'

John took the mace from his belt. 'I would be only too happy to use force to compel you to come, Heraclius.'

The patriarch stopped struggling. 'That will not be necessary.' He tied his robes about him and strode stiffly through the door, John at his back. The sergeants fell in around them.

It was a short walk under clear winter skies from the patriarch's palace to that of the king. Their escort left them at the palace gate, and John took Heraclius by the arm and guided him to the king's large audience chamber. The vaulted hall was crowded. Guards lined the walls and barons and courtiers stood before them. At the centre of the hall, Guy stood with his wife Sibylla and his brother Amalric. The two men shifted nervously. Sibylla stood unmoving, her head held high. She wore a tight-fitting caftan that accentuated her slender figure. Her long auburn hair hung loose down her back, and she had decorated her eyes with kohl.

Baldwin sat on his throne across from Sibylla. He wore full regalia, an ermine-lined cape over his shoulders and the crown of Jerusalem on his head. The silver mask hid his face. He clutched a scroll in his right hand. A second throne had been set beside him and on it sat his nephew, Sibylla's son Baldwin. The sickly child also wore royal robes and a thin crown. Behind the throne stood Agnes, straight-backed and regal. Raymond, Joscelin and Balian flanked her, along with Peter, the bishop of Tripoli, whom Baldwin had named chancellor to replace William.

John guided Heraclius to stand beside Guy and then went to join the others behind the throne. 'I have brought Heraclius, Your Grace,' he whispered to the blind king.

'All are present?' the king asked.

'The traitors stand before you,' Agnes told him.

'Then we will begin.' Baldwin raised the scroll and tossed it to land at Amalric's feet. 'What is the meaning of this?'

The constable picked up the scroll and unrolled it. His forehead creased in confusion. 'I have never seen this document.'

Beside him, Guy had paled. 'My lord, I never wished to be king. I—'

'Silence! I do not wish to hear you snivel. I know well enough that this plot was not hatched by you, Guy. You and your brother are too simple for such treachery.'

Guy bowed. 'Thank you, Your Grace.' Beside John, Balian sniggered.

'This bears the stamp of Heraclius and my sister,' Baldwin said.

'It was Sibylla!' Heraclius squealed. 'She asked my advice on how to draw up such a document. I gave it to her, nothing more. I will swear it on the True Cross itself.'

'What do you say to this, Sister?'

Sibylla looked down her thin nose at her brother. 'I am a

princess and heir to the throne. I will not suffer this charade of a trial. Do what you will to me and be done with it.'

'Very well.' Baldwin cleared his throat. 'Amalric, I believe you innocent. You are a brave man. If you swear to serve me faithfully, then you shall continue in your post as constable.'

'I swear it, Your Grace.'

Baldwin turned his sightless eyes in the direction of the Patriarch. 'Heraclius, you have your post by the will of God; it is not for me to gainsay Him. But to demonstrate your loyalty, the Church of the Holy Sepulchre shall contribute fifty thousand bezants to the Crown for the defence of the Kingdom. John assures me that you have the sum.'

Heraclius looked ill. 'Yes, Your Grace.'

'Guy of Lusignan,' Baldwin declared, 'you are regent no longer.'

'And who shall rule?' Sibylla asked with a smirk. 'You, Brother? You are no king. You are a cripple.'

The silver mask hid Baldwin's expression, but his silence betrayed his anger. When he finally spoke, his voice grated like two stones rubbing together. 'From this moment, my nephew Baldwin will rule beside me. When I die, it is he who will succeed me, not you, Sibylla.'

'You cannot do this, Brother! The Haute Cour—'

'– has already sanctioned my command.'

'But, Your Grace,' Guy ventured. 'Young Baldwin is only a child of six.'

'Raymond of Tripoli shall serve as regent until the boy comes of age. You, Guy, will take that scheming wife of yours and return to Ascalon. If either of you shows your face in Jerusalem without my permission, I will have your head.'

Sibylla glared at her brother for a moment longer, and then the arrogance left her. She slumped to the floor and began to weep. 'Brother, please! For the love I bear you, do not do this!'

'Save your false tears, Sister. They will not move me.'

Sibylla rose, her tears gone and her face now red with rage.

87

She pointed to Agnes. 'This is your doing! You always favoured that diseased cripple over me. You will pay for this!' She stormed out. Guy followed.

'That went well,' Balian murmured.

'Do not take Sibylla's anger lightly, Balian,' Agnes cautioned. 'There is much of me in her. She is dangerous, more dangerous than a thousand Saracens.'

Chapter 6

'Your Grace,' John called softly from the doorway. The candle had burned out, and though dawn light was beginning to filter through the window, the room remained dim. He could just make out the king. Baldwin sat beside the bed where Agnes's body had been laid out. He was slumped forward, his head on his mother's chest, his face away from John. He had not moved at the sound of John's voice. John crossed the room and touched his shoulder. 'Your Grace, it is time.'

Baldwin lifted his head. It was the first time John had seen him without the silver mask since the king had woken from his illness. His cheekbones were prominent over sunken cheeks that were covered with red lesions. A lump like a gnarled root deformed his right brow. His nose was shrivelled and misshapen, the left nostril eaten away by disease. The king's sightless eyes were red from weeping. He turned his head in John's direction and spoke in a hoarse voice. 'I prayed once to be free of her, John. Now she is dead.'

'It is not your doing, Your Grace. Agnes has lost much of her hair, and her nails are yellowed. She was poisoned.'

'Zirnih.' Baldwin whispered the name of the poison. 'I know the signs all too well. This was Sibylla's doing, I have no doubt. She is her mother's child.'

'What will you do?'

'Annul her marriage to Guy and send her to Europe. Perhaps Philip of Flanders will still want her hand.'

'It will be difficult to annul the marriage without the Patriarch.' Rather than pay the fifty thousand bezants Baldwin had demanded, Heraclius had fled to France. Men at the docks in Acre said they had seen him loading chests full of gold aboard his ship.

'Nevertheless, it must be done. I shall not live for much longer, John. I'll not have Sibylla and her fool husband scheming for the throne when I am gone. I want her far away. And we must have peace.' Baldwin reached out and found John's hand. The king's own was gnarled and covered with white nodules. 'I am sending you to Damascus to treat with Saladin.'

'The last time we met it was with swords in hand. You should send another.'

'There is no one else I trust. William is still in Rome. Raymond must stay in Jerusalem in case I die. It must be you, John. Render me this last service.'

John nodded. 'I will not fail you, Your Grace.'

'Good. Good.' Baldwin turned back to his mother and found her hand. The sun rose higher and light spilled through the window to illuminate her, turning her blond hair gold. Agnes was still beautiful, even in death. Seeing her like this, it was easy for John to remember why he had loved her once. Part of him, he realized, loved her still.

'We must go,' he said, his voice thick with emotion. 'The vigil is over. She must be taken to the church for burial.'

Baldwin nodded. He kissed his mother's hand. 'Had she not kept me safe during my illness, I might be dead now. She stood by me, in the end.'

'She did, Your Grace.'

Baldwin leaned back in his chair. 'Porters!'

Four men entered the room and carried him out. When they had gone, John leaned forward and kissed Agnes's cheek.

It was cold. He brushed away a tear as he strode from the room.

JANUARY 1185: DAMASCUS

The sun hovering over the hills west of Damascus glowed like iron fresh from the forge and sent John's shadow racing before him as he led his mule into the courtyard of one of the caravan-serais outside the city. Stable boys were already tending to the camels and horses of the caravan he had joined. He preferred to travel with Saracens rather than an escort of Frankish sergeants, who would only cause trouble. A slight boy no older than seven came to take John's mule. The child's eyes went wide as John handed him a silver denier. 'See that she is brushed, her hooves picked, and she is well fed and watered, and you shall have another,' John told him in Arabic.

'Yes, sayyid.' The boy bowed and led the mule away.

'Juwan!'

He turned to see Dhameer, the merchant who had organized the caravan. He was dressed in expensive silks, but his broad shoulders and rough, scar-lined hands spoke of a previous life as a soldier. He smiled and held out his hand palm upwards. John had joined the caravan in Acre, where he had paid Dhameer three deniers. The rest of the fee was due now that they had reached their destination. John took a gold bezant from the pouch at his belt and placed it in Dhameer's hand.

Dhameer made to give the coin back. 'I am no thief. This is too much.'

'Keep it.' It was no secret that those who paid well were afforded better protection by the caravan guards. 'Consider it an expression of my thanks for having delivered me safely to Damascus. I trust I will be welcome in your caravan for the return journey?'

'Of course. We leave in one week's time.'

'I will see you then.' John headed for the gate.

'Where are you going? Stay with us, Juwan. Tonight we feast our safe arrival.'

'I have business in Damascus.'

'You must hurry then. The city gates close at sunset.'

John checked the sun. The lower rim was touching the hills. He left the caravanserai and walked briskly down a path that cut through the orchards. The orange trees were heavy with fruit, and their scent filled the cool evening air. Ahead, he could see the Bab al-Faradis, or gate of paradise. Only the top of it was lit by the setting sun; the lower half was bathed in shadows. In the dim light, and dressed in a dusty caftan and keffiyeh, John looked much like any other Saracen. The guards at the gate hardly spared him a glance. No sooner had John passed through than he heard the creak of it being closed behind him. Muezzins began to chant the call to prayer. 'Allahu akbar! Allahu akbar! Allahu akbar! Allahu akbar! Ash-hadu an la ilaha illallah!'

The streets were filling with men heading towards the great mosque at the heart of the city. John joined the crowd. The palace lay just beside the mosque. He went straight to the men who guarded the bridge across the moat.

'What do you want?' the captain of the guards demanded.

'I am an emissary of King Baldwin of Jerusalem. I have come on his behalf to speak with Al-Malik al-nasir Saladin.'

'King Baldwin, eh?' The guard let out a sharp bark of laughter. 'Saladin's next public audience is Tuesday. Come back then.'

John reached into his caftan, and the guards lowered their spears towards him. He slowly took a scroll of paper from the tube around his neck, unrolled it, and handed it to the captain. The scroll was covered in Arabic and bore the king's seal. The guard's forehead creased as he squinted at the writing. John guessed he could not read. That was good. The illiterate often had an almost superstitious respect for the written word.

'It says that I am John of Tatewic, abbot of Mount Sion,

archdeacon of the Church of the Holy Sepulchre, and councillor to King Baldwin. I come on his behalf to treat with Saladin.'

The captain stared at the paper a moment longer before rolling the scroll and tucking it into his belt. 'Show him inside. I will inform the Malik.'

John was taken to a small room off the entrance hall of the palace. A servant brought him water and a bowl filled with cubes of watermelon. After that, John saw no one for a long time. He paced the room. Would Yusuf receive him as a friend or as an enemy? Finally, John knelt to pray in order to calm his nerves. The single candle that lit the room had shrunk so that it was guttering in its own wax when the door finally opened. Imad ad-Din stepped inside.

'John! It is really you.'

John embraced him. He had known Imad ad-Din since the scholar was a young man tutoring Yusuf in history and politics. Now, Imad ad-Din had grey hair and a lined face. 'It has been too long,' John told him. 'Will he see me?'

'I will take you to him.'

They crossed the palace through marble-clad halls and climbed a stairwell to Yusuf's private quarters. Saqr stood guard at the door. 'The Malik is waiting,' he told John and pulled the door open.

Yusuf sat amidst cushions on the far side of the small audience chamber. John hardly recognized him. Yusuf's cheeks were hollow, his hair and beard more grey than black. There were dark circles under his eyes.

'John.' He sounded weary. 'Why have you come?'

'King Baldwin has sent me. He desires peace between our kingdoms.'

'But why you? He could have sent another emissary.'

'He chose me, friend.'

'You are not my friend. You have chosen your side. You made that clear at Montgisard.'

'I spared your life.'

'And saved Baldwin's. This war could have been over.' Yusuf sighed. 'Your king and I are enemies, John. So long as you serve him, so are we.'

'We do not have to be.'

'You are wrong.'

'Perhaps.' John decided to try a different tack. 'You need peace with us in order to deal with Mosul.' He waited for a reply, but Yusuf did not speak. 'I have my orders, Yusuf. I will not leave without peace.'

'Very well.' Yusuf raised his voice. 'Saqr!' The mamluk entered at once. 'Have John shown to guest quarters and see that he is comfortable. Post guards at his door. He is not to leave without my permission. He will be staying with us for a very long time.'

Yusuf rode through the camp that sprawled along the Barada River to the south-east of the city. There were thousands of tents: the ordered rows of the mamluks from Egypt; the brightly coloured tents of the emirs who had come with their own mamluks; and the sprawling sheepskin structures of the Bedouin who had joined the army in the hope of spoils. Yusuf could see another tribe of Bedouin on the horizon, kicking up a cloud of dust as they rode towards Damascus. The rainy season was over, and the lands east of the city were once more hard and dry. It would be time to march soon. In Aleppo, Yusuf would meet the rest of his men, including the emirs of Al-Jazirah – Gökböri, Nu'man and Muhammad.

He reined to a halt before a tent of saffron-yellow silk. Al-Mashtub strode out. The huge warrior smiled broadly, showing teeth that had yellowed with age. He held Yusuf's stirrup for him to dismount. Yusuf embraced him and kissed his cheeks. 'I am glad you have come, friend.'

'I would not have missed it. Life in Banyas is dull. The Franks in Hunin have not left their castle in months. I fear they have lost their stomach for battle.'

Talk of Banyas made Yusuf think of John. They had taken the city together, back when Nur ad-Din ruled. John was still confined to his quarters in the palace. Yusuf had not seen him since he arrived more than two months ago.

'When do we leave for Mosul?' Al-Mashtub asked.

'In two weeks. Tonight, you will dine with me at the palace.'

'Do you still have that cook you took from Aleppo?' Yusuf nodded, and Al-Mashtub grinned. 'Then it will be my pleasure.'

Yusuf continued on his way, greeting half a dozen more newly arrived emirs and sheikhs before returning to the palace. Imad ad-Din met him in the entryway. 'A bird has come from Jerusalem, Malik.' The secretary lowered his voice. 'King Baldwin is dead.'

'Who rules in Jerusalem now?'

'Baldwin's young nephew has been crowned king, with Raymond of Tripoli his regent. What will you do, Malik? Will you invade the Kingdom?'

'I will think on it.'

Yusuf returned to his chambers to find his wife Shamsa waiting for him. She and the children had joined him from Cairo last month.

'You have heard?' she asked.

Yusuf nodded. 'It is no surprise. Baldwin has been ill for years.'

'Some will take it as a sign that he died when you have an army ready at hand. Your men will want to attack Jerusalem.'

Yusuf knew that tone. 'But?'

'If you turn away to attack the Kingdom, Izz ad-Din will invade from Mosul. He might take Aleppo.'

'Not with Selim there.'

'Even your brother cannot win against overwhelming odds. I know the news from the north as well as you, Husband. Izz ad-Din has allied with the Seljuk prince Jahan Pahlavan. Together, they have besieged your ally, the emir of Ibril. If you do not oppose them, they will move on to take Mardin and Nisbin, then Saruj and Edessa. The emirs of Al-Jazirah who have pledged their swords to you will join them. Aleppo will be next.'

Yusuf kissed her on the brow. 'I have missed you, my clever wife.'

'So you will move on Mosul?'

'Perhaps. The regent, Raymond, will be eager to start his rule with a victory. If I march on Mosul, the Franks will strike at Damascus.'

'Not if you make peace with them.'

Yusuf scowled. 'After Montgisard, I swore to drive the Franks from the Holy Land.'

'And you will, in time. But you cannot fight on two fronts, my love. You must put your own house in order before you turn to the Franks.'

'*Hmph.*' Yusuf went to the window and stood with his arms crossed over his chest.

Shamsa came to stand beside him. She touched his chin and gently turned his face towards her. 'I know you are angry with John, habibi, but do not let your anger cloud your judgement. Would you still resist peace had the Franks sent a different emissary?'

Yusuf opened his mouth to protest, but then thought better of it. She was right. 'You know me better than I know myself.' He kissed her, then pulled away and raised his voice. 'Saqr! Bring me John.'

John's palms began to sweat as he followed a guard through the halls of the palace. It was the first time he had left his room in months. He had passed the days reading, gazing out of the window and practising his arguments for peace. Hope had begun to fade, but now Yusuf had summoned him.

They had reached the audience chamber. The guard knocked and pushed the door open. Yusuf sat in the same position as the last time John had been there. 'Your king is dead,' he said when John had sat.

John blinked. 'What? When?'

'Yesterday.'

And he had not been there. John felt as if a great weight were pressing on his chest. He should have returned after Yusuf's initial refusal. Perhaps he could have done something.

'You chose him over me once, John.' Yusuf met his eyes. 'I ask you to choose again. Join my service.'

John shook his head. 'I swore an oath.'

'To Baldwin. Baldwin is dead.'

'I am a priest. I swore an oath to God as well.'

'There is only one God, John. I serve him. I fight his battles.'

'War is no business of God. I must return to Jerusalem. Allah yasalmak, friend.' He rose.

'You said you would not go without peace.'

John paused at the door. 'Peace?' Why now, when the Kingdom was most vulnerable? He searched Yusuf's face, but found no answer. John's forehead creased in thought. When Guy took over as regent, he had sent Reynald raiding into the Hijaz. Perhaps Yusuf feared another such attack from Raymond. But why fear a Frankish army, unless . . . 'You plan to march on Mosul.'

'Perhaps. Tell me of the new king. The truth, John.'

'Young Baldwin is a sickly child. He is not likely to live to his majority.'

'And the regent, Raymond.'

'You have met him. You know him to be a good man.'

'But is he a good soldier?'

'You will not find the Kingdom an easy prize while he rules, if that is what you mean.'

Yusuf met John's eyes. 'One more question, John. Answer me true; your peace depends on it. Can I take Jerusalem?'

John opened his mouth, prepared to lie, but then thought better of it. He could not deceive Yusuf. They knew one another too well. 'Yes, you can take it. But it will cost you dearly, and you will not be able to hold it, not if you must send men to protect Aleppo from the emir of Mosul.'

Yusuf nodded. He held out a sheet of paper.

'What is this?'

'A truce, John. Four years.'

John took the treaty, held it to his heart, and bowed. 'Shukran allah.'

Yusuf shook his head. 'Do not thank me. Once Mosul is in my power, there will be nothing to prevent me from turning to the Kingdom. When the four years are up, I am coming for Jerusalem.'

Chapter 7

Yusuf felt as if his insides were on fire. Sweat beaded on his forehead, and he grit his teeth as he squatted over the chamber pot. When he had finished shitting, he stepped outside the private section of his tent and a servant went in to retrieve the pot. As it was carried out, Saqr looked inside and frowned.

'Malik—'

Yusuf waved away his concern. Mosul was almost his. He could not afford to be weak. 'It is nothing. Have water brought and help me with my armour.'

Saqr helped him pull on a shirt of heavy mail and then laced up the vest of golden scale armour that Yusuf wore over it. Yusuf buckled on his sword belt, pulled on his helmet and stepped outside. The morning sun flashed off his golden armour and the gilt crown of his helmet. It was important to look the part of a king, no matter how miserable he might feel.

Yusuf's tent had been set on a low ridge two miles west of Mosul. The tents of his khaskiya covered the face of the slope before him, and beyond them the camp stretched to within half a mile of the city, on the far side of which the Tigris River flowed past, its waters glittering reddish gold. From here, Mosul's tall walls – the same dusty brown colour as the land around them – looked small enough to step over. The emir, Izz ad-Din, was trapped behind those walls. His ally, the Seljuk

Pahlavan, had fled when Yusuf crossed the Euphrates. After his withdrawal, many of the emirs east of Mosul had gone over to Yusuf's side. The city was isolated. It held less than half as many men as Yusuf's army. Yet after five months of siege, it still stood.

A servant arrived with a cup of water. Yusuf forced himself to drink, though his stomach still burned. Perhaps the water would help to quench the fire. As he sipped, he watched the catapults at work, hurling chunks of rock taken from ruins in the hills across the Tigris. The catapults pounded day and night, but they did little damage. Izz ad-Din had sent out sorties to drive away Yusuf's sappers before they could get close enough to undermine the walls. Yusuf would have to starve the city into submission. He could well imagine how the people must be suffering. As a young emir, Yusuf had spent four months under siege in Alexandria. He still remembered the gnawing hunger in his gut. It had eventually become so much a part of him that he almost ceased to notice it.

Yusuf lowered his cup as he noticed a flurry of activity atop the nearest gate. Helmets flashed in the sun as more men joined the guards that were there. A horn sounded from amongst the men Yusuf had posted to watch the gate. A moment later, the gate opened. Yusuf's men quickly formed a line to blunt the charge of any sortie. Below Yusuf, the camp sprang to life as men dropped their breakfast to reach for swords and spears. Al-Mashtub galloped up the ridge and slid from the saddle before Yusuf.

'Malik, the gate!'

'So I see,' Yusuf replied calmly. 'Inshallah, Izz ad-Din will be fool enough to attack. You will lead the Egyptian regiments against him. When the enemy charges, hold fast in the middle and send your flanks to cut them off from the city.'

'Yes, Malik.'

'And make sure the guards at the other gates stay alert. This may be only a feint before he attacks in force elsewhere.'

Al-Mashtub climbed into the saddle and galloped away shouting orders. Yusuf turned his attention back to the gate. If it was a sortie, Izz ad-Din's men were taking their time about it. Any element of surprise had long since past. Finally, two dozen men rode out. Even from this distance, Yusuf could see that the three men at the centre were not soldiers. They wore no armour, which would have reflected the morning sun. Emissaries. The gates swung shut behind them.

Yusuf turned to one of the dozen messengers who attended him. They were young mamluks, selected for the speed with which they rode and their ability to accurately remember his instructions. 'Tell Al-Mashtub to keep a careful watch,' Yusuf told him. 'This may be some trick.' The man nodded and sprinted for his horse. 'You four, have Gökböri, Nu'man, Muhammad and Imad ad-Din attend me in my tent. And you, see that Izz ad-Din's messengers are shown here. Saqr, have food and drink prepared for our guests.'

Yusuf entered his tent and seated himself on a camp-stool. Imad ad-Din came in first and the emirs arrived shortly thereafter. Gökböri was still chewing on a roasted chicken leg. Muhammad was dressed immaculately in silk robes of emerald green decorated with a floral motif in silver. Nu'man waddled in last of all, wearing the hard leather and stained mail that never seemed to leave his back. The three men joined Imad ad-Din at either side of Yusuf's stool.

'You think they have had enough, Malik?' Gökböri asked.

'Inshallah,' Muhammad said. 'Sieges are a tiresome business.'

'And expensive,' Imad ad-Din added. 'Each day costs thousands of dinars in food and pay for your mamluks, Malik. Even the coffers of Egypt will run dry at some point.'

'Izz ad-Din's treasury is filled with gold,' Nu'man said. 'We will have all we need when the city falls.'

'Malik.' Saqr stepped inside. 'Izz ad-Din has sent his wife, the khatun Asma umm Arslan, and her two eldest daughters.'

Saqr held the flap aside, and the women entered. The two daughters were dressed in caftans of white – a symbol of purity indicating that they were virgins – and wore niqabs that covered all but their eyes. Izz ad-Din's wife Asma wore robes of yellow silk and her face was uncovered. She was an attractive woman, with brilliant golden eyes that had the beginnings of crow's feet at their corners. Her hair showed no trace of silver and her face was round. She, at least, had not suffered from a lack of food during the siege. She met Yusuf's gaze boldly.

'Ahlan wa-Sahlan,' Yusuf welcomed them. He gestured to the food that had been set out. It was the hospitality due any guest. 'Sit. Eat and drink.'

'Shukran Allah, Malik,' Asma said. 'Your welcome honours us.' She sat first, followed by her daughters. They each took a small bite of bread and a sip of water, then set the food aside.

'After months surrounded by only warriors,' Yusuf told Asma, 'it is a joy to look upon beauty such as you and your daughters possess. It is like finding an oasis in the desert.' Yusuf was more concerned with their message than their looks, but certain formalities had to be observed.

'I see your reputation for courtesy is as well earned as your reputation in war, Malik. I hope to find that your reputation for mercy is equally well founded.'

That was well done. This Asma was clever. 'Those who admit their faults and accept my judgement will find me ever merciful,' he told her.

'Then I beg mercy for the people of Mosul. They have done nothing to offend you, yet it is they who suffer most from this siege. Grain is worth its weight in gold. Men have been murdered over a loaf of bread. Hundreds of starving children beg in the streets. Be merciful, Malik. If you will not lift your siege, at least send food for our people.'

Food that would no doubt go to feed Izz ad-Din's soldiers. 'If your people want food, they have only to open the gates to me.'

Asma shook her head. 'Our people are loyal before all else. They will never betray Izz ad-Din.'

'We shall see, khatun. It is said that a hungry belly knows no loyalties.'

Asma's eyes narrowed. When she spoke again, there was an angry edge to her voice. 'You claim to be the servant of Islam, Malik. Why, then, are you here in the east fighting your brothers when the enemy lies far to the west in Jerusalem?'

'You know well enough why I am here. I cannot fight the Franks so long as I fear a knife in my back the moment it is turned.'

'You use clever words to hide your ambition. If all you seek is to secure your borders, then make peace with Mosul. Do not destroy it.'

Finally, they had reached the heart of the matter. Yusuf nodded for her to continue.

'Izz ad-Din offers a ten-year truce. My daughters will marry your sons. You will free the emirs east of Mosul of their oaths to you. In return, Izz ad-Din will allow you to keep the lands to the west.'

Yusuf arched an eyebrow. 'He will allow me? He cannot stop me. I do not seek a truce, khatun. I have come for Mosul, and it will be mine.'

One of the daughters sniffled. She began to weep loudly. The other joined in. Yusuf almost smiled, the ploy was so transparent. Asma herself made as if to wipe away a tear. 'You would leave us with nothing?' she demanded, her voice quaking. 'You would kill your Muslim brothers? You would condemn my daughters to a life of squalor, make them the whores of your soldiers? I see that the legend of your piety is false. You are no man of God.'

Yusuf smiled gently. He, too, could play this game. 'I do not wish any harm to your good daughters, khatun.'

'Then you will make peace?'

'If Izz ad-Din kneels before me as my subject, then I will

103

grant him his life and spare his men and the people of Mosul. I will give your husband the province of Sinjar to rule.'

'Sinjar?' Asma said the word as if it left a bad taste in her mouth. She rose, and her daughters did likewise. 'Izz ad-Din is the descendant of the great Imad ad-Din Zengi. He will never bow before a Kurd such as you.'

'Then he will die and Mosul will fall. When that day comes, not even your daughters' tears will save you. Go and tell your husband that.'

Yusuf hunched beneath his cloak as he rode out from camp for his evening inspection of the men on guard. The siege had reached seven months and winter had come. Heavy wet snow collected on the hood of his cloak and his horse kicked up mud, spattering Yusuf's legs. They might be starving in Mosul, Yusuf reflected, but at least they had roofs over their heads. He could hardly remember the last time he was warm. The winter chill seemed to have got into his bones. And the ache in his stomach was worse than ever. Today was the last day of Ramadan; perhaps when the daily fasting was through, he would feel better. He glanced at Saqr who rode straight-backed, his head uncovered. He seemed to not notice the cold. *Ah, to be young again.*

Through the snow ahead, Yusuf spied ranks of mamluks. The guards stationed outside Mosul's northernmost gate stood to attention as he approached. He knew the men were worse off than he. Some were shaking with cold as they clutched their spears. They knelt in the mud as he passed.

'Saqr,' Yusuf called. 'Send a messenger back to camp. Have the cooks prepare a hot soup and see that it is brought to the men on guard.'

'Yes, Malik.'

Yusuf continued on towards the next watch. The fire in his belly was growing worse. He felt a sudden, sharp stab of pain, like a hot poker thrust into his gut. He dismounted and fell to his hands and knees in the mud as he retched violently. His vomit was red with blood.

Saqr was at his side immediately. 'Are you well, Malik? I will call the doctors.'

Yusuf waved him away. 'Leave me be.' He tried to rise, but his head was spinning and his legs weak. He collapsed and rolled on to his back. The last thing he remembered was the touch of the wet snow on his hot cheeks. And then the world went black . . .

He did not know for how long he was unconscious, but after a time, images came to him. He saw his son Al-Salih as a young babe, crawling towards him from the darkness. The baby became a man, holding a golden sword with a wide, curving blade. When he spoke, Al-Salih's voice was hollow and cold, the voice of a dead man. 'Vengeance, Father. I will have vengeance.' He swung his blade, and Yusuf skipped back out of the way. He was in armour now, with a sword in his hand. He met his son's next blow and turned it aside. Yusuf countered and his blade opened up a gash in Al-Salih's stomach. No blood appeared.

Al-Salih attacked again, hacking down. Yusuf sidestepped the blow and impaled his son. Al-Salih laughed, a hollow sound, like bones clacking together. 'You cannot kill me, Father. I am already dead.' He reached for Yusuf with his hands, and as they closed around Yusuf's throat, Al-Salih transformed into his mother, Asimat. Yusuf pushed her away, but she came back, raking at his face with long nails. Her hand closed again on his throat and began to squeeze. Yusuf grabbed her arms and tried to pull her hands away, but her grip was like iron. He was growing desperate for air.

'I know,' she rasped. 'I know what you did.' The flesh of her arms began to decay in his hands. Her face became grey, the skin sloughing off to reveal white bone. 'I know!' Her fingers closed tighter and tighter, choking the last air from him. He sank into darkness once more.

Yusuf awoke in a dim room. He was lying in a soft bed and above him shadows played on the ceiling, cast there by a candle that flickered on the bedside table. He tried to call for a servant but only produced a strangled croak. His throat was impossibly dry. He made to get up, but sank back into the feather mattress, his head spinning. He heard voices and turned his head, locating the door. It was open. Outside, he saw dim figures speaking in hushed tones.

'He must not be disturbed,' one of them said. Yusuf did not recognize the man's voice. 'He needs rest if he is to recover.'

'Yes,' agreed another strange voice. 'More *hashah* to dull the pain and allow him to sleep.'

'He has had sleep enough.' That was Selim. What was he doing here? He was supposed to be in Aleppo. 'While my brother lies in bed, men are conspiring to steal his kingdom from him and his children. I must speak with him. You will do whatever it takes to wake him.'

'I dare not,' one of the doctors protested.

'Let—' Yusuf managed to rasp. It felt as if the words were clawing their way out of his throat. 'Let. Him. In.'

'Brother!' Selim entered and knelt at Yusuf's bedside. He looked back to the doctors. 'Bring water at once.'

One of the doctors entered with a cup. He was a compact man with a beak of a nose and a black beard with a few streaks of grey. He looked familiar, but Yusuf could not place him. It did not matter. He took the cup and drank greedily. When he spoke again, it was easier. 'Where am I?'

'Harran. Your men carried you here four weeks ago.'

'Four weeks? What of Mosul?'

'The siege was abandoned. I came from Aleppo as soon as I could.'

'I heard you talking. What are these conspiracies you speak of?'

Selim glanced towards the door. 'It would be best to speak in private. I know a place where we will not be overheard.'

Yusuf nodded. 'Help me up.'

Selim put his arm behind Yusuf's back and helped him to sit. Yusuf looked down at his legs. They were impossibly thin beneath his linen tunic. He raised a bony arm and examined it.

'At first, you could keep nothing down,' Selim told him. 'You lost two stones before the doctors managed to feed you a little broth. Do you want food?'

'Later.' Yusuf tried to rise, but the world was spinning. He put his arm around his brother's shoulder, and Selim helped him to stand. 'I wish to speak with Imad ad-Din as well. Have him come with pen and paper.'

'You heard the Malik,' Selim told the doctors. 'Fetch his secretary.'

Selim helped Yusuf down the hall to a windowless room. He eased Yusuf on to a stool. Yusuf sat hunched forward, sipping from the cup of water until Imad ad-Din arrived.

'I am so pleased to see you well, Malik. Allah has answered my prayers.'

'Close the door,' Selim instructed. He turned back to Yusuf. 'Rumours of your death have been enough to fray the seams that hold your kingdom together, Brother. Your emirs are scrambling to secure what is theirs or to add to it. Our cousin Nasir ad-Din is the worst. It seems he is not content with Homs. He has made arrangements to take Damascus when you die.'

'Are you sure of this?' Yusuf rasped. He knew that Nasir ad-Din was given to excess, but he had not thought him a traitor.

'It seems he resents you. I am told that he said you treated him worse than the lowest of your emirs.'

'I spared his life when I could have had him hanged,' Yusuf growled. 'Tell me of this plot of his.'

'One of the men he sought to buy told Al-Muqaddam, who informed me. The plan was for the emirs of Damascus to take your son Al-Aziz hostage. Nasir ad-Din would then rule as regent. The boy was to be disposed of before he came of age.'

'My own family turns against me.' Yusuf shook his head and looked to Imad ad-Din. 'Write to Al-Muqaddam in Damascus. Have him distribute alms in celebration of my recovery. Five thousand dinars should be enough to remind the people who their rightful ruler is. Selim, you will return to Cairo.'

'But Brother—'

'You have done enough in the north. If Damascus is restive, Cairo will be as well. Egypt is the key to my kingdom. I need you there. On your way south, you will deal with Nasir ad-Din. Our nephew has a fondness for wine. That will lead to his death, if he is not careful.'

'I understand, Brother.'

'Good. Now go; you both have much to do. Have food brought for me and send in Al-Mashtub, Gökböri and Nu'man. I must prepare to return to Mosul.'

Imad ad-Din frowned. 'So soon, Malik?'

'My enemies and allies alike will think me weak after my illness. If I do not show them otherwise, the emirs of Al-Jazirah will start to shift their allegiance back to Izz ad-Din. Mosul would slip through our fingers. That must not happen. I will ride within a fortnight. A show of force may be enough to bring peace.'

'Peace, Brother? I thought you had determined to take Mosul.'

'And Allah has shown me my error. Izz ad-Din's wife said I was a godless man, and Allah struck me down. I am done fighting my Muslim brothers. It is time to turn to the kingdom of the Franks. Now go.'

Imad ad-Din opened the door. Selim let him leave, then closed the door and turned back to Yusuf. 'I have one last thing to tell you. Your wife Asimat was involved in the conspiracy to put Nasir ad-Din on the throne of Damascus.'

An image sprang into Yusuf's mind: Asimat as a corpse, her cold hands clasped around his throat. He shuddered. 'Are you certain?'

Selim nodded. 'She claims you killed her son.'

Yusuf's stomach began to burn. He had told her that Izz ad-Din killed Al-Salih. How had she discovered the truth? The Hashashin were sworn to secrecy. Yusuf sat up straight. The doctor! He remembered where he had seen that face. 'The doctor who attended me, the one with the beaked nose, bring him to me.'

'If you feel ill, perhaps you should lie down, Brother.'

'I am fine. Do as I say.'

The doctor entered and shut the door behind him. 'Malik.'

'Rashid ad-Din Sinan,' Yusuf greeted him, and the head of the Hashashin bowed. 'You are far from Masyaf. Are you so concerned for my health?'

'I am, Malik. You have been a good friend to my people, but that is not what brought me here. I came to apologize.'

'Asimat.'

Sinan nodded.

'How did she learn the truth?'

'She is a stubborn woman. She tortured and bribed the palace guards until she found the man responsible. He had been serving as one of Al-Salih's private guards.'

Yusuf frowned. 'The Hashashin are sworn to secrecy.'

'Yes, but we are only men. My *fidai* would never have given in to torture, but Asimat is a beautiful woman. She can be most convincing.'

'I see. Where is this man now?'

'Dead. As for your wife . . . That is why I am here, to learn your will.'

Yusuf met the assassin's dark eyes. 'You will visit her yourself. Traitors must be punished.'

Yusuf sat in his tent eating a bowl of boiled wheat. That and a thin chicken broth were all that Ibn Jumay allowed him. The doctor had arrived from Damascus two weeks ago. He had also forced Yusuf to cease making his twice-daily rounds of the men on watch. So Yusuf had to be content to wait in his tent while his army besieged Mosul. He turned to Imad ad-Din, who sat across from him sorting through the correspondence they had received that day.

'What do you have for me?'

Imad ad-Din held up two letters. 'A letter from your brother and another from the Hashashin's leader, Rashid ad-Din Sinan.'

'Start with my brother.'

Imad ad-Din broke the seal and scanned the letter. 'Your cousin Nasir ad-Din is dead. Apparently, he died of an excess of drink.' Yusuf knew better. As per his instructions, Selim had drowned Nasir ad-Din in a barrel of wine. 'His son – a boy named Shirkuh, like your uncle – is to succeed him.'

Yusuf set his bowl aside. He found no pleasure in vengeance. It had taken his appetite. He held out his hand. 'I will read the letter from the Old Man of the Mountain myself.'

'Yes, Malik.'

Imad ad-Din handed over the letter. Yusuf broke the seal and read: *Greetings Al-Malik al-nasir from your friend and ally Rashid ad-Din Sinan. I regret to inform you that your wife, Asimat, has died of a heart attack. She died quickly. There was no pain.* Yusuf stopped reading. He felt a sudden burning in his chest and tasted bile. I only did what I must, he reminded himself. He dropped the letter in the brazier of coals that had been set beside him for warmth. He watched it burn before turning to Imad ad-Din. 'Asimat has died. Distribute alms in her memory, and see that her tomb is suitably splendid. Spare no expense. That is all for now.'

Imad ad-Din departed without a word. Yusuf rose and began

to pace his tent. His legs felt weak. Was that an effect of his long illness? Or was it Asimat's death? He tried to remember her face as he had first seen it, when he was a young boy just come to the court of Nur ad-Din. But he could only see her as a corpse, as she had come to him in the dream.

'Malik!' Imad ad-Din called as he re-entered the tent.

'What is it?' Yusuf snapped.

'Izz ad-Din. He wishes to speak with you.'

'He is here?'

'He waits before the walls of the city.'

Yusuf stepped outside and looked to Mosul. Outside the western gate, a rider sat surrounded by forty soldiers on foot. Yusuf raised his voice. 'My horse! Saqr, prepare the guard.'

Yusuf rode from camp at the centre of fifty mamluks. He signalled for them to halt when they were still a hundred yards from Izz ad-Din. 'I will ride on alone.'

Yusuf's men parted, and he rode through. Izz ad-Din came forward to meet him. The two men stopped only a few feet apart. Izz ad-Din was ten years Yusuf's junior and was a handsome man with sharp features and not a trace of grey in his long hair. He smiled, showing even white teeth.

'As-salaamu 'alaykum, Saladin. I am pleased to meet with you at last.'

'Wa 'alaykum as-salaam.'

Izz ad-Din's eyes narrowed as he examined Yusuf more closely. 'I understand you were ill, Malik. I thank Allah for your recovery.'

'I have not come to exchange flatteries and platitudes, Izz ad-Din. Say what you have come to say.'

'Very well. The war between us has cost us both much. How much more are you willing to lose to take Mosul?'

Izz ad-Din was a proud man. Admitting that Mosul would eventually fall was as close to an offer of peace as Yusuf was likely to receive. 'It is your men I want,' he told the emir of Mosul, 'not your city. Acknowledge me as your overlord, pay tribute and send your men to fight with me against the Franks, and you shall keep Mosul.'

'Mosul and the lands to its north and east.'

Yusuf nodded.

'Then I am your man, Malik.' The emir of Mosul dismounted and took hold of Yusuf's stirrup.

Yusuf dismounted and embraced him, exchanging the ritual kisses. 'We are brothers, Izz ad-Din. Now, the Franks will tremble before us.'

Chapter 8

John set the sheet of parchment back on the table and rubbed his eyes. He had arrived at the Church of the Holy Sepulchre before sunrise after a late night at the Abbey of Mount Sion. The abbey's cellarer – a wiry, toothless old man who had been at the abbey long before any of the other brothers arrived – had died in mid verse during lauds. Selecting a new cellarer had proven no easy task. The prior, the treasurer and the sacristan all had their own candidates. John knew better than to choose amongst them. That would only make enemies of the men whose candidates had been rejected. In the end, he had chosen the kitchener. He was an honest man and a terrible cook. By making him cellarer, John would spare the brothers his cooking.

John picked up the parchment again and squinted at the rows of figures. They recorded the church's monthly revenues: sheep, wool and grain from their land holdings; coin donated by worshippers or earned by the sale of pilgrims' badges; more gold and silver from the shops, mills, ovens and markets that the church owned in Jerusalem; and money sent by pious overseas rulers who could not come to the Holy Land themselves. With Heraclius gone, John had charge of the church. There would be no more money wasted on silk robes and fine perfumes. He looked to the treasurer seated across from him. He was a portly man with sagging jowls and eyebrows like hedgerows.

'Only forty-seven sheep?'

'It has been a brutal summer, Archdeacon. The shepherds had to slaughter much of their flocks, or lose them.'

'I see.' John gave the figures a final glance and set them aside. 'Store the grain. Set ten sheep aside for the Feast of the Assumption. Sell the rest at market, and the wool, too. Half the coin should be used to buy provisions. The cellarer may use his discretion, but I want foodstuffs that will last. The rest should go to hiring more sergeants.' The Holy Sepulchre owed a thousand men to the king's service, but it had not provided that number for some years. John would remedy that.

The treasurer's forehead creased, bringing his bushy grey eyebrows together. 'What of the canons, Archdeacon? Their monthly prebends are due.'

John scowled. The canons would have little enough use for that money if they were dead. But he knew better than to withhold their pay. He might wake with a knife in his belly. 'Pay them.'

'The roof of the chapel of Saint Helen is leaking.'

'We will deal with it later.'

'Two plates were broken last week in the refectory, and two spoons are missing from—'

'Later. All of it later. We need soldiers, not spoons. Is there anything else?'

'No, Archdeacon.'

'Then you are dismissed.'

John pulled on his cloak and preceded the treasurer out the door. He left the archdeacon's residence and stepped into the street south of the church just as the sun rose above the gilt roof of the Templum Domini. John walked the other way, past the pig market and south to the palace. The guards at the gate stepped aside for him. He entered and went to the chancellery, a large room dominated by an oak desk. The shelves lining the walls were bowed under the weight of papers and tomes. John sat in a wooden chair, its seat well worn from use. A stack of correspondence had been placed on the table. John checked the pigeon post first. He unrolled a letter from Tripoli that reported Bedouin raids in the countryside. The next message was from Ascalon. Guy was hiring mercenaries; building an army. John reached for another of the tightly rolled scraps of paper. This one was from a spy in Aleppo. John read it, then left immediately for the king's chambers.

'Is the King receiving?' he asked the guard at the door.

The guard nodded. 'The regent Raymond is with him.'

John strode through the receiving room to the king's bedroom. Morning sunshine slanted through an open window to illuminate young Baldwin, who lay abed under a thin linen sheet. The king was nine years old and small for his age. He was as pale as freshly shorn wool, with feverish cheeks. Baldwin had always been sickly, and he had only grown worse since becoming king a little over a year ago. The doctors feared he would not see his tenth birthday. On their advice, he would soon move his residence to Acre. It was hoped the wet sea air would quench the fire in his lungs.

Raymond sat on a stool beside the bed. The regent's brow was creased and his back hunched, as if he carried the weight of the Kingdom. John was about to make that burden even heavier. He handed Raymond the message. The regent's lips moved as he read.

'By his wounds,' Raymond whispered. He crumpled the paper in his hand. 'Now it begins.'

'What—' Baldwin was stopped short by a fit of coughing. He clenched the sheets in his fists as his chest shook. The coughing subsided, and Baldwin spit bloody phlegm on to a cloth. 'What begins, Uncle?'

'Izz ad-Din, the emir of Mosul, has bent the knee to Saladin. The Saracen kingdoms are united.'

And we are not. Guy and Sibylla were gathering an army in Ascalon to seize the throne when Baldwin died. Balian of Ibelin and Reginald of Sidon were marshalling their own troops in order to press the claim of Sibylla's sister Isabella and her husband Humphrey. Civil war was on the horizon.

Young Baldwin was wide-eyed. 'What will we do, Uncle?'

'I will deal with this, Your Grace. You must rest. You will need your strength in the days to come.' Raymond rose and drew the curtains.

'If Saladin invades, can I fight?' Baldwin asked. 'Will I have my own suit of armour?'

'Of course, Your Grace. And your own sword, too. Sleep now.'

John followed Raymond into the receiving room and closed the door behind him. Raymond went to a side table and poured himself a cup of wine. 'This is evil news, John. We must put our house in order before the truce with Saladin expires.' He took a long drink. 'I must pull Guy's teeth, and Humphrey's too.'

'Publish Baldwin's decree.'

Before his death, the elder Baldwin had drawn up a decree declaring that if the younger Baldwin died without an heir, Raymond was to rule as regent until the Pope and the kings of France and England decided between the claims of Sibylla and Isabella.

Raymond shook his head. 'I can think of no better way to start a civil war. If I make the decree public, the barons will think I mean to seize the throne.'

'Something must be done. The boy will not live long. You know it as well as I.'

'I will call the Haute Cour and let the barons decide. They will choose Humphrey and Isabella.'

'It is not their decision to make. Baldwin's will is clear.'

'Baldwin is dead, John. If he were alive now, he might think differently.'

'We will never know. Humphrey is not yet twenty, and lost the one battle he fought. If we are to face Saladin, the Kingdom needs a strong hand. Baldwin knew this. He wrote the decree to buy us time. While the kings of England and France decide, Humphrey can learn to rule and you will protect the Kingdom.'

Raymond grimaced. He drained his cup. 'I never wished to rule, but damn it, you are right, John. The Kingdom needs me. It's all the more reason not to make the decree public. Now is not the time to show our hand. We must bide our time, and when the moment comes, move against Sibylla and Isabella before they can strike at us.'

AUGUST 1186: ACRE

'Hellfire,' Raymond muttered. He and John were riding along a tree-lined stream at the head of five hundred sergeants. 'Hellfire! God damn it!' His outburst startled a host of sparrows from a nearby tree.

'Easy, Raymond. It is a grave sin to take the Lord's name in vain.'

'What more can God do, John? Saladin in control of Mosul. Two kings dead in little more than a year.' He shook his head. 'These are dark times.'

It was not the first time during the journey from Jerusalem to Acre that Raymond had given voice to his sombre thoughts. John made no reply. There was nothing he could say to cheer his companion. Young King Baldwin had died three days earlier. Raymond and John had set out at once for Acre. They rode to pay their respects and to retrieve the body for burial at the Holy Sepulchre. More importantly, they would also secure the city and retrieve the crown and the royal seal. Without them, Sibylla or Isabella would have difficulty pressing her claim to the throne.

Raymond gestured to the valley that stretched to either side of the stream they were following. Canals channelled water away from the stream into green fields, where native Christian and Muslim peasants worked bare backed under the hot summer sun. Beyond the fields rose hills covered with olive trees.

'Sometimes I fear we are not meant to hold these lands,' the regent said. 'Perhaps the Saracens have the right of it. Why else would God visit these afflictions upon us?'

'Enough, friend,' John told him with mock severity. 'Soon enough you'll be talking of fire and brimstone and shouting at your men to repent. You will leave us priests with nothing to do.'

The corner of Raymond's mouth twitched, and he smiled. 'You are right, John. Forgive me.'

They rode on in silence. The sun had sunk to hover huge and red before them when they finally left the hills and rode on to the coastal plain. They could already see Acre's massive walls, which divided the promontory on which the city sat from the mainland. As they rode closer, John could make out flags on the towers that dotted the wall. There was the black cross of the Hospitallers and the red cross of the Templars. They headed for the Gate of Saint Anthony, over which flew the Jerusalem cross. There was no sign of Guy's lions rampant or of Humphrey's golden bull. That was good.

Raymond paused in the shadow of the gate and called to the captain of his men. 'Ernault! Take three hundred of our men and take charge of the walls. Put another hundred on patrol around the city. The rest will come with me.'

'Yes, my lord.'

The brief ride to the palace stirred up old memories for John. It was his first time in Acre since he had arrived in the Holy Land thirty-eight years ago as a boy of sixteen. They passed the fountain where he had nearly come to blows with a native Christian that he had mistaken for a Saracen. They passed the bathhouse where he and Rabbit had bathed. Rabbit. John had not thought of the boy with the large ears and twitching nose in years. What had his real name been? He could not remember.

John followed Raymond into the palace courtyard. Their men trooped in after them. Ten took charge of the gate and the rest took up positions around the courtyard. As John and Raymond dismounted, Joscelin of Courtenay strode out to meet them. The seneschal's wavy blond hair had been cut short, and there were dark circles under his sky-blue eyes. 'Welcome to Acre, Lord Regent, Father Abbot,' he greeted them.

'Show us to the King,' Raymond told him.

They passed through the palace entryway and down a dim hallway. 'You will want to see his doctors as well,' Joscelin said as he led them up a broad stairway. The implication was clear.

'The boy was sickly, Jos,' Raymond replied. 'No one believes you had a hand in his death.'

'They may not believe it, but some will find profit in spreading lies.' They reached a door framed by two guards in mail. 'Fetch the doctors,' Joscelin told the men, and then pulled the door open.

Inside the room, the soft light of the setting sun shone through the open windows and illuminated the dead boy king. He was laid out on his bed. Raymond knelt at the bedside. 'If only he had lived a few years longer,' he said in a low voice, as if the king were sleeping and he feared to wake him.

'The doctors say his heart stopped,' Joscelin said. 'I believe the crown was too heavy a burden for the boy.'

Raymond kissed Baldwin's hand and rose. 'Now it is my burden.' He took a sheet of vellum from his vest and handed it to Joscelin. At the bottom, the document bore the king's seal showing the Tower of David, the Church of the Holy Sepulchre and the dome of the Templum Domini, all surrounded by the words *Civitas Regis regnum omnium* – City of the King of Kings. 'This decree is by the hand of the elder Baldwin, made before his death. I am to rule until a decision is made between his sisters Sibylla and Isabella. The Pope and the kings of France and England are to decide our next ruler.'

'*Hmm.*' Joscelin sucked at his lower lip. 'That will take months, maybe years.'

'I will write to England, France and Rome and urge them to

quickly select Isabella,' John said. 'In the meantime, Raymond will summon Sibylla and Isabella to Jerusalem, where they will be kept under guard until a queen is chosen. We have sent the chamberlain Balian to Ascalon to fetch Sibylla, and the constable Amalric to retrieve Isabella from Nablus.'

Joscelin was sucking at his lip again. 'Do you think that wise, Raymond?'

'I must act firmly or risk civil war between Guy and Humphrey.'

'Yes, but if you proceed as John suggests, then you will bring war as surely as night follows day. You know that there are those amongst the barons who believe you seek the throne. If you seize Jerusalem and Acre and put the rightful heirs under lock and key, then their suspicions will seem justified. The barons will turn against you. There will be war.'

'I am no usurper, Jos.'

'Then you should bend your knee before your rightful queen.' Joscelin gestured to the window.

John could hear the clatter of hooves. He looked out to see fifty knights ride into the courtyard, followed by over two hundred sergeants on foot. The lions rampant and silver crosses of Guy flew above them. A knight shouted for Raymond's men to lay down their arms. One of Raymond's men drew his blade and there was a brief struggle. When it was over, four men lay dead, their blood staining the stones red. The rest of Raymond's men had been herded into a corner.

'What is the meaning of this?' Raymond hissed.

Joscelin only nodded to the courtyard below. The knights dismounted and knelt. A moment later, Sibylla rode into the courtyard with Guy at her side.

John grabbed Joscelin by the collar and slammed him against the wall. 'What have you done?' he growled. 'What did she promise you?'

Raymond pulled John away from Joscelin, who spread his hands in a gesture of innocence. 'Why, John! You wound me.

I seek no more benefit than the health of the Kingdom. I know as well as you the threat Saladin poses. Now is no time for civil war. We must unite behind our queen. Come, let us go and meet her.' Joscelin went to the door, but neither John nor Raymond moved. 'Or shall I have the guards bring you?'

'That will not be necessary,' Raymond muttered.

The guards at the door fell in behind the men as they left the room. They met Sibylla and Guy in the palace entryway. Joscelin went to one knee. 'My queen.'

'Kneel before your queen,' the guard behind Raymond growled.

'I see no queen here.'

The guard swung the shaft of his spear and struck Raymond in the back of the legs, dropping him to his knees. The other guard did the same to John.

'Enough!' Sibylla snapped. She went to Raymond and offered him her hand. Raymond ignored it as he got to his feet. 'I apologize,' Sibylla said sweetly. 'That was not necessary.'

John also stood. 'Save your false courtesies. We know your true nature. You are a murdering bitch. You have no right to the throne.'

Sibylla turned her icy blue eyes on him. Her tone was now decidedly less friendly. 'Silence, priest. I have not forgotten your part in having me exiled to Ascalon. Were it not for Jos, I would have your head on a pike already. But he believes you may be useful. I warn you, though: if you do not cooperate, then I will be only too happy to see you killed.'

'Poisoned? As you poisoned your mother?'

'No. A hangman's noose should do for the likes of you.' She returned her attention to Raymond. 'The priest is wrong. As Amalric's eldest child, I have every right to the throne. The Patriarch agrees. Heraclius has returned from France and will crown me queen in one week's time.'

'The barons will not stand for it,' John protested.

Sibylla nodded ever so slightly, and guards grabbed John's

arms and dragged him into the corner. He began to struggle, but Raymond shook his head.

'The barons have already agreed,' Sibylla continued. 'Reynald, Reginald of Sidon, my husband Guy and Humphrey have given their assent, as has Joscelin, the new Lord of Toron.'

So that was why Joscelin had betrayed Raymond. John shot him a hard look. Joscelin shrugged. 'Do not act so indignant, John. The Queen has seen fit to reward me for my years of good service, nothing more.'

'You, Raymond, are the only great lord who has yet to swear loyalty,' Sibylla concluded.

'And I never will.' Raymond gestured to Guy. 'I will die before I see this fool on the throne.'

Guy's face turned crimson. He reached for his sword, but Sibylla touched his arm. 'I am not unreasonable, Raymond,' she said. 'Many of the barons feel as you do. I have agreed to divorce Guy, if they acknowledge my right to rule.'

Raymond looked to Guy. He nodded curtly. 'It is for the good of the Kingdom.'

'And what of Baldwin's will?' John asked.

'Baldwin was a fool,' Joscelin cut in. 'The kings of England and France are always at one another's throats. If Henry claimed a glass was half full, Philip would go to war to prove that it was half empty. They will never agree on a ruler for the Kingdom.'

'Nor should they,' Guy added. 'Why should men who know nothing of the Kingdom choose our queen? Sibylla is the elder. That should be an end to the matter.'

'And after you take the throne?' Raymond asked Sibylla. 'A woman cannot rule alone. You will need a husband to lead our armies in war. Who will rule beside you?'

It was Joscelin who answered. 'The other barons have agreed that Sibylla will choose her new husband.'

'I see.' Raymond drew his sword and a dozen other blades hissed from the scabbard as Sibylla's men also drew. Sibylla had not moved. Her eyes were locked with Raymond's. After a moment, he knelt and laid his sword at her feet. 'My sword and the arm that wields it are yours, my queen. I will serve you.'

All eyes turned to John. His heart was pounding and his palm itched for the feel of his mace. He wanted to fight, but that would only get him killed. He dropped to one knee. 'As will I.'

'Good.' Sibylla's features softened. She smiled, and for a moment, John saw her mother in her. The thought both encouraged and frightened him. 'Now come. We have a coronation to plan.'

SEPTEMBER 1186: JERUSALEM

John sat in his stall in the choir of the Church of the Holy Sepulchre and watched as Heraclius held the crown of the kingdom over Sibylla's head. The patriarch was dressed in spectacular white robes that glittered with gold and jewels. A jewel-encrusted mitre sat atop his head. John could smell his heavy perfume from a dozen feet away. In contrast, Sibylla's royal robes of red silk seemed plain. She stood straight-backed looking out on the audience of nobles and great merchants. Her long auburn hair had been plaited to form a wreath around her head, where the gold crown would sit.

'*In nomine Patris, et Filii, et Spiritus Sancti,*' Heraclius declared in nasal tones that echoed off the limestone walls and vaulted ceiling. 'I pronounce you Sibylla, first of her name, Queen of Jerusalem.' He lowered the crown on to her brow. John knelt in his stall, and the canons followed his example. The crowd beyond the colonnade that separated off the sanctuary had also knelt. John spotted Guy in the front ranks. He was dressed like Sibylla in robes of red silk and wore a smug smile on his face. Sibylla had made Heraclius annul their marriage, as promised, but Guy had been allowed to keep his lands in Ascalon and Jaffa. Reynald was beside him, while only a few feet further along the colonnade Raymond knelt. The Count of Tripoli's brow was furrowed and his mouth stretched in a thin line. He had worn the same pained expression ever since he had sworn fealty to Sibylla.

The sound of booted feet on the marble floor brought John's attention back to the sanctuary. Balian, the royal chamberlain, strode to the edge of the sanctuary and raised his voice. 'Long live the Queen!'

'Long live the Queen!' the crowd echoed, and John with them. It was the third monarch he had seen crowned. The elder Baldwin had reigned only eleven years. His nephew had sat on the throne for scarcely more than a year. John wondered how long Sibylla's rule would last.

The queen strode forward to stand beside Balian. Heraclius followed. 'And now,' he said, 'Her Highness wishes to address her people.'

John tensed. This was unusual. Customarily, the patriarch would now pray over the new monarch and deliver a sermon urging her to rule righteously. Those in the crowd who had started to leave early for the coronation feast stopped and turned back towards the sanctuary.

'My people!' Sibylla began. 'By the grace of God, I have been crowned. I did not seek the throne, but God called me, and I am not one to turn aside from my duty.' There were sniggers amongst the people. Sibylla glared at them and continued. 'Now, I am your queen, and I must choose the man who shall rule beside me, who will offer his wisdom in council and his steel to defend our kingdom.'

Sibylla paused to allow the suspense to build. There were murmurs in the crowd. No doubt they were as surprised as John. He had thought Sibylla would take her time, maybe choosing a French or English husband who could bring desperately needed money and men to the Kingdom. John noticed some of the single barons in the crowd leaning forward in anticipation, hoping she might choose them.

'I choose –' a smile played at the corner of the Queen's mouth – 'the lord of Ascalon and Jaffa!'

'No,' John murmured under his breath. There were gasps in the crowd.

'Rise, Guy of Lusignan!' Sibylla continued as if oblivious to the consternation she had caused. 'Join me.'

A broad smile on his face, Guy stood and strode through the colonnade that separated the crowd from the altar and the choir. There were scattered cries from the barons of 'No!' and 'This cannot be!' Guy stopped before Sibylla, and she signalled brusquely to Heraclius. The patriarch brought forth a second crown. Sibylla took it and held it over Guy's head.

'Stop!' Raymond shouted. He stepped forward and gripped one of the thin, ornate columns of the colonnade. 'You cannot, Sibylla! You swore an oath!'

'I swore to divorce my husband, and I did. I did not swear not to remarry him.' She lowered the crown on to Guy's brow. 'Guy of Lusignan, I pronounce you King of Jerusalem!'

Raymond's face had gone purple with rage. He started towards Sibylla, but two of his liegemen held him back. 'This will not stand!' he shouted before turning and storming from the church. John took careful note of those who followed: Balian of Ibelin, Reginald of Sidon and, after a moment's hesitation, Humphrey of Toron. If John were to undo Sibylla's scheme, he would need those men. He rose and headed for the night stair at the back of the sanctuary.

'Archdeacon!' the precentor hissed. 'The service is not yet complete.'

John did not stop. He had more important business to attend to.

The cross hanging from John's neck glinted in the light shed by the crescent moon as he waited outside the gate of the Abbey of Mount Sion. John had one hand on the cross; in the other he held his mace. It was just past midnight. From inside the abbey, he could hear the brothers chanting nocturnes.

A form emerged from the darkness – a man in a black cloak with a hood over his head. He was framed by two soldiers in mail. John's grip on the mace tightened. 'Who goes there?' he asked, speaking as loudly as he dared.

'It is I.' The voice belonged to Raymond.

'Were you seen leaving the palace?'

'I think not.'

'Good.' John rapped softly at the gate – two knocks, then another, then three more. The gate opened a crack. 'The Queen is in Nablus,' John whispered, and Aestan pulled the gate open. The sergeant wore mail and had a sword in his hand. 'Aestan will show you to the crypt,' John told Raymond. 'Your men can wait in the courtyard. The others will join you soon, God willing.'

Balian came next. He greeted John with a smile and slipped through the gate. Then came Reginald. 'I am too old for this skulking about,' he grumbled in greeting. The few hairs Agnes's former husband had left had greyed long ago.

'I am glad you came,' John told him.

'*Hmph.* Is Humphrey here?'

'He will arrive soon.'

'I pray he does, or you are risking our necks for nothing.' Reginald went inside, leaving John to wait.

The brothers finished chanting nocturnes, and still Humphrey did not come. John began to pace. Finally, he heard footsteps. A lone figure strode towards the gate. He stepped into a pool of moonlight, which illuminated fleshy cheeks and a weak chin. Humphrey. He looked more a prosperous merchant than a king, yet all their hopes rested on him.

'Thank God you have come,' John greeted him.

'John, I must—'

'Best to talk inside.'

Once they were inside the gate, John turned to Aestan. 'Keep a careful watch. No one is to enter. No one.'

'Yes, domne.'

John led Humphrey across the courtyard and into the church. Dark shadows shifted in the flickering light shed by a candle on the altar. John took the candle and led them down narrow steps beneath the apse. At the bottom, they found themselves in a tunnel cut into the rock on which the church was built. John moved forward, stooping to avoid bumping his head. A door appeared after a few feet. The man guarding it nodded to John and pulled it open. John and Humphrey stepped into the church's crypt. It was a small room with burial niches cut into the walls. Half of them were occupied with stone sarcophagi holding the remains of former abbots. One day, John would be buried with them.

But tonight his business was with the living. Raymond, Balian and Reginald waited around a stone table. As the guard shut the door, all eyes turned to John. He had summoned them. It was for him to speak first. He took a deep breath.

'Thank you all for coming. You know why I have asked you here. We agreed to make Sibylla queen on the condition that Guy would not take the throne beside her. She has betrayed her promise to us. We cannot allow this outrage to stand. The Kingdom is in greater danger than ever before, and Guy is not the man to defend it from Saladin.'

Everyone but Humphrey nodded. 'Fit or not, Guy has been crowned,' he said.

'An empty gesture,' John replied. 'Until he remarries Sibylla, he is no king. We must not let that marriage happen.'

Reginald rubbed his bald head. 'She is queen now. That ceremony was valid enough. And we promised she could pick her husband. I do not like it any more than you, John, but if we move against her, we are committing treason.'

'No,' Raymond said. 'We are protecting the Kingdom. John is right; Guy is no leader of men. He changes his mind each time the wind blows. If we allow him to remain on the throne, then we betray our oaths to defend the people.'

Reginald looked from Raymond to John. 'What would you have us do? Rebel? We dare not. Saladin controls Mosul now.'

'All the more reason to act now,' John countered swiftly. 'Saladin is coming for Jerusalem. Do you want Guy in command when he arrives?'

'The truce still has two years to run,' Humphrey noted.

'When Guy was regent, he did not rule two months before he set Reynald to violate our treaty with Saladin. Do you want to risk it happening again?'

'What is our alternative?' Balian spoke now. 'Raymond as regent again?'

Raymond shook his head. 'I have no wish to rule, nor do I have a claim.'

'Humphrey does.' John turned to the young man. 'You are married to Sibylla's sister Isabella. Your forefathers have served the Kingdom faithfully since the beginning. It should be you on the throne.'

John's pronouncement was met with silence. He stepped back from the table. He has said his part. Now it was up to them.

Reginald rubbed his head again. He turned to Humphrey. 'I knew your grandfather, the constable Humphrey. He was a great warrior and an honest man. If you are half the man he was, then you will be a worthy king. If you make a bid for the throne, I will support you, Humphrey.'

'As would I,' Balian echoed. Raymond nodded his assent. All eyes turned to Humphrey.

'I – I do not know,' he ventured. 'It is Sibylla who has been crowned, not Isabella.'

'And what sort of queen will Sibylla be?' Raymond demanded. 'She has stripped your ancestral lands from you and given them to Joscelin. Will you allow her to disgrace your family?'

'I was compensated for Toron.'

Reginald snorted. 'With gold. Is your honour for sale, then?'

Humphrey bristled. 'Do not speak to me of honour, old man.

Reynald is my father-in-law, and he supports the Queen. Would you have me turn against my own kin? Is that the honour of which you speak?'

'And what of your wife, my stepdaughter?' Balian asked. 'She is your kin, too. Would you deny her the throne that is rightfully hers?'

Humphrey said nothing. He began to fidget with the clasp of his cloak.

'Speak, man!' Reginald urged.

'I tried to tell you earlier, John. I – I cannot. Sibylla and Guy have been crowned before the eyes of man and God. It is not for me to undo what God has done.' He took a candle from the table and left the room. John could hear his footsteps echoing on the steps up from the crypt.

Reginald cleared his throat. 'Perhaps it is for the best. The boy is not his grandfather. He has no backbone.' Reginald raised the hood of his cloak. 'I am off to bed, sirs. I must rise early tomorrow to lick Guy's royal arse.'

'Reginald speaks true,' Balian said. 'We must all make peace with the King.' He followed Reginald out.

Raymond placed a hand on John's shoulder. 'You tried, John.'

'I failed. What will you do?'

'I will not swear loyalty to Guy, no matter what threats he levels.'

'There will be more than just threats. He will come for you.'

'My castle at Tiberias is strong.'

'Not strong enough to hold against the army of the Kingdom. You need allies.' John took a deep breath, for what he was about to say was treason. Yet he saw no other way. 'Saladin would support you.'

Raymond looked as if he had been slapped. 'No, John. I will not betray the Kingdom.'

'Nor would I ask you to. Ally with Saladin to protect your lands, nothing more.'

Raymond rubbed his beard. 'I will think on it. What of you, John?'

'There is no future for me in Jerusalem. Sibylla wishes me dead. She has made no secret of that. I will come with you, if you will have me.'

'You are always welcome in my hall.' Raymond forced a smile. 'Perhaps fortune will smile on us yet. As Humphrey said, the truce with Saladin still has two years to run. Much can happen in two years.'

Chapter 9

'Your son Az-Zahir writes from Aleppo to say that the Seljuks are gathering in the north, Malik.'

Yusuf turned away from the window of his private study. His secretary sat cross-legged before him, a writing desk balanced on his lap. 'What else, Imad ad-Din?'

'The caliph An-Nasir has sent an envoy to congratulate you on your overlordship of Mosul and to encourage you to make war on the Franks.'

'*Hah*. You mean to encourage me to send the gifts he feels are his due.'

'As you say, Malik. Your brother writes from Egypt. The Almohads are moving in the west. They threaten to retake Tripoli.'

'If it falls, it falls. Tell my brother that peace with the Almohad caliph is more important than Tripoli.'

'And the rest, Malik? The Seljuk army numbers in the thousands. Perhaps it would be best to delay your pilgrimage to Mecca until your borders are secure?'

'No. I have delayed long enough.' The hajj was a duty that every Muslim was expected to fulfil at least once in life. There would be no better time than now. The truce with the Franks still had two years to run. After that, he would go to war. Yusuf wanted Allah's blessing first. He already wore the clothes of a pilgrim – sandals and the ihram, a sort of toga comprising two white sheets held at the middle with a sash. The ihram was meant to demonstrate that all pilgrims were equal before Allah. It was also a reminder to focus on pure thoughts. Yusuf should not be conducting affairs of state in it, but he had no choice. He was a king. He could not shed his responsibilities as easily as his royal robes.

'Write to Az-Zahir,' he told Imad ad-Din. 'Tell him that if the Seljuks march against us, he is to wait for reinforcements before attacking. Al-Mashtub will lead the army of Damascus north to add to his strength. As for the Caliph's envoy, my son Al-Afdal will meet with them. See that he sends the envoy on his way with the appropriate gifts. Fifty horses and a hundred silk robes should be sufficient.'

'Yes, Malik.'

'Anything else?' Yusuf asked, and the secretary shook his head. 'Then go.'

Yusuf returned to the window. It was a clear winter evening and he could see to the walls and the plain beyond, where hundreds of cooking fires winked in the twilight. Men and women from as far as Homs and Edessa had come to join the royal caravan. Tomorrow, Yusuf would lead them south on the pilgrim road. It was paved near Damascus, but for the rest of the journey it was nothing more than a track in the desert, formed by the passage of countless feet over countless years. Forts along the route, many dating to Roman times, would provide shelter and water. They would pass through Mafraq, Zarqa, Jiza and Qal'at al-Hasa. They would ride within twenty miles of the crusader castles of Kerak and Shawbak before reaching Ayla. Even accounting for the winter rains, which each year turned the floor of the great Wadi Al-Hasa south of Kerak into a sea of mud, the journey would take no more than two weeks. From Ayla, Yusuf and his private guard would take a ship for the week-long journey down the Red Sea to the port of Jeddah. From there, it was a two-day ride to the Holy City. He would arrive a week before the start of the festivals associated with the

hajj. Yusuf was taking the sea route to save time. He had already
sent much of his household – including his sister Zimat and her
two eldest daughters – ahead with a caravan led by Al-Muqaddam.
They would take the safer land route, heading south from Ma'an
instead of going on to Ayla.

'Habibi.' Shamsa stood in the doorway of his study. Her
caftan of tight-fitting red silk showed off a form that was still
slim and athletic, despite giving him two sons and three daughters. And her dark eyes still held that mixture of challenge and
invitation that had first drawn him to her. She came to his side
and leaned her head on his shoulder. 'I shall miss you, my love.'

'I shall return before the barley is ripe in the fields.'

'You make too much haste. The Red Sea is dangerous. Imad
ad-Din speaks of pirates, of hidden reefs that tear the bottoms
from ships.'

'If you would see me sooner, then you should be glad of
the route I have chosen. Travelling by sea will save me two
weeks.'

She wrapped her arms around his waist. 'You could stay.'

'I will only be gone for two months.' Two months free of the
daily burdens of rule. On the road to Mecca, he would be just
one more pilgrim. He could feel the tension in his gut easing
at the thought. He kissed Shamsa's forehead. 'I have been gone
much longer on campaign. Why are you now so reluctant to
see me go?'

'Perhaps because you go to war only reluctantly,' she pouted.
'You could at least pretend you will miss me.'

'You could come with me, Shamsa.'

Her nose wrinkled. 'I have been on the hajj, with my father
just after I became a woman. I will never forget the crowds –
thousands of sweating men packed together in the scorching
desert heat. More people than stars in the sky, it seemed to me.
During the stoning of the devil, a man missed one of the
columns and his rock struck me in the face. I had a black eye for
weeks.'

Ramy al-Jamarat, the stoning of the devil, commemorated the trials suffered by Abraham on the way to sacrificing his son Isaac. The story went that when Abraham was leaving the city of Mina, only a few miles east of Mecca, he came to a rocky defile where the devil appeared to him beside a column of rock. Abraham threw seven stones to drive him away. The devil appeared again beside another heap of stones, and then again. Each time, Abraham drove him away with seven stones. The stoning was re-enacted on the third day of the hajj, and then again in the following days. It was one of the most dangerous parts of the hajj, both because of the crushing crowds and the flying rocks.

Yusuf gently brushed Shamsa's cheek. 'No one would dare to cast a stone at you now.'

'Perhaps not, but even you cannot protect me from the hot sun or the stink of the crowd. I will stay.' Her hand moved down his side and she began to untie the sash that held up the lower half of his ihram. 'I shall have to give you a reason to hurry back to me.'

He caught her hand. 'I wear the ihram. My thoughts should be on Allah.'

Shamsa smiled wickedly. 'You will be thanking him soon enough.' She kissed his neck as she finished untying the sash. She kissed his chest and next his stomach as she knelt before him.

There was a knock at the door. '*Yalla*!' Yusuf cursed. 'Will they not leave me one moment of peace?'

Shamsa rose. 'I will be waiting for you,' she said as she stepped into his bedroom.

Yusuf secured his ihram around his waist. 'Enter!'

'Malik.' Imad ad-Din's face was pale. He clutched a scrap of paper in his hand. 'Forgive me for disturbing you.' He held out the paper.

Yusuf's jaw clenched as he read. 'I will kill the bastard myself! I swear it.'

'Who?' Shamsa stood in the doorway to the bedroom. 'What has happened?'

Yusuf was too angry to speak. It was Imad ad-Din who answered. 'The one called the Wolf raided the pilgrim caravan from Damascus. Al-Muqaddam and his men fought him off, but not without many losses. Reynald has thrown his captives in dungeons at Kerak. He raped and murdered many others—' Imad ad-Din's voice trailed off.

'My sister was one of them.' Yusuf's voice was flat. 'Zimat is dead.'

Shamsa went to him. 'I am sorry, my love.'

Yusuf shrugged her off. 'This is not the time for sorrow. Reynald's butchery has broken our treaty with the Franks. Imad ad-Din, send letters to every corner of the kingdom. Tell my emirs to come with all their men. The hajj can wait. Come summer, we are going to war.'

JULY 1187: LA SEPHORIE

Sergeants in mail and native Christians in vests of leather or padded cotton stepped reluctantly aside as John and Raymond rode into the Christian camp at La Sephorie. The Saracens had crossed the Jordan, and a mighty army had gathered to face them. The men's angry faces were lit by the flickering light of cooking fires. Some spat as Raymond passed. Others grumbled curses. A pair of Lombards made the sign of the evil eye, touching their thumb and forefinger and shaking them.

'They look at me as if I killed the Templars myself,' Raymond muttered. 'Cresson was not my doing. If Gerard were not such a rash fool—'

John placed a hand on Raymond's arm. The grumbling amongst the men had grown louder. 'Best to keep such thoughts to yourself,' he said in a low voice. Right or wrong, these men blamed Raymond for the massacre at Cresson. It was not a good idea to speak ill of those who had died or been captured there.

It had been an unexpected disaster. Three months ago, when Guy had gathered an army to force Raymond to recognize him as king, Raymond had looked to Saladin for support. Saladin had sent his son Al-Afdal with several thousand men. Raymond had never intended to bring the Saracens into battle against his fellow Franks. They were a bargaining chip, nothing more, a way to force Guy to stand down.

But everything had gone horribly wrong. Raymond had given Al-Afdal permission to ride across his lands to scout. On their way back, a troop of Templars and Hospitallers had attacked them at Cresson. The Templar Grand Master, Gerard, led the knights in a charge, leaving his foot-soldiers behind. But Al-Afdal's retreat had only been feigned. The Saracens turned and slaughtered the two halves of the Frankish force separately. Every single knight was killed, the Grand Master of the Hospitallers amongst them. Gerard was taken prisoner. When he was ransomed a few weeks later, he returned to the Kingdom raging against Raymond and blaming him for the disaster. He was not alone in calling for Raymond's head.

Now, the Saracens had invaded with an army larger than any John had ever seen. Raymond had put aside his hatred of Guy and marched his men to join the Christian army at La Sephorie. John had joined him. Judging from the murderous looks of the men they had passed, they might well be riding to their deaths. They were through the camp now and at the base of the hill on which the squat keep stood. They dismounted, and John handed his reins to Aestan.

'You're not likely to receive a warm welcome, domne,' the sergeant said in a low voice. 'There is still time to leave. We could ride for the coast, take a ship for the old country.'

'We are needed here.'

'You'd best hope King Guy feels the same way. If you hang, I'll see that you're buried properly.'

John followed Raymond up the hill. A dozen of the king's men, their surcoats emblazoned with the gold Jerusalem cross, guarded the entrance to the keep. Their captain spat at Raymond's feet. 'Your weapons, *milords*.' He said the last word as if it tasted of shit.

Raymond unbuckled his sword belt and John turned over his mace. The guard led them into the keep and up a narrow flight of stairs to a thick, iron-bound door. The guard pounded on it, and it opened a crack. 'Raymond of Tripoli to see the King.'

There was a short pause, during which Raymond leaned close to John. 'We must master our passions,' he whispered. 'We are here to fight in defence of the Kingdom. Nothing else matters.'

The door swung open. John had to duck as he passed through the low doorway. Inside, Guy sat at the centre of a long table set with food and drink. To his left and right, all facing the doorway, sat his brother Amalric, Reynald, Humphrey of Toron, Reginald of Sidon, Gerard of Ridefort and William of Montferrat, known as William the Old to distinguish him from his son of the same name. He had fought in the Second Crusade and the year previously had returned to fight again. He was a short, compact man with a ruddy face and hair so blond that it was almost white.

Gerard, the Templar Grand Master, was the first to break the silence. 'So, the butcher of Cresson dares show his face.'

Raymond ignored him. 'I have come to fight for the Kingdom.'

'If you wanted to fight, you should have stayed in Tiberias,' Reynald said. 'Saladin is there now, besieging your wife. It seems you are running away from battle yet again, Raymond.'

Raymond's jaw clenched, but he swallowed his anger and managed to speak in a calm voice. 'My men would do no good trapped inside the castle.'

'So you admit you run.' Reynald turned to Guy. 'Gerard is

right. You should string him up, Your Grace, him and his Saxon lapdog. They are traitors.'

'Traitors?' John demanded. 'It is your madness that has put the whole kingdom at risk, Reynald. Had you not broken the treaty by attacking the pilgrim caravan, we would still have peace.'

'You would like that, wouldn't you?' Reynald smirked. 'Peace with your friend Saladin.'

'Better than a war that might destroy us all,' Raymond put in.

'We must fight them sooner or later. We are not all of us willing to bend the knee to Saladin.' Reynald looked to John. 'Or to bend over for him.'

John's hands balled into fists, his nails digging into his palms. He would have liked to beat Reynald senseless, but that might well end with John dangling from a rope. He ground his teeth, not trusting himself to speak.

Reynald rose and came around the table to stand before John. He leaned close, and John could smell the wine on his breath and the grease that had dribbled into his grey beard while he ate. 'You do love the sand devils, don't you, Saxon? I found your Saracen whore when I raided the caravan. She spoke of you when she begged for her life. She said you would ransom her. What was her name again?'

'Zimat,' John growled between clenched teeth.

Reynald sneered. 'Ah, yes. That was it.' He leaned close and whispered in John's ear. 'If she had not mentioned you, I might have spared her. I raped the bitch before I gutted her.'

John slammed his shoulder into Reynald's chest and drove him backwards into the table. Plates and goblets clattered to the floor as the two men grappled. John's hands closed on Reynald's throat. Reynald head-butted him, and John stumbled back.

'Enough!' Guy shouted. 'Guards!'

John ignored him. He raised his fists and surged towards Reynald, but before he reached him, he was grabbed from behind. Two guards dragged him back across the room; a third man held a knife to his throat. John ceased struggling.

Reynald pointed a thick finger at him. 'You see! He is a demon. He should be hanged as a traitor.'

'Sit down, Reynald!' Guy commanded. He stepped around the table to face Raymond and John. 'I am glad you have come, both of you. We can use every man we can find. But I will not have you if you are not willing to serve. I must have your oaths.'

Raymond and John knelt and clasped their hands before them as if in prayer. They spoke in unison. 'I promise on my faith that I will be loyal to you, King Guy, loving all that you love, shunning that which you shun, according to the laws of God and the order of the world. My men, my sword, and the arm that wields it are yours.'

'I accept your fealty.' Guy returned to his place at the table. 'You must be hungry after your travels. Sit.'

A place was made for John and Raymond at one end of the table, beside bald Reginald of Sidon. Servants entered to clear away the mess and to bring more food and wine. The roast lamb was tough and the wine sour, but they were welcome all the same.

'Raymond!' Guy called from down the table. 'Before your arrival, we were discussing marching on Tiberias. You know these lands better than any of us. What do you say?'

'I council against it, Your Grace.'

'You would leave Tiberias to the enemy?' Gerard demanded. 'He condemns himself with his own words, Your Grace.'

'Enough, Gerard!' Guy snapped. 'I will hear him out.'

'For twenty years and more,' Raymond began, 'I have fought the armies of Islam, but I have never seen a force equal to the one that Saladin has brought against us. He has more than twelve thousand mamluks, with an equal number of Bedouin and Turkmen. We have had to empty all our garrisons to gather a force that can match him. If we are defeated, there will be no one left to defend the Kingdom.'

John nodded. 'It is not just the size of the enemy army that should give us pause. Raymond and I have just ridden from Tiberias. Saladin controls the southern road, along the valley. We will be forced to take the north road – fifteen miles across arid land with only a few wells. If we stay here, Saladin's army will have to cover that ground. They will be tired; their mounts will be thirsty and weak. If we march, it will be we who suffer. We must stay at La Sephorie. Saladin will withdraw again, as he did the last time he invaded.'

'I remember the last time.' Reynald turned to Guy. 'You did not fight, Your Grace, and it cost you the regency. Baldwin had you exiled to Ascalon. Raymond opposed your crowning. Now, he seeks to make a fool of you, to undermine your reign and cheat you of your chance at glory.'

'He made a treaty with the infidel,' Gerard added. 'He let the Saracens into his lands. He is responsible for Cresson!'

'And I have come to wipe the stain of that day from my honour,' Raymond said stiffly. He leaned over the table so he could meet Guy's eyes. 'I want victory as much as the next man, Your Grace. But how much are you willing to risk in order to achieve it? If we suffer defeat, the Kingdom will fall. Make no mistake, Your Grace.'

'We will not lose!' Reynald insisted. 'Saladin's host is vast, yes, but so is ours. We have never before gathered so many men – twelve hundred knights, over eight thousand light cavalry and nearly ten thousand sergeants. We must not let them go to waste.'

Raymond opened his mouth to reply, but Guy held up a hand, silencing him. 'I have heard enough.' The king took a long drink of wine. 'You have made your arguments. Now I would have your council. Who favours marching on Tiberias?'

'We must attack, Your Grace,' Gerard declared.

'Aye,' Reynald agreed.

Young Humphrey nodded his assent. 'As my father-in-law says.'

Guy waited a moment, but no one else spoke. 'And those against?'

Raymond and John spoke first. Reginald joined his voice to theirs, and to John's surprise, so did the constable, Amalric. William the Old spoke last. 'I fought during the Second Crusade, Your Grace. I saw what lack of water can do to an army. I say we stay here. If Saladin wants a fight, then let him come to us.'

'Five against three, Your Grace,' Raymond said. 'The choice is clear.'

Reynald shook his head. 'You are a king, Guy. Your duty is to lead, not count votes. The decision lies with you.'

Guy licked his lips. 'We will stay.'

John woke with a start. Someone outside his tent was shouting. 'Get your lazy arscs up!' The man banged his sword against his shield. 'Up, I say! We march at sunrise!'

John stepped outside. The day had only just dawned and the horizon to the east was turning a purplish red, like a bruise. He looked about. Last night, tents had stood for as far as he could see in every direction, their shapes silvery in the moonlight. Now the plain around La Sephorie was almost bare. Men were calling to one another as they stowed the remaining tents. Others pulled on their armour or sharpened their swords. At the heart of the camp, the cooking fires were roaring. John could smell baking bread. His stomach rumbled. He spotted Aestan striding towards him.

'Morning, domne.' The sergeant handed John a piece of steaming bread.

'Why are we breaking camp?'

'I'll be damned if I know. I was sound asleep when that bastard started shouting outside my tent. I had half a mind to gut him, but he was in full mail.'

'Whose arms did he wear?'

'Reynald's.'

John felt a hollow feeling in the pit of his stomach. 'Help me with my armour, Aestan.'

Dressed, John headed for the keep. He had reached the hill on which it stood when he saw Raymond coming down towards him. The lord of Tripoli's face was grim. 'By the devil's hairy balls!' he cursed. 'Of all the boil-brained, senseless—'

'My lord,' John greeted him.

'John. You had best start praying, friend.'

'Tiberias?'

Raymond nodded. 'I had it all from the king. Gerard and Reynald came to him late last night. They persuaded him to march. It seems they have spent the gold that King Henry of England sent ahead for when he comes on crusade. They used it to hire more men-at-arms. Gerard has convinced Guy that if they do not have something to show for the coin they spent, there will be hell to pay when Henry finally arrives. Guy might even lose his throne.'

'He will lose it just as surely if Saladin defeats us.'

'I know it, John, but he will not be swayed. By his nails! I cannot believe I knelt to that spineless bastard.' He took a deep breath. 'Maybe it is God's will, as Gerard insists. Perhaps we shall be victorious again, as at Montgisard.'

'Perhaps.' John looked up to where ravens were circling overhead. 'Perhaps we will all be food for crows before the day is done.'

'The Horns of Hattin,' Raymond declared. In the distance, two round hills with a saddle between them rose to dominate the surrounding plain. Their steep sides were covered with scrubby brush. 'On the far side the land slopes down to the lake, three miles distant.'

John nodded. His mouth was too dry and sticky to speak. The army had marched all day while the summer sun beat down and transformed the arid plain around them into a sea of mirages. The Saracens had harassed them continuously, swarming about the two-mile-long column and filling the sky with arrows. Few lives were lost, but the march had slowed to a crawl as the foot-soldiers drew together and shuffled along with their shields overlapped. The villages they had passed had all been burned to the ground. When the men went to water their horses, they found that the corpses of dogs had been thrown in the wells. John had finished the last of his water before they were halfway to Tiberias. By mid afternoon, his horse was lathered in sweat and he had a blinding headache. Some of the men had become so desperate for water that they removed the dead animals from the third well they reached and drank. Within a mile they were sick, dropping to their knees on the side of the road to retch.

The day finally began to cool as the sun sank towards the horizon, casting long shadows ahead. They had nearly reached the Horns when William of Montferrat came galloping up the column to join them where they rode in the vanguard. 'Guy has called for a halt,' the old crusader said.

'Why?' Raymond demanded.

'He did not see fit to share his reasoning with me.'

'We cannot stop,' John said. 'We must reach the lake.'

'I will speak with him,' Raymond said.

'I will come with you.'

They cantered down the column to where the king's banner flew. They found Guy nervously licking his lips while Reynald and Reginald of Sidon shouted at one another.

'Are you blind as well as stupid?' Reginald roared. He pointed to the horizon. 'The lake is there! We cannot stop now.' He fell silent as John and Raymond approached.

'Why have we stopped, Your Grace?' Raymond asked.

It was Reynald who replied. 'We will not reach the lake before sunset. It is best to make camp before dark falls.'

'No. Reginald is right. We must push on.'

Reynald sneered. 'Afraid of a night under the stars, Raymond?'

John answered for him. 'The men and the horses are thirsty.

If we wait until tomorrow, they will be in no condition to fight.'

'That's what I tried to tell him,' Reginald grumbled.

'You would have us stumble on in the dark?' Reynald asked. 'We will march straight into a Saracen ambush.'

John shook his head. There was no use trying to speak reason to this fool. He turned to the king instead. 'Your Grace?'

Guy licked his lips. 'We will halt.'

'But my lord—' Reginald began.

'I have made my decision.' Guy raised his voice. 'Make camp! Where are my squires?' He walked his horse away from the column. Reynald followed.

Reginald spat dust from his mouth. 'This is madness.'

'We have no choice.' Raymond grimaced. 'Guy is our king. We are sworn to follow him.'

'Straight to hell,' John muttered.

Chapter 10

The night was dark; the moon only a thin sliver in the sky. The camp was silent save for a faint rustle as a wind from the east blew over the tents of the mamluks, Bedouin and Turkmen. But Yusuf could not sleep. He never could on the eve of battle. He stood outside his tent, which had been erected on a ridge overlooking the plain where the Franks had camped. Yusuf could see their white tents, lit a hellish red by the brush fires blazing around them. The smoke would rob the Franks of sleep, leaving them awake to be tormented by their thirst. The fires had been Ubadah's idea. Yusuf's nephew had grown into a valuable commander. Tomorrow, he would command the army's right wing.

From near by, Yusuf heard the slow rasp of a whetstone on steel. He motioned for Saqr to stay behind and walked amongst the luxurious tents of his emirs until he found the source of the sound. Al-Afdal was seated outside his tent with a sword in hand. Yusuf stopped in the shadows of a nearby tent and studied his son. Al-Afdal had narrow shoulders like his father, but his hands were strong and his forearms well muscled. He had his mother's sharp cheekbones, covered now with a thin adolescent beard. His son was nearly sixteen. When had he become a man? Yusuf frowned. He had seen little enough of his father as a child, and he had resented Ayub's distance. But he had been no better with his sons. No, he had been worse. There had been no time. He had a kingdom to rule.

Perhaps it was not too late. Yusuf stepped from the shadows. 'Trouble sleeping?'

Al-Afdal looked up, startled. He set the sword aside. 'Father. I – I wished to be certain my blade was sharp.'

The dry grass crunched beneath Yusuf as he sat. 'You did well at Cresson, my son. I am proud of you.'

'I killed five men.' It was not a boast. Al-Afdal's voice was soft and his eyes were fixed on the moon above. 'The last was a foot-soldier, one of their sergeants. I struck him from behind as he fled. He fell, and I dismounted to finish him. He rolled on to his back . . .' Al-Afdal trailed off. He took a deep breath. 'He was no older than me. When I raised my sword, he begged me to spare him. "Please! Please!" Those were his last words.'

Yusuf wanted to put his arm around his son's shoulders, to whisper words of comfort to him, but he could not. His son was a man now. Instead, Yusuf took up his son's sword and whetstone. He tested the blade's edge with his thumb, and began to sharpen it with long, practised strokes. 'I killed my first man when I was ten.'

Al-Afdal looked up, curious.

'It was at Damascus. A great host of Franks had come from overseas to lay siege to the city, but we drove them off. My father rode out with the other warriors to harry the Franks as they withdrew. He was unhorsed and my brother Turan and I rode out, thinking to save him.'

'Did you?'

Yusuf shook his head. 'I was a foolish child playing at war. Were it not for my brother, I would have died.' Yusuf stopped short. He had not thought of Turan in years. The memory made his stomach churn. *Forgive me, Brother.*

'And the man you killed? Do you remember him?'

'He was an old man with scrawny arms and a long white beard. His clothes were little better than rags and he fought with a pitchfork. He had a mouth of brown, rotting teeth. I split his skull with my sword . . .' If he closed his eyes, Yusuf could still see the mad grin on the old man's face as blood ran down his cheeks to stain his white beard scarlet. 'You never forget your first, but it grows easier with time.'

Al-Afdal nodded but said nothing. The only sound was the rasp of the whetstone. Yusuf tested the edge again, rose and handed the sword to his son.

'Will there be battle tomorrow?' Al-Afdal asked.

'The Franks have no choice. They must have water, and we block their path. In their arrogance, they have wandered into our trap.'

Al-Afdal grinned, and Yusuf could see the boy in him again. 'It will be a great victory.'

'Inshallah. I will see you at sunrise, my son.'

Yusuf returned to stand outside his tent. His conversation with Al-Afdal had got him thinking of the past. It had been after the battle at Damascus that Yusuf had first met John. He had found him caged and dying in the slave market. Yusuf exchanged the sandals on his feet for the man who would become his closest friend. He looked again towards the Christian camp. Through the smoke, he glimpsed the True Cross rising in the midst of the tents. John was there with the Franks. If Yusuf triumphed tomorrow, then his friend would likely die.

He frowned. Such thoughts were unworthy of him. What he did, he did for Allah. What did the life of one more Frank matter?

'Well, bugger me,' Reginald grumbled as he ran a hand over his bald head.

John had to agree with the sentiment. His lower back ached after a restless night on the hard ground. The smoke had kept him awake, praying for dawn, but when it came, he soon regretted his prayers. He now stood with Guy and the other great lords atop a small rise at the centre of the Christian camp. Black smoke was thick in the air. A sudden gust of wind blew it aside, and John could see the Horns of Hattin in the distance to the north-east. The wind shifted again, revealing the road to Tiberias. Thousands upon thousands of mounted Saracens lay across it.

Reginald spat. 'As thick as flies on a corpse.'

'We will never fight through that way.' John's voice was scratchy after a night of inhaling smoke, but he had no water to ease his raw throat.

'And retreat is not an option,' Raymond said. He nodded to the west. The smoke was thinner there, and they could see the force Yusuf had sent to block the road back to La Sephorie.

'A charge will break those lines,' Reynald retorted. 'There can be no more than five thousand men there.'

'The force is small for a reason,' John said. 'Saladin wants us to go that way. Another day without water and our horses will fail.'

'The men will give out before the horses,' Reginald said. 'If I tell my sergeants they must march back to La Sephorie, I'll have a mutiny on my hands.'

Reynald looked to Guy. 'What do you say, Your Grace?'

'Reginald is right. La Sephorie will not do. We must reach water, and soon.' He licked his lips. 'These are your lands, Raymond. Is there another way? A well or spring north or south of here?'

'The Springs of Hattin lie to the north, beyond the Horns. They are only three miles distant. But the Saracens will oppose our march, and if the springs are poisoned like the wells we passed yesterday—'

'A chance we must take,' Guy decided. 'Amalric, prepare the army to move.'

'Yes, Your Grace. Raymond, you know the way. You will march in the vanguard. Reynald, the King and I will follow with the Cross. John, you will march with us. Joscelin and Reginald will form the rearguard, along with the Templars and Hospitallers. The native cavalry will stay to our left, to protect us in case the Saracens seek to flank us. The foot-soldiers will march between us and the enemy, to shield our horses from their arrows. You must all see that your sergeants stay in formation. Tell them that any man who leaves the column will be hanged.'

'We will march before the day grows hot,' Guy concluded. 'God save you all.'

John fell in with Raymond as they headed for their tents. 'If I die,' Raymond told him, 'give my love to my wife Eschiva. Tell her that my last thoughts were of her.'

John nodded.

'Is there anyone—?'

'No.' No one would care if John died, except perhaps Yusuf, and he stood with the enemy.

Raymond stopped at his tent and put a hand on John's shoulder. 'Good fortune, friend. God willing, I will see you at the springs.'

'God willing. Guard yourself well, Raymond.'

John continued to where his tent had stood. It had already been struck and his one hundred and fifty sergeants formed up in a square. The men had dark circles under their eyes and stood with shoulders slumped. The smoke had left many with loud, ragged coughs. John went to Aestan, who stood ready with his horse.

'The men are thirsty and tired, domne. They're in no mood to fight, unless they are fighting for water. They'd kill Christ himself to reach that lake.'

'It will not come to that.' John pulled himself into the saddle and raised his voice. 'Men! We march for the Springs of Hattin, where we will find water. They lie beyond the Horns, no more than three miles from here. The Saracens will press us close, but if you stay in close formation, their arrows will be wasted. If you leave the column, you will die. If the Saracens do not kill you, the King will.'

His speech was met with sullen silence. 'You're not much of a one for words, are you, domne?' Aestan whispered. 'Perhaps you ought to say something to fire their blood?'

John's forehead creased. He had ridden beside Yusuf for years, and his friend had always seemed to find the right words to encourage his troops. What would Yusuf say now? 'We march for God to face the infidel,' he told the men. 'We march with the True Cross at our back. We must not let it fall!' A few men were listening intently now, but many more still stood dejected, their eyes on the ground. John changed tack. 'We are the last shield of the Holy Land,' he shouted. 'If we fall, there will be no one left to defend your homes, your wives, your children.' More were listening. Some were nodding. 'We march for the King! For our home! For Jerusalem!'

Perhaps half of the men returned the cry. 'For Jerusalem! Jerusalem!'

'For water!' someone shouted, and this time the men took up the cry enthusiastically. 'For water! Water! Water!'

'We'd best reach those springs soon, domne,' Aestan murmured as he pulled on his great helm, a flat-topped steel cylinder with slits for his eyes and mouth.

John led his men to join the column and then rode on to where Amalric and a hundred knights with lances in their hands were clustered under the king's standard. More knights joined until their ranks had swelled to five hundred, with twice as many native Christian cavalry. A dozen Templars approached with the True Cross, which was mounted on a cart drawn by two mules. The king and Reynald came behind the cross.

'Are the men ready?' Guy called. His brother Amalric nodded. 'Give the order to march.'

'*For Jerusalem!*' Amalric roared. '*For the Kingdom!*'

'*For the Kingdom!*' a few men shouted. 'For water! For water!' cried others, drowning them out.

Amalric's squire blew a long note on a curved ram's horn. A moment later, Raymond's vanguard moved forward, followed by the king's men and then the rearguard. They left behind the smoke thrown up by the still smouldering brush. John could now see the enemy more clearly. There were tens of thousands of men on horseback, arrayed in a crescent. They held formation as they began to ride north. The tip of the crescent now blocked the path of the Christian army. A horn sounded amongst the Saracens, followed by the loud beat of drums. *Boom. Boom. Boom.*

'They are coming,' John said.

Several thousand mamluks broke away from the formation and rode at a trot for the Christian column. The drums beat faster and the Saracens spurred their horses to a gallop. A wave of sound swept over John as the enemy shouted their war cry. '*Allah! Allah! Allah!*'

'Shields up, men!' Amalric roared. 'Close together now! Hold formation!'

The sergeants on the outside of the column stepped close to one another so that their shields overlapped. A moment later, arrows began to skitter off them. The Saracens were streaking towards the line, shooting as they rode. Near John, a sergeant fell screaming, an arrow through his calf. The thunder of approaching hoofbeats now drowned out the Saracen war cries. John could feel the ground shake beneath him.

Amalric was shouting to be heard over the din. 'Keep those shields together! Spears out!'

The line bristled with spears. The Saracens turned their horses just before reaching them. They galloped along the line, shooting arrows into the men. One mamluk rode too close and a spear jabbed out from the Christian ranks, plucking him from the saddle. The rest of the Saracens peeled away to return to the main body.

A ragged cheer went up amongst the men, but it died out as another wave of Saracens came on. Arrows again filled the sky, clattering off shields and hissing amongst the knights. John grunted as a shaft hit his chest. The arrow lodged between the links in his mail. As he broke off the shaft, another arrow pinged off his helmet, jarring him. The knight beside him screamed as a shaft struck him in the eye. The man yanked it out, taking blood and gore with it, then slumped from the saddle.

The Saracens came at them in wave after wave as the column crawled towards the Horns. The sun climbed in the sky, and soon heat rose in waves off the dry land. John's horse began to labour, despite the slow pace. The poor beast was flagging after the previous day's long march with no water. The foot-soldiers stumbled along beneath their heavy packs. Their shield arms grew heavy and the shields dropped lower, leaving them vulnerable. Each wave of Saracens left more and more fallen sergeants in its wake. The sun stood straight overhead by the time Raymond's vanguard marched between the Horns of Hattin, the tops of which rose steeply to either side, more than two hundred feet above the surrounding plain.

'Stay tight, men!' John shouted to his sergeants. 'The springs lie only two miles beyond the Horns!' The men shuffled on, too tired to cheer.

Ahead, the vanguard was moving faster now, striding up the slope towards the pass between the Horns. The Saracen attack had abated. John could see Yusuf's men cantering away to the south, no doubt circling around the Horns to block the Franks on the far side, where the level ground would be more to their advantage. As he rode between the Horns, John lost sight of them.

Raymond's men were also out of sight, having marched over the pass. John heard cheering from ahead and was forced to urge his horse to a trot to keep up with the column as the foot-soldiers surged forward.

'Amalric, stop them!' Guy shouted. 'What is happening?'

At the top of the pass all was revealed. Lake Tiberias glittered to the south. John knew that it was nearly two miles away, but the water looked tantalizingly close. And there was nothing but brown grass between them and the water. Raymond's sergeants had broken ranks and were rushing towards the lake. Two of the foot-soldiers near John left the column to join them.

'You there, stop!' Amalric shouted. 'Another step, and I'll have your heads!'

The men stopped. They looked back for a moment, but turned and ran. Three more men joined in, then a dozen, then the entire column of infantry broke for the lake.

'Stop! Stop, damn you!' Amalric shouted, then gave up. 'Bloody hell!'

Beside him, Guy had gone pale. 'Without the sergeants to protect our horses, the Saracen will cut us to pieces.'

Reynald turned to John. 'You wished to prove your loyalty to the Crown, Saxon. Now is your chance.'

Guy nodded. 'You must get them to turn back.'

John had a strong urge to smash his mace into Reynald's smirking face, but instead he secured his kite-shaped shield on his left arm and nodded to the king. 'As you command, Your Grace.'

He spurred after the foot-soldiers, his mount's hooves throwing up divots as it flew across the gently sloping field. 'Turn back!' he shouted as he caught up to the rearmost sergeants. 'Turn back!'

'To hell with you!' one of the men shouted back.

'You'll never reach the lake, you fools! Turn back! We must stay in formation or the Saracens will slaughter us!'

The men ahead of John slowed. Some stopped and turned back. 'Back to the King!' he cried. 'Form the line!' More and more men turned to run. He had done it. A moment later, he looked beyond the foot-soldiers and his stomach turned. It was not his words that had stopped the sergeants. The Saracen army had rounded the Horns to the south, blocking the path to the lake. They had reformed their formation and the left branch of the crescent was surging towards the sergeants, who were streaming past John. 'To the King!' he shouted in desperation. 'Rejoin the column!'

But the men did not listen. The king and his knights were far, and the southern hill of the Horns close. They headed up its slope, seeking the high ground. The mamluks poured after them.

Fighting together, in close formation, the sergeants could have turned back the charge. Fleeing in panic, they were easy pickings. The Saracens' fastest riders caught up to the rearmost sergeants and began to run them down, spearing them from behind.

John rode towards the slaughter. 'Stand and fight!' he shouted. 'We must stand and fight!' Ten men rallied to him, then ten more. 'Form a line! Shields together. Spears out!' More men rushed to join in. They were two hundred strong now, but thousands of Saracens were galloping towards them, setting the earth atremble. The mamluks reached their line and split, like waters flowing around a rock.

'Back now, men!' John shouted. 'Bring in the wings! March in step! Stay together!'

The line retreated, bowing as the ends curved in to prevent the Saracens from flanking them. But the sergeants were too few to hold against so many. The men at the ends of the line were not falling back fast enough. They were flanked and began to fall as the Saracens attacked them from behind. The line broke suddenly as the men at the centre panicked and fled past John. He found himself alone, facing a wall of charging Saracens. And then they were on him.

A bamboo spear shattered against John's shield and another slammed into his shoulder. The point did not penetrate his mail, but the blow knocked him back in the saddle. He recovered and lashed out, feeling a jolt in his arm as his mace made contact. The man he struck rode past before John could see what damage he'd done. He knocked another spear aside with his shield and swung his mace, catching a mamluk in the throat. The man fell wide-eyed, his windpipe crushed and his screams dying in his throat. John was raising his mace to strike another rider when he felt his horse give out beneath him. A mamluk had planted his spear in the beast's chest. John rolled clear as the horse fell. A Saracen was galloping straight for him. John huddled in a ball and felt a rush of wind as the animal galloped past.

John staggered to his feet. He had lost his mace. Another

mamluk was bearing down on him, his spear raised. John bent down and wrested the spear from the hands of the dead sergeant at his feet. Just before the mamluk reached him, he raised the spear and planted its butt against the ground. The Saracen rode straight on to the weapon, and the tip burst from his back, carrying him from the saddle. His horse galloped past, and John turned to give chase.

'Waqqaf!' he called. 'Waqqaf.' The horse slowed to a walk, but as John caught up to the steed, it whinnied and pranced away. 'Easy! Hudû.' John managed to catch the reins. He gently stroked the horse's neck and pulled himself into the saddle.

The left wing of the Saracen formation had ridden past, chasing the sergeants up the slope. The Christian foot-soldiers were not putting up much of a fight. The rush for the lake had taken the last of their strength. Many had already thrown down their weapons and collapsed, exhausted. John looked away. The rest of the Saracen army had moved on to confront the knights. As John watched, Raymond's vanguard of five hundred men charged the northern wing of the enemy. The Saracens resisted for a moment, then split to let Raymond's knights ride through. Once past, Raymond paused for a moment before leading his men galloping from the field.

Only six hundred knights, and twice as many native Christian cavalry, remained grouped around the king. Eighteen hundred men against more than twenty thousand. And many of the Christians were on foot, their horses having been shot out from under them. They were retreating, following the True Cross up the slope of the northern Horn while the Saracens massed below for the final assault. The battle was all but over.

Then John spotted Yusuf's eagle standard flying over the centre of the Saracen ranks. Saladin. If he killed his friend, John might just save the Kingdom. It was their only chance. But he could not do it alone. 'Yalla!' he shouted and spurred his horse towards the northern Horn.

★

Yusuf sat in the saddle behind his lines and watched as Raymond of Tripoli's men galloped north, leaving the battle behind. Beside him, his son Al-Afdal frowned. 'Why did you let them escape, Father?'

'By letting them go, I weaken our enemy. Raymond of Tripoli is not the one I want. I want the King.' He could see Guy's standard. It was flying beside the True Cross atop the northern Horn, where the king and his knights had retreated, leaving the lower slopes littered with the bodies of dead warriors and horses. As Yusuf watched, the king's red tent went up atop the Horn. It was to serve as a rallying point, but there was no one to rally. The Christian foot-soldiers were trapped atop the other Horn. Yusuf saw a single knight gallop from the southern Horn to join the king. He was halfway up the slope of the northern Horn when a dozen mamluks met him. The knight soon had so many arrows protruding from his mail that he looked like a porcupine. A dozen knights from the top of the Horn rode to his rescue, driving off the mamluks. Together, they managed to reach the king.

'A brave man,' Yusuf noted.

'A fool, Father. He would have done better to throw down his arms. The Franks have lost.'

'Not yet. Not until the King's tent falls. Saqr, signal the final attack.'

Haa-room! Saqr blew a loud blast, and the mamluks massed at the foot of the Horn surged forward. The sides of the hill turned black as they rode up it from all directions. They looked sure to overwhelm the knights; but they were fighting uphill, and the knights' armour was strong. The wave of mamluks crashed against the knights ringing the top of the hill and was thrown back. Yusuf's men surged forward again, but they could not break the Christian lines. For every knight that fell, four or five mamluks died. Yusuf clenched his reins, twisting the leather in his hands. A horn sounded from the hilltop.

'Perhaps it is a signal to surrender, Father.'

'No.' Yusuf could see the few knights whose horses still lived gathering atop the hill with lances in hand. 'It is a signal to attack.'

'Ride for the eagle standard!' John shouted to the knights grouped around him. 'If Saladin falls, his men will not stand!'

'This is suicide, Saxon,' Reynald grumbled.

'We will die either way. This is our only chance.' John's grip tightened on the sword he had taken from a dead knight. He raised it over his head. 'Follow me. For the Kingdom!'

The knights holding back the Saracens parted, and John galloped past and straight into a crowd of mamluks. His horse shouldered aside one of their mounts, and John cut down a second mamluk. A spear glanced off his shield, and then he was through, charging down the hillside with forty knights thundering after him. Hundreds more mamluks galloped towards them, and John charged straight into them. The knights on their destriers came close behind, encased in thick mail and wielding death. They drove through the Saracen ranks like a sword through cloth. John struck out to his left and right. He caught a man in the neck and a spray of blood filled the air. He could see Yusuf's standard only fifty yards distant.

But the ranks of men ahead grew thicker and thicker. Spear after spear shattered against John's shield. One dug into his left shoulder, penetrating the mail just enough to send a wave of agony down his arm. A sword glanced off his right side. Another flashed towards his face. He ducked, and the blade struck the crown of his helmet, setting it to ringing. The men facing him now wore the saffron-yellow surcoats of Yusuf's private guard. John spurred his mount, trying to hack his way through, but the Saracens were pushing back. The charge stalled, and John found himself fighting for his life. He swung his sword in wide arcs, trying to keep the enemy at bay. Out of the corner of his eye, he saw a mamluk raise his sword to strike, but suddenly the man fell, impaled from behind. It was Reynald. Ten more knights joined them, driving back the Saracens.

'Are these men all that remain?' John shouted over the cries of combatants and the clash of steel.

Reynald grunted in affirmation. 'Where is that bastard Saladin?'

John looked beyond the sea of men before him and spotted Yusuf only twenty yards away, waving his sword to rally his men. 'There! With me, men! For Christ! For the Kingdom!'

John spurred forward, driving into the enemy ranks. The knights came after him, hacking their way through the mamluks. John could clearly see Yusuf's face now. He was only ten yards away. His eyes widened as he recognized John. Then John heard shouting from behind.

'This way, men!' Reynald roared. 'With me if you want to live!'

John looked back to see that Reynald had veered away from Saladin and towards a weak point in the Saracen line. The knights were following. They burst through the mamluk ranks and out on to the plain. Reynald galloped away without looking back.

'Bastard!' John growled. He gave a final glance in Yusuf's direction, turned and galloped after Reynald. He followed him north across a field of brown grass and towards a wadi that led into low hills. Arrows began to fall around him, and he looked back to see hundreds of mamluks giving chase. John's mount was lathered and tiring, its breath coming in laboured bursts. '*Yalla! Yalla!*' he shouted, flicking the reins and urging one last effort from the beast. It surged forward and John pulled alongside Reynald.

'We must turn back!' he shouted. 'We must strike Saladin!'

Reynald ignored him. John slashed backhanded and his blade caught Reynald in the chest, tearing his surcoat but not penetrating the mail beneath. Reynald countered, and his sword slammed into John's forearm. John felt his arm go numb, and his sword dropped from his hand. He turned his horse into Reynald's and grabbed him, pulling Reynald from the saddle. John fell with him. He hit the ground and rolled several times before coming to a stop. His lower back felt as if a sword had been plunged into it, and each breath brought a stab of pain in his chest. He pushed the pain from his mind and climbed to his feet. He was facing the northern Horn. The king's tent had fallen. John turned to see the other knights galloping on without them. A few feet away, Reynald was on his hands and knees, crawling towards his sword. He grasped it and rose.

'You traitorous shit!' he roared as he staggered towards John.

John looked about for a weapon, but there was only knee-high brown grass. He backed away.

'Come here, Saxon,' Reynald growled. 'I'll kill you before I die.' He lifted his sword over his head and charged, then stopped short as an arrow struck him in the wrist, the arrowhead bursting out the far side. Reynald cried out and dropped his sword. Three more arrows slammed into his chest, and he staggered backwards.

John turned to see hundreds of mamluks galloping towards them. An arrow struck John in the stomach and lodged in his mail. He turned away and crouched low to make himself a smaller target.

Reynald had fallen to his knees and was cradling his wrist. 'Fool!' he snarled at John. 'We could have escaped. You have killed us both.'

John began to smile, but then winced in pain; he had split his lip. 'So long as I see you die first, I shall die happy.'

Chapter 11

Crows flapped among the bodies that littered the slope of the northern Horn, pecking out eyes and tearing at the soft flesh of faces. Yusuf kicked at one, and it cawed in protest as it flapped away. He continued up the slope, striding past dead knights, their mail armour stained reddish-brown with dried blood, their swords sill clutched in their hands. He passed a big Frankish destrier with arrows protruding from all over its body. Its eyes were rolled back in its head and the poor beast had bitten through its tongue. The horse had struggled as it died, thrashing and kicking up chunks of earth all around it. Beyond the horse, Yusuf came upon a dozen dead mamluks, fallen almost one atop the other. They had been facing a single man. The Frank lay dead, his surcoat so stained with blood that it was impossible to make out the arms he wore. His great helm hid his face. Yusuf felt a sudden stab of pain in his gut as he thought of John. He knelt beside the knight and removed his helmet. The dead man had white hair and green eyes that stared sightless into the heavens.

'Malik,' a voice croaked from behind. Yusuf turned. One of the mamluks he had thought dead moved, propping himself up amongst the dead. 'Malik!'

Yusuf went to him. The mamluk was a young man, not much older than Al-Afdal. An ugly gash on his thigh went to the bone. It was oozing blood, but too little. The young man was bled out. He would die soon. Yet when he clutched Yusuf's arm, his grip was surprisingly strong.

'Have we won, Malik?'

'We have.'

The mamluk smiled. His teeth were red with blood. 'I shall boast of our victory in paradise.' His eyes fluttered and then closed. A moment later, his grip on Yusuf's arm relaxed.

Yusuf blinked back tears as he rose. The boy's death had moved him in a way the rest of the carnage had not. He turned to Saqr, his shadow, always by his side. Al-Afdal stood a short distance away, watching as some Bedouin stripped a fallen knight of his armour and boots.

'Remember this, my son,' Yusuf called. He pointed to the body at his feet. 'The scribes will write of this as a day of glory. Never forget its true nature. Never forget the cost of victory.'

Yusuf continued up the hill. The slope grew steeper, and the muscles in his thighs were burning when he finally reached the top. The bodies were thicker here, mamluks and Franks fallen one on top of the other. He had to pick his way so as to avoid trampling on the dead. Ahead, a ring of mamluks stood guard around the surviving knights. Only two hundred remained – two hundred knights out of more than a thousand. Several hundred had escaped with Raymond, but the rest lay on the field. The survivors before Yusuf looked more dead than alive. They sat slumped on the ground, their heads hanging. Not one of them looked up when Yusuf stepped into the circle.

Yusuf addressed them in French. 'Where is your king?'

At the centre of the knights, a man rose wearily to his feet. He was broad-shouldered and tall, with long blond hair and a turned-up nose that gave him a piggish appearance. His face was smeared with blood that had dried almost black. 'I am Guy, King of Jerusalem.'

'Come here.'

After a moment's hesitation, Guy started towards Yusuf. His men moved aside to let him pass.

'Your men are dead or captured, your army destroyed,' Yusuf told him. 'Do you yield?'

Guy's voice was hollow. 'I yield. I am your prisoner.'

'Where is the Wolf, the one you call Reynald?'

'The last I saw, he was charging your lines. He meant to kill you.'

Yusuf turned to Saqr and spoke in Arabic. 'Find him, dead or alive, and bring him to me. Have the King taken to a tent, one befitting his status, and kept under guard. The noble lords will be kept together until they can be sent to Damascus to await their ransom. The other knights, sergeants and camp followers will be sold.'

'What of the Crossed, Father?' Many of the survivors wore the hated red or black crosses of the Templars and Hospitallers. They were the most implacable of Yusuf's foes, fanatics who fought without regard for their lives.

'Their kind do not take prisoners, nor shall we. Execute them.'

Yusuf turned and started back down the slope. He had not got far when a rider galloped up. 'We have found the Wolf, Malik!' the mamluk cried as he slid from the saddle.

'He lives?'

The mamluk nodded. 'He was captured along with one of their priests.'

The sword blade flashed, lit gold by the light of the setting sun, and descended in a blur to connect with the Templar's bare shoulder with a sickening *thwack*. The Templar fell forward on his hands and knees, screaming in agony as his blood gushed forth, turning the dusty ground to mud. Yusuf grimaced and looked away.

So many had clamoured for the honour of killing one of the hated Templars or Hospitallers that Yusuf had had them draw lots. This executioner was one of the imams who travelled with the army and he handled his heavy sword clumsily. He swung again, striking the templar in the back and knocking him flat. It took him two more blows to kill the man, and three more after that to sever his head. It was impaled on a spear, joining the others that framed the entrance to Yusuf's tent.

'Fifty-three,' Imad ad-Din murmured as he recorded the number on a piece of parchment. 'Thank Allah that is done with.' The scribe's cheeks had taken on a greenish tinge.

'It was necessary,' Yusuf told him. 'We shall carry the heads before us in battle as a warning to the enemies of Islam.' He rose and turned to his emirs. 'Ubadah, bring King Guy to my tent. Saqr, fetch Reynald.'

Yusuf went inside and poured a cup of water. The executions had left a bitter taste in his mouth. He rinsed and spat, but the foul taste remained. Perhaps it was due to the smell of corruption already coming from the thousands of corpses lying in the hot sun. His men were busy digging graves for their fallen comrades, but Yusuf had decreed that the bodies of the Christians be left. He took another drink and sat.

Guy entered a moment later, escorted by Ubadah and two guards. The king's eyes were wide after passing between the rows of impaled heads, and his legs were shaking.

'You are tired,' Yusuf told him. 'Please, sit.' He gestured to a camp-stool and then raised his voice. 'Bring food and cool water for the King.'

As Guy slumped on to the stool, two servants entered with a platter of fresh bread and goat's cheese and a glass of water chilled with ice from Yusuf's private stores. Beads of water had formed on the outside of the cup. The king took a long drink and sighed. The servant refilled the cup and he drained it again. 'You have my thanks, Saladin.'

The king was taking another drink when Saqr led Reynald inside. The Wolf of Kerak was clutching his right hand, which was bandaged with a bloody cloth. He glared at Yusuf and sat without being asked. Guy handed him the cup. He drank greedily. Reynald wiped his mouth with the back of his hand. 'What do you mean to do with us?' he demanded.

Yusuf met his eyes. 'To kill you, Reynald.'

Reynald held up the cup and smirked. 'Do your own laws mean nothing to you? You have given me drink. That makes me a guest in your tent.'

'Your king gave you drink, not I.' Yusuf stood and drew his sword.

Reynald paled. 'You cannot do this.'

'Guards!

Saqr and another mamluk grabbed Reynald by the arms and lifted him from the stool. 'Do not be a fool!' he cried. 'I am the lord of Oultrejourdain. My ransom will be worth a fortune!'

'No amount of gold would be as precious to me as your death. You have made vows and broken them. You have slaughtered innocents and sought to profane the holy places. You have sworn peace only to attack the moment our backs are turned.'

Reynald straightened. 'I am a ruler. I did what I must.'

Yusuf stepped closer, so that his face was only inches from Reynald's. 'You killed my sister,' he hissed. He stepped back and nodded to the guards, who forced Reynald to his knees. Saqr placed a leather strap around Reynald's neck and pulled his head down on to one of the stools. Yusuf raised his sword.

'You cock-sucking pig!' Reynald snarled. 'Shit-faced—'

Yusuf brought his sword down. The first blow killed Reynald and spattered Guy with blood. The second severed Reynald's head. It landed on the floor and rolled to the feet of Guy.

The king blanched. He slid off the stool and went to his knees, his hands clasped before him. 'Please, great king, spare me! It was Reynald who broke the treaty! I will give you gold. I—'

Yusuf raised a hand. 'Your life is safe. A king does not kill a king. You will be ransomed, but first you must swear to never again take up arms against Islam.'

'I swear it.'

'On your cross.'

'On the True Cross and by the blood of the Saviour, I swear it.'

'I will hold you to that oath.' Yusuf pointed to Reynald's corpse. 'Remember the fate of those who betray their word. Guards, take the King to his tent.'

When Guy had been led out, Ubadah turned to Yusuf. 'I have something to ask of you, Uncle.'

'You fought well today, Nephew. Ask, and if it is in my power, you shall receive it.'

'We captured the priest, John of Tatewic. Let me kill him.'

Yusuf's brow knit. 'Were it not for John, the Wolf would have escaped. I mean to spare him.'

'You cannot. He betrayed you to serve the Franks, Uncle.'

'He saved my life.'

'And he took that of my father!' Ubadah shouted. 'I was only a child, but I remember. He killed Khaldun.'

'Khaldun died in the great earthquake.'

'He died trying to defend my mother's honour.' Ubadah went to his knees. 'Please, Uncle. I beg you.' He gestured to Reynald's headless body. 'You have had your vengeance. Give me mine!'

'You do not know what you are asking, Nephew. I cannot let you kill him.'

Ubadah stood. His knuckles whitened around his sword hilt. 'You cannot stop me.'

'I am your king!' Yusuf snapped. 'You will do as I say.'

'Not in this. Do to me what you will. I swore to Allah I would kill John, and I mean to fulfil my oath.' Ubadah started for the tent flap.

'Wait! John did not kill your father, Nephew.'

Ubadah stopped with his hand on the tent flap. He turned and met Yusuf's eyes. 'What do you mean?'

'He – John is your father.'

'You lie!'

'Look in a mirror, Nephew, then tell me if I lie.'

Ubadah's hand fell from his sword and his shoulders slumped. 'You . . .' he began, but faltered. 'I will never forgive you.' He spat at Yusuf's feet and left the tent.

Yusuf felt suddenly weary. He went to his stool and sat slumped forward, staring at Reynald's body. He had wanted the Wolf dead for so long, yet he could take no joy in it. He had promised his sister to never tell Ubadah the truth. But Zimat would have understood that he had to protect John. She had loved him, too. Yusuf straightened and looked to Saqr. 'Bring me John, before Ubadah does something foolish.' He gestured to Reynald's body. 'And have this mess removed.'

Reynald's body was being dragged out as John entered the tent. He grimaced, but then noticed the head still sitting on the carpet. He met Yusuf's gaze. 'Shukran, Yusuf.'

'It is I who owe you thanks. My men told me what you did. Reynald would have escaped were it not for you. Sit. Drink.'

John winced in pain as he lowered himself on to one of the stools. He took a long drink of water. 'What now?'

'I told Ubadah the truth.'

John's eyes widened. 'Why?'

'He would have killed you otherwise. He may try to kill you still.'

John's forehead creased. 'You mean to let me live?'

'You delivered my greatest enemy to me. For that, I grant you your freedom. You should leave the East, John.'

'My duty lies here.'

'Your death, you mean. The army of Jerusalem has been shattered, John. There is no one left to defend your lands. I will take every last town from the Christians. I will drive them into the sea, and you with them, if you remain.'

John shrugged. 'If that is my fate, so be it.' He took another drink. 'I saw the Templars and Hospitallers. The Yusuf I knew would not have done that.'

'The man you knew would not have won this victory.'

'You won, yes, but at what cost? You told me once that a great king must lead a holy life.'

The pain in Yusuf's gut was back. He looked away from John's blue eyes. 'I do not wish to be great, John. I am a servant of Allah, nothing more.'

'Evil done in the name of God is still evil, friend. I know that all too well. Smell the air. Does that smell like virtue to you?'

'Enough. It is time you were gone. I cannot guarantee your safety so long as you remain in my camp. You shall have a horse and supplies for three days.'

'Again, shukran.' John moved to leave, but stopped at the tent flap. 'You have it in you to be better than this. I shall pray for you, friend.' And with that, he was gone.

Chapter 12

'Too many people on this road,' John observed to no one in particular. He wished, not for the first time, that he had someone with whom he could share his worries. But Aestan had died at Hattin, and Raymond had succumbed to a lingering wound not long after John reached Tripoli. Reginald of Sidon was a prisoner of Saladin, along with Guy and most of the other great lords. 'Too many mouths to feed,' he muttered, 'and not enough swords.'

He had left Tripoli with fifty sergeants. As they made their way down the coast, they had been joined by refugees carrying their possessions on their backs and their young children in their arms. After they turned inland towards Jerusalem, the band following them had swollen into the thousands. The people came from every corner of the Kingdom. Tiberias had surrendered the day after Hattin. Acre, the Kingdom's main port and most populous city, had fallen a few days later. After that, Saladin's army had split up and swept through the Kingdom. The list of their conquests was sobering: Nazareth, La Sephorie, La Fève, Daburiyya, Mount Tabor, Jenin, Sebaste and Nablus in the south; Haifa, Caesarea, Arsuf and Jaffa along the coast; Toron and Beirut north of Acre. In the last few weeks, the southern strongholds of Ascalon and Gaza had surrendered after long sieges. Only scattered outposts remained. Kerak and Shawbak were in Christian hands but were isolated and besieged. Tyre had been rescued when Conrad of Montferrat arrived from Europe with his men. And at the heart of the Kingdom, Jerusalem still stood. For now.

Saladin was marching north from Ascalon to besiege the Holy City. The men and women on the road knew this as well as John. He could see it in their eyes. They were dull, devoid of hope. Yet what choice did they have? They had nowhere else to go. John would do his best to protect them, but his steel would not save them from hunger. With so many people flooding into the city, food would run short after only a few days. The people would be reduced to eating rats. And when the rats were gone, they would turn on each other. It would make hell look a pretty place.

The road ran upwards through olive groves, and when they reached the top of the slope, Jerusalem came into view. Refugees clogged the road leading to the city. The pace slowed to a crawl, giving John ample time to study the city's defences. Mangonels had been mounted on the walls, which had been hung with leather skins and bales of hay to reduce the impact of a bombardment. That was good, but there were far too few men walking the walls. John counted only twenty heads over David's Gate and only two men each on the square towers that dotted the wall to the north and south. As he rode closer, John saw shirtless men working with picks to deepen the dry moat that circled the city. Guards in mail framed David's Gate. They briefly stopped each refugee. As John approached, a broad-shouldered guard with a thick beard stepped forward.

'You're a welcome sight, si—' He blinked as he noticed the gold cross hanging from John's neck. 'Father. Nice to see a man with steel at his side instead of just another hungry mouth.'

'How many are in the city?'

'God only knows. More than I can count.'

Another guard laughed. He held up his two hands and wiggled his fingers. 'You can't count past ten, Ragenaus.'

'Twenty,' Ragenaus shot back. 'You forgot my toes.'

John was glad to see them joking. When food grew short, humour was the first casualty. 'Who rules in the city?' he asked.

'Balian. You'll find him at the palace. Your men can stay in the Temple.'

'What of the Templars?'

Ragenaus shrugged. 'What Templars? They're all dead on the fields of Cresson and Hattin. Only priests, old men and stable-boys remain. You'd best move on now, father.' He nodded to the long line behind John. 'Or I'll have a riot on my hands.'

Inside the city, the press on David Street was so great that John had to dismount and lead his horse. Most in the crowd were newly arrived refugees, stumbling along glassy-eyed as they searched for a place to stay. The earlier arrivals lined the narrow street with hands out. Some offered to buy food, giving as much as a gold bezant for a handful of apples, and a few amongst the new arrivals were fool enough to take the money.

John noticed that many of the boys begging had shaved heads. One of them, a bony young lad with a face smeared with dirt, grabbed at John's tunic. 'Please, father. Food. Food for a starving child.' The boy had a high, fluting voice and green eyes that seemed impossibly large in his thin face. He had delicate features for a boy.

A thick-necked man saw John staring and pulled the child away. 'Keep away from my daughter!'

John reached into his saddlebag and held up an orange. 'Why have you shaved her head?'

The man's eyes widened at the sight of the fruit. 'I don't want the Saracens raping her. If they think she's a boy, maybe they'll leave her be.'

John tossed the man the fruit and continued into the square where David Street met the Street of the Armenians. He handed his reins to one of his sergeants. 'Take the men to the temple and see that my horse is stabled. I will meet you there this evening.'

John turned south towards the palace. The Street of the Armenians was less crowded, although he did pass several families who had set up camp on the side of the road. He came upon a procession of monks with scourges in their hands, their upper bodies bared to reveal bloodied backs. They were chanting, begging God for mercy. Every four steps, they whipped themselves. John hurried to the palace. The guards recognized him and waved him through the gate. After the chaos of the streets, the courtyard was an oasis of calm. The guards had kept the populace out, and other than a pile of horse dung, the cobbled courtyard was empty. John crossed to the palace doors, where the guards told him that Balian was in the king's chambers with the queen.

John entered to find Sibylla lounging against the window. She wore a belted silk tunic that showed off her slim figure. Her auburn hair fell loose to her pale shoulders. She would have looked lovely were it not for the scowl that marred her features.

Balian was standing beside the cold fireplace. He too was glowering, but when he saw John, his face brightened. 'John! Thank God you have come.' He embraced John and nodded towards Sibylla. 'Perhaps you can talk some sense into her.'

John turned to Sibylla and knelt. 'My queen.'

Sibylla nodded coolly. She pointed at Balian. 'This fool refuses to ransom my husband, his *king*.'

'Saladin demands fifty thousand dinars. We cannot pay, my queen. You have seen the people crowding into the city. We need every last denier to purchase food.'

'We need our king!'

John cleared his throat. 'Forgive me, my queen, but Balian is in the right.'

Sibylla's face had flushed red before John finished speaking. She drew herself up and looked down her thin nose at him. 'You are traitors, both of you,' she hissed. 'When Guy is freed, he will have your heads!' She stormed out, slamming the door behind her.

'You see what I have been dealing with, John?' Balian went to a side table and poured himself a cup of wine. He took a long drink. 'She grows worse each day. I should send her out to walk the streets. There are more than eighty thousand people in Jerusalem – three times the population before Hattin – and more are arriving every day. Food is already short and Saladin has not even arrived.' He took another drink. Balian had always been strikingly handsome, but now his face was lined and there were dark shadows under his eyes. 'Your arrival is the first good news in weeks. You have brought men?'

'Fifty sergeants.'

'No knights?' John shook his head. 'What of Raymond? You come from Tripoli. Will the count march soon?'

'He is dead.'

Balian's cup froze halfway to his mouth. 'God help us. How?'

'At Hattin an arrow penetrated his mail and lodged in his chest. It was not a deep wound; but it mortified and the foul humours entered his lungs. He died two days after I reached Tripoli.'

'Who rules now?'

'His godson, Raymond.'

'Bohemond of Antioch's boy?'

John nodded. 'I tried to persuade him to march for Jerusalem, but the young Raymond chose to follow his father's lead. Both Tripoli and Antioch have signed a truce with Saladin. Raymond, at least, gave me leave to take volunteers. The fifty men who came with me were all I could find.'

'By his nails!' Balian took another drink. 'How many knights do we have?'

'True knights? One – me. But I have knighted several hundred sergeants, and I have also made it known that I will knight any man over sixteen who will bear arms. Thus far, I have raised an additional thousand knights.'

'They are farmers and tradesmen with swords, Balian, not knights.'

'Aye.' Balian raised his cup again, only to find it empty. He frowned and set it aside. 'But they are all we have.'

The muezzins in camp began to cry the call to morning prayers as Yusuf emerged from his tent. It had been erected atop the hill called Golgotha – Place of the Skull – so named for the caves that made the hillside look like a grinning skull, or perhaps for the executions carried out there in ancient times. This was where the prophet Jesus had been crucified; unless you believed the Christian priests, who claimed that the hill they called Cavalry was at the site of the Church of the Holy Sepulchre. 'Church of the Dunghill,' Yusuf's people called it, and the name adequately conveyed their opinion of whether or not Jesus had died there.

Yusuf could see the dome of the church from where he stood. It towered over the western portion of the city. His gaze moved from it to the Dome of the Rock, its gilt roof glinting in the morning sun. Movement along the wall caught his eye, and he looked to see that a postern had opened. A dozen sergeants marched out, followed by two men riding under a white flag. Another delegation had come to negotiate the city's surrender. Fifty mamluks galloped out to meet them. They surrounded the Christians and led them into camp. Soon after, Qaraqush cantered up the hill and slid from the saddle before Yusuf.

'Who did they send this time?' Yusuf asked.

'Balian of Ibelin, who commands the city, and John the priest. They must be truly desperate.'

Or they know that after last night they are finally in a position of strength.

Yusuf stroked his beard as he stared at the breach that his sappers had opened in the wall the previous night. He had sent in thousands against the Christians, but their greater numbers had not mattered in the narrow gap. Two hundred and twelve of his bravest men had died. Their bodies had been removed, but the debris remained, spilling out to fill the moat before the wall. At the high point of the rubble, the Franks had erected a wooden palisade. The catapults would make short work of it, but still, taking the gap would be no easy thing. The Franks had shown that much. The siege was ten days old. How many more days would be needed to take the city? How many more lives? Yusuf knew his men were prepared to martyr themselves. They wanted revenge for the slaughter the Franks inflicted when they took Jerusalem. But John's words echoed in Yusuf's head. Evil done in the name of God was still evil.

'Show the Franks to my tent,' Yusuf said. 'And have my emirs and secretaries come as well.'

Qaraqush scowled, but that was the extent of his disapproval. 'Yes, Malik.'

Inside the tent, a servant helped Yusuf don his golden scale armour and wrapped a black turban lined with gold about his head. He had just sat down on his camp-stool when Imad ad-Din arrived with ink and paper. The emirs of Al-Jazirah, fat Gökböri and squat Nu'man, entered after him, followed by Al-Afdal. Ubadah entered a moment later. Yusuf could smell wine on his breath as he took his place standing beside Yusuf. His nephew had taken to drink after learning the truth of his parentage. He only emerged from his tent when absolutely necessary.

Qaraqush came last of all. 'Balian of Ibelin and John of Tatewic,' he declared.

Balian entered first, and Yusuf studied the knight carefully. He was a handsome man of middle age, with long dark hair and a curly beard that looked as if it had once been neatly groomed but had recently been allowed to grow unchecked, leaving it long along his jaw and shorter at his neck and cheeks. John followed, and Yusuf noticed Ubadah's jaw clench. John was thinner than when Yusuf had last seen him, and there was even more silver in his sandy hair. He and Balian knelt.

'You are welcome in my tent,' Yusuf told them, speaking in Arabic. He knew Frankish well enough, but he wished them to see that he was the master here.

John translated for Balian. 'Greetings, Al-Malik al-nasir,' the knight said. 'We are honoured to be in your presence.'

'Sit.' Yusuf gestured to the two stools set before him. 'You have come to beg for the lives of your people?'

'We have come to save lives, yes, both yours and ours,' Balian replied.

Ubadah snorted upon hearing John's translation. 'Idle threats. There is no need to bargain with these hell-bound dogs. Let us crush them! The blood they shed when they took Jerusalem cries out for revenge!'

The other emirs nodded their agreement.

'Ask the men who died last night if our threats are idle,' Balian said. 'Many thousands of men stand ready to defend our city. More men even than in your army.'

'Pig farmers and cloth merchants,' Gökböri spat. 'Not warriors.'

John translated, and Balian's brow knit. 'Some are common men, yes, but even common men will fight like warriors if given no choice. At the moment, they keep away from the walls, hoping to be spared as you have spared those in the other towns you have conquered. But if the people of Jerusalem see that death is inevitable, then by God, every last one of them will take up arms, ready to die as martyrs.'

'We have our martyrs as well, father, men who will gladly sacrifice their lives to retake Jerusalem,' Al-Afdal put in. 'You will find thousands of volunteers ready to try the breach again. You have but to ask.'

John replied at once, without having bothered to translate. 'You may take the city by storm, Yusuf; I do not deny it. But if you do, your prize will turn to dust in your hands. Before the city falls, we will kill our children and wives so you may not rape and enslave them. We will burn our homes and

175

possessions. We will slaughter our Muslim prisoners, kill every horse and animal we possess. We will leave behind nothing but blood and ashes.'

Nu'man stepped forward. 'If they wish to slaughter themselves, let them,' the short man said in his harsh voice. 'It is nothing less than they deserve.'

'You may not care for the lives of our women and children,' John said, 'but what of your holy places? Do you wish to conquer the city, only to find the Al-Aqsa mosque a smoking ruin?'

'Ruins can be rebuilt,' Nu'man replied.

Gökböri nodded. 'The blood the Franks have spilled must be avenged, Malik.'

'Enough,' Yusuf said. 'Leave me with our guests. All of you.'

The men trooped out. Ubadah spat at John's feet before leaving. When they were alone, Yusuf turned to Balian and spoke in French. 'John says you will leave Jerusalem a smoking ruin rather than see it in our hands. What do you say to this?'

'He speaks truly. And after the slaughter is done, the blood of the dead will cry out to be avenged. When Edessa fell to the sword, men came in the thousands to avenge it. If Jerusalem falls the same way, how many tens of thousands will cross the sea to take it back?'

'If I spare your people, then how am I to know that I will not soon find myself defending these very walls from them?'

'Your man spoke true,' John replied. 'Most of those inside are farmers and craftsmen. They will fight for their lives, but they will not fight to retake Jerusalem. And if you doubt it, then take their weapons before they go.' John's blue eyes found Yusuf's. 'You are better than the man who slaughtered the Templars at Hattin, Yusuf. I know it. Do not stain Jerusalem's holy places with the blood of innocents. These people do not need to die. Reynald was a murderer of women and children. You are better than that. You are a righteous man.'

Was he? Yusuf felt the familiar stab of pain in his gut. Would a righteous man kill his brother? His wife? Yusuf swallowed the bile that had risen in the back of his throat. He looked to Balian. 'What do you propose?'

'Give us three days to prepare, and we will turn the city over to you. Allow those who wish it to leave. We will march to Tyre, and Jerusalem will be yours.'

'You will march to Tyre and take your riches with you. That will not do. You may take as much as you can carry, but no beasts of burden will leave the city. As for your people, their lives are in my hands. You have told me so yourself. If they wish to have them back, they must pay for them. Ten dinars a head.'

'And what of those who have no money?' John asked.

'Let them sell what they possess to my men. Any who still cannot pay at the end of forty days will be enslaved.'

Balian's jaw set. 'I will not send my people into slavery.'

'Slavery is preferable to death.'

'Very well,' Balian muttered. 'But ten dinars is too much.'

'It is a low price to purchase a slave.'

'A male slave, perhaps,' John said. 'The price should be lower for women and children.'

'That is fair. Five dinars for women. Two for children under twelve.'

'And old men?' John asked. 'What use are they as slaves?'

'I will let those too old to be of use go free.'

Balian looked to John, who nodded. Balian stood. 'John said you are an honourable man, Saladin. I am pleased to see he was right.' He extended his hand. Yusuf rose and clasped it. 'In three days, Malik, Jerusalem will be yours.'

John sat on his bed in the archdeacon's residence at the Church of the Holy Sepulchre and listened to the bells ringing to call the people to morning prayers. It would be the last time those bells sounded. In but a few hours, Jerusalem would cease to be a Christian city.

He rose and began to gather his things. Of most value was his priest's garb: the alb and amice of white linen; the maniple and long silk stole; the chasuble, heavily embroidered with gold and silver. He stuffed them into a rucksack, along with the dried fruit, salted beef and hard cheese he had purchased in the market the Saracens had set up in the city. No horses or beasts of burden were allowed to leave Jerusalem, so he would have to carry his possessions on his back. He already wore his boots, a pair of linen breeches, a plain cotton tunic and cloak, and the gold cross that always hung round his neck. He took his mace from where it lay on his bed and ran a finger along the worn leather of the handle before setting it down. He would have to leave it behind. Saladin had decreed that no weapons would leave the city.

John left the archdeacon's residence through a narrow stone passage that led directly to the sanctuary. He frowned. The tapestries had been removed from the church's stone walls and the candelabra taken. Even the gold inlay had been stripped from the altar. Only two of the canons had bothered to come to prayers. Their voices sounded small in the vastness of the church. John knelt before the sepulchre and crossed himself. He whispered a prayer for the people of the city and then exited into the southern courtyard. Three large wagons stood there, each piled high with crates, barrels and burlap sacks. Since horses could not leave the city, men had taken up the traces. Heraclius stood at their head. He was studying a sheet of parchment as he spoke with the treasurer.

'The hangings?' Heraclius asked. 'You are sure you packed them?'

The treasurer nodded, setting his fat cheeks to jiggling. 'Yes, Your Beatitude. I believe so.'

'You believe?' Heraclius's eyebrows arched. 'Those hangings are worth more than you are, you fool. Make certain.'

The treasurer nodded and scurried off. John crossed the courtyard to confront Heraclius. 'What is the meaning of this?'

'Have you not heard, John? The city has fallen. The treasures of God must be protected. I am taking them to Tyre.' He went back to examining the sheet.

John plucked the parchment from his hand. It was a list of the church's wealth – the silks, the golden candelabra and goblets, the relics in their ornate reliquaries, the chests of gold and silver. 'There are more than fifteen thousand people who cannot afford their ransom,' John said. 'There is wealth enough here to free them all. Balian will hear of this.'

'He already knows.' Heraclius sneered. 'He has no power over me. These treasures belong to God, not the poor.'

'The women will be raped, Heraclius, and their children sold into slavery.'

The patriarch looked down his nose at John. 'And their suffering shall reap them a great reward in the next life. Blessed by the Spirit are the poor, for theirs is the—'

John punched him, and Heraclius landed hard on his rump, blood trickling from his broken nose. John raised his fist again, but two knights of the Holy Sepulchre held him back. John spat, catching Heraclius in the face. 'You will burn in hell,' he growled as he shrugged off the knights' hands and strode away.

He walked south, heading past Saint George's Church on his way towards David's Gate. The pig and grain markets that normally stood near the church had been transformed into huge bazaars featuring every sort of good imaginable. John saw chairs and tables, rugs, pots and pans, a table laid out with a blacksmith's tools and another with the mortar and pestle, scales and vials of a druggist. Anything the Franks of Jerusalem could not carry with them, they sought to sell here. Even themselves. Young women, their tunics torn down the front to reveal their cleavage, lounged amongst the goods, hoping to sell their bodies for enough to buy their freedom. They were desperate, and the price was correspondingly low. Saracens and the Syriac Christians who had been allowed to stay in the city were snapping up women and goods for next to nothing.

Past the markets, John joined the line of refugees waiting to leave, their possessions slung over their backs as they shuffled forward with heads bowed. Half the day was gone before he reached the gate. It was framed by mamluks who demanded the ransom due from each person leaving. When they paid, their coins were handed to a scribe, who made a note of the money collected and dropped the coins in an iron-bound chest. Some sought to pay in kind. If the scribe approved, he would give a curt nod. If he rejected the offering, then the guards would roughly shove the unfortunate soul back into the city.

When John's turn came he counted out ten bezants. Balian had given him a hundred to see him back to England, but John had kept only twenty. The rest he had returned to Balian to purchase the freedom of poor Franks. John handed the coins over, and the mamluks waved him through.

Beyond the gate, he joined the crowd on the road to Jaffa. From there, they would head north, following the coast road to Tyre, the last Christian stronghold in the Kingdom. At the port, John hoped to find a ship that would take him to England. There was nothing left for him in the Holy Land. He was abbot and archdeacon of churches in Saracen hands. The women he loved were dead, as were Raymond and Baldwin. The only people he still cared for were amongst the Saracens, and they had become his enemies.

The refugees ahead of John were stepping off the road to make way for a troop of mounted mamluks. John also stepped aside, and as the mamluks passed, he caught a flash of gold. It was Yusuf in his vest of gold jawshan, coming to claim the city. He rode looking straight ahead, and passed John without noticing him.

John felt a sudden heaviness in his chest. It was the last time he would see his friend, he was sure. He waited until Yusuf had entered Jerusalem, and then turned his back on the city.

★

Yusuf felt oddly numb as he rode through the Gate of David. The last time he had passed through the arch had been twenty years ago. He had been a hostage to King Amalric. Now, he was a conqueror. The moment was not how he had dreamed it. Instead of cheering crowds, Frankish refugees lined the road-side, held back by a line of mamluks. The Christians glared at Yusuf with undisguised hatred. A red-haired woman spat as he passed.

Yusuf's son Al-Afdal saw it. 'Guards! Bring me that woman's tongue!'

'Leave her be!' Yusuf commanded. 'I have promised to spare these people, Al-Afdal. I will not have you make a liar of me.'

'But she insults you, Father.'

'Look at these people. I have taken everything from them but their lives. Let them insult me if they wish. It is all they have left.'

Yusuf continued up David Street. The way narrowed and grew steeper until he was forced to dismount and lead his horse up a series of steps to the top of the hill, from where he could see the Dome of the Rock glinting in the distance. That was his destination. He mounted again and rode down into a valley, then up and across the bridge that led through the Gate of the Moors to the Haram Ash-Sharif, what the Franks called the Temple Mount. The Al-Aqsa mosque, which the Templars had claimed as their headquarters, sat to his right. The dome rose high on his left.

'Al-Afdal, you will see that the cross is taken down from the roof of the Dome. And make certain that Al-Aqsa is cleansed in time for next Friday's prayers.'

'Yes, Father.'

Yusuf dismounted and headed up the steps to the Dome of the Rock. 'Wait here,' he told his guards. 'I wish to pray alone.'

Inside, his boots sounded loudly on the marble floor. Light filtered in through windows above, illuminating the bare walls. The elaborate mosaics and Koranic inscriptions that had once covered them had been plastered over by the Franks. Yusuf would have them restored.

He crossed to the rock, which sat directly beneath the dome. The Christians had built an altar over it, but part of the smooth white stone was still exposed. The iron grate the Christians had installed in order to stop pilgrims chipping off pieces had already been removed by Yusuf's men. He stepped on to the rock, turned to face Mecca and began to pray, speaking the words of the sura al-fatiha. 'In the name of Allah, the Most Gracious, the Most Merciful: all Praises to Allah, Lord of the Universe. The Most Gracious, the Most Merciful . . .'

When he had finished his prayers, he remained kneeling on the hard rock. It was from here that Mohammad had ascended to heaven. Yusuf looked up to the ceiling. Might the words he spoke here reach paradise?

'I have done as you commanded, Father,' he whispered. 'I have driven out the Christians—' Yusuf stopped short as he thought of John and of the others he had lost: Zimat, Faridah, Shirkuh, Turan, Asimat. 'I sacrificed everything, Father. Those who stood in my way, even those I loved. I did it for you and for Allah.' Yusuf rose. When he spoke again his voice was loud and firm. 'But now my task is done. No more lies. No more murder. Once the last of the Franks are driven out, I will return to Damascus. I will see my daughters married. I will raise my sons to be better men than I. I will create a kingdom of peace and plenty, and when I die, I will be remembered for the good that I did, not the men I killed.'

Part II
Lionheart

Acre, the crown jewel of the Kingdom. Its vast harbour welcomed ships from Egypt, Italy and Constantinople. Its markets produced more wealth than the rest of the Holy Land combined. And it was there, before its mighty walls, that the fate of the Kingdom would be decided. On the one side stood Saladin, conqueror of Jerusalem. On the other was Richard, King of England. Lionheart, they called him, and it was a fitting name. He was the fiercest warrior I have ever known. It was the greatest battle of Saladin's life, a battle in which victory could only be bought at the ultimate price . . .

The Chronicle of Yahya al-Dimashqi

Chapter 13

John's hood was pulled up in a vain attempt to keep out the rain, and he leaned heavily on his staff as he trudged into Harthill. It was a tiny village, almost indistinguishable from the dozens of others like it that he had trudged through in his trek north across England to Yorkshire. The street was unpaved, and his heavy wooden clogs sank into the mud with every step. He passed scattered wooden longhouses and sunken huts until he came to one with a tankard hanging over the door – the sign that ale was being served. Most villagers were brewers and turned their homes into impromptu taverns whenever a fresh batch was ready. John pushed the door open and stepped inside.

The room was dim, the ceiling and walls dark with smoke from a fire that guttered in the hearth on the far wall. John hung his cloak from a peg over the fire and leaned his staff on the wall. Two simple tables – boards set atop trestles – ran the length of the room. At the far end of one, two men sat across from one another. One gripped his tankard with strong calloused hands that were black under the nails. He had broad, muscled shoulders and a back bent by labour – probably at the whetstone quarry that John had passed on his way into the village. John did not like the look of the other man. He also gripped his tankard with thick fingers, but his nails were clean and his back was straight. He wore his cloak indoors. There was no reason to do so unless he was hiding something – armour, or perhaps a weapon. The men lowered their tankards and glared at John with undisguised hostility.

John had grown accustomed to rude welcomes. More than a year had passed since he left Jerusalem. He had marched to Tyre, but the city's new ruler, Conrad of Montferrat, had refused to open the gates to the flood of pilgrims. He feared that if Tyre were besieged, it would run short of food as Jerusalem had. John and the other refugees were forced to continue north to Antioch. By the time they arrived, the sailing season was over and John had to wait until March. Refugees continued to pour into Antioch. They crowded the docks, forcing up the price of passage to Europe. John had to sell his cross, and even then he could only afford a passage to Venice. He did not have sufficient coin for a horse, so he had crossed Europe on foot. The rucksack with his vestments and prayer book had been stolen while he slept at a church in Turin. His leather breeches had held up well enough, but his tunic was ragged and his cloak so riddled with holes that it looked as if a thousand moths had made a meal of it. His boots had fallen to pieces as he crossed the Alps, and soon enough his feet were raw and blistered, leaving him leaning on his staff as he limped along at a snail's pace. After seeing his tattered feet, the Benedictines in Lyon had been kind enough to provide him with a pair of clogs. The inside of the right one had cracked somewhere outside Paris when John stepped on a sharp rock. The crack opened and closed with every step, pinching his foot.

John had stayed in churches and monasteries along the route of his journey. At first, the abbots and archbishops had been delighted to welcome the archdeacon of the Church of the Holy Sepulchre. He had shared their tables and slept in well-appointed rooms. But as the road took its toll on his appearance so the welcomes cooled. By the time he had reached Bayeux, near the channel coast of France, he was lucky to find a place in the stables. In England, his appearance brought hostile looks wherever he went. Harthill it seemed, was no exception.

John ignored the men's glares as he took a seat on the far side of the room. The tavern keeper entered from the back. He was a skinny man, all elbows and knees, with a bulging Adam's apple. He scowled when he saw John and his hand moved to clutch something beneath his leather apron.

'A tankard of small ale,' John told him in English. The skinny man did not move. John held up a silver coin – his last – and the man muttered something as he went into the back. John looked about. Now that his eyes had adjusted, he noticed a third man in dark priest's robes sitting in the far corner. He was a portly fellow, and his head was resting on the table while he snored softly, his tankard of ale still in hand. The village priest, no doubt.

The tavern keeper came back with a full tankard. John took a sip and childhood memories came flooding back. The ale was sweet, with a bitter aftertaste. There had been nothing like it in the East. 'A good brew.'

The tavern keeper grunted. He was still standing by the table, his hand beneath his apron. 'You speak queer. You're no Frenchman, nor an Englishman neither.'

It was John's turn to frown. 'I have spent some years in the East. I come from the Holy Land.'

'A pilgrim.' The man said the word as if it were an insult. 'What brings you to Harthill, stranger?'

'I am a priest, on my way to Tatewic.'

The priest in the corner sat up, setting his double chin to jiggling. 'A priest? Have the White Brothers sent you? To take over the grange in Tatewic?'

The White Brothers were Cistercian monks. They had owned no farmland in Tatewic when John was a child. He wondered to which abbey the grange belonged. 'I have come to speak with Tatewic's lord,' he said. He looked back to the tavern keeper. 'Tell me, is it still Rangaldr's son, Caelin, who sits in the hall?'

'Aye, same as it's been these last forty years and more.' The man's eyes narrowed. 'What's your business with him, priest?'

'I come on behalf of Geoffrey, the bishop of Lincoln, bearing this message.' John took a scroll of paper from inside his tunic and unfurled it on the table. In fact, he had not passed through Lincoln. In Bayeux, the bishop had been shocked to learn that the archdeacon of the Holy Sepulchre and abbot of Mount Sion was sleeping in his stables. In a transaction of dubious legality, John had sold the posts in return for passage to Portsmouth. The scroll was a record of the transaction. The tavern keeper squinted at it, but it was clear he could not read. John would be surprised if even the fat priest were lettered. Most village priests were as ignorant as their parishioners.

The tavern keeper was nodding, clearly impressed by the document, as John had hoped he would be. 'Tatewic is less than three miles north, father, just past the woods.'

'Tell me of Caelin,' John said as he rolled up the scroll. 'Is he a good lord?'

'*Hmph*.' The man in the cloak slammed down his tankard and rose. John could hear the clink of mail as he stomped to the door and stepped outside.

The man he had been drinking with turned on his bench to face John. 'He's good enough, when he's here. He and our lord Serlby spend most of their days in France, campaigning for the King.' The quarryman spat. 'His wars bring us nothing but trouble.'

'Aye,' the tavern keeper agreed. 'Lord Serlby was here only yesterday. He spoke of a new tax to fund King Henry's crusade.'

The priest in the corner lowered his tankard. 'A holy cause!' he declared and then belched.

'A waste of good coin, if you ask me,' the quarryman grumbled.

The tavern keeper nodded. 'Henry has been planning his crusade for longer than I can remember. It's only another excuse to tax us. He won't leave France, not now. Lord Serlby says that

Richard has allied with Philip of France to make war against Henry. The Lionheart aims to take his father's throne. Our good lords Serlby and Caelin have returned home to squeeze yet more silver from us to pay for the war that's coming.' The man snorted. 'God save us from kings.'

'Amen.' John finished his ale and placed his last silver on the table. He went to the fire and pulled on his still damp cloak. He had reached the door when the tavern keeper called to him.

'What's this?' he demanded as he held up the piece of silver. 'I've never seen a coin like this.'

'Silver is silver.'

The tavern keeper grunted and pocketed the coin. John stepped outside with staff in hand. The rain had stopped, but the road north was still muddy and pockmarked with puddles. He slogged his way past sloping fields where sheep grazed on the stubble left from the recent harvest, and entered an old wood. The occasional towering grey-trunked ash, already bare of leaves, stood out amongst the golden foliage of field maples and elms. A thick layer of leaves crunched under foot, and John breathed deeply of their rich scent. He had walked these very woods as a child. They smelt of home.

He entered a clearing. On the far side stood a stand of ancient oaks with gnarled trunks so thick that ten men could not have encircled them. Pigs were rooting for acorns beneath. As John approached, two men stepped out from behind the trees. One clutched an old, chipped sword and the other held a knife. The one with the sword had a thick blond beard and wore rusted mail. The other was a huge man in leather armour so old it was falling apart. He had close-set eyes and a simpleton's slack-jawed smile. Outlaws. John had come across such men more than once during his long journey. Most were commoners who had joined their lord in his wars, and when they were done, had decided they did not wish to return to a life behind the plough.

John's grip on the staff tightened. 'I have no quarrel with you, good sirs.'

'Sirs? D'you hear that, Walter?' The man in mail roared with laughter, but his eyes remained cold and hard. Walter chuckled along with him. The man's laughter stopped suddenly and he spat. 'We're no lords. And might be we have a quarrel with you.'

'I am a poor priest. I carry nothing of value.'

'We'll see about that, father.'

A branch cracked behind him, and John whirled about. Just in time. A third outlaw lunged at him with a dagger. John sidestepped the blade and brought the butt of his staff up, cracking it against the side of the man's skull. The outlaw fell, unmoving. John could hear the crunch of leaves and the jingle of mail as the other men rushed him. He turned to see the bearded man charging from his left with his sword held high. Walter rushed from the right. John stood his ground until the last moment and then stepped towards the man in mail and jabbed with the tip of his staff, catching him in the face. Walter was almost on John, and he spun away from the huge man's clumsy blow and brought the staff around to catch him in the back of the knees. Walter fell face first, stabbing himself in the shoulder with his dagger. He rolled on to his back and lay screaming.

The man in mail was backing away. Blood ran from his nose to stain his beard crimson. 'What sort of priest are you?'

John leaned casually on his staff. 'The kind who baptizes with blood – yours.'

The man turned and ran. The outlaw who had attacked John from behind was still unconscious, an ugly bruise already forming at his temple. John recognized him as the cloaked man from the tavern. He took his dagger and tossed it into the woods and then turned to Walter. The huge man's eyes were wide. 'Please! Please!' he begged. 'Don't kill me.'

'Hold still.' John knelt and wrenched the dagger from his shoulder. Walter squealed in pain. John made the sign of the cross over him. 'May God save you from your evil ways.' He tucked the dagger into his belt and strode away.

John left the woods behind and came upon a meadow where

there grazed a single cow, its udder bulging with milk. Beyond the meadow lay Tatewic – two dozen wooden longhouses huddled around a well. The rain had started again by the time he reached the edge of the village where an imposing stone residence with glass windows stood. It had not been there when John was a boy. It had to be the grange.

Men and women came to their doors and stared at John as he made his way down the village's only street. They were farmers mostly, kept inside by the rain, but one was a miller in an apron dusted with flour. Men and women alike had broad faces with red cheeks and eyes narrowed in suspicion. John did not recognize any of them, no more than they did him.

He reached the well and turned right between two houses. Tatewic hall lay straight ahead. It was a rectangular, two-storey building with narrow windows and walls of thick stone. It was separated from the village by a moat, but the drawbridge was down. As he crossed, John saw fat carp swimming in the water below. He reached the door and pounded on it with his fist. There was no answer. He pounded again, and a man in mail answered.

'If you've come to beg,' the guard growled, 'you'd best be off.' He had a grey beard that covered sagging jowls. His eyes were the bright green of spring leaves. John recognized those eyes.

'Edwyn? I have come to see your lord.'

The guard blinked. 'And who might you be?'

'His brother.'

'I have half a mind to have you whipped,' Caelin said. John's brother had not risen from the table where he had sat when John entered the great hall. Indeed, Caelin had not even looked up from his leg of lamb. When John had left, his younger brother had been a boy of thirteen. Now he was a man, thick of chest, with a fleshy face and full sandy-brown beard. He took a sip of wine and looked over the rim of the cup towards John. 'My brother Iain died more than forty years ago.'

Iain. No one had called him that in many years. 'I am called John, now. And I did not die. I took the cross and went to the Holy Land. See for yourself.' John held out the scroll the Bishop of Bayeux had given him. His brother unrolled it and then set it aside.

'I do not read.'

'It says that I was archdeacon of the Church of the Holy Sepulchre and abbot of Mount Sion. I ceded the posts to the Bishop of Bayeux.'

Caelin picked up the paper. 'Turstan!' he called to the guard. 'Have Father Hugh examine this. I wish to know what it says.' Caelin sat back and turned his pale-blue eyes on John. 'And why have you returned after so many years?'

'Jerusalem fell. Only Tyre, Antioch and Tripoli remain in Christian hands. Surely you must have heard?'

'We hear much and more from overseas, most of it lies.' Caelin took another drink and his eyes narrowed as he examined John more closely. 'You have Iain's eyes and jaw. You could almost be him.'

'I am him, Caelin. I was there when you dropped Father's favourite carving knife down the well, when you kissed Fat Sally down by the smithy. I played at knights with you in this very hall.'

Caelin set his cup aside. He pushed back his chair and rose to stand before John. He gripped his shoulders with strong hands and stared into John's eyes. Then he embraced him. 'By God! It is you!' Caelin stepped back, and when he spoke again, his voice had an edge. 'Why are you here, Iain?'

'Do not fear, Brother. I have not come to dispute your claim to Tatewic. I am a priest now.'

'As Father wished.' Caelin smiled and embraced him again. 'Welcome home, Brother. Sit. Steward, wine!' A thin young man brought another bottle and a cup. Caelin poured for John. 'We thought you dead, Iain. You left without a word.'

'I had good reason. Our brother, Ranulf—'

'Was a piece of shit. No one here has forgotten what he did, the rebellion he invented to win the Earl of York's favour. He cost a dozen families their land. Father was hanged because of his lies. No one blamed you for what you did, Iain. I would have killed Ranulf myself, had I been older.'

'Earl William would not have been so understanding.'

'William is dead and gone, and we have a new king. I have fought beside him. Henry is a good man.'

'I am glad to hear it.' John took a sip of wine. It tasted of burnt wood and mushrooms, but he swallowed nonetheless. 'It is good to see you, Brother. When I left, you were only a boy.'

'And you a beardless youth.' Caelin sighed as he twisted in his chair to stretch his back, which produced a loud crack. 'We have grown old, Brother.'

'How is Mother?'

'Gone these five years.'

John frowned. 'And Aedwyn?'

'Our sister is married and a mother of six.' Caelin slapped the table. 'By the devil! I can scarcely believe you are here. I could hardly be more surprised if Christ himself visited my table. What are your plans, Brother? The King is gathering his lords in France. Will you come to war with me?'

'I have had enough of blood and death. I wish only for a place to live out my days as a simple priest.'

'That you shall have. The brothers at Roche Abbey have a grange in Tatewic with a well-appointed house for the overseer of their lands. He died some weeks ago and has yet to be replaced. The abbot owes me a favour. I shall speak with him on your behalf.'

'You have my thanks.'

Caelin grinned and slapped John on the shoulder. 'By God, it is good to have you back.'

'It is good to be home, Brother.'

Chapter 14

T *he day will soon come when I hold you in my arms once more,*
Shamsa. My conquest is almost complete. My men have swept
through Antioch, taking Al-Arqah, Jabala, Latakia, Sayhyun,
Burzey, Saminiqa, Bakas Shoqr, Darbsaq and Baghras. In the south,
the great fortress of Kerak has finally fallen.

Yusuf's quill paused over the sheet of parchment. Near the
end, the defenders of Kerak had been so desperate that they had
sold their women and children to the besiegers in return for
food. Not even that measure had saved them. They had been
slaughtered to a man when the fortress fell, but Shamsa did not
need to know the grisly details. Yusuf dipped his quill in the
inkpot and continued.

Now all that remains to our enemies are the cities of Tyre, Antioch
and Tripoli and a few scattered fortresses. My army is at the castle the
Franks call Beaufort, what we know as Qala'at al-Shaqif.

'The castle high on the rock.' It was a fitting name. Yusuf's
tent sat in the shade of Beaufort, which sat at the edge of a cliff
that rose over a thousand feet above the plain below. It was a
mighty citadel, but its imposing limestone walls could not
protect its defenders from starvation.

Once Beaufort falls, Tripoli will be next, then Tyre and Antioch.
And then I will come home. And once he did, there would be no
more war. Yusuf would build, not destroy. He would construct
mosques and places of learning. He would secure the caravan

routes to encourage trade. He would rebuild Jerusalem into a thriving city. Yusuf dipped the quill a final time. *And once I return, nothing will drag me from your side. You have my word, habibi.*

Yusuf was rereading the letter when the tent flap opened and Az-Zahir stepped inside. Looking at him was like looking into a mirror that reflected a younger version of himself. Yusuf's third son had a dark adolescent beard, a thin face and narrow shoulders. His armour was covered in dust. Az-Zahir looked to have just returned from Tyre, where Yusuf had sent him to keep an eye on the Christians. Conrad of Montferrat had refused Guy entrance to Tyre, and in response the King of Jerusalem had brought his knights and laid siege. Yusuf had stayed clear, happy to let his enemies tear one another apart.

Yusuf rose and kissed his son on the cheeks. 'As-salaamu 'alaykum, Az-Zahir.'

'Wa 'alaykum as-salaam, Father. I bring dark news from Tyre. Christian warriors from overseas have arrived outside the city. King Guy has taken command of them. He has left the city and is marching on Acre with an army of three thousand men.'

Yusuf frowned. Three thousand men were not enough to take Acre, which was garrisoned by over four thousand mamluks under Qaraqush. Still, he had hoped that after Hattin, he was done with Guy. 'When I freed him, the King swore he would never again take up arms against Islam.'

'I spoke with some merchants who had visited Guy's camp. They say King Guy wished to sail for France, but his wife Sibylla refused. It is she who urges him on.'

'Sibylla swore no oath to me. Guy did. The man is an oath breaker, and he shall be punished accordingly. We will march for Acre. Have my emirs meet me here.'

Az-Zahir did not move. 'There is more, Father. The merchants also spoke of a new crusade.'

Crusade. The word struck Yusuf like a punch to the gut. For the first time in months, his stomach began to burn.

'The French and English kings are gathering troops,' Az-Zahir continued. 'And the German emperor Barbarossa is said to already be on the march. One of the merchants saw his army cross the Danube. He said he had never seen so many men. He said the army is without number, like the stars in the sky.'

Yusuf forced himself to remain impassive. 'Go. Bring my emirs,' he said curtly. But when Az-Zahir had left, he slumped against the tent pole. He was tired of war, so very tired. Now it was coming again. A host without number. And that was just one of three armies. How could he defeat so many? Even if he gathered every mamluk, Bedouin and Turcoman in all his kingdoms and emptied the treasuries to purchase mercenaries, he could not field an army larger than thirty thousand men. Yusuf took a deep breath and stood straight. He had to be strong for his men. He poured himself a cup of water to quench the fire in his gut. He was drinking when Gökböri entered, followed shortly by Al-Mashtub, Nu'man and Imad ad-Din. Yusuf's sons Al-Afdal, Al-Aziz and Az-Zahir entered together. Ubadah did not come.

'King Guy is marching on Acre,' Yusuf told his emirs. 'It is the key to Palestine. It must remain in our hands. Imad ad-Din, you will send word to Saif ad-Din to bring the army of Egypt north. When our forces are combined, we will grind the Franks to dust against the walls of Acre. I mean to have Guy's head on a pike.'

'Guy's men are no threat to Acre,' Nu'man pointed out. 'Why not wait to march until after we have taken Beaufort?'

'Because Guy must be defeated quickly. The Christians' Pope has called a new crusade, larger than any before it. The Franks are coming in the thousands.'

His words were met with silence. Imad ad-Din looked as if he might be sick. Al-Mashtub and Gökböri were scowling. They were old warriors who had seen the second crusade and knew what Yusuf's words meant. Nu'man's face was impassive. Al-Afdal and Al-Aziz both grinned. They were too young to know better.

'Let the Christians come!' Al-Afdal exclaimed. 'More fuel for the fires of hell.' The older warriors glared at him, and his smile faded.

'The Franks will outnumber us by many thousands,' Yusuf continued. 'We have fought these many years to drive them from our lands. Now, we fight for our very survival. Al-Aziz, you will go north and secure the passes that lead to Antioch. You will halt the Germans before they reach our lands.' Yusuf spoke firmly, disguising his own doubts. In truth, Al-Aziz had as much chance of stopping the emperor's vast army as a fly had of halting a rolling boulder. 'Inshallah.'

'Inshallah,' the emirs murmured.

'The rest of you go and prepare your men to march. We leave tomorrow for Acre.'

Yusuf followed his emirs out. The sun had set and the light was fading fast, draining the world of its colours. He strode across the camp to Ubadah's tent. He waved the guards aside and entered to find his nephew flat on his back with a woman riding him. Yusuf recognized her as a Frankish slave that Ubadah had taken at Hattin. She was plump and pale, with hair as red as flame and large breasts that bounced with each thrust of Ubadah's hips.

'Nephew!' Yusuf snapped.

Ubadah's eyes widened. He pushed the girl off and pulled a robe about himself as he rose. 'Leave us, Elena!' he shouted. His voice was slurred with drink.

Yusuf watched the girl go. He turned to his nephew. 'I have been patient with you, Ubadah, but my patience is at an end.'

Ubadah stared at the carpeted floor of his tent, refusing to meet Yusuf's eye. He swayed and grabbed the tent pole to keep from falling.

'Look at you! You can barely stand. I expect more from you. You are one of my most important commanders. You are my nephew.'

'And the son of a Frank.' Ubadah looked up, and Yusuf could

see hurt in his eyes. 'Is it any wonder I drink like an infidel?' He pushed past Yusuf and left the tent.

Yusuf followed and grabbed his nephew's arm. 'It is your actions that matter, Ubadah, not your parentage.'

'Is that why you lied to me?' Ubadah snarled and shrugged off Yusuf's hand. 'You were ashamed of the truth. Ashamed of me!' He was shouting now. 'I am nothing, Uncle! I am the son of a dog!'

'You are wrong,' Yusuf replied evenly. 'John is honest, and he is the bravest man I have ever known. A better man than Khaldun was.'

His nephew struck him, a backhanded blow that snapped Yusuf's head to the side. Behind him, Yusuf could hear the whisper of steel leaving the scabbard as Saqr drew his blade.

The blood had drained from Ubadah's face, but he did not flinch when Yusuf met his eyes. 'You knew!' Ubadah hissed. 'You should have killed him, and instead you did nothing!'

'I love you, Nephew, else I would have your hand for striking me. Hate me if you will, but do your duty. That is all I ask.'

'Yes, Malik.' Ubadah's voice was stony. He strode away, and Yusuf watched him disappear into the darkness before heading for his tent. He sat heavily on his camp-stool and leaned forward, his head in his hands. His gaze fell on the letter to Shamsa. Yusuf picked it up and held it to a lamp until it caught fire. He dropped the still burning scrap in his brass chamber pot and went to his portable desk to start a new letter.

OCTOBER 1189: ACRE

Yusuf stood before his tent at the edge of a low, flat-topped hill. The day had dawned clear, and he could see the mighty walls of Acre one mile distant. Beyond those walls, the city sat on a promontory that curved out into the waters of the Mediterranean. The sea was indigo now, but when the sun rose higher, it would transform into a brilliant turquoise. A gust of chill wind blew off the water, bringing with it the tangy smell of the ocean.

Yusuf's gaze shifted from the sea to the enemy. The Frankish besiegers were concentrated south of the city, along the banks of the Belus River where it entered the sea. To protect themselves from Yusuf's army, they had built a line of earthen bulwarks topped with spears and fronted with ditches. The Frankish ramparts ran from their camp near the river to the coast north of the city, cutting Acre off from the mainland. Another set of ramparts facing the city protected the camp from sorties by the Muslim garrison. Dozens of different flags flew in the space between the ramparts. In the month since Yusuf arrived at Acre, two thousand Franks from overseas had joined Guy. There were Danes and Frisians, Frenchmen and Germans, and two cohorts of Italians, all eager to avenge the fall of Jerusalem. And as of last night, another new flag flew above the camp. It was silver and crowned with a band of scarlet – the arms of Conrad of Montferrat. The marquis had set aside his differences with Guy and come from Tyre with nearly two thousand men, a hundred of them knights. Although Yusuf still had more men when his forces were combined with those in the garrison, the Christians now outnumbered his army in the field. Selim could not arrive from Egypt soon enough.

'Malik,' Saqr said as he appeared at Yusuf's side. 'Your horse is ready.'

'Good. Ride with me.'

Yusuf climbed into the saddle and started down the hillside. He made a tour of the lines each morning and evening. His uncle had taught him that. 'You must be one of the men before you can lead them,' Shirkuh had said before giving Yusuf his first command. Yusuf had never forgotten those words. Even now, when he was king of Egypt and Syria, and the conqueror of Jerusalem, he knew that he was only as strong as the men who fought for him. And those men would fight harder for a leader they could see and hear than for one who remained aloof in his tent.

Yusuf had ordered his troops to pitch their tents in a crescent that mirrored the enemy lines. He headed for the left flank. On the way, he passed through the camp market. At first, it had been only a few tents, but it had grown larger every day as merchants flocked to serve the army. Now the market sprawled across the coastal plain, spreading for a quarter-mile in every direction. There were hundreds of shops, selling everything from armour to fine carpets to Frankish slaves. Near the heart of the market, Yusuf heard the clang of steel on steel. Some of the hundreds of blacksmiths in the market were already at work, repairing armour or weapons. Further on, he passed cooks busying themselves at giant kettles. Just beyond them were the baths. A dozen holes had been dug in the ground and lined with clay. A series of wooden stalls had been built over them. A line of soldiers stood waiting to pay their two fals admission. For a silver piece, they could even have hot water.

Yusuf continued on to a cluster of tents pitched beside the smooth waters of the Belus. Mamluks returning from the night-watch were removing armour before crawling into tents. Others sat breakfasting beside fires. They recognized Yusuf in his gold armour and rose as he passed on his way to the front lines, where yawning men were leaning against an earthen bulwark topped with spears. The mamluks straightened as Yusuf approached. Their commander stepped forward.

'Morning, Malik.' Husam's gold tooth glinted as he spoke. A seasoned warrior ten years Yusuf's senior, he commanded Shirkuh's old regiment, the Asadite mamluks. They were Yusuf's most trusted troops, which was why he had placed them across from the Christian's main camp.

'Anything to report?' Yusuf asked.

'Last night five of our men crossed the lines to visit the red tents.'

Yusuf scowled. A week ago, three shiploads of Frankish

whores had arrived and set up their red tents just beyond the Frankish palisade, where they could cater to Christian and Muslim alike. For only a dirham, they would raise their ankle bracelets to touch their earrings and let the men have their way.

'Shall I cut off their balls?' Husam asked.

'No.' If he cut the balls off of every man who visited those tents, he would soon have an army of eunuchs. 'Ten lashes for each of them.'

'Yes, Malik.'

Yusuf continued up the line, nodding to the men and stopping to speak with those he knew well. He passed Gökböri's men; then the Kurdish troops under Al-Mashtub. The huge emir was leaning against the barricade and breakfasting on a roast leg of lamb.

'What news?' Yusuf asked.

'Nothing, Malik. The Franks are as silent as death.'

Yusuf looked towards the enemy ramparts, which began a hundred yards from his own. Beyond them, he could see tents topped by standards fluttering in the wind. 'They celebrated late into the night after Conrad's arrival,' he noted. 'No doubt they are still sleeping off their excesses. Keep a careful eye on their lines, nonetheless.'

'I always do.'

Yusuf urged his horse on to the centre of the line, where he had placed his personal mamluks, who were commanded by his sons Al-Afdal and Az-Zahir. Az-Zahir had the morning watch, and he smiled at him as Yusuf rode past. Only fifteen, Az-Zahir still had a boy's enthusiasm. The ground was higher here, and Yusuf could see the line of his men stretching away before him: the Mosul regiments under the emir Zahir ad-Din, Nu'man's men from Diyar Bakr, the mamluks of the eunuch Qaimaz an-Najmi and finally Ubadah's men securing the far wing. Yusuf was just approaching Nu'man when a horn sounded in the Frankish camp. *Ahh-hoo.* Others joined it. *Ahh-hoo. Ahh-hoo. Ahh-hoo . . .*

'I don't like the sound of that,' Nu'man grumbled. The short man pulled the battle-axe from his back and scrambled to the top of the barricade.

Yusuf pulled on his helmet, dismounted and joined him. The call of the Frankish horns faded, and the only sound was the distant crash of the waves. Yusuf searched the Frankish lines but saw no activity. His stomach twisted with nervous tension. 'Bring more men forward,' he told Nu'man. 'Send the message—'

His voice was drowned out by a mighty roar from the Franks. All down the enemy line, sergeants poured over the barricades. Crossbowmen came first, followed by spearmen, all screaming war cries. 'For Christ!' 'For the Kingdom!' 'Death to the infidel!' As the Franks sprinted across the open ground between the lines, archers took to the ramparts behind them and let fly, filling the sky with arrows.

'Get down, Malik!' Nu'man shouted as he pulled Yusuf down behind the barricade. The arrows hissed past to shatter on the earth behind them. Others buried themselves in the top of the earthen barricade.

Yusuf ignored the arrows as he ran for his horse. He swung into the saddle, drew his sword and waved it over his head. 'To the barricade, men!' he shouted as he rode down the line. 'To the barricade!'

The mamluks on watch had already mounted the bulwarks and were shooting arrows into the onrushing Franks. More men were rushing towards the lines. Yusuf galloped past a half-dressed man, his mail worn over bare legs and feet. Another soldier rushed by in only a tunic, his spear and shield in hand. Yusuf reached the centre of the line and reined in. He shouted for Az-Zahir and then saw his young son on the rampart. The first Franks were reaching the line and scrambling up the earth bank. Az-Zahir hacked a man down with his sword. He impaled another. Then he fell.

Yusuf slid from the saddle and sprinted for the barricade. He could hear Saqr shouting, but he ignored him. He ran up the rampart, but saw no sign of his son. All along the line, Franks were swarming up the barricade. Some stopped to yank out the spikes that Yusuf's men had placed on the face of the slope. Others paused to loose crossbow bolts. One zipped past Yusuf. He saw another Frank about to shoot and raised his shield just before a quarrel slammed into it. He shifted his shield to block a Frankish blade and lunged, slicing through his attacker's throat. Saqr joined Yusuf on the wall and began shouting orders. Three mamluks stepped in front of Yusuf to protect him, and Saqr pulled him away from the fighting.

'Az–Zahir!' Yusuf shouted. 'Az–Zahir!'

'Here, Father!'

The boy sat ten feet away, at the edge of the rampart. He was clutching his leg, and as Yusuf knelt beside him, he saw that there was a crossbow quarrel through his son's calf. The boy was fighting back tears. Yusuf turned to Saqr. 'See that he is taken to safety and his wound looked after.'

Saqr's reply was swallowed up by another roar from the Franks. Yusuf looked north down the line to where hundreds of fresh troops were striking the right flank. They swarmed up the barricade and Ubadah's men gave ground, retreating down the far side of the rampart.

'*Yaha!*' Yusuf cursed. He had hoped that Ubadah's troubles were over. He should never have given him such an important command. 'Saqr! Go and bring my personal guard to strengthen the right flank.'

'What of Az–Zahir?'

'I will see to him. Go!'

Saqr scampered down the face of the rampart and mounted his horse. He was galloping away when Az–Zahir struggled to his feet and pointed towards the enemy lines. 'Look, Father!'

Directly across from Yusuf, one of the gates that closed off a gap in the Frankish bulwark had opened and dozens of knights were charging forth, their mounts' hooves kicking up plumes of dirt as they raced across the sandy soil.

'Stand fast!' Yusuf shouted to the men around him. 'Spearmen to the fore!'

A line of mamluks stepped forward and braced the butts of their spears against the ground. Yusuf took a spear and joined them. The knights had reached the mid-point between the two barricades. They slowed to a walk so they could form a line, their horses shoulder to shoulder. The knights lowered their lances as they picked up speed again. The Frankish sergeants scattered to either side as the knights approached at a gallop. Yusuf dug his feet into the loose earth atop the bulwark and raised his shield.

The knights charged up the slope, shields in hand and lances couched. 'For Islam!' Yusuf shouted, and his men echoed his cry. The shout of the mamluk to his left was cut short as he was skewered by one of the Frank's long lances. Yusuf took a lance on his shield and was knocked on his back. He curled into a ball as a horse galloped overhead. He started to rise when a hoof caught him in the ribs. He fell flat, struggling for breath. He spotted Az-Zahir a few feet away, crouched behind his shield. Yusuf crawled to him. 'Can you walk?' he shouted, and Az-Zahir nodded.

Yusuf looked about him. The knights had crashed through the line, leaving dead men in their wake. They were now galloping past tents as they drove deep into the Muslim camp. On the other side of the rampart, the Frankish sergeants were rushing towards the gap opened by the knights.

'We must fall back; lean on me.' Yusuf put his son's arm around his neck and together they stumbled and skidded down the rampart. The first tents were only fifty yards from the barricade, but their progress was slow. Az-Zahir cried out in pain with every step. Yusuf glanced back to see the first sergeants cresting the ramparts. 'Hurry!' he urged his son. Az-Zahir gritted his teeth and limped faster. From behind, Yusuf could hear the Franks' battle cries. He dared not look back. The hairs on his neck rose. He could almost feel the point of a Frankish spear driving into his back. And then they reached the tents. He pulled Az-Zahir behind the second one they came to. A sergeant rushed past a moment later, followed by another, and another.

'Go on!' Az-Zahir told him through clenched teeth. Tears were streaming down his cheeks, and it was all he could do to stand. 'You will stand a better chance without me. You must rally the men.'

Yusuf nodded. He lowered Az-Zahir to the ground.

'Give me a knife, Father.'

'No.' Yusuf knelt before him. 'Do not throw your life away. If they find you, yield. I will ransom you.'

Az-Zahir shook his head. 'I will not dishonour you, Father.'

Yusuf slapped him. 'This is no game, boy! Honour counts for nothing if you are dead. Do as I say.'

Yusuf did not wait for a response. He turned and ran, dodging between the tents. He heard shouting from behind. 'There! The one in gold! He's their king!' Yusuf swerved left behind a tent, where he ran headlong into a man on foot, knocking both of them down. The man Yusuf had hit was a fellow Muslim, and judging by the stains on his tunic, a cook. Wide-eyed, he scrambled to his feet and grabbed the three saddlebags he had dropped. A thief. The man sprinted away, but he had not got ten feet when a knight at his back ran him down. The knight's lance hit him between the shoulder blades and exploded from his chest in a shower of blood. The knight reined to a stop as he tried to free his lance from the dead man's body. He saw Yusuf rushing at him, but too late. Yusuf's thrust caught the knight in the armpit, where there was no armour. The Frank's eyes widened in surprise, and he mouthed a silent *Oh!* Then he slumped to the ground, landing with a crash.

Yusuf pulled himself into the saddle and quickly surveyed the field. Ubadah's wing had rallied and was now pushing the

Franks back. On the left, Gökböri had led his men in a charge, covering for Al-Mashtub, who had brought his mamluks down the line to cut off the Franks who had broken through. The Frankish foot-soldiers had spread out to loot the tents of Yusuf's men. Most of the knights had continued into camp and surrounded the hill where Yusuf's tent stood. A hundred members of Yusuf's private guard stood atop the hill, fending off twice that number of Franks. If the tent fell, then Yusuf's men would think him dead. The entire army might collapse.

Yusuf waved his sword over his head. 'Your king is here! To me, men! To me!'

Men stepped out from behind the tents where they had been hiding. Soon, a dozen mamluks surrounded Yusuf, with more on their way. 'You,' he instructed a man. 'Run to Taqi ad-Din. Tell him to send men to my tent. You, go to Al-Mashtub and say the same. The rest of you, come with me.'

There were thirty mamluks with him now. As they came clear of the tents, Yusuf spurred his horse and shouted, 'For Allah!' His men echoed the cry and sprinted after him. They struck the Frankish knights in the rear. Yusuf drove between two men. His sword glanced off the helm of the one on the right, and he slammed his shield into the face of the one on his left. His men came after him and dragged the knights from their saddles. Yusuf pressed on, hacking left and right. He felt a sword glance off his side. Another struck the side of his helm, setting his head ringing. He roared and swung blindly. He felt his sword dig into flesh, and when he swung again, a spray of crimson blood flew from the blade.

On the hill above, the men of his khaskiya had seen him and were fighting with renewed vigour, pushing the Franks back. Yusuf lowered his gaze just in time to see a Frank driving his sword towards his gut. He twisted out of the way and hacked down, catching the Frank on the wrist and severing his hand. Another knight raised his sword to strike, but he was grabbed from behind by his mail coif and pulled from the saddle. Ubadah rode over him as he came alongside Yusuf. His nephew's face was spattered with blood.

'Shukran, Nephew.'

Ubadah had struck the knights' flank with three dozen mamluks, and fifty more, with Saqr and Al-Mashtub at their head, were driving into the Christians from the other side. One of the knights shouted for the retreat. The Franks wheeled their horses and drove past the mamluks that Yusuf had led into battle.

'For Allah, men!' Yusuf shouted. 'With me!' He galloped after the knights, across the plain and in amongst the tents. The Frankish foot-soldiers were also retreating, lugging their loot with them. Yusuf slashed one of them down from behind. Another sergeant dropped the heavy bag he was carrying and turned to give battle. Yusuf took his spear thrust on his shield and slashed down, catching the man in the neck. The Frank twisted as he fell, spraying blood in an arc.

Ahead, knights were riding over the barricade and sergeants were scrambling after them. Yusuf struck down two more as he rode up the rampart. Before him, the Franks were sprinting for the safety of their lines. To his right, he could see that Ubadah's men were driving the Franks before him. On the left flank, Gökböri's men had reached the ramparts of the Frankish camp. A horn sounded behind the Frankish lines, and Yusuf saw sergeants running from the rampart facing the city to reinforce the barricades across from Yusuf's camp. The blast of the horn had hardly faded before the gates of Acre opened and the Muslim garrison poured out to strike the now abandoned ramparts. Some of the sergeants turned back to meet the threat. Others milled about, unsure what to do.

'We have them now!' Yusuf shouted. 'We will drive the infidels into the sea from which they came! Yalla! Yalla!' He spurred his horse down the far side of the bulwark and galloped across the sandy ground. He raised his sword as he closed on the rearmost of the fleeing sergeants.

'Malik! Malik! Stop!'

Yusuf pulled back on the reins. Ubadah, Al-Mashtub and Saqr drew alongside with only a dozen mamluks. 'What has happened? Where are the rest?' Yusuf looked back and his eyes widened in disbelief. His men had turned back and were returning over the barricade and into camp. The men on the left and right flanks had also turned back. 'We had victory in hand. Where are the cowards going?'

'We had best join them, Malik,' Al-Mashtub urged. 'We cannot remain here.'

Yusuf gave a last look to where the Franks were still fleeing towards their camp. He had been so close. When he spoke, his voice was as sharp as a well-honed sword. 'To camp, men.'

As they reached the top of the bulwark, Yusuf dismounted and took Ubadah aside. 'You fought bravely today, Nephew. You saved my life.'

'Each time I kill a Frank, I pray that he is John. That is why I fight; not for you.' Ubadah turned and stalked away.

'Father!'

Yusuf looked to see Az-Zahir limping up the rampart. His anger faded, and he went to embrace his son. 'Alhumdillah. You are safe.' Yusuf pulled back and then noticed that the camp before him was nearly empty of men. 'Where is the army?'

'The merchants and some of the rearguard thought we were defeated when the Franks breached our lines. They plundered our own men's tents and fled. I tried to stop them, Father, but they would not listen. When our men saw what was happening, they abandoned the attack to retrieve their belongings.'

The stupid fools! Yusuf's jaw clenched, and he could feel the veins at his temples throbbing. He turned to where his emirs where gathered. 'Saqr! Gather up the enemy dead and have them dumped in the river, downstream of our camp. Al-Mashtub, round up the thieves. Bring all that they have taken back to camp and see that it is returned to its owners.'

'And the men who took it?'

'I will have no thieves in my camp. They ran from the Franks; let them keep running. Take everything they own, including their clothes, and send them on their way.'

Rain drummed on the roof of Yusuf's tent. He stared at the cup in his hand before draining it. The medicine left a bitter taste in his mouth, but it worked. His gut had been troubling him again. It felt as if there were coals burning in his stomach. The medicine extinguished them, if only for a time. 'Shukran, Ibn Jumay.'

The Jewish doctor touched Yusuf's forehead. 'You are feverish.' He poured another cup of water, to which he added several powders from his supplies. 'Drink this as well.'

'What is it?'

'Crushed coriander seeds and anise with poppy extract. It will ease the pain in your head.'

Yusuf swallowed the draught and grimaced at the taste. He waved to Ibn Jumay, dismissing him, but the doctor did not leave. 'May I speak with you, Malik?' he asked, and Yusuf nodded. 'You push yourself too hard. You are only human. Remember what happened at the siege of Aleppo. You almost died.'

'I did not have you with me that time.'

'I am no miracle worker. My medicines can ease your pain, but they cannot cure what ails you. Only rest can do that, Malik. Pull back, at least until the men of Egypt arrive.'

'And let the Franks fortify their position even more?'

'It is not the Franks you should fear, Malik. Sickness in the enemy camp is spreading. You must pull your men back or risk infection. Disease will kill more surely than the Franks, and you cannot fight it.'

'I will think on what you have said.'

Ibn Jumay bowed and departed. Yusuf rose and the world spun for a moment, then steadied. *The air is too close in my tent.* He pulled on his cloak and stepped outside. After a few deep breaths, his head cleared. He could just make out the Frankish camp through the rain. Since the battle, they had spent their days digging a deeper trench before their bulwarks. They had also built a wooden wall around their camp. They had begun to extend it along their lines, starting at the river and moving north. Men were at work on it even now, despite the rain. Beyond them, Yusuf could see pyres burning in the empty piece of ground between the Franks' two ramparts. The Christians were burning their dead.

Every day saw more bodies on those pyres. The Franks had pulled the bodies of their dead from the river, but too late. The flux was loose in their camp, and hundreds had died already. If the disease spread to Yusuf's men, hundreds more would join them. Ibn Jumay was right to be afraid. Yet Yusuf could not retreat. Not now. If the Franks finished that wall, their siege would be that much harder to break. And their numbers were growing. For every one that burned on the pyre, three arrived from overseas. The spring would bring even more of them. And meanwhile, the German emperor Barbarossa had reached Constantinople. Yusuf had to strike now.

'Saqr!' he called. 'My horse!'

Another wave of dizziness swept over him as Yusuf climbed into the saddle. He swayed but managed to straighten.

'Perhaps you should rest, Malik,' Saqr suggested. 'One of your sons can inspect the lines.'

'I am well enough,' Yusuf grumbled and set off into camp. At the barricade, the men had erected canvas shelters and were huddled beneath them to keep out of the rain. Yusuf noticed that some were pale, with tight skin and dark circles under their eyes. He kept his distance. Had sickness already come to his camp? How?

'Malik.' Husam stepped out from beneath one of the shelters. He coughed – a deep, chest-rattling cough – and spat. 'Three more men caught visiting the red tents last night.'

The red tents. That was it. 'Show them to me.'

Husam barked an order and two of his men jogged off. They

returned a moment later marching two men in tunics before them. The men were shivering in the cold. Their faces were drawn and their eyes red. 'Where is the third man?' Yusuf asked.

'Too sick to walk, Malik,' came the reply from one of the mamluks. 'He collapsed in the mud, just outside the prison tent. I thought it best not to drag him here.'

'You did well.' Yusuf turned to Husam. 'These men are to be placed in a tent on the edge of camp. Give them a guard and their own cook. No one else is to have contact with them. And the next man to be caught visiting the red tents will be beheaded. Let it be known.'

'Yes, Malik.'

Yusuf continued down the line. He rode in silence, nodding at the men as he passed. His teeth were soon chattering. He drew his cloak more tightly about him. He was always cold of late. Near the middle of the line, he rode up the rampart to look at the enemy lines. The wall the Franks were building now extended along a quarter of their line. In a week, maybe less, it would be complete.

'Saqr,' he called. 'Have the emirs gather in my tent. I will want to speak to them when I return.'

Yusuf rode back down from the barricade. His mind was busy planning as he continued up the line. He would strike tomorrow. Tonight, he would need to send a message to Qaraqush in Acre to coordinate the attack. One of Yusuf's mamluks – a man named Isa – had already delivered several messages. Isa was a great swimmer. He would enter the sea to the south of the Frankish camp and swim under their ships and into the harbour of Acre.

Yusuf returned to his tent and dismounted. He had to lean on his horse for a moment to steady himself. Ibn Jumay's medicine was wearing off. The pain in his gut had returned. He entered his tent to find his emirs waiting. He strode past them and sat heavily on the camp-stool.

'We have waited long enough,' he began. 'Tomorrow, we

will strike. We—' He paused and his hand went to his head. The faces of the men before him blurred. He blinked, but they refused to come into focus.

'Father!' he heard Az-Zahir say, but his son's voice seemed far away. The world was spinning again. He felt himself falling. Then everything went black . . .

Chapter 15

John sat at a simple oak desk, the accounts for the grange open before him. The previous overseer — a layman hired by the abbey — had kept poor records. John suspected the man had been stealing. If so, that was only one of the sins for which he was, no doubt, suffering in hell. John had learned from the miller — a talkative man who was happy to gossip so long as John bought his ale — that the previous overseer had died of an attack of apoplexy while fucking the blacksmith's wife. Her screaming had drawn half the village, including her husband, who the miller assured John had been busy buggering one of the acolytes from the abbey.

John squinted at the rows of numbers and made a notation. He set the quill aside and rubbed his hands, trying to bring warmth back to his aching knuckles. It was no use. He rose and added another log to the fire. He poked at the blaze until it was roaring merrily, but still the chill in the room remained. The grange was a fine home with a study, a well-appointed bedroom, a great hall and a separate kitchen, but the thick stone walls made it as cold as a tomb.

Something howled outside. It sounded like a baby crying. John went to the window and pushed open the shutters. Snow was falling, and the square below was blanketed in white. On the far side was a pack of boys, some not yet old enough to help in the fields, others with downy cheeks. They stood in a semicircle before the wall of the miller's house, where they had nailed up a cat by its tail. The poor animal was hissing and thrashing, its claws scrabbling against the wall as it sought to free itself. One of the boys stepped forward and head-butted it. He came away with a bloody gash on his cheek. The other boys cheered. The cat howled.

John closed the shutters. He did not need to see more to know how the boys' sport would end. They would butt the cat until it died, and whoever killed it would be declared the victor. It was a savage game. John had played it himself when he was a child. He had been a savage, too. He grimaced. Since returning to England, he sometimes felt like a man living amongst beasts. A very, very cold man. He returned to the fire and his hands began to tingle as they slowly thawed. He had cursed the heat of the Holy Land more times than he cared to remember, but the cold was much worse. He closed his eyes and imagined himself standing on the sandy shore south of Acre and looking out over the clear turquoise waters of the harbour. He could almost feel the hot sun beating down, its warmth balanced by the cool sea breeze.

There was a tentative knock on the door. 'Enter!' John called.

It was his servant, Caesarius. The boy was a novice from the abbey, and he could hardly have had a more ill-fitting name. Caesarius was a gangly lad, forever tripping over his own feet, and he was so shy that he could hardly string together more than three words when in John's presence. He set a bowl of stew down on the table and hurried from the room without a word.

John sat and poked at the stew with his spoon. Turnips, carrots and some sort of boiled meat were floating beneath a thick film of grease. He knew it was better than most of the villagers ate, but just looking at it made his stomach turn. He sometimes found himself dreaming of fresh mangoes and oranges, of spiced lamb and thin, crisp bread. If he had the coin to take ship, he would have returned to the East months ago, but he was not about to trek across Europe, not again. His trip north had nearly killed him.

This stew looked likely to finish the job. John pushed the bowl away and donned his heavy cloak. Outside, the air was so cold it burned his lungs. His boots crunched in the snow, and he left fresh tracks behind him as he crossed the square. The boys had finished their sport. Only one remained. He was furtively carrying the dead cat away.

'You there! What are you doing?'

The boy froze. He looked to be no older than ten, with saucer-like eyes and smooth cheeks marked by the cat's claws. 'I – I was going to bury it,' he murmured.

'Bless you, son.' John made the sign of the cross and continued to the door of the miller's house. He knocked.

The fat-cheeked miller Edgar greeted him with a smile. 'John! Come in, come in.'

John hung his cloak by the door and sat before the fire crackling in the hearth. The miller's food was no better than John's, but at least it was warm here. And Edgar's wife brewed a fine ale.

'Let me get you something to drink,' the miller said.

'That would be kind of you.'

'Don't mention it.' Edgar stepped into the next room but continued talking. 'I'm glad you came, John. My wife is visiting her sister up in Thurcroft. Mabil is pregnant.' Edgar crossed himself as he returned with a tankard in hand. 'A winter babe. God help it.' He took a hot poker from the fire and dipped it in the ale, which foamed over the sides. He handed the tankard to John and sank into the chair beside him.

John sipped at the warm brew. It was rich and sweet, with a bitter aftertaste and a hint of spice. John raised his eyebrows. 'Cinnamon?'

Edgar grinned. 'And a touch of honey and ground ivy.'

'Where on earth did you find cinnamon?'

'I have my ways.' Edgar's smile faded. He took a sip from his own tankard. 'Mabil's child . . . if it dies early, will you baptize it, John?'

John nodded. Baptizing the dead was a common enough practice. No mother wanted her child to go to hell, so the babes were brought to priests who waited for a sign of life – sweating or movement – and then quickly baptized the child. The parents could then bury it with a clear conscience. John had seen enough dead men to know that the signs of life were nothing of the sort, but he was happy to provide what comfort he could.

'Good, good. That will put my wife's mind at ease.' Edgar took another drink. 'How is the grange, Father?'

'Cold.'

'*Hah*! That it is. The man who built it was a fool. I told him those glass windows were good for nothing.' Edgar took up a poker and stirred the fire, sending sparks racing up the chimney. 'Ah well, nothing a fire and warm ale can't fix, eh?'

'Amen.' John took a long drink.

There was a knock on the door, and it swung open, bringing with it a swirl of snowflakes. Caesarius stood uncertainly in the doorway, shifting from foot to foot.

'Don't just stand there, boy!' Edgar cried. 'Get inside.'

'What is it, Caesarius?' John asked as the boy closed the door.

'Your – your—' Caesarius's gaze fell to the floor. He licked his lips and started again. 'Your brother has returned, father.'

'He is in the castle?'

The boy nodded.

'My thanks for the ale, Edgar.' John retrieved his heavy cloak from beside the door. 'Caesarius, see that the fire in my room stays lit. I want it roaring when I return.'

Outside, the snow was falling so heavily that it had already filled Caesarius's footsteps. John trudged through the storm to the manor. The guard at the gate nodded to him. 'He's in the hall, father.'

John found Caelin slouched in his seat at the end of the table. A bowl of stew sat untouched before him. He had a mug of ale in hand, and he took a long drink as John entered the hall. Last spring Caelin had left for France to join King Henry in battle against his son, Richard. He had left on a sunny spring day and had been in high spirits. He had ridden a magnificent chestnut destrier, and his mail had been scoured so that it gleamed to match his bright smile. Now his armour was rusted and rent at the shoulder. An angry scar ran down his right cheek.

'Brother!' Caelin called. He was missing his two top front teeth. He took another swig from his mug. 'Sit. Eat. I have no stomach for food.'

John sat beside him and glanced at the stew. 'I am not hungry.'

'Ale for my brother!' Caelin ordered.

A young boy came forward with a mug. John accepted the warm ale gratefully and took a long drink. 'What has happened to you, Brother?'

'Have you not heard? The King is dead.'

'News travels slowly. We heard rumours.'

'It is more than rumours. In June, we met to parlay with Richard and King Philip of France. They offered outrageous terms, which Henry refused. We returned to Le Mans.' Caelin shook his head and took another drink. 'A truce had been called for the parlay. Richard attacked before it ended. We were caught unprepared. Richard broke into Le Mans and set it afire. We fled, but Richard and Philip caught up to us at Ballans. They crushed us. Afterwards, Richard forced Henry to recognize him as his heir instead of John. Two days later, Henry was dead.'

'At Richard's hand?'

'Henry was old, but he was not dying, not until Richard drove him from Le Mans in the midst of a raging storm. Henry took ill, and he never recovered. Richard may not have struck him down, but make no mistake, he killed his father.' Caelin drained the mug and slammed it down on the table. 'More ale!' The servant boy hurried forward with a mug, sloshing ale as he set it on the table.

'So Richard is king?'

Caelin nodded. 'And a right bastard he is, too. His men call him Cœur-de-lion, Lionheart.' Caelin snorted. 'But the man has no heart.'

'The brothers at Roche Abbey say he is a religious man.'

'His only religion is blood and steel. Richard has taken the cross, but do not think it is for God. He is using his crusade as an excuse to squeeze his father's allies dry. He would not let me leave court until I paid him a hundred pounds.'

'But he will march for Jerusalem?'

'Aye. He is in London now, collecting coin and men. An army of cut-throats and murderers, if you ask me. He's promised a full pardon to any who take the cross. The gaols of Wales and England have emptied.' Caelin shrugged and took a long drink from the fresh mug of ale. 'I suppose a few more thieves hardly matter; most of his knights are brigands.'

A crusade. This was John's chance to return to the Holy Land. 'Do you suppose Richard would take a priest?'

Caelin set his mug down and gripped John's arm with surprising urgency. 'Do not think of taking the cross, John. You do not want to serve under Richard. He is a man without honour.'

John thought of Reynald and Guy. 'I have fought for men without honour before. God can use even the basest of tools to achieve his purposes.'

Caelin released John. 'If the grange does not please you, Brother, then I will find you another residence. You are always welcome in my hall.'

'It is not the grange, Caelin; it is England. I am a stranger here. My place is in the East. Richard is going there, and I mean to join him.'

Caelin gave his brother a long look. He nodded. 'Very well. I will see that you are fitted out with armour, weapons and enough coin to see you to London.' He shook his head again. 'God save you, Brother.'

John smelt London long before he saw it. The damp air over the Thames was heavy with the reek of decaying waste, rotting meat, offal and shit, all overlaid with the sharp scent of wood smoke. He wrinkled his nose. The captain of the small merchant ship noticed and laughed. He was a red-cheeked man with thin arms and an enormous belly. 'You should smell her in the summer, priest. Today she's sweet as a rose by comparison.'

John had ridden the short distance to Hull, from where he had taken a ship, preferring to chance the winter seas rather than the muddy roads leading to London. The captain had hugged the coast, and the voyage had passed uneventfully. John spent most of it below decks retching. Better this, he had told himself, than weeks spent riding south through the bitter cold. After they entered the mouth of the Thames, his seasickness had abated and he had come on deck. He could see the Tower of London now, a massive keep looming above grey walls on the north bank of the river. A ray of sunshine escaped the clouds and illuminated the keep, causing it to shine like fresh snow.

'The White Tower,' the captain said. 'Newly built of limestone. A pretty site, but I wouldn't want to go there. Richard uses it as a prison for those who displease him.'

Beyond the Tower, the city of London squatted behind its walls. It was a jumble of wood and stone houses and taller church towers, all pressed up against one another. A bridge spanned the river, connecting London to Southwark across the Thames. The bridge was under construction. The section nearest the walls was built of stone and the rest of wood.

'What are you doing?' John asked the captain. The boat was angling away from the city and towards the south bank. 'You promised to take me to London.'

'And so I have. It's cheaper to dock at Southwark, father. It's only a short walk to the city.'

Men busied themselves about the deck, and the sails came

down as the boat glided towards a pier. Sailors jumped ashore to tie the ship off. John waited until they had lowered the gangway. He crossed himself as he stepped on to the pier. The waterfront was crowded with sailors, merchants and whores. He shouldered his way into the crowd. Beneath his fur-lined cloak, he wore a coat of mail that his brother had given him, and most of the men and women in the crowd stepped quickly aside when they felt it. But one young whore, hardly more than a child, clung to his arm. She leered at John. 'Fancy a fuck, good sir? I'm newly arrived from the country, fresh as new linen.'

John pulled away and pushed on. The crowd thinned as he left the waterfront behind. The streets of Southwark were paved, but the stones were slick with snow and filth. John stepped carefully as he made his way to the bridge. A stone gatehouse stood at its head. He joined the line of people tromping across the drawbridge that separated it from the town. When he reached the gate itself, a soldier in mail stopped him. 'Two pence to cross on foot.'

John handed over the coins and shuffled forward with the crowd. The bridge was wide enough to accommodate sixteen men abreast, but the sides were lined with merchants' booths and pedlars hawking their wares. In between, singers, fire-eaters and jugglers were entertaining the crowd. Near the middle of the bridge, John passed a barber pulling a man's tooth before a crowd of onlookers. The barber was a bear of a man with muscled shoulders and meaty forearms covered in thick black hair. More hair protruded from the collar of his thick wool shirt. He grabbed hold of the man's tooth with iron pinchers and jerked it free in one pull. His patient fell forward, blood dribbling from his mouth, while the barber held up the tooth for all to see.

After crossing the stone portion of the bridge, John entered the city. Narrow wooden houses crowded close on either side, casting the street in dark shadows. He stopped at the first intersection. A small stone church sat at the south-west corner. At the far end of the street to the right, he could make out the walls of the Tower of London. Ahead, the road ran straight through the city for as far as he could see. The street to his left curved slightly so that he could only see a short way up it. He had no idea where to go. A man with a white crusader's cross sewn on his cloak stepped out of the church. He wore boiled leather beneath his cloak. A soldier. The man was clean-shaven and had a broad nose and full lips.

'God keep you, good sir,' John greeted him.

'And you, sir,' the man murmured as he made to pass on by.

John fell in beside him. 'I see you have taken the cross. I also wish to join Richard's crusade. Might you tell me where his army is gathering?'

The man stopped. He examined John and frowned. 'I'll tell you, but I don't think they'll take you, old man. Richard is looking for warriors – young, strong men.' He nodded towards the street that curved away to the left. 'Follow Watling Street out past Newgate. The army is camped north of the city on the banks of the Fleet.'

'You have my thanks.'

The soldier grunted and continued on his way. John turned up Watling Street. Patches of melting snow dotted the way, and a mixture of night soil and God knows what else drained down the middle. John caught his reflection in a pool of murky water. His hair, more grey than blond now, had receded at his temples. Crow's feet stretched out from the corners of his eyes and his forehead was marked by deep creases. When had he grown so old? He still remembered arriving in the Holy Land as if it were yesterday. He had been sixteen. That was forty-two years ago.

He continued up Watling Street and crossed a wooden bridge over a stream. The waters smelt foul, but women were washing clothes in them. A child scooped up a pail of water and lugged it away. Further on, the road branched. To the left it ran to a massive, half-finished church, the nave open to the elements at one end. He took the right branch and soon came to a vast square with half a dozen streets leading from it. In front lay a grain market where merchants haggled with farmers who had brought carts loaded with wheat or barley. John was halfway across the square when he heard a loud scream behind him, followed by shouting. He turned to see another market at the far end of the square. Four of the houses that bordered it were burning. A crowd had gathered before each of them, but the people were not attempting to extinguish the blaze. They were shouting at the occupants. One particularly strident voice reached John. 'There's a taste of hell for you, Jew!' A man ran from one of the houses. His hair was on fire. The crowd closed on him, and he disappeared amidst swinging fists and kicking feet.

John turned away and went to the stall of the nearest grain merchant. Its proprietor was a thin, bald man with long fingers that had thick, red knuckles. He sat on a stool, huddled beneath thick furs. 'What is happening?' John asked.

'The Jews.' The merchant spat. 'They sent men to the King asking to have their portion of the Saladin tithe decreased. The King turned them out. Someone at the palace gate struck one of the Jews, and a crowd gathered. I saw them parade by with one of the Jew's heads. Bad for business, that.' The merchant spat again. 'The crowd isn't content and has come looking for more Jews. They're burning them out of their homes.'

John watched the buildings burn. The crowd was growing louder, shouting taunts. Suddenly, a man jumped from the second storey of one of the houses. He landed in the crowd, knocking three men down, and was up instantly and running. He managed to get free and sprinted down the street towards John. The crowd gave chase. The man flashed by. He was young and had a short black beard. He turned sharply and ducked into a church. The crowd gathered outside and shouted for him to come out. Finally, four men headed in after the Jew.

John thought of his friend, Ibn Jumay. The Jewish doctor had saved John's life more than once. John would likely never see him again, but perhaps he could return the favour. He pushed through the crowd and into the church.

The interior was dim, and it took a moment for his eyes to adjust. He walked forward between shadowy pews. There was the Jew, crouching behind the altar as the four men approached. Two of them wore leather armour and carried clubs. One wielded a cleaver. The fourth was in mail and held a sword.

'Leave him be!' John shouted. 'That man has sought shelter in a house of God.'

The man with the sword turned. He was a handsome youth with long blond hair that framed an angular face. He was a lord. Over his mail he wore a velvet doublet emblazoned with the arms of his house: a field of ermine bordered with a band of scarlet containing six gold horseshoes. 'This is no business of yours, old man,' he snapped in French.

'I am a priest, ordained by God. What happens in His house is my business.'

'God don't care about his sort, father,' the man with the cleaver said. He wore a bloody butcher's smock.

John took his mace from his belt. His voice was hard and edged with menace. 'You will not shed blood in the house of God.'

'Do not make us hurt you, grandfather,' the young lord scoffed.

'You are welcome to try.'

The lord smirked. 'I shall do quite a bit more than try.'

The butcher held back, but the other three advanced together, the lord flanked by the men in leather. John let them come. The man on the right swung his club for John's head. John sidestepped the blow and grabbed the man's arm. The lord lunged at John, and he swung the man he held on to the lord's sword point. The man in leather screamed and fell to the floor, blood seeping between his fingers where he clutched his gut.

The young lord stood wide-eyed, staring at the blood on his

blade. 'I am a king's man,' he hissed. 'You will pay for that with your life.'

John's only response was to raise his mace.

'Stop! This is a house of God!' someone called behind him. He turned to see a thin man in white priest's robes. John saw a flash of gold as the priest swung the heavy cross that he had taken from the altar, and then pain exploded in his temple and the world went black.

'Get up!'

John started awake as the toe of a boot dug into his side. A man in mail stood over him; he was holding a torch. John squeezed his eyes shut against the light. His head was pounding. He felt just above his ear, where the priest had struck him. His hair was sticky with blood.

'Get up!' the guard said again. 'The King wants to see you.'

John pushed himself to his feet. He was in a windowless room with smooth stone walls and a thick, iron-banded door. The guard led him out into a dim hallway. They went up a flight of stairs and down another hallway, this one with windows looking out on the Thames. John could see London in the distance, a haze of wood smoke hovering above it. He followed the guard up more stairs. The halls here were covered in thick carpets that swallowed up the sound of their footsteps. The guard stopped at a door decorated with flowery steelwork. He knocked. A square-jawed man with curly auburn hair and hard grey eyes answered.

'The prisoner, milord,' the guard said.

The man nodded and opened the door. John stepped into a small room with a beamed ceiling and walls hung with tapestries that depicted hunting scenes in bright colours. The room was dominated by a large table, which left barely enough space for the crowd of courtiers. A young man with a sparse red beard lounged against the window embrasure to John's left while a stooped old man with pale, sagging skin leaned on the side of the table. The rest stood. They were hard men in the prime of life. Two were dressed in bishop's robes. The others were lords with arms embroidered on their doublets. Amongst these last, John noticed a man with the same arms as the young lord he had confronted in the church. His hair was more white than blond and his cheeks more hollowed, but he had the young man's same angular face. John guessed that this was his father.

Behind the table sat a man so handsome that he might be called beautiful. He was clean-shaven and strong-jawed, and had reddish gold hair that fell to his shoulders. His eyes were the blue of Acre harbour on a sunny day. He wore a thin circle of gold on his head. This was King Richard.

The man who had let John in took his arm and pulled him forward to stand before the table. 'The prisoner you wished to see, Your Grace. The one who tried to save the Jew.'

'And killed one of my son Henry's men,' the hollow-cheeked man said.

'Your son killed him,' John replied.

'Liar!'

'Enough, Walchelin.' Richard's voice was a rich baritone, and he spoke in the curt tone of one accustomed to command. The king looked to John. 'You heard Lord de Ferriers. He claims you killed one of his men and threatened to kill his son in order to protect a Jew. He has asked for your head.'

'The Jew had taken shelter in a church, Your Grace.'

'What does that matter? Young de Ferriers was doing my bidding, and God's work. I need gold for my crusade. I've already sold every lordship and parcel of land that I can find buyers for. I'd sell London itself if I could, but no one wants this shit-hole. So I need the Jews' coin. I have asked for twenty-five per cent of what they own. They came to me wheedling and pleading that they be allowed to give less. Such impertinence must be punished. You can be sure the Jews from the rest of my kingdom will pay readily enough now.'

'Evil done in God's name is still evil, Your Grace.'

Richard smiled at that, showing even white teeth. 'You are either a bold man or a fool to speak thus to your king. How are you called?'

'John of Tatewic.'

'From near Yorkshire, Your Grace,' said the wrinkled old man leaning on the table.

'And what brings you to this stinking cesspool of a city, John of Tatewic?'

'I wish to join your crusade.'

The young man by the window laughed, though his green eyes showed no sign of mirth. Richard smiled again. 'A crusader who loves Jews and an old man at that. What use would I have with you?'

'I have spent most of my life in the Holy Land, Your Grace. I fought in King Louis' crusade. I was at Hattin and at Jerusalem when it fell. I served as Archdeacon of the Church of the Holy Sepulchre and as Abbot of Mount Sion. I lived among the Saracens. I know the enemy you will fight and the lands on which you will fight them.'

Richard's blue eyes narrowed. 'Perhaps I shall have to spare you after all.'

'He is no abbot,' Walchelin put in. 'And I doubt if he has ever sailed beyond our shores. He lies to save himself, Your Grace.'

'We will know the truth of it soon enough.' Richard nodded to the stern man who had opened the door. 'De Chauvigny, bring Heraclius.'

While they waited, Richard poured himself some wine. He filled a huge goblet – gold and encrusted with jewels – that held half the pitcher. He had drained it and poured another by the time Heraclius entered.

The patriarch wore his ceremonial garb: gold-embroidered robes of white silk; a stole of shimmering golden silk around his shoulders; and atop his head a mitre encrusted with jewels that glittered in the candlelight. His eyes widened when he saw John.

'Patriarch Heraclius,' Richard addressed him. 'Thank you for attending me. Do you recognize this man?'

Heraclius weighed his answer for a moment before he shook his head. 'I have never seen him before.'

'You bastard!' John growled. He lunged for the patriarch, but two men held him back. One of them twisted John's arm painfully behind his back.

Heraclius's full lips curled into a sneer. 'Whoever he is, he seems quite the savage.'

Walchelin's hand went to the dagger at his belt. 'Let me kill him, Your Grace.'

'Not yet.' Richard studied John. Their eyes met. 'Leave us, all of you.'

'Your Grace!' Walchelin protested.

'Go! I wish to speak with him alone.' When the courtiers had shuffled out, Richard rose and came around the table to stand before John. The king was a big man, half a hand taller than John and with broad shoulders and strong hands. 'I know a liar when I see one,' he said. 'How long did you spend with the Saracens, John of Tatewic?'

'Fifteen years, Your Grace.'

'How did you come to be amongst them?'

'I was captured at the siege of Damascus and sold as a slave. I served in the household of Najm ad-Din. I was the personal slave of his son, Saladin.'

'The same Saladin who took Jerusalem? You know him well?'

John nodded. 'I was the captain of his private guard. We were like brothers, once.'

'God has sent you to me for a reason, John.' Richard clapped him on the shoulder. 'I have need of you. Heraclius is a prating fool. He has travelled across Europe begging men to take up the cross, but he cannot tell me one useful thing about the enemy we will face. One thing I learned from my father, may the devil piss on him, is to never move forward without knowing the lay of the land. With you at my side, I will not be marching blind.'

'I will serve you as I am able, Your Grace.'

'You will be my secretary. The march to Palestine will take months. I expect you at my side every day. By the time we arrive, I will know everything there is to know about our enemy.'

'Your Grace, if I may?' Richard nodded, and John continued. 'You speak of marching to the Holy Land. I have trod that road in the army of King Louis. The emperor in Constantinople gave us little help, and in Anatolia the Turks harassed us day and night. We lost more than half our men before we reached Acre. You would be better served taking a ship.'

'You prove your worth already, John.' The king grabbed his goblet and took another drink. 'But ships are damnably expensive. We'll need to kill more Jews.'

Chapter 16

Yusuf sighed as he sank into the pool. When his feet touched the bottom, the steaming waters came up to his chin. A bath attendant poured a bucket of hot water over his head. Yusuf brushed the wet hair from his eyes and leaned back, resting the back of his head against the edge of the pool. Sunlight filtered through the cracks in the wooden roof. Where the rays passed through clouds of steam, they looked almost tangible, as if one could reach out and grasp them.

Ibn Jumay had prescribed frequent baths to help him recover from the illness that had laid him low last autumn. For weeks he had been confined to bed, racked by terrible pain that felt as if someone were twisting a dagger in his gut. His shit was red with blood. Ibn Jumay had prescribed him a diet of only water, boiled wheat and, once a week, a rich broth made of drippings from roasted meat. Slowly, he had recovered. By the time the winter rains ceased, he was able to resume his daily inspection of the lines. Still, he was weaker than he would have liked. The ride down the lines left his legs aching and his shoulders tight.

Yusuf closed his eyes and concentrated on breathing slowly and steadily, like in one of the drills he had done as a child, back when he was struggling to overcome the suffocating fits that had afflicted him. The tense muscles in his shoulders relaxed, and the sounds of the camp seemed to fade away. He could have been anywhere – in Damascus or even in his favourite palace, the one in Cairo, with the windows that looked out over the city to the Nile and the pyramids beyond. He could almost hear Shamsa's voice calling to him from the next room.

'Saladin! Malik!'

Yusuf's eyes snapped open. Saqr stood at the edge of the pool. 'Az-Zahir has seen something from the tower,' the mamluk said.

'More Franks?'

After the winter storms had passed and the seas had become navigable again, the Franks had begun arriving in the hundreds – Danes, Frisians, Flemings, Frenchmen, Germans, Lombards and Hungarians. Two weeks ago, Conrad had returned from Tyre, where he had wintered, with yet more men and supplies to build siege engines. Yusuf had written to the caliph asking for men or money to fight the infidel. The response had come three days ago. The caliph sent two loads of naphtha, a few spear shafts, five experts in Greek fire and a letter of credit authorizing Yusuf to borrow twenty thousand dinars in his name. Such a paltry sum would pay his army's expenses for no more than a week.

Saqr was shaking his head. 'This is something different. The messenger Az-Zahir sent was most urgent.'

Yusuf climbed from the bath, and the flesh on his arms and legs prickled in the morning cool. He towelled off and dressed: leather breeches and boots; a padded vest; a mail hauberk that reached to his knees and wrists; over that his vest of golden jawshan; a coif to protect his neck; and lastly his gilt helmet, a golden eagle at its crest. He buckled his sword and dagger about his waist as he stepped outside.

Seagulls shrieked and wheeled overhead, riding the cool sea breeze. The camp was already full of life. A long line of men waited outside the bathhouses; another, longer line stretched away from the clay ovens where the army's bread was baked.

Yusuf saw a mamluk step away from the ovens only for a gull to swoop down and carry off his piece of steaming flatbread. The man cursed at the bird.

Yusuf took a deep breath of the salty sea air and set out for the centre of the line. Past the baths, the ovens and the sprawling camp market, he entered amongst the tents of his men. These tents belonged to the Egyptian troops. They had arrived last November and replaced the men of Al-Jazirah, who had returned home for winter before heading north to defend the passes into Antioch from the German king. Selim had brought from Egypt a thousand mamluks and close to five thousand infantrymen. He had brought siege engines, too. A line of ten catapults stood just beyond the tents. Day and night, they hurled stones large and small into the Frankish camp. After any skirmish between the two sides, they would hurl the bodies of dead Franks. Next to them were four ziyars – huge crossbows that shot bolts four feet long. They were wicked instruments. Yusuf had seen a single bolt skewer four men, like pieces of meat on a spit. As he passed, one of the ziyars fired, sending a bolt arcing through the sky and into the Frankish camp.

The tower loomed at the end of the line of siege engines. It had been his son Az-Zahir's idea, and Yusuf had rewarded him by giving him charge of the siege equipment. The tower was sixty feet tall, the base built of whole pine trunks taken from the hills north-east of Acre. The sides were covered with hides that the men kept wet to protect the tower from flaming arrows. From the top, lookouts could see down into the Frankish camp. Yusuf would not be surprised by his enemies again.

He climbed the twisting staircase to the top and found Az-Zahir looking out towards Acre. His son heard Yusuf's footsteps and crossed the tower to greet him. The injury to his calf had healed, but Az-Zahir still limped slightly.

'As-salaamu 'alaykum, Father.'

'What have you seen?'

'Look for yourself.'

One side of the tower was open save for a wood railing to prevent falls. Standing at the rail, Yusuf could see dozens of Frankish ships riding at anchor on the glittering waters outside the harbour of Acre. Fifty Egyptian galleys had managed to force their way past the blockade to resupply the city, but that had been in late October, more than five months ago. Food had to be running short in the city. Qaraqush and his men would be suffering.

Yusuf shifted his gaze to look at the enemy siege lines, which cut the city off from Yusuf's army. The Franks had completed their wall while he lay ill. It was wooden, ten feet tall and fronted by a ditch four feet deep. Winter had turned the land between the Frankish and Muslim lines into a sea of mud, making attack impossible. Yusuf had been forced to bide his time until the spring.

Winter, at least, had taken a heavy toll on the Franks. Dozens of men had deserted. They had crossed the lines to Yusuf's army, willing to be taken as slaves if only they would be fed. The deserters brought horrible stories. Food was so scarce that the lords began to eat their horses. King Guy was said to be nothing more than skin and bones, and his wife Sibylla was losing her hair in clumps. For the common men, it was worse. There was no horsemeat for them. Some of the truly desperate had eaten the dead, of which there was a rich supply. Starving men were easy prey for disease, and the bloody flux had swept through the Frankish camp. Pyres had burned day and night. Disease had struck Yusuf's camp as well. He had isolated the sick, but nevertheless, nearly three hundred men had died. At least his men had not suffered from hunger. The camp market had continued to grow throughout the winter. There were now dozens of bread ovens and soup kettles, along with more than a hundred blacksmiths and several thousand small shops selling provisions and comforts.

Yusuf looked from the Frankish ramparts to their tents, which were clustered beside the river. He saw men sharpening swords or sitting on the ground to eat their breakfast. A dozen men were practising swordplay in the open square at the centre of the camp. Along the river, men were fishing.

'What am I looking for?' he asked Az-Zahir.

'Look at the ramparts facing Acre. Near where the Belus enters the sea.'

Yusuf looked and saw that a ship's hulk had been pulled up on the beach. The deck had been removed, and Frankish carpenters were at work pulling apart the rest. At least one other ship must have already suffered the same fate, because there was a large pile of timbers further up the beach. The Franks were using them to build three towers. One already rose fifteen feet. The others were less than ten feet high, but judging by the size of their bases, they would be at least nine times that tall when complete. Each had huge wooden wheels to make it mobile.

'They are making quick progress,' Yusuf noted. 'They must have started under cover of darkness.'

Az-Zahir nodded. 'And look there.' He pointed to Acre. Dozens of Franks were digging up the ground near the walls and dumping cartfuls of dirt into the moat. 'They mean to roll those towers to the walls. As at Jerusalem.'

Yusuf did not need to be reminded of what had happened at Jerusalem. When the Franks first conquered it, they had used mobile towers just like these to enter the city.

'The towers will be complete in two or three days,' Az-Zahir continued. 'The moat may take up to a week to fill. When that is done—'

Yusuf finished for him. 'Allah save Qaraqush and his men.'

Aah-hoo! Aah-hoo!

Yusuf woke to the sound of a horn. He had slept in his armour, and he grabbed his sword as he left his tent. It was still dark. Saqr stood at his post beside the tent flap. Yusuf's brother Selim, who had had charge of the night-watch, was striding up the hill towards him.

'What is happening?' Yusuf called.

'The towers. The Franks have rolled them to the walls.'

The towers had been completed a week ago and the moat filled in earlier that day. Yusuf had wondered how long the Franks would wait before they attacked. Not long, it seemed. He peered in the direction of Acre. Torches on the wall flickered in the darkness like stars in the heavens, but he saw nothing of the towers. Then a bright flame shot from his camp, hurled towards the walls by one of the catapults. It arced through the night sky and exploded against one of the towers, outlining it in flames. The tower was over ninety feet tall, and it loomed high over the wall. Franks on the top levels were shooting arrows and crossbow bolts down on the wall's defenders, while men at a lower level tried to force their way on to the ramparts. A moment later, the flames went out, and the tower and the men were swallowed up by the night. Yusuf had watched the Franks cover the towers with skins soaked in vinegar. It was a better fire retardant than water.

Five more jars of naphtha were hurled towards the towers. These missed, shattering against the wall of the city and coating it in the viscous, burning liquid. By the light of the flames, Yusuf could see all three towers, side by side. At the foot of the wall, a ram with a peaked roof over it was rolling towards the land gate. Yusuf heard a loud boom as the ram struck for the first time.

The flames burned out, and in the darkness, Yusuf spotted another jar of naphtha arcing towards the towers. This one went over the wall and into Acre. 'Messenger!' Yusuf called, and one of the dozen young mamluks stationed outside his tent stepped to his side. 'Tell Az-Zahir to stop firing. He will burn down Acre before he destroys one of those towers.' The messenger sprinted down the hill into the darkness. 'My horse!' Yusuf shouted. 'Saqr, sound the call to arms.'

Saqr took the horn that hung from his belt and blew a long blast, followed by two more. As the last note faded, deep drums began to beat throughout the camp, calling the men to the line. *Boom. Boom. Boom.*

Yusuf rode down the hill followed by Selim and Saqr. In the camp, men were stumbling from their tents and heading for the line. Yusuf reached the barricade to see that the night-watch had already taken up their posts along the top of it. His commanders waited for him beside the tower. Ubadah and Gökböri were grim-faced. They knew the danger the towers posed.

'With me,' Yusuf told them. He dismounted and climbed to the top of the rampart. The defenders in Acre were now shooting flaming arrows at the towers. It was all they had. There were no fire masters in the city who knew how to make naphtha. Each tower was bristling with burning shafts, but the flames were guttering out before the flames spread.

Yusuf turned back towards his emirs. 'We must draw the Franks from the walls. Az-Zahir, throw fire at the Franks' tents. That should bring them running. While their tents burn, we will attack along the Frankish rampart. They cannot concentrate on taking the city if they must also defend their own lines. Keep half of your men in reserve. This will be a long battle. So long as those towers stand, we fight. Each of you, send a man to let me know when you are ready to strike. Go, and Allah protect you.'

His emirs left to prepare their troops. 'Ubadah!' Yusuf called, and his nephew turned back.

'Yes, Malik?' There was a hostile tone in his voice. Yusuf had hoped Ubadah would have forgiven him by now.

'You have served me well these last few months, Nephew. You have my thanks.'

'I know my duty, Malik,' Ubadah said stiffly. After a pause, he continued, 'What is it all for, Uncle? If you love John and the Franks so much, then why do you fight them?'

Yusuf opened his mouth to reply, but then stopped. Once, he would have had an easy answer. Now he was not so sure. He took a deep breath. 'I should have told you about your father, Ubadah, but I feared you would hate Zimat, hate yourself.'

'Instead, I hate you, Uncle.' Ubadah met his eyes. 'If you wish to thank me, then send me away from here, from you.' He strode away down the rampart.

Yusuf grimaced as he watched him go. He had raised Ubadah as a son, and his hatred stung. But Yusuf had done what he could. He had extended his hand, and Ubadah had slapped it away. Perhaps his nephew was right. Time away might cool his anger.

Yusuf turned to watch the battle at the city wall. He could hear the regular boom of the Frankish ram. A flaming jar of naphtha arced over him towards the Frankish camp. It flew too far and was extinguished in the waters of the Belus. The next jar exploded amongst the Frankish tents, scattering fire in all directions. Several tents went up in flames. Another jar hit, spreading the fire. Yusuf could see men in the camp rushing to the river with buckets in hand. A jar fell amongst them, and the men became staggering columns of flame. They stumbled shrieking into the river. The naphtha continued to burn as it floated atop the water.

A messenger rushed up to Yusuf. 'Saif ad-Din's men are ready,' he reported. More messengers arrived, bringing the same message from different points along the line. Az-Zahir's catapults continued to hurl naphtha into the Frankish camp. As the last commander reported, a jar fell short and burst against the Frankish wall, covering it in flames.

Yusuf turned to Saqr. 'Sound the attack.'

Haa-room! Saqr blew his war horn, and it was joined by the sound of other horns from down the line. The drums started again, beating faster this time. *Ba-boom. Ba-boom. Ba-boom!* Yusuf's men rushed forward screaming their battle cry: 'For Allah! *Allah-Allah-Allah!*' To his right, men disappeared into the darkness between the two lines. On the left wing, Yusuf could see his men, who were lit by the flames licking up the Frankish wall. A few of the onrushing mamluks fell to Frankish arrows. The rest reached the wall, where the bowmen spread out and began to shoot up at the defenders. Other men raised ladders or hurled grappling hooks over the wall. Yusuf saw two mamluks head up a ladder, only for it to be pushed back. Another man started to climb a rope, but was cut down as he reached the top of the wall. Yusuf looked back to Acre. The combatants were lit by the flaming arrows protruding from the towers. Below, the ram slammed against the gate again. *Boom*!

Yusuf began to pace, his hands clasped behind his back. His men swarmed up the Frankish wall again and again. Here and there they reached the top, only to be pushed back. The bodies of the fallen mounted at the foot of the Frankish rampart. At Acre, the garrison bravely held the walls, but the Franks were pouring arrows into them from the towers. Qaraqush had to be losing many men. And the boom of the ram sounded again and again, regular as a heartbeat.

Yusuf's legs had grown weary from pacing when the sun crested the hills to the east. His standard still flew over Acre. The three towers still stood, though the skins that covered them were blackened. Along the Frankish ramparts, hundreds of dead mamluks lay amidst the remains of broken ladders and cut ropes. The fighting had slackened; both sides were clearly exhausted.

'Saqr!' Yusuf called. 'Send messengers. Tell the emirs to pull back their men and send in fresh troops.'

'Yes, Malik.' Saqr hesitated. 'Perhaps you should also retire to your tent for a moment.'

'I will stay here. Bring my breakfast.' Yusuf's eyes were on the towers. Sooner or later, the Franks inside them would overpower the garrison and take the city. All the arms and gold that Yusuf had stored there would go over to his enemies. Worse yet, the Franks would control the greatest port in the east, giving them a secure base to which to bring more men from overseas. If Acre fell, the rest of Palestine might follow. He had to destroy those towers. 'And Saqr!' he called. 'Bring me one of the fire masters.'

Yusuf sat on a camp-stool atop the rampart and chewed on a spoonful of boiled wheat as the sun rose behind him and bathed the city in soft light. He had not left the ramparts in eight days, not since the Frankish attack began. The stool was his only concession to Saqr and Ibn Jumay's fears for his health. He dozed off occasionally while seated, but never for long. The boom of the ram would wake him. There it was now. *Boom.* Yusuf counted to ten and it came again. *Boom.*

The days had taken on a sort of routine. After that first night, Yusuf had divided his men into four waves, which alternated their attack on the Frankish ramparts. They had lost hundreds without breaching the Franks' walls. Inside the Frankish camp, at least half their tents had been turned to ash. The rest had been struck to save them. At Acre, the Franks continued to pour forth from their towers, and the garrison turned them back again and again. At least the rain of arrows from the Franks had ceased. They had run out of ammunition. And all the time, the ram continued its work. Eventually, it would break through, or the Franks would force their way on to the wall. Unless Yusuf's plan worked . . .

The previous night, he had sent one of fire masters into the city. He had gone with the swimmer, Isa. The two of them had slipped through the Frankish fleet at night and swum for the walls. Or so Yusuf hoped. They might just as easily have drowned, or been spotted and killed. If they had made it, Yusuf would know soon enough.

Haa-Room! A horn sounded, and the mamluks attacking the Frankish ramparts fell back. Fresh troops jogged across the open space between the lines to take their place. Yusuf turned his tired eyes back to the walls of Acre. It was nearly noon when he saw it: a jar flew from the city and soared over one of the towers. Three more were launched before one smashed against the side of the tower. There was no fire. Another jar flew, and another and another. Still no flames. Had his plan failed? Had the fire master drowned, or was he a fraud who did not know the secrets of naphtha?

More jars came from the city, dozens of them hurled into each of the towers. Yet there were no flames. A gust of wind came from the sea, and for a moment Yusuf could hear the jeers of the Franks at the wall. Then a jar with flame trailing it flew from the city and hit the middle tower. The tower exploded, the fire so bright that Yusuf was momentarily blinded. He looked away, blinking tears from his eyes. He looked back to see that the tower was engulfed in flames. A flaming jar hit another tower, and it too was transformed into an inferno. The wind gusted again, and this time it brought with it screams of agony.

'Allah is giving the Franks a foretaste of hell,' Saqr murmured.

Yusuf said nothing. The wind had also brought the stench of roasting flesh. It made his stomach turn.

The last tower went up in flames. A moment later, several jars were dropped on the ram. The Franks manning it fled long before the last, flaming jar fell. The ram burst into flames and was quickly consumed. The Franks who had survived began to stream back to their camp, while behind them, the towers collapsed into piles of ash and charred timbers. The screams of the dying had ceased but the smell of roasting meat had grown stronger.

'Father!'

Yusuf turned to see Al-Afdal striding up the rampart, Az-Zahir trailing him. 'You have done it! The city is saved!'

'Alhamdulillah!' Az-Zahir cried.

Yusuf nodded. He could not share their joy. Acre was saved, yes, but for how long? All their attacks had failed to dislodge the Franks, and more of the enemy arrived every day. Yusuf's gaze went to the sea. He remembered the crusade of his childhood, when he had watched in secret as his father and uncle talked in hushed tones about the barbarians from overseas. Now they were coming again. The German emperor's great army was marching across Anatolia, creeping ever closer. And from across the sea came the King of France and the English King Richard, the one they called Lionheart.

Chapter 17

'Sit still, man!' Philip snapped. The French king was as ugly as Richard was handsome, and though he was eight years Richard's junior, he somehow looked older. Philip had broad shoulders, thick stubby fingers and a plain face that would have suited a peasant better than a king. His hair was wild and unruly, and he had lost sight in his left eye, which drifted aimlessly, making it impossible for John to tell where he was looking. It was disconcerting.

'I said stop,' the king repeated, 'or I'll have your head.'

John stopped pacing. He had worn a path on the ground before Richard's tent. He turned in the direction of Messina. The city was out of sight beyond a range of hills, but when the wind blew from the east, he could hear distant cries of agony and rage, overlaid with the clash of steel. The latest breeze brought a whiff of smoke, too.

John had arrived in Sicily two months ago after a long journey from England. He had stayed at Richard's side throughout. In spring, they had crossed to France, where Richard had marshalled his men: a hundred knights, four thousand experienced men-at-arms, two thousand Welsh bowmen and another two thousand common soldiers, mostly thieves and farmers. Pincushions, Richard called these last. He considered them good for nothing but to serve as human shields. In July, they had joined forces with Philip at Vézelay, a fortress town three days' march east of Orléans. Philip brought with him over six hundred knights – more than John had ever seen gathered in one place. Each knight had two horses and at least one squire. There were also five hundred French men-at-arms, though their purpose seemed to be mostly to see to the baggage train.

Despite their differences, or perhaps because of them, Richard and Philip were as close as brothers. They had fought together against Richard's father, and as youths they had spent time together in Aquitaine. John had overheard old Sir Ranulf of Glanville muttering to one of his men that Richard had buggered the French king half a dozen times. But such rumours were always present in an army. When he asked Robert Blanchemains about Ranulf, the lord high steward had frowned. 'Stay clear of that one, priest. He fought for Richard's father. The King does not favour him.'

The two armies had marched south together until Lyon, where the French had turned east for Genoa. Philip had contracted with an Italian fleet to carry his men. Richard led his army to Marseille, where an English fleet thirty ships strong met them. Once at sea, both fleets had been caught in violent autumn storms that forced them to take shelter at Messina, in Sicily. It had not been long before Richard had fallen out with Tancred, the king of the island.

Richard's younger sister, Joan, had been married to the previous king, William. When he died, the throne had been disputed. Joan had backed the losing side, and when Tancred took the crown, he had placed her in prison. When Tancred refused to immediately free Joan, Richard had left Messina in a rage. He had marched south and seized the castle of La Bagnara from one of Tancred's vassals. Now he had returned with blood on his mind.

The plan was for a hundred French and English knights to approach the city's northern gate under cover of darkness. A dozen men with grappling hooks would climb over the wall, kill the guards and open the gate. Once inside, Richard was counting on surprise and confusion to win the day. 'If we make enough noise,' he had said, 'they will think our whole army is inside the walls. They'll run before they even see us.'

It was a bold plan. A mad adventure, Philip had called it. The French king had elected to stay in camp. The sun was now nearing the mid-point in its daily journey across the sky, and he and John were still waiting for news of the battle.

'Will you sit still!' the king said.

John had not realized he was pacing again. 'My apologies, Your Grace.' He sat on a camp-stool beside Philip.

The king was reading from the second volume of a travel-sized version of *De re militari*. The military treatise had been written by a Roman over eight hundred years ago, but it remained popular amongst the nobility. Philip swore by it. In private, Richard had told John that he feared the French king cared more for books than battle. 'If wars were won with a pen in hand instead of a sword,' he had said, 'then King Inkpot there would be mighty indeed.' John did not share Richard's scorn for scholarship, but nor could he understand how Philip could sit calmly reading while his knights were risking their lives.

Philip noticed John staring and lowered the book. He seemed to guess what John had been thinking. 'Richard finds a reason for bloodshed wherever he goes. Tancred is no fool. Just last week, he invited Richard to Messina to discuss their differences. He thrust out his hand in friendship, and Richard pissed all over it. Lives will be lost because of it, the lives of my men and his. And what will be gained? A few pieces of gold, perhaps?' He shook his head. 'It is not truly the gold Richard wants. It is the fight.'

'Why did you not try to stop him?'

Philip smiled, showing crooked teeth. 'I would as soon stand before an arrow to halt its course. I could never stop Richard.'

The king looked away, his attention drawn by the sound of pounding hooves. John followed his gaze and saw an approaching knight. It was Peter de Preaux, one of Richard's favourites. He was a handsome young man with curling blond hair and a bright smile that he flashed often. He had made his name at tourneys in Normandy and Aquitaine. Though he was not yet twenty-six, Richard had given him the honour of carrying the king's standard in battle. John had heard other knights grumble about that.

Peter slid from the saddle and knelt before Philip. 'Your Grace, Richard bid me tell you that the battle is won. Messina is ours, or what's left of it.'

Philip raised an eyebrow. 'What exactly did Richard do?'

'Once we were inside the walls, we put the city to the torch, and went charging through town, shouting like madmen. When Tancred's troops saw the smoke and heard us coming, they panicked and fled. It was hardly a battle.'

'I heard screams – shouts of battle,' John said.

'Begging your pardon, father, but the women do scream sometimes when you stick it to them.'

John noticed Philip wince. 'And Richard is well?' he asked.

'Not a dead man among us, though Lord Chauvigny won't be sitting for some days. He took a crossbow bolt in the arse. Richard has invited you to feast his victory with him in the palace.' De Preaux turned to John. 'You are invited as well, priest.'

'See to your horse, sir,' Philip said. 'We will find our own way.' He shook his head as de Preaux sauntered off. 'The fool plays at war as if it were a game.'

A dozen knights rode with Philip and John to the city, which consisted of a few churches and a sprawling palace set among hundreds of white stucco homes, all clustered at one end of a crescent-shaped harbour that opened on to the Straits of Messina. The western gate stood open. Inside, Messina had been reduced to a smouldering ruin. Their horses' hooves kicked up clouds of ash as they rode. Only one building in ten still stood. The rest had collapsed into piles of blackened timbers. To the south, the fires still burned, leaping high into the sky. John could feel their heat from a quarter-mile away. He passed a man in a blacksmith's smock lying in the street in a pool of his own blood, his throat slit. Near by, a woman was trying to cover herself with the torn remains of her tunic as she sat weeping in the doorway of one of the few standing homes. John's grip on the reins tightened. The scene reminded him of the needless butchery that he had once seen in Egypt.

At the palace, an English man-at-arms showed them inside and down a cool, tiled hallway that opened out on to an expansive garden. There were hundreds of rose bushes, their last petals fallen and their leaves now tinged red. Orange trees stood around the edge of the garden, their branches heavy with green, unripe fruit. At the centre of the garden was a fountain, water spouting from the breasts of a full-figured bronze mermaid. Richard stood beside it. His face was blackened with smoke and ash. His white surcoat was red with blood.

'Congratulations on your victory, Cousin,' Philip greeted him.

Richard's scowl deepened. He gestured to the fountain. 'This should be torn down. It is unholy.'

Philip laid a hand on his shoulder. 'It will be seen to, Cousin. We have other matters to attend to first. Do you have Tancred? Joan?'

'He escaped south towards Catania. He took my sister with him.'

'That is unfortunate.' Philip hesitated before he continued cautiously. 'You might not have burned the town, Cousin. We cannot leave Sicily until we have recovered your sister, and that means we shall be forced to winter in Messina. Where will the men live?'

'You will find a place for them, Philip.' Richard turned to John. 'A word with you, priest.' He led John to a corner of the garden. 'I wish to confess my sins, father.'

John suppressed a frown. He had taken confession only a handful of times, and had never grown accustomed to sitting in judgement of his fellow men. 'I am but a humble priest. Hubert Walter is the bishop of Salisbury. Perhaps he would be better suited.'

'My soul is heavy with sin. I must confess now.' Richard knelt and bowed his head. 'I confess that I have kept to my baptismal vows worse than I promised our Lord, and my rank, which I ought to have kept in praise of God and for my own eternal salvation, I have held unworthily.'

'If you truly repent and mend your ways, the Lord will be forgiving.'

Richard's head snapped up. 'Do not go lightly on me, John. Give me the penance that I deserve.'

'I will. What other sins have you committed?'

'I killed men today, at least a dozen. I have not the exact number.'

'These were the defenders of Messina?'

Richard nodded.

'Then you slew them under compulsion, for they were your enemies.' John tried to recall the penance recommended in the penitential he had studied before becoming a priest. 'You will fast for one year, consuming only bread and water, then for two years, you will fast each Wednesday. What other sins have you committed?'

Richard's voice was almost a whisper. 'I raped a woman. A maid. She can only just have come into her womanhood. She had dark hair, dark skin. She screamed in a foreign tongue when I took her.'

John's jaw set. His brother Caelin had been right about Richard.

The king looked up at him, and John was surprised to see tears in his eyes. 'Give me my penance, father.'

John hesitated. He had known plenty of men who raped and pillaged without a second thought. Richard's remorse seemed genuine enough. 'The penalty for taking a maid in fornication against her will is excommunication. But as you were stoked with bloodlust and thus not in your right mind, I shall lessen your penance to one additional year of daily fasting, and six more years of fasting each Wednesday. Have you anything else to confess?'

'No, father. I ask you to be my witness on Doomsday regarding these sins, so that the devil might not gain power over me and the Lord not judge me overharshly.'

'I will, and if you perform your penance faithfully and repent your deeds truly, the Lord will surely show you mercy.'

Richard rose. The cloud over him seemed to have lifted. 'My thanks, John. There is nothing like a good shriving after a battle.' He took a deep breath. 'How many years did you say I must fast? I lost count.'

'Two years daily, my lord, and each Wednesday for eight more years.'

'My men will share my fast with me these next three days, and the food they would have eaten will be distributed to the people of Messina. Eight thousand men for three days: that adds up to well over ten years of fasting, yes, father? Good. Now, I have another task for you. Tancred has taken my sister. You will go to Catania and treat with him for her release. Now that he has lost Messina, perhaps the King of Sicily will be more accommodating.'

John was still digesting Richard's rather cavalier attitude towards penance. He was less than eager to serve his king. 'I am only your secretary, my lord. Tancred will be more likely to listen to someone of higher rank. He might even see my presence as an insult.'

'Tancred will not want to listen to any of my men, not after today. You are from the Holy Land and archdeacon of the Church of the Holy Sepulchre. That is why I am sending you. But you are right; rank also has its value. Bishop Walter will accompany you.' Richard gripped John's shoulder. 'Make certain my sister is well and bring her back to me. With her dowry.'

The palace in Catania stood behind tall, strong walls on a cliff overlooking the sea. Behind the palace, gardens had been planted to provide food in the event of a siege. They stretched to the very edge of the cliff, where there was no wall – the sheer slope offering adequate protection. When they arrived, John and Walter were led there. They found Tancred seated in the shade of a lemon tree and looking out to sea. The sun was setting behind them, turning the waters to shimmering gold.

The king had wavy brown hair, a thin nose, pointed chin and shrewd eyes. He stood as they approached. His right leg was bandaged around the thigh, and he leaned heavily on a crutch. When he spoke, his voice was tight with pain. 'Richard has sent you with his terms?'

'Yes, Your Grace. I am Hubert Walter, Bishop of Salisbury, and this is John of Tatewic, formerly Archdeacon of the Church of the Holy Sepulchre and at present the secretary to King Richard. We—'

Tancred raised a hand. 'Let me save time by telling you what you will say. Richard wants Joan, and her dowry and inheritance, too. He will not settle for less. We shall have time enough to discuss what Richard wants. The autumn storms are here, and the seas will be unsafe for months to come. Now, I am sure you will wish to make certain Joan is well. My men will take you to her.' He turned his back to them and lowered himself on to the bench.

Tancred's guards led them back to the palace, where bishop Walter excused himself, saying he wished to rest after their journey. John was shown to Joan's quarters. She looked to be six or seven years younger than Richard, in her mid twenties, but other than that the resemblance between the two was striking. She had his reddish-gold hair, his clear blue eyes framing a straight nose and his prominent cheekbones. Her beauty was only marred by her shoulders, which were broad for a woman. She sat with two maids in a thickly carpeted room, the walls of which were hung with tapestries portraying the goddess Diana at hunt. A single window looked out over the sea. Joan and her maids had been talking, but they fell silent as John entered.

'My lady queen, I am Father John of Tatewic, secretary to your brother Richard.'

'You are welcome, father.' Joan touched her maids lightly on the arm. 'Leave us. I wish to speak with him alone.' The maids passed through a door to the next room, and Joan patted one of the seats they had vacated. 'Sit beside me, father.'

John was careful to move the chair further away before he sat. He was uncomfortably aware of Joan's beauty. Her lips were full and her fair skin almost luminescent. It had been years since he had been this close to such a woman. It made him feel old. He cleared his throat. 'Your brother has sent me to see that you are freed, my lady.'

'My brother cares nothing for my freedom,' Joan replied curtly. 'It is my inheritance and dowry that he wants, to pay for his wars. I will be disposed of quickly, married off to a man of his choosing. What sort of freedom is that?'

'I assure you, my lady, your brother cares for you.'

Joan laughed. 'You are a fool or an innocent, John of Tatewic. Richard is a stranger to me, and I to him. I came to Sicily as a girl of eleven, to be married to King William. I have not seen Richard for fourteen years and more. Sicily is my home now. I have no wish to leave.'

'But Tancred holds you prisoner.'

'I will deal with Tancred in my own way. There is much that he has not told you, or Richard. Roger of Andria has the support of the barons in Apulia, the land across the straits. Even now, he leads an army south, with the backing of the German emperor. He will crush Tancred, and once he does, I will marry Roger's son Robert. We are of an age, and Robert is to my liking. Our union will solidify Roger's claim to the throne. He will be king, and in time, I will be queen again. So you see, father, I have no need of my brother, nor of you.'

The guard outside Tancred's chambers pushed the door open. 'My lord,' he declared. 'John of Tatewic to see you.'

John was ushered into the king's quarters. Tancred sat before the fire, his injured leg propped up before him. He waved John forward. 'Sit. Would you like a glass of mulled wine?' He did not wait for an answer, but gestured to a servant, who brought John a glass of the steaming beverage. It smelt of cloves and orange peel. Tancred sipped at his own wine. 'You have spoken with Joan?'

'I have, Your Grace.'

'So you have seen what a scheming bitch she is. I will be glad enough to be rid of her. I might even pay to have her gone, but I must be certain that Richard will take her from Sicily. She must be married, and not to a German or an Italian lord. I will not have her children coming to seek my throne.'

'If what Lady Joan says is true, then you are in no position to make such demands.'

'She only knows half the truth. She believes my chancellor has betrayed me. She gives him letters for Roger, and he delivers the replies. They are forgeries. Roger is dead, betrayed by his friends. The count of Acerra turned him over to me for gold. His son Robert will join him in the grave soon enough. Joan's would-be husband is besieged at the fortress of Sant'Agata.'

'If that is true, then why the charade? Why not tell Joan the truth?'

'Why indeed?' Tancred sipped at his wine as he stared into the fire. The flames reflected in his brown eyes. 'Her letters have proved most instructive. In them, she sometimes names fellow conspirators of Roger, men in Sicily who are waiting to join his side when he arrives. Some of them I put to death, others I am content to watch. It is good to know your enemies, John of Tatewic. That is a lesson your King Richard would do well to learn.'

'What do you mean?'

Tancred waved the question away. 'Enough idle talk. We have much to discuss. Why have you come here, John?'

'To treat on behalf of my king.'

'Yes, yes. To free Joan and take my coin. I know that. But what do *you* want?'

'I am only a simple priest, Your Grace. What I want is of no importance.'

'Oh, but it is, John. It is. You are not like Richard. You are older, and wiser, I hope. You are a priest, which I presume means you do not share his taste for bloodshed. You saw what he did to Messina. You have seen the sort of man he is.' He leaned forward. 'Tell me, why do you serve him?'

John was unnerved. Tancred had read him as if he were an open book. Still, he saw no harm in telling the truth. 'I wish to return to the Holy Land. It is my home.'

Tancred sat back. 'Ah, yes. I see it now. Then you wish Richard on his way just as much as I. We are of one mind.' The king smiled shrewdly. 'So tell me, John, what must I give up before Richard will leave my lands and you can return home? And more importantly, what is your king prepared to give me?'

Chapter 18

'Any word from the Almohad caliph?' Yusuf asked.

Imad ad-Din flipped through the stack of letters at his side. He shook his head. 'Still nothing, Malik.'

Two months earlier, Yusuf had sent a request for aid to Al-Mansur, who ruled most of North Africa and Iberia from his capital in Marrakesh. With the request, he had sent rich gifts: a Koran covered with jewels; musk, aloe and balm of Judea; a dozen amber necklaces; and a hundred bows, seven hundred arrows, twenty saddles and the same number of sword blades. The gifts looked to have been wasted. Yusuf sighed and rubbed his temples. He could have used those bows. The German army had sacked Konya months ago and was due to arrive at Acre any day. Some said their king marched with twenty thousand men; others said it was fifty thousand or even a hundred thousand – so many men that the line of their march stretched for five miles and the broad trail of trampled ground left behind looked like a huge scar upon the earth.

'What do you have for me?' Yusuf asked.

Imad ad-Din had brought the previous day's correspondence to Yusuf's tent, as he did every day after noon prayers. He selected a tiny scrap of paper from the pigeon post. 'Your nephew Taqi ad-Din has reached Aleppo.'

Yusuf had sent Ubadah north to raise troops. When his

nephew had taken his leave, Yusuf had embraced him. 'God keep you safe, Nephew,' he had told him.

Ubadah had returned the embrace stiffly. 'Farewell, Malik.' He had mounted his horse and ridden away without looking back. Yusuf hoped that when they met again, they could put the past behind them.

Imad ad-Din finished scanning the message from Ubadah. 'He writes that the city is well ordered and that he has been able to secure an additional one hundred mamluks. He is sending them—' Imad ad-din stopped short as Az-Zahir rushed into the tent.

'Father! The Germans are here!'

Yusuf rose at once. He stepped out of the tent and squinted against the bright winter sunshine. He could see the Frankish lines – the deep ditch backed by a spiked rampart with a pal-isade built atop it. He scanned the line but saw nothing out of the ordinary. 'Where are they?'

'There.' Az-Zahir pointed north.

Yusuf could just make out a distant line of men marching along the coast. 'There can't be more than five thousand of them. Where are the rest?'

'That is all of them, Father. You can see better from the tower.'

By the time Yusuf reached the top of the tower, the first Germans had reached the Frankish lines and he had a clear view of them. They stumbled into the camp looking like disinterred corpses. Their cloaks were tattered, and he could see rents in their armour. And they were painfully thin. With each step they took, many of the men's legs shook, hardly able to support them.

'What do you think happened to them?' Az-Zahir murmured.

'I do not know, but I thank Allah for it.'

This was the first good news in some time. Yusuf had attacked the Franks twice last spring, but his men had broken against their fortifications. The last supply ships to force their way through the Frankish blockade had arrived months ago, and Qaraqush and his garrison must be desperately short of food. Yusuf did not know for sure, because in August the swimmer Isa had washed up dead on the shore, a Frankish arrow in his back. Yusuf now had no way to communicate with the defenders in the city. Worst of all, the Franks continued to come from overseas in wave upon wave. Just after Isa died, three thousand more had arrived with Henry of Champagne. He had taken command of the siege. The cousin of both Richard and Philip, he was a great lord and a clever man, though you would never guess it to look at him. When Yusuf had first met him, he was surprised to see a dough-faced young man with lumpy features and muddy brown eyes.

Yusuf, meanwhile, was struggling to hold his army together. With winter looming, dozens of his emirs had returned home. The emir of Ibril had died of a fever while in camp, and Gökböri had left for Al-Jazirah to take possession of his lands. With Gökböri and Ubadah gone, Yusuf had given his sons Al-Afdal and Az-Zahir command of the right and left wings. They were brave but still young; only nineteen and sixteen. Still, Yusuf had been no older when he won his first battles. If they were not tested, they would never learn to lead.

Yusuf looked back to the Germans. There, at last, was a reason to smile. Yusuf knew that food was short in the Frankish camp. The pyres had been lit again to burn those who had died from disease or hunger. Most days they consumed several dozen corpses, though Yusuf's men had once counted as many as two hundred men laid upon the pyres. And from the tower, he had seen fights break out at the stew pots as the men accused each other of taking more than their fair share. From the look of them, the Germans brought no food, only more mouths.

Yusuf turned to Az-Zahir. 'Let us make the new arrivals welcome. Send a messenger to invite their commander to supper. Invite Henry of Champagne as well. And the king, Guy.'

★

That evening, Yusuf stood in the private section of his tent and examined his reflection in a silver mirror. He had bathed and had his servants oil his hair and perfume him with the scent of jasmine. He was dressed in a black silk caftan with geometrical patterns stitched in gold at the collar and cuffs. He wore sandals decorated with emeralds and sapphires, and tucked into his belt was his dagger with the gold hilt in the shape of an eagle. He would have preferred a simple cotton tunic and leather sandals, but tonight that would not do. He wished to impress his Christian guests. He wanted them to return to their camp with stories of his fabulous wealth. They could not know that the once seemingly inexhaustible coffers of Egypt were now issuing glass in lieu of coin; that he was not sure how much longer he could keep his men in the field on half pay. So Yusuf would dress as a great king, though in truth these robes were the last he had. He had sold the rest of his finery to pay his men.

It was a game, and it was not the first time he had played it. The siege was fifteen months old, and it had long since grown tedious. The winter rains had set in the previous month, turning the battleground into a sea of mud. Both camps huddled behind their barricades and tried to stay warm. Two months ago, Yusuf had decided to invite the Frankish commanders to dine with him in order to relieve the tedium. At first, the Franks had been wary, but now it had become a regular practice. They came for the food, and he was happy to feed them in return for information.

Saqr stuck his head through the curtain that separated Yusuf's quarters from the rest of the tent. 'The Franks have entered camp, Malik. They will arrive shortly.'

Yusuf stepped out into the main portion of the tent. In the centre was a low table surrounded by silk cushions piled high on the thick goat-hair carpet. The table was set with gold plates and goblets. Before each setting was a basket of steaming flatbread and a bowl filled with an aromatic dip of eggplant, toasted walnuts and raw onion. He had obtained a barrel of wine for his Frankish guests. That would help to loosen their tongues.

Yusuf sat on a camp-stool to wait. He had learned as much about the German commander as he could before the meal. It seemed that Frederick Barbarossa was dead. The Germans were now led by one of his sons, a man named Frederick of Swabia, wherever that might be.

Saqr entered. 'Your guests, Malik.' He stepped aside and held the tent flap.

Frederick entered first. He was a tall man with a long, gaunt face, a ruddy complexion and hair so blond it was almost white. He looked about the tent and frowned. Henry of Champagne entered next, wearing hose and a blue tunic that ill-suited his bulky figure. Guy followed. When Yusuf had last seen him, at Hattin, the king had been a heavy-set man. Now he was painfully thin, his skin hanging in folds from his jowls and neck. Yusuf was surprised to see a fourth man enter. He was stooped beneath his luxurious priest's robes and the greyish skin of his face was as lined as the dry desert floor east of Damascus. He seemed half dead but for his eyes, which were a deep turquoise blue.

'And who is this?' Yusuf asked in French.

'The Patriarch Heraclius,' Guy replied. 'He has recently returned from England. I thought you would wish to meet him.'

Yusuf nodded to the priest. 'God grant you joy. You are welcome in my tent.'

'We are honoured by your invitation,' Henry replied. He made a small bow. Heraclius shuddered as he coughed into a silk cloth. Guy and Frederick remained stiff-backed. The German murmured something to Henry in a harsh, guttural tongue. Henry answered quietly.

'What did he ask?' Yusuf queried.

'He wished to know why there are no chairs save yours, Malik. You must forgive him. Frederick is new to these lands.'

'Of course. Please, sit.'

All save Frederick settled on the cushions around the table. The German remained standing for a moment but finally sat, awkwardly folding his long legs beneath him. Yusuf addressed him in Latin. 'I apologize for not speaking your tongue.'

Frederick's eyes widened. 'How do you come to speak Latin?'

'My father thought it wise that I know my enemy.' Yusuf gestured to the food. 'Please, eat.'

Yusuf scooped up some dip, whispered 'Bismillah' and ate. The Franks murmured their own prayers before eating. Henry, Guy and Heraclius eagerly scooped up the dip. Frederick stared at it for a long time before dipping his index finger and tasting it. He nodded and scooped up more dip. He finished his piece of bread in three bites and grabbed another. Yusuf signalled for a servant to bring more bread.

'Frederick,' he said. 'Allow me to offer my condolences for the death of your father.'

'A terrible blow.' The German's voice was hollow. His eyes tensed, as if he had seen something painful. He started to speak again, and the words tumbled out. 'We had come across Anatolia with the army intact – twenty thousand men, three thousand of them knights. They all rushed to my father's banner when he took up the cross. A mightier force you have never seen. We reached a river in Armenia, the Saleph, may God curse it. There was a bridge, but it was small and the crossing slow. My father grew impatient. He decided to ford the river on horseback. His horse stumbled, and he fell. He disappeared beneath the waters and hit his head on a rock. By the time I found him, he had drowned.'

'When God issues his summons, none can refuse,' Yusuf said, 'not even kings.'

Frederick shrugged and took a long drink of wine. 'After that, the army fell apart. We were less than a hundred miles from Antioch, but many of the lords decided to return home.

As our numbers dwindled, the Turks attacked with increasing impunity. We lost hundreds to their arrows, and hundreds more to your men guarding the passes leading to the Holy Land. After that, supplies ran short. Thousands died of hunger during the long march to Acre.' Frederick shook his head. 'I feel as though I have seen hell.'

'And you have come through it.' Yusuf raised his glass of water. 'To your safe arrival.' Frederick and the other Franks drank glumly. Yusuf whispered 'Alhumdillah' before he drained his glass. Surely Frederick's death was the work of Allah.

Servants entered with the next course: a dish of jazariyyah – tender chunks of lamb swimming in a rich sauce alongside carrots, whole garlic cloves, pearl onions and toasted walnuts. The conversation ceased as the Franks ate. They were like hungry wolves after a long winter. Yusuf was content to let them fill their bellies. He made certain that the servants kept them well supplied with wine. He had instructed them to refill the Franks' cups after each time they took so much as a sip.

The food and wine proved too much for Frederick, who nodded off where he sat. He snorted, and his head jerked up. He murmured something in his guttural tongue and his chin fell back to his chest.

'Forgive him,' Henry said. 'He travelled far today.'

'Forgive him? We should be thanking him,' Guy muttered. 'The man is an interminable bore. All he speaks of is death. He's much better company asleep.'

'I wish him pleasant dreams,' Yusuf said. 'We must all seize any opportunity to escape the suffering around us. I see the pyres have been lit in your camp. It pains me to see your people suffer so. Hunger and disease are cruel enemies.'

Heraclius nodded. 'We have lost good men.' He paused to cough into his handkerchief. From the look of him, Yusuf guessed Heraclius would be joining those men soon enough. 'And women, too,' the priest added, looking to Guy.

The king drained his cup and held it up for more. 'My wife

Sibylla is dead,' he said flatly. 'The flux took her. Her hair fell out first, her beautiful hair. My daughters . . .' He trailed off and took another drink of wine.

Henry shot Guy and Heraclius a sharp glance. 'Surely Saladin does not wish to hear of our suffering. It will rob him of his appetite.'

'On the contrary, I am happy for any news you care to share. The siege drags on day after day, month after month, and there is little enough to entertain me.' Yusuf paused as the next course arrived. Two servants carried a platter whereon pieces of roasted lamb were piled on a bed of chickpeas and bread, which soaked up the juices from the meat. More servants entered with bowls of spiced lentils for each of the guests.

'It's a bloody mess,' Guy stated. His words were slurred from drink. 'With Sibylla dead, Conrad has challenged my claim to the throne. The bastard thinks he should be king.'

'Guy!' Henry hissed.

'He will know soon enough, Henry,' Heraclius said. 'There are no secrets in our camp.' The priest turned to Yusuf. 'Sibylla's sister Isabella is next in line for the throne. Conrad has annulled her marriage to Humphrey of Toron and married her himself, although some say he left a wife behind in Constantinople. They have returned to Tyre, where Conrad has declared himself King of Jerusalem.'

'The cocksucker!' Guy put in.

'I see.' Yusuf would need to find a way to take advantage of this split amongst the Franks. He would send an envoy to Conrad. Perhaps if Yusuf recognized him as king and agreed to support his claim, Conrad would agree to withdraw his troops from Acre.

Guy finished another cup of wine and slammed it down on the table. 'It will all be settled soon enough. Richard and Philip will be here come spring, and Conrad will be put in his place.'

'Spring? So the French and English kings have decided to winter on Sicily?'

Henry's lips pressed into a thin line. 'King Guy was only speculating. We have had no news from Sicily.'

'Yes, of course,' Guy slurred. 'I misspoke.'

He was a poor liar. So Richard and Philip would not arrive until spring. That was a small reprieve, but a welcome one. It gave Yusuf four more months to prepare; four more months to try to save Acre.

Thick clouds hid the moon, and the night was dark and cold. Yusuf was sure his breath was fogging in the air, but he could not see it. He could just make out the dim shapes of the three thousand men around him. The loud crash of waves drowned out the jangle of their mail. They were volunteers all, each carrying a heavy pack filled with grain. They would be led by Al-Mashtub. The giant mamluk stood in the surf, waves foaming about his feet. He was staring out to sea.

'The men are ready?' Yusuf asked as he approached him.

'Yes, Malik.'

'The tide is out. You should just be able to round the Frankish ramparts if you stick close to the water. With the help of the dark and the roar of the waves, you should be inside their camp before they know you are there. Send a dozen men screaming towards the heart of their camp. That will be our signal to attack. In the confusion, you will push on to Acre. If you make it into the city—'

'Send up three burning arrows,' Al-Mashtub finished for him. 'I know, Malik.'

Yusuf gripped his shoulder. 'You do not have to go.'

Al-Mashtub turned towards him. The mamluk's face was lost in shadows. When he spoke, his voice was soft. 'I have known Qaraqush for fifty years and more. We trained together to become mamluks. We were freed in the same year. He has held the city with no reinforcements for a year now. He needs my help.'

Yusuf embraced him. 'Keep yourself alive, friend. I need you, too.'

Al-Mashtub grinned, and Yusuf could see his teeth in the dark. 'I don't plan on dying, Malik. It will take more than a few thousand Franks to kill me.'

'Allah yasalmak, Al-Mashtub.'

'Allah yasalmak.'

Al-Mashtub moved away. Yusuf called softly after him. 'Al-Mashtub.' The mamluk stopped. 'If Acre is lost, then all we have done will start to unravel. Do not surrender the city.'

Al-Mashtub nodded and went to join his men. He issued several whispered orders, and the mamluks formed a column. They set off at a jog for the Frankish ramparts, which were lit by torches burning along the palisade. Farther in the distance, lights winked on the wall of Acre.

Yusuf mounted his horse and rode back to camp with Saqr at his side. The two men climbed to the top of the tower. Looking towards the sea, he saw no sign of Al-Mashtub and his men. That was good. He stood with his hands clasped behind his back and forced himself to appear calm, though his stomach was churning with nervous tension.

'Saqr,' he said. 'Do you remember the night I found you?'

'Of course, Malik.'

'It was a night much like this. Dark, with low clouds. Not a breath of wind.'

'I do not remember the weather, Malik. I was hiding beneath a dead man – my uncle – with a knife in my hand. I thought you were one of Reynald's Franks, come back to kill me.'

'I remember.'

There was a loud shout from the direction of the Frankish camp, and Yusuf's gaze snapped to the line. There was another shout, and then a loud war cry, taken up by a dozen men. Yusuf could faintly hear it: 'Allah! Allah! Allah!' Al-Mashtub's men were behind the Frankish lines. There were answering shouts of alarm amongst the Franks.

'Sound the charge,' Yusuf called.

Saqr sounded his horn, and Yusuf's men surged forward. He could hear the clink of mail and the drumming of their feet, but he saw nothing of them in the darkness. Then there they were, lit up by the Frankish torches. As the light hit them, they roared their battle cry. Horns sounded in the Frankish camp, and men rushed to the barricades. Soon, Yusuf could hear the clash of steel alongside screams of rage and pain. But the battle was not what interested him. His gaze moved to the wall of Acre in search of arrows. Al-Mashtub had fought beside him since Yusuf was a boy, since his first command at Tell Bashir. He had always been there. He was a rock that Yusuf could lean on.

He glanced back to the battle at the Frankish ramparts. A mamluk reached the top of a ladder and clambered over the palisade, only to be hacked down from behind by a huge Frank wielding a war-axe. The Frank was speared in the side by the next man up the ladder and tumbled off the wall. Yusuf looked back to Acre. Still nothing. The battle continued and the night crawled on. A gap in the clouds let in the moonlight, turning the sea silver. There was no sign of Al-Mashtub's men on the coast. The clouds closed again. At the barricade, the battle began to slacken as the combatants tired.

'It has been too long,' Yusuf murmured. 'They should have reached the city by now.'

'There, Malik!'

Yusuf looked in the direction Saqr was pointing and saw a flaming arrow arcing from the wall of Acre to fall in the ocean. Another arrow followed, and then another.

Saqr grinned. 'They made it.' He blew his horn to signal the men at the barricade to fall back.

'Alhamdulillah,' Yusuf whispered, his voice swallowed up by the blast of the horn. 'Thank God.'

Chapter 19

John bent over the ship's rail and retched. His stomach had emptied long ago, and nothing came up but bitter bile. He spat. The first time he came to Acre, he had also been puking. He raised his head to gaze at the horizon. He saw only endless waves. But he knew that before day's end, they would make landfall in the Holy Land. Home. And Richard was coming to destroy it.

John had harboured doubts about Richard after Messina. They were confirmed on Cyprus. They had set sail from Messina in April, but during the voyage a storm had split the English fleet. Joan and Richard's new fiancée, Lady Berengaria of Navarre, had landed on Cyprus, where the ruler, Isaac – a renegade from the Roman court in Constantinople – had taken them captive, hoping to ransom them back to Richard. That had been a mistake. Guy and several of the other crusader lords had sailed from Acre to join Richard, and instead of paying, he had brutally subdued the island. He and his men had waded ashore through a hail of arrows to crush the Cypriot army, and had sent them fleeing across the island. Since Isaac was a fellow king, Richard had promised not to place him in irons. He had shackled him with silver chains and turned him over to the Hospitallers for safekeeping. The common people had not been so lucky. Those who had surrendered saw their homes ransacked and their women raped, but at least they escaped with their lives. The few who resisted had been killed, slowly, and their heads set on spikes as a warning to others.

John had urged Richard to show mercy, but the king had refused. 'If I show them mercy now, John, then they will have their knives out the moment my back is turned. I must teach them the cost of defiance.'

Perhaps John would have more success in the Holy Land, where Richard would need his guidance. He prayed that it was so, for the king desperately needed someone to curb his passions. Cruelty and bloody-mindedness were not irredeemable faults in a king – many believed they were virtues – but Richard's impulsiveness made him his own worst enemy. On Sicily, he had no sooner come to terms with Tancred than he broke with King Philip. Tancred had agreed to turn over Joan, along with her dowry and half the inheritance owed her. He had also 'voluntarily' contributed four thousand tari – the equivalent of a thousand gold dinars – to the war chests of both Richard and Philip. Tancred was glad to pay, for he had obtained the thing he coveted most: both kings had recognized him as the rightful ruler of Sicily.

The feast to celebrate the agreement was attended by the three kings, the Lady Joan and Berengaria of Navarre, a drab little thing with mousy brown hair framing a round face that would have been pretty were it not dominated by a long, sharp nose. Berengaria had been escorted to Sicily by Richard's mother, Eleanor, ostensibly for the purpose of marrying the next king of Jeruslaem. But in the middle of the feast, a very drunk Richard had declared that he would marry Berengaria. Philip was furious. Richard had been betrothed to his sister Alys, and he saw this new marriage as a personal attack. Richard did not help matters when he called Alys his father's whore and loudly swore he would never go where Henry had been before. Philip had stormed from the hall. Two days later, he and his men left Sicily without Richard. They were, no doubt, already at Acre.

'Father John. May I join you?'

He turned to see Joan approaching. Her fair face was even

paler than usual, and there were faint circles under her eyes. She had at last learned the truth about Roger of Apulia's death, and the king's treaty with Richard had sealed her fate. She was little better than Richard's property now, to be disposed of as he pleased.

John bowed. 'Lady Joan. Are you well?'

She nodded to the front of his robe. 'Better than you, I should think.' She placed her elbows on the rail, and together they looked out to sea. 'What is the Holy Land like?' she asked.

'Not so different from Sicily.'

'And the Saracens? I understand you once lived amongst them.'

John nodded. 'They are people like any other. There are good and bad men amongst them.'

Joan placed her hand on his arm. He turned, surprised, and she met his eyes. 'I need your help, John,' she whispered urgently. 'I—'

'John! There you are!' Richard strode across the deck and slapped John's back. For reasons John could not fathom, the king had taken a liking to him. Perhaps it was because John was not afraid to speak the truth to him.

'The lookouts have spotted land!' Richard declared. He frowned as he turned to Joan. 'You should get below, Sister. The sun will do your complexion no favours.'

'Yes, Brother.'

She left, and Richard took her place at the rail. He pointed to a smudge on the horizon. 'There it is, John. That prophet Tancred kept at his court, what was his name?'

'Joachim, Your Grace.'

'Joachim, yes. He said I would not lose a battle in the Holy Land.' Richard patted the sword at his waist. 'I will take Jerusalem, John. I swear it. And I will have Saladin's head.'

'May God's will be done,' John murmured. Silently, he prayed God would spare his friend.

★

The sun was halfway to its mid-point, turning the waters of Acre harbour turquoise, and Yusuf was nearing the end of his tour of the barricades. The sky was clear and the day already warm. That was bad. Fair weather meant the Frankish diggers would make more progress.

Yusuf reached the end of the right wing, where ten mamluks had gathered to talk or perhaps to play a game of chance. They were leaning casually against the rampart, their spears propped up near by. One mamluk, younger than the rest, stood apart holding his spear. Yusuf was not wearing his gold vest, and the men did not recognize him until he was almost upon them. It was the young one who saw him first. 'Malik!' he gasped.

The other men snapped to attention. One grabbed for his spear and knocked the rest over. The men froze as their weapons clattered to the ground.

'Pick those up,' Yusuf said quietly. 'Form a line.'

The men retrieved their spears and formed a line at the foot of the rampart as Yusuf slid from the saddle. He walked slowly before them. He touched at a spot of rust on the mail of the second man. 'See that this is cleaned.' He reached the end of the line, where the young mamluk stood. He was rangy and had sandy hair and wide-set blue eyes. Yusuf was reminded of John, and wondered briefly where the mamluk had come from. His coat of mail was so clean it gleamed in the sunshine. 'What is your name?'

'Dhameer, Malik.'

'A good name.' It meant 'conscience'. 'You have only recently become a mamluk?'

'I was freed one month ago, Malik.' All mamluks began as slaves, purchased between the ages of eight and twelve. They trained until age eighteen, at which point they were freed and became full mamluks, in the pay of their lord.

Yusuf stepped back to address the men. 'Do you hear that? One month ago. I came upon you lounging about like women gossiping at the well. How is it that only this boy knew his duty?' There was no response. The men stared at the ground. 'It has been a long siege, men. We have all lost friends to the Franks, and if not to them, then to cold or sickness. I have not seen my wife or home for years. I know the same is true of you. It has been hard, and if you do not wish these sacrifices to have been in vain, then you must remain vigilant. Look to Dhameer's example. He commands this ashara now.' The young mamluk was wide-eyed. The former commander had flushed red, but he held his tongue.

'I will need all of your spears in the days to come,' Yusuf concluded. 'I am sure you will not fail me.' He mounted and rode back down the line and towards the tower. Such scenes with his troops had become all too common. The siege was nearing its second year, and victory grew less certain with each passing day. Yusuf had to spend more and more time shoring up the morale of the men. His tours, which had once taken little longer than the time it took him to ride the length of the barricades, now lasted late into the morning.

Yusuf reached the tower and climbed the stairs. This, too, had become part of his morning ritual. The lookouts bowed and stepped to the back of the viewing platform. Yusuf stood with his hands clasped behind him as he looked out. His eyes went first to the tent of King Philip. The simple canvas tent would have been hard to find had Yusuf not known precisely where to look. It was much smaller than those of Leopold of Austria, Frederick of Swabia, Guy or even many of Philip's own vassals. From the top of the tent flew the king's standard – rows of golden fleur de lys on a field of azure. Yusuf had invited Philip to dine with him, but the king had refused. Shortly thereafter, the French king had ended the practice of granting safe-conducts that allowed men to pass between the two armies. Philip was a more serious foe. The siege had made more progress since his arrival seven weeks ago than it had in the previous twenty months.

Yusuf shifted his gaze to the city wall. It was pitted and

cracked, and the battlements were crumbling in many places. There had been seven trebuchets when Philip arrived; now there were seventeen, and more were being built. The machines were in essence huge slings that worked by means of a heavy counterweight, which was affixed to one end of a long arm. A sling was attached to the other end. The weight was winched high in the air, and when it fell, the arm swung up, pulling the sling after it. A trebuchet could hurl stones over a quarter of a mile. Philip had built two huge ones, which could sling rocks weighing up to twenty-five stones.

But the trebuchets were not what most worried Yusuf. Hundreds of Franks with picks and shovels were at work digging under the city wall. As they tunnelled, they put up braces to keep the wall from collapsing on them. When they had dug all the way under the wall, the braces would be burned, and the wall would collapse.

Trumpets blared in the Frankish camp, and Yusuf looked that way. The camp was abuzz with activity, but at first, Yusuf could see no reason for it. He noticed men rushing towards the coast and looked out to sea. He saw the ships of the Frankish blockade, which were riding at anchor. On the horizon beyond them was a single sail; then another, and another. Yusuf counted thirty ships in all. The wind was at their back, and they grew quickly in size. They were large transport ships, each capable of holding at least three hundred men and fifty horses. One was larger than the others. From its mast flew a scarlet flag emblazoned with three lions.

The ship made anchor and a longboat was lowered. Eight sailors, two men in priests' robes, and half a dozen warriors in mail climbed down into it. One of them was much taller than the rest. Even from this distance, Yusuf could see that he had long hair of reddish gold. He sat in the stern while the sailors rowed the ship to shore. The trumpets blared again, and the Franks from the camp waded into the surf to meet the longboat. The tall man jumped from the boat into waist-deep water to meet them. The Franks cheered him, and the sea breeze carried their voices to Yusuf.

'Lionheart!' they shouted. 'Lionheart! Lionheart!'

King Richard had arrived.

Smoke stung his eyes as John approached another bonfire. Richard seemed not to notice the smoke, or the heat on his face. He grinned as he approached the men crowded around the fire. They cheered. Upon his arrival, Richard had distributed food and wine to every man in camp. For some, it was their first taste of wine in over a year, and they were good and drunk. Someone had had the idea to build a bonfire to celebrate Richard's arrival, and soon a dozen of them were blazing on the beach. The one that John and Richard were approaching was the biggest of the lot. Huge beams had been leaned against one another and set on fire to create a blaze that soared thirty feet into the air, sending sparks racing up towards the heavens.

The men at the fire surrounded Richard, basking in his presence. The king slapped backs, grasped men by the arm, laughed when they showed him their scars and showed them his own in turn. The men loved him. Richard had his faults, but he was made for this.

'Men!' he roared and motioned for quiet.

'Quiet now!' someone shouted. 'Quiet for the King!' others echoed. 'Quiet for the King!'

Richard waited until the only sound was the crackle of burning wood. 'It has been a long journey from England,' he began, 'and I give thanks to God that I am here at last. I see Englishmen amongst you, and Frenchmen, too. I see Frisians, Scandinavians, Flemings, Sicilians, Genoese and Germans. Good men, all. Brave men. Tonight, I have heard many tales of your courage, of your skill at arms, of the infidels you have killed –' he winked – 'of the women whose fields you have ploughed!' A few of the men cheered at this. 'I thank you for saving the fairest maiden of them all for my arrival. There she sits!' He pointed to the walls of Acre. 'You have laboured these many months to spread her legs wide. Are you ready to take her?'

The men's shouts of approval were louder this time. Richard started speaking again before the last shouts had ceased. The king's voice was softer, his tone measured. The men quieted instantly. They leaned forward, straining to hear.

'Some of you have fought here for weeks, some for months, a few for nearly two years. I have arrived only today, but do not think that I do not understand the sacrifices you have made, the scars that you bear. You have faced not only the Saracens but hunger and disease. You have lost good friends. I have seen the pyres where you burn the dead.' Richard paused and bowed his head. The men around him had grown sombre. When the king spoke again, his voice was firm and strong. 'I have not come to steal their glory, but to honour them. Their deaths will not have been in vain!'

His voice rose in volume. 'You have no doubt heard tales of me, of my valour, my bravery, my skill at arms. Stories are only words. I will let my actions here speak for me. But I will tell you this: I am a man of my word, and I give it to you now. Your long wait is over.' He pointed again to Acre. 'The bitch will be ours before summer is through. And after that, I will not rest until Jerusalem is once more in Christian hands!'

The men were completely under his spell. They were nodding, their eyes shining in the firelight. It would take only one word to release them, and Richard gave them that word. He raised his voice into one final roar. 'To Jerusalem!'

'Jerusalem!' the men shouted back. 'Jerusalem!' The call was mixed with cries of 'Lionheart!' The cries grew in number until the men around the bonfire were chanting as one. '*Lionheart*! *Lionheart*! *Lionheart*!'

Richard moved on, leaving the chants behind. John followed, along with the other lords and knights of the king's retinue. He gave more or less the same speech at each of the bonfires. Each time it was greeted with the same enthusiastic response. By the time Richard finished at the last fire, his cheeks were flushed and sweat had soaked through his mail to wet his surcoat.

'Are you well, my lord?' Robert Blanchemains asked. 'Perhaps you should retire to your tent.'

Richard shook his head. 'I have no desire for sleep. John, come with me. The rest of you go.'

John followed Richard away from the bonfires, through the tents of the camp and up the bank of the rampart. The guards moved away respectfully. Richard stood with his hands on the palisade, his face lost in shadows, and stared out at the Saracen camp. 'You have told me about the Saracens' training and the tactics they employ, John. I wish to know more of their leader, this Saladin. You have said he is an honourable man.'

'He is.'

'Some of the men say he threw the bodies of our dead into the river to poison the waters. Thousands of our men died in pools of their own shit, struck down by the flux. Where is the honour in that?'

John's brow knit. There was no easy answer. The Yusuf he had known would never have done such a thing. 'We slaughtered women and children when we first took these lands,' he said. 'In some places, we even ate the dead. Perhaps Saladin only wishes to revisit upon us the atrocities we visited upon his people.'

'*Hmph.* If it is blood and suffering he wants, I shall give him both.' Richard stared at the lights of the enemy camp for a long time. Finally, he turned away, bringing his face into the flickering light cast by the torches on the wall. Sweat was beading on his forehead and his eyes were rimmed with red. The flush on his cheeks had spread to his neck as well. The king looked ill. When he spoke, his voice sounded strangely hollow. 'Philip did not come to greet me. I have lost him, John.'

'No doubt he was occupied, my lord. Perhaps you should retire to your tent.'

'No,' Richard snapped. 'You all peck at me as if you were hens. I will retire to my tent when I am ready.'

John decided to take another tack. 'Your wife will be missing you, my lord.'

Richard and Berengaria had been married on Cyprus in the midst of Richard's sack of the island. The king frowned at the mention of her. 'Berengaria will be glad I am gone. I frighten her, John. On our marriage night, she would not stop crying after I took her. I had to sleep in another room.'

'Nevertheless, you must do your duty by her, my lord. You must strive to produce a son.'

'My duty . . .' Richard nodded. 'Come, then.'

The king's lords were waiting for him inside his tent. When Robert Blanchemains saw Richard, the steward's eyes widened. 'My lord, you are not well. Bring a doctor at once!'

'I am well enough,' Richard protested weakly. He sank into a folding chair.

When the doctor arrived, he took one look at Richard and scowled. 'Why was I not sent for sooner? He has camp fever. He must be bled to cool his blood. Lay him down.'

Men came to carry Richard to his bed, but he waved them off. 'I'm not an invalid,' he growled. He pushed himself to his feet and leaned against the tent post. 'Set my cot up there,' he said, pointing outside the tent. 'I wish to see the walls. I have waited months to reach Acre. I'll not miss the siege while lying in my tent.'

Chapter 20

'My lady, you wished to see me?' John asked as he stepped into Joan's tent. The dim interior was a relief from the brutal summer day outside. The heat rose in waves from the sandy ground between the Frankish camp and the city, making the walls of Acre seem to dance.

Joan sat between two handmaids, one of whom was reading. Joan was sharpening a knife with smooth, practised strokes. She wore a light cotton tunic, through which John could see the outline of her small breasts and flat belly. Sweat glistened on her arms and in the hollow at the base of her neck. John forced himself to look away.

'Leave us,' Joan told the handmaids. 'Sit, father.' John moved towards a stool in the corner. 'No. Here.' She pointed her dagger towards the stool beside her.

John sat, but as far from Joan as he could. 'What do you want of me, my lady? Do you wish to confess your sins?'

Joan's laugh was deep and throaty. 'What sins could I have possibly committed? It is almost a month since we reached Acre, and I have hardly set foot outside my tent. My dear brother says he fears for my life and honour.' Her blue eyes met John's. 'I want you to help me, father.'

'I will help as I am able, my lady.'

'I pray that is true, John. It is no secret that I wish to be free of my brother. I am just as much a prisoner here in this tent as

I was in Sicily. At least Tancred was content to let me live in peace. Richard will marry me to some fat old lord in France or Spain in order to forge an alliance. He will tell me it is my duty to obey.' She gave the dagger a last angry stroke with the whetstone and set it aside. 'But I tell you, I am not some pretty thing to be disposed of. I am not the innocent maid that I was when my father sent me to Sicily. I have known men.'

John took note of the plural, but said nothing.

'I have been a queen,' Joan continued. 'I will choose my own fate. I thought that King Isaac might help me on Cyprus. When the storm struck, it was I who urged the captain to make for the island. I gave Isaac a choice. He could have disposed of Berengaria and the others and said I died with them at sea. I would have lived at his court in secret and married him once my brother returned to France. Or, I offered him money in exchange for a ship to sail on to Constantinople. The fool chose neither. He threw me in prison and sent ships to find Richard and demand a ransom. My only consolation is that Isaac paid for his idiocy.'

'Does Richard know of this?'

'No, and I would deny it if you told him. Besides, what would it matter if he did know? I am his sister and a lady. Richard may be a bloody-minded fool, but he is nothing if not honourable where women are concerned. High-born women, at any rate. He would never harm me. I am more useful as a bride.'

John was frowning. 'But even Richard could not forgive this. You asked Isaac to kill his wife.'

'I was doing her a favour. Better death than a life married to my dear brother.'

'I am sure Berengaria would see things differently. The girl never did you any harm.'

Joan raised a thin eyebrow. 'Did Saladin do Richard any harm? Men kill one another every day, fighting for gold or land or titles. Why should women do any differently?'

Joan might be beautiful, but she was deadly as a snake. She

reminded John of Agnes. 'I will pray for you, my lady,' he said curtly and rose. 'But I cannot help you.'

'Sit, father. I am not done with you.' She had the same steely voice of command as her brother. John thought she would have made a formidable commander had she been born a man.

He sat. Joan turned so she was facing him and leaned forward, allowing him to see down her tunic to the curves of her breasts. He looked away. 'Say what you will, my lady, and be done with it.'

'You served Saladin once. I hear he is an honourable man. When he took Jerusalem, he did not allow his men to rape and pillage. If I went to him and threw myself upon his mercy, what would he do?'

'Surely you cannot be thinking—'

'And why not? Perhaps I might marry one of Saladin's sons. Better a Saracen husband of my choosing than to be sold by Richard.'

'Saladin would treat you honourably, but to marry a Saracen, you would have to convert to their faith.'

'If I must. My soul is a small price to pay for my freedom.'

'You would not be free, my lady. You would be kept in a harem, secluded from all men who were not part of your husband's family. You would not be allowed in public without a veil and guards to accompany you.'

She laughed again. 'You think my present life so different, John? I have not been without guards or handmaidens since I was a child.' She placed a hand on his knee. He could feel the warmth of her touch through his leather breeches. 'Help me. I can escape camp, but I need you to present me to Saladin, to tell him who I am.' She ran her hand up his thigh. 'I will reward you as I am able,' she whispered as she lightly traced the bulge beneath his breeches.

John caught her wrist and pulled her hand away. There was a time when he might have taken her, as he had once taken

Agnes. But he would not make that mistake again. He was too old for such foolishness, old enough to be Joan's father. 'I am sorry, my lady. I cannot help you.'

Joan snatched her hand away. This time her voice was cold. 'You disappoint me, John. I had thought you a bolder man.'

'I am a man of honour.'

'Honour.' She said the word with scorn. 'You are a fool, father. Honour will not win you friends nor buy you drink or warm your bed. Take your honour and go.'

A rumbling sound, like a distant rockslide, drowned out her last words. It was followed by shouting. Then a horn sounded. John hurried outside to find the camp in chaos. Men were rushing towards the city, and he looked that way. Philip's diggers had finally undermined the wall. A stretch twenty yards across had collapsed. Smoke from the fires the diggers had used to burn the tunnel's supports rose from the debris in the gap. The first Frankish soldiers were just starting to clamber up the rubble. Thousands more were rushing towards it. John saw Peter de Preaux sprint past him, and William de Roches at the head of a dozen knights. Robert Blanchemains rode past, accompanied by Andre de Chauvigny.

God save the city's defenders. No, not God. It would have to be him. He turned the other way and strode into camp to find Richard.

The king was pulling on his boots as he sat on a stool outside his tent. The camp fever had taken its toll. Richard had lost weight and there were bags under his eyes. The rest of his face was bright red, the skin peeling. Despite John's council to the contrary, Richard had scorned any offer of shade and spent his first day in the Holy Land lying outside his tent as he watched the bombardment. He said that he had spent his life in the field and had never had any reason to fear the sun.

'My armour!' the king roared at one of his squires. 'Bring my mail, you fool!'

Just then, another skinny young man stumbled from the tent with Richard's mail slung over his shoulder. Richard took the armour and pulled it over his head. The squire laced up the collar and helped him into his surcoat. The first squire had not moved.

'What are you still standing there for? Fetch my shield and helm. You, bring my sword and battle-axe.'

The king's doctor had been standing by, wringing his hands. He now stepped forward. 'My lord, I must council you to return to bed.'

'I have had enough of lying about. I've not come all the way from England to miss the battle.'

'But you are ill, Your Grace.'

Richard raised a mailed first. 'I'll make you ill, by God.' The doctor backed away. Richard noticed John and grinned. 'A battle at last, father! It will do me more good than lying in bed.'

John was not so sure. The king's condition was much improved, but he had been desperately ill, hardly able to eat for days. The doctor no doubt had the right of it, but if John wished to curb the bloodshed that would start once the city fell, he would need Richard at his side. 'As you say, Your Grace. We must hurry, or we will miss the fight.'

Richard slapped him on the back. 'I knew that the mail you wear is not just for show. Squire, bring the priest a shield, too!' The king buckled his sword belt about his waist. The squire handed him his battle-axe, a huge double-bladed weapon which the king slung across his back. The second squire came forward with two shields and the king's helm. Richard took the tall kite-shaped shield on his left arm and handed the other one to John. He tucked his helm under his free arm. 'Come, John.'

Richard set out through the camp with determined strides, but by the time he and John reached the barricade facing the city, the king was breathing heavily. King Philip stood atop the rampart under the flag of France and surrounded by his nobles. Richard stomped towards a gate in the barricade without sparing his fellow king a glance. The two had hardly spoken since Richard's arrival at Acre.

'Where are you going, Cousin?' Philip called down from above.

'I am joining the fight.'

'Why in God's name? Acre is almost ours. The last thing we need is for you to get yourself killed. You should return to your tent and rest. I have matters well in hand.'

'Forgive me, Cousin, but it looks to me as if you are taking no hand at all in this battle.' Richard pulled on his helmet and strode through the gate.

John walked at his side. He had a better view of the action now that they were on the flat plain leading to the city. The steep pile of rubble that filled the gap rose thirty feet. The Muslim garrison had been prepared for the wall's collapse. They had brought forward mantelets – overlapping mobile walls seven feet high and four feet across – and placed them across the gap. The hundreds of knights and men-at-arms who had scrambled up the rocky slope were keeping their distance from the man-telets, and John soon saw why. A sergeant ran forward and leapt, grabbing hold of the top of a mantelet. He had begun to pull himself up when a spear tip burst from his back. As he fell, John saw the spear pulled back through one of dozens of holes in the face of the barrier. The sergeant lay dead at its foot, joining a score of other Franks.

Richard was puffing as he climbed up the uneven slope in his heavy mail. An arrow shot by a Saracen archer on the still stand-ing portion of the wall hit him in the chest. John froze, but Richard only grunted and snapped the shaft off. It had not penetrated his mail. Robert Blanchemains came skidding down the slope towards them. 'Your Grace! We did not look for you at the battle.'

'Well here I am.' Richard paused to catch his breath. 'What progress have—?' Another arrow hissed through the air and slammed into his shield. 'By the devil's hairy balls! You there!'

The king pointed to an archer who had just arced an arrow over the mantelets. 'Quit wasting arrows and make yourself useful. Gather your fellows and keep those archers off the walls.' Richard turned back to Blanchemains. 'What progress have you made, Rob?'

'The gap is small, Your Grace. We have many thousand men eager to fight, but cannot bring all our force to bear. We have tried to push through the mantelets, but it is no use. They spear any man who gets too close.'

'So our men stand about like flies on a horse's arse while their archers pick us off one by one. Is that the way of it, Rob?'

'Yes, my lord.'

Richard squinted against the glaring sunshine as he stared up at the wall of mantelets. 'Fetch me twenty men with grappling hooks and rope, Rob. We'll have that wall down soon enough.'

Men were sent running to camp to fetch the hooks. Richard and John climbed to the front of the line, where Richard's knights gathered around the king. When the men with the hooks arrived, Richard drew his sword and held it aloft so that the sun flashed off the blade. 'Men, are you ready to give those bastards a taste of your steel?' he roared. Richard turned to the men with the hooks. 'Throw them over the wall, men, and we'll pull it down.'

The men stood in a line and swung their hooks in wider and wider arcs before letting fly. Many of the hooks fell short or bounced off the mantelets. Others flew too far. The Saracens on the far side of the wall grabbed the ropes and pulled them forward so they snaked over the wall. But two were thrown just right. They hooked over the top of the same mantelet, and the lines went taut as the men who had thrown them started to pull. Other men took up the ropes and added their weight.

'Pull, men!' Richard shouted. 'Heave! Heave!'

The mantelet tilted forward and then fell over with a crash. The men roared and rushed at the gap. The first to reach it was a French knight, his shield emblazoned with a castle. He ran straight into a flaming jar of naphtha, tossed by one of the Saracens. The jar shattered against the knight's chest and the naphtha ignited, turning him into a human torch. He stumbled forward and was impaled on the spear of one of a dozen mamluks who had stepped forward to defend the gap.

The charge faltered as the men edged back from the burning knight. None were eager to follow him into what looked to be sure death.

Richard stepped forward. 'With me, men! For Christ!'

Before any of his lords could stop him, the king charged. John was the first to follow. As he neared the gap, he could see a jar of naphtha arcing towards the king. Richard raised his shield and the jar burst against it, coating it in flames. Richard flung the burning shield forward into the Saracens and rushed after it. He sidestepped a spear and hacked the shaft in half. His backswing nearly took the mamluk's head clean off. Another mamluk thrust his spear at the king's back, but John stepped forward and took it on his shield. Richard had continued forward, inside the reach of the enemy spears. A splash of naphtha clung to the crown of his helmet, burning there like a halo. He impaled a mamluk and left his sword in the man's gut. Richard took his battle-axe from his back and lay into the enemy with huge swings. He was a head taller than the Saracens surrounding him, a giant amongst men. He fought his way forward, his axe snapping spear shafts, slicing through mail, severing limbs.

John came close behind, protecting Richard's flank and finishing those the king missed. He blocked a spear and smashed the attacker's face with his mace. A sword sliced through his breeches and opened a cut on his thigh. As John fell to one knee, de Preaux stepped past and hacked down the man who had struck him. John pushed himself to his feet and was swept up in the wedge of Franks driving forward through the enemy. Richard was still at their head, a dozen paces up ahead. The king was hacking his way through the enemy ranks. Then he came face to face with Al-Mashtub.

The huge mamluk was even taller than Richard, and much thicker, with a chest as wide around as a barrel of wine and arms as thick as most men's thighs. He held his four-foot blade with both hands. Richard swung for him with his axe, but Al-Mashtub caught the blade with his sword and kicked out, catching Richard in the gut. The king stumbled back into the men behind. The charge stalled.

Now that the Franks were no longer driving forward, the Saracens closed from all sides. John found himself fighting for his life. He parried a sword thrust and brought his mace down on his attacker's forearm, shattering the bone. He glanced towards Richard. The king had tossed aside his flaming helmet. He snarled as he hacked at Al-Mashtub with mighty blows. The mamluk turned them aside easily. John had seen Al-Mashtub fight dozens of times. He knew how deadly he could be. If Richard had not been ill, he would have been a match for him, but the king's fever had weakened him. Even a glance was enough to tell John that Richard was going to die. His crusade would die with him. All John had to do was let it happen.

A flash of pain exploded in John's ribs as a sword slammed into him. He staggered to the side and turned to face his foe, a squat mamluk with a long black beard. The man swung again, and this time John knocked the blow aside with his mace. There was another stab of pain in his side. He must have cracked a rib. John gritted his teeth and swung backhanded, catching the bearded man in the side of the head and caving in his helmet. As the mamluk fell, John turned back towards Richard. The king was on the defensive now. He turned aside a thrust. Al-Mashtub swung his blade back, and Richard recovered just in time to block it.

'Christ's blood!' John cursed. Richard might be a bastard, but he had sworn to serve him. He pushed through the battle towards the king. A sword flashed at him and he dropped to one knee. He slammed his mace into the attacker's gut and the man crumpled. Richard was only a few strides away. The king was clearly labouring, his chest heaving as he struggled for breath. As he blocked another blow, his axe went spinning from his hands. Al-Mashtub hacked down at him. Richard tried to sidestep the blow, but it glanced off his shoulder, driving him to his knees.

The pain in John's leg and side vanished and the sounds of battle faded until all he could hear was the blood pounding in his ears. He sprinted forward. A mamluk appeared before him, and John deflected the man's blade and then slammed his shoulder into him, knocking the man aside. Al-Mashtub was raising his sword to finish Richard. John stumbled and lunged forward swinging. He caught Al-Mashtub in the side of the knee. The huge mamluk crumpled, screaming in pain.

Richard had grabbed his axe and pushed himself to his feet. He looked about at the Saracens swarming from all sides. 'There are too many! We must fall back.' He raised his voice. 'All together, men! Fall back! Fall back!'

John and Richard fought side by side as they retreated towards the gap. They were the last of the Christians through. As they emerged on the other side, men surrounded them. They were shouting, their voices so loud that it took John a moment to understand them. 'Lionheart!' they screamed. 'Lionheart! Lionheart!'

Richard swayed and leaned against John to keep from falling. John noticed that the mail at the king's shoulder was rent and bloody, but the king was grinning despite his injuries. 'Sieges sap men's courage, John. These men need only shed a little blood to become brave again.' Richard pushed away from him and started down the slope unaided. Men lined the path back to the camp. 'Lionheart!' they cheered. 'Lionheart!' As they passed through the gate in the rampart, John looked up and found Philip. The French king stood with his arms crossed, scowling as he looked down upon Richard.

★

Yusuf stood atop the tower and chewed on a piece of flatbread. It was all he could stomach. His gut had been troubling him ever since the breach was opened in the wall. That had been a week ago. He looked to Acre. The night after the breach was made, the garrison had built a wooden wall atop the rubble, behind the line of mantelets. The Franks had burned that wall the next day. The garrison built a new one, and that, too, had been burned. Another wall now protected the gap, but it would not last long. Even now, Franks bearing torches were launching another attack.

Yusuf knew the garrison could not hold out for much longer. They were losing hundreds of men each day. Yusuf had kept up a steady attack on the Frankish lines to draw some troops away from the battle, but yesterday he had pulled back his men and sent a messenger to the Franks, offering to start negotiations for the surrender of the city. If he could not save Acre, he at least wanted to see that its garrison was spared. His messenger had been sent back with no answer.

The Franks were hurling their torches at the base of the wall. The defenders were prepared. Some met the Franks with arrows while others poured buckets of water to extinguish the flames. A jar of naphtha flew from behind the wall and shattered amongst the Franks, covering half a dozen men with clinging flames. The rest scattered. Acre would hold a little longer.

Movement along the Frankish line caught Yusuf's eye, and he turned his gaze in that direction. A gate opened in the barricade, and two men rode forth under a white flag of truce. Yusuf could not see their faces from this distance, but they were clearly not Philip and Richard. He scowled. He turned to the messengers who waited at the rear of the tower. 'Go to my brother. Tell him the Frankish negotiators are coming, and he is to treat with them.'

Yusuf already had a tent prepared for the negotiations. The men at the line had been instructed to lead the Franks there. Yusuf would not go. He had asked to speak king to king, and he would not lower himself by meeting with their representatives. He left the tower and returned to his tent to await Selim's report. His stomach was twisting with nervous tension. He tried to read the *Hamasah* to settle his nerves. He had not finished the first poem when Saqr stepped into the tent.

'Your brother has sent one of the Franks to you, Malik.'

Yusuf's brow creased. 'I instructed him to treat with them.'

'He thought you would want to meet this one in person. It is John.'

Yusuf thought John had returned to England. Had he come with Richard? Or had he been in the enemy camp all along? He set the book aside. 'Show him in.'

It had been four years since Yusuf had last seen him, but John seemed to have aged more than that. His hair was more silver than blond now, and the lines on his face had deepened. He still stood straight-backed, though, and walked with a firm step.

'Ahlan wa-Sahlan,' Yusuf greeted him.

John gave a small bow. 'As-salaamu 'alaykum. Thank you for seeing me.'

Yusuf gestured for him to sit. 'I had thought you in England.'

'I was.' John sat across from Yusuf. He smiled ruefully. 'I spent so many years dreaming of home. But when I finally reached Tatewic, I realized my home is here. I joined Richard's crusade so I could return.'

'And now you fight by his side.'

'God help me, but I do.'

'What sort of man is he?'

'He is a bastard. He can be cruel and impulsive, headstrong and hot-tempered. And he is worse when he drinks.' John met Yusuf's eyes. 'But I have never seen a braver warrior, nor a better leader of men. Not even you, Yusuf.'

'Can he be reasoned with?'

'You cannot buy him off, if that is what you mean. Richard has set his sights on Jerusalem. He has vowed not to stop until he has taken it.'

'I will stop him.'

'Do not be so sure. I would not lie to you, Yusuf. Richard is unlike anyone you have faced. There was a prophet on Sicily who predicted Richard would not lose a battle in the Holy Land. I thought those were just words, but after seeing Richard at Messina, then on Cyprus, and now here at Acre . . . I believe him.'

'Allah is my shield, John. Prophecies to not frighten me.'

'Perhaps not, but Richard should.'

Yusuf sat back and stroked his beard. He could tell that John was in earnest, and it troubled him. Until now, he had hoped this most recent flood of crusaders would be content with Acre. Even if Yusuf lost the city, and all the gold and weapons it contained, he would retake it once the Franks returned overseas. But if what John said were true, then the Franks would not return to their homes, not until they had taken everything that Yusuf had sacrificed so much to gain.

'Let us speak of Acre,' he said. 'I will offer Richard the town and everything in it if he spares the defenders.'

'He will not accept. He will have Acre anyway, and he knows it.'

'And if I offer the True Cross?'

John shook his head. 'Richard may lack cunning, but the French king Philip does not. He is negotiating directly with Al-Mashtub and Qaraqush in Acre. He believes they are more desperate than you, and so will grant better terms.'

And he is no doubt right. 'Acre is not yet in Frankish hands. You will lose many more lives to take it. And even if it does fall, my army is still here. If your kings will not make a reasonable peace, then we shall have war.'

'That is precisely what Richard wants,' John said grimly.

'If war is all Richard wants, then why did you come here, John?'

'To warn you, and to ask you something. They say you threw the bodies of the dead in the river to poison the waters.'

'I did.'

John grimaced. 'There is no honour in that.'

'Such things do not please me, John, but dead is dead. An arrow to the gut or a sword to the throat kills as surely as the flux. What does it matter?'

'It mattered to you once. It should still.'

Yusuf sighed. John had only voiced his own doubts. He had missed him. No one else would speak the truth to him. 'Perhaps you are right, friend.'

'Am I still your friend, Yusuf?'

'I hope so.'

'Then heed my warning. The garrison will surrender soon, perhaps as early as tomorrow. Do not think to save Acre. It is lost. Now, you must do all you can to save your kingdom.'

'I see.' Yusuf rose, and John did likewise. 'Thank you for coming, John.'

John nodded. 'Allah yasalmak, Yusuf.'

When he had gone, Yusuf stood alone for a moment, considering what John had told him. Then he raised his voice. 'Saqr!'

The head of his guard stepped into the tent. 'Yes, Malik?'

'Have the emirs come to my tent. We attack tonight.'

Sunrise found Yusuf standing atop the Muslim ramparts. As the sun crested the horizon at his back, his shadow stretched out towards Acre, running down the side of the rampart and on to the ground between the lines. It stretched over the body of a dead mamluk, the feathered shaft of an arrow protruding from his eye. It ran over a severed arm; over another dead man, lying face down on ground muddied by his blood. The shadow stopped short of the real carnage. Bodies were piled up against the Frankish palisade. There were more than six hundred dead, and all for nothing.

Yusuf had sent his men against the Frankish line again and again. He had held no one back. Twice, his men had made it past the palisade. The first time, they had scaled the wall with ladders and gained a foothold. Over a hundred mamluks had got behind the Frankish lines. But Richard had rallied the enemy. When the mamluks tried to open one of the gates in the barricade, they were surrounded and slaughtered.

The second time, Yusuf's men had managed to set fire to a portion of the Frankish palisade. A stretch ten men wide had burned. It was still smoking now. That was where the fighting had been at its fiercest. Yusuf's men had charged the gap more than a dozen times. Each time, Richard had thrown them back. Dozens of corpses lay all around.

Aah-hoo! A horn sounded in Acre, and Yusuf looked to the walls. He saw his eagle standard hauled down and Frankish flags begin to go up. He recognized Philip's flag – rows of golden fleur de lys on a field of blue. And there were the three gold lions passant on a field of red – the flag of Richard. Yusuf had come to hate that flag.

There were shouts of alarm amongst Yusuf's men on the barricade. They rushed to take up their spears and string their bows. A gate in the Frankish barricade was swinging open. Two men walked out. The taller one limped heavily and was leaning on the shorter man. The gate closed behind them, and they set out towards the Muslim lines. Yusuf squinted. He knew those men.

'Qaraqush! Al-Mashtub!' He strode down the face of the rampart to meet them. The two emirs looked grim. Al-Mashtub's jaw was clenched in pain, and he winced with each step. Qaraqush was a shadow of his former self, his flesh hanging in loose folds from his face. Yusuf embraced him and then Al-Mashtub. 'Thank Allah you have lived.'

'I wish I had not.' Qaraqush's voice was hollow.

Yusuf squeezed his shoulder. 'You did all you could.'

The grizzled old emir shook his head. 'I failed my men. I left them.'

'Their King Philip made us go,' Al-Mashtub explained. 'We agreed to terms with him this morning. He feared you would not believe the terms of the surrender unless they were delivered by men you trust.'

'What are these terms?'

Qaraqush grimaced. 'The Franks are holding all three thousand men of the garrison for ransom. You are to pay two hundred thousand dinars. You must also release five hundred common Frankish prisoners and one hundred nobles to be named. And you must turn over their True Cross. You have two months to deliver all this, or the men of the garrison will be sold into slavery.' He hung his head. 'Forgive me, Malik.'

'You did what you had to do, Qaraqush. Better that than sacrifice the lives of your men. I would have done the same.' Though that did not make it any easier to stomach. He was already short of coin to pay his men. Where would he find another two hundred thousand dinars?

'Come,' he told them. 'You look like you need a good meal, Qaraqush. And you shall have a doctor see to your leg, Al-Mashtub.' He led them up the rampart, where mamluks took the two emirs and carried them into camp. Yusuf stayed to watch the Franks enter the city. A new flag had appeared above one of the towers on the wall. It was a field of red bisected by a thick white horizontal stripe. It had hardly been unfurled when it was pulled down again. Richard's standard took its place. He wondered why.

'Brother!' It was Selim, approaching along the barricade. 'A dark day.'

Yusuf nodded.

'Some of your emirs have asked leave to depart. They say they have been too long gone from their lands.'

It was starting already. His men had followed him without question so long as he led them to victory after victory. Now that he had been defeated, they were scattering like birds fleeing before a sandstorm. 'Tell them they may go when the first rains fall, not before.'

'I will tell them, Brother . . . But some have already left.'

Yusuf's hands clenched at his side as sudden blinding anger swept through him. How dare they? How dare they leave now, when he needed them most? He took a deep breath, and when he spoke, his voice was even. 'Tell them that the next emir to leave without my permission will forfeit all his lands. And tell them that this battle is far from over. It has only begun. Richard did not come for Acre. He came to retake the Holy Land. He came for Jerusalem. I mean to stop him.'

Chapter 21

John heard shouting as he approached the council chamber in the palace at Acre. 'It must be Jaffa!' It was hard to tell who was speaking through the thick wood of the door. 'It is the most direct route to Jerusalem!'

A quieter voice replied, 'You will never take Jerusalem without food and water. We must head east. The lands are rich in the valley of Jezreel.'

'If you wish to conquer villages and fields, then go. I have come for Jerusalem!'

'Have you not heard a word I said? If you march south, you will never take the Holy City!'

The guard outside the chamber nodded to John. 'They are in fine form today, father,' he said as he opened the door.

John stepped into a tense silence. The lords standing around the council table turned from glaring at one another to stare at him. To his right were the grim-faced native lords: Reginald, Balian and Garnier of Nablus, the new Grand Master of the Hospitallers. Nablus was a tall, powerful man with thick black hair and bushy eyebrows that formed a single bar over his green eyes. Conrad stood at his side. Guy stood across the table from Conrad. This was no surprise; the two had been at one another's throats over who was the rightful king of Jerusalem. Guy gave John a sour look. Hugh of Burgundy – a man with a great belly and bulging eyes – stood with Guy. He had taken charge of the remaining French knights following Philip's departure, and Guy had been cultivating his support. Richard's men – Robert Blanchemains, Bishop Walter, de Chauvigny, his cousin Henry of Champagne and de Ferriers – lined the table between the two factions. De Ferriers scowled. He was the one who had called for John's head back in London.

Richard stood on the far side of the table. He swatted at one of the flies buzzing about his head. The king's face had gone from bad to worse; the sunburnt skin was now peeling and blistered. Juice from the aloe plant provided relief, but it also attracted flies. When he spoke, there was an irritated edge to his voice. 'Where have you been, priest?'

John went to stand with Reginald and Balian. 'At the gates, Your Grace, meeting with Saladin's emissaries. They have delivered one hundred thousand dinars.'

Guy's eyes widened at mention of the sum. 'His coin is most welcome. My men have not been paid in years.'

'The money is not yours to dispose of,' Bishop Walter countered. 'It belongs to the King.'

'I am king. I began this siege and—'

'And Richard finished what you could not,' Walter concluded.

Guy was red-faced. He opened his mouth, but Richard spoke first. 'One hundred thousand dinars. That is only half the sum agreed upon.'

'It will take time to raise the full amount, my lord,' John replied. 'Saladin still has three weeks before the rest is due.'

Blanchemains shook his head. 'Three more weeks here will be the death of us. We are short of food. Most of the coin Saladin sent us will only go back to him to purchase grain.' A week ago, Saladin had opened the market in his camp to the Franks. He was as desperate for gold to pay the ransom as they were for food. 'God help us if the Saracens close their markets to us.'

De Ferriers rubbed the stubble on his hollow cheeks. 'The

food we have would go further without three thousand extra mouths to feed. If we executed the Saracen prisoners—'

'We gave our word those prisoners would be spared,' Balian said coldly. 'I do not know your customs in France, sir, but here in the Kingdom, that means something.'

'I am a man of my word, Lord Balian,' de Ferriers replied, his voice rising. 'I swore to deliver Jerusalem, and I will kill as many infidels as needs be to do so.'

'Then you lack brains as well as honour,' Reginald replied in his gravelly voice. 'Slaughter those prisoners and you turn them into martyrs. If you wish for fewer mouths to feed, then I say we start with yours.'

De Ferriers looked to Richard. 'You hear, Your Grace? This brute dares threaten me. I would not be surprised if he were responsible for my murdered men.'

De Ferriers was not the only one at the table to have lost men. The lords of France, England and the Kingdom were constantly at one another's throats, and the quarrels were taken up by their men. Drunken brawls were common, and each morning men were found dead in the streets of Acre.

'I am no murderer in the night,' Reginald growled. 'I too have lost men.'

Guy pointed across the table. 'Conrad is to blame. Last night, I lost a dozen men to his troops.'

'Your men struck first,' Conrad said evenly, 'yet I lost only five men-at-arms. I cannot be blamed if my soldiers bested yours.'

'Your men lay in wait for mine. You speak nothing but lies, usurper!'

'I am the rightful king of Jerusalem. My wife Isabella is queen. None can dispute her claim.'

Hugh of Burgundy sniggered. 'How many wives do you have, sir? I hear Isabella is your second. Or is she your third?'

'I'll have your tongue for that!'

'You can try. I—'

He stopped short as Conrad came around the table and rushed him. Hugh got off a punch, but Conrad knocked it aside with his left arm before delivering a straight right to the Frenchman's jaw. Hugh went reeling back into Henry of Champagne. Blanchemains and Bishop Walter grabbed Conrad to hold him back. Reginald shoved Walter away from Conrad, and the bishop turned and swung. John was ready and caught his arm. Then Guy slammed into John from the side, sending him sprawling on the floor.

'Enough!' Richard slammed his fist against the table. 'Out! All of you!'

The men exchanged angry glances as they trooped out. John rose to follow.

'You stay, John.' Richard poured himself a cup of wine and drained it while the last men filed out. 'A bunch of prattling fools,' he muttered. 'But Blanchemains has the right of it. We cannot stay here. I have already lost the Germans and the bulk of the French. Three more weeks and I will have no army.'

And you will have only yourself to blame, Your Grace. Richard had driven his allies away. Leopold, the duke of Austria, had taken command of the Germans after Frederick of Swabia died of camp fever. During the negotiations with the Saracen garrison, Leopold had insisted that the Germans deserved a full third of the ransom. 'We fought and suffered for months before you arrived,' he had told Richard and Philip. 'We earned that gold with our blood.'

Richard had mocked his claims. 'You fought for months and what did you accomplish? It was our arrival that settled the matter. You accomplished nothing, and you will have nothing.'

When the city was taken from the Saracens, Leopold had sought to stake his claim by running his flag up on the wall. Richard had torn it down and pissed on it. Leopold and his men set sail six days later.

Philip had followed within two weeks. Ostensibly, the King of France had left to settle the disputed inheritance of Flanders, but it was no secret that he and Richard were on poor terms. The split between them that began with Richard's marriage to Berengaria had widened after the fall of Acre. Philip felt that his trebuchets and tunnelling had brought Acre to its knees, and Richard had only delivered the final blow. Yet the men hailed Richard as the conqueror of Acre. Philip's parting words had been, 'Let us see how much my cousin conquers without me.'

Richard poured more wine. He took a sip as he studied the map of the Holy Land laid on the table before him. 'We must go now,' he repeated. 'The men need a goal to unite them. This infighting will cease once we face a common enemy.' He pointed to a city on the map. 'Jaffa. It is the closest port to Jerusalem. Once it is in our hands, we can ship the siege equipment from Acre by sea. From there, we will head inland for the Holy City.'

'A bold plan, Your Grace, but a hazardous one,' John cautioned. 'You propose to march sixty miles over rough country, with multiple river crossings, in the height of the summer and with a larger Saracen army still in the field. Such an undertaking would be difficult in the best of circumstances. With the Muslim hostages in tow, it will be impossible. And with Philip and Leopold's men gone, we do not have enough troops to safely leave three thousand Saracens prisoners behind in Acre.'

'You are right, John.' Richard drained the cup. 'The hostages must die.'

John blinked. He had seen women raped and men beheaded. He had watched armies starve to death. He had seen sons kill their fathers, and priests who cared more for gold than the lives of their flocks. He had seen Richard himself in all his savage glory on Cyprus. He had thought there was nothing left in this world that could shock him. He had been wrong. 'But Your Grace, you gave your word they would be spared.'

Richard only shrugged and poured himself more wine.

'You will stain your soul forever, Your Grace.'

'You will absolve me, priest.'   •

'I cannot, my lord, not from this.'

'Bishop Walter, then. I will have my men fast for me.'

'Your Grace, the penance for the murder of three thousand hostages would be more than twenty thousand years of fasting. You do not have enough men or coin for the absolution. The blood of those you kill will follow you to the grave.'

Richard lowered his head. His knuckles showed white as he clenched the edge of the table. Finally, he looked up and met John's eyes. 'No, it will follow me only to Jerusalem. When I take the Holy City, God will forgive my sins.'

The first light of dawn filtered through the windows high above as John knelt before the altar in the small church near the palace of Acre. His head was bowed and his hands clasped in prayer. The church was empty. Most of the Christians were headed outside the walls to watch the slaughter of the Muslim prisoners, while the Muslim citizens were holed up in their homes, afraid they might suffer a similar fate. 'Lord God forgive me,' John murmured, not for the first time. He had advised Richard, fought at his side and saved his life. Now thousands of defenceless men would die because of his efforts.

The door to the church creaked open, and John heard the slap of sandals on stone. He kept his head bowed. The newcomer stopped beside him. 'John? I had thought you would be at the execution.'

John looked to see Joan kneeling beside him. She wore a hooded grey cloak that blended with the stone of the church. 'I want no part of it,' he said.

'You have no stomach for blood?'

'For murder, no.'

'Does that mean you come to pray for our enemy? How charitable of you.'

'What do you pray for, my lady? You do not strike me as the religious sort.'

She gave him a pointed look. 'Prayer is all I have, though it is but a poor substitute for a willing man. I had hoped that with time, you might have come to reconsider.'

'If you have come to offer to be my whore again, the answer is still no.'

Joan flushed. 'No, John. I was wrong to offer myself to you, but, God forgive me, I have grown accustomed to dealing with men of a baser sort. You are a man of honour. That is why I believe you will help me. Take me to Saladin. What better time than now, when the entire city is distracted.'

'I have given you my decision.'

'And my brother swore to spare the Saracen prisoners. Yet today they will die.' John winced, and Joan took note. 'You despise my brother, don't you? You should, John. He is an animal.' Her clear blue eyes met his. 'Will you leave my fate in his hands?'

'Richard is my king.'

'He is a murderer. You said it yourself.'

John bowed his head and closed his eyes, as much to block out Joan's searching gaze as to gather his thoughts. She had voiced his doubts. He felt her touch on his arm.

'Your prayers will not help the Saracens,' Joan said softly. 'You should go to Richard. Perhaps you can still stop him.'

'What of you, my lady?'

She shrugged. 'I am not heartless, John. You should not concern yourself with me when thousands of men are facing their death.'

Were her words only a ploy to win him to her side? John searched her face, but found no answer. Perhaps he was wrong to distrust Joan. He would not have wanted his fate to hinge on Richard's whim. 'I will do what I may to help you, my lady. If you truly wish to marry amongst the Saracens, I will speak of it to Richard.'

'Thank you, father. Now go.'

The streets of the city were empty at first, but they grew crowded as John approached the land gate. A long line of

Saracen prisoners was filing out, walking into the light of the rising sun. Beside each man walked a Christian soldier. The captives' hands were tied behind their backs, and they were roped together at the neck in chains of ten, making it impossible to resist. Those few who tried to run or to strike out at their captors soon found themselves on the ground, tangled up with their fellow prisoners. Their captors would kick at them and slap them with the flat of their swords until they got to their feet. All they won for their bravery were bruises and bloodied lips.

John strode past the line of men and out the gate. The prisoners were being lined up atop the far barricade of the Christian siege camp. There was no sign of Richard's standard. John turned to one of the guards at the gate. 'Have you seen the King?'

The guard shrugged. 'Probably in the palace waiting until these sand devils are all lined up for their trip to hell.'

John would wait for Richard. He took up a position just inside the gate. In the meantime, he would do what he could to ease the Saracens' passage from this life to the next. 'Today you will gain paradise,' he murmured in Arabic as a hostage trudged past. 'Today you will gain paradise,' he repeated to the next man, who nodded in thanks. John knew that his words offered little solace, but they were all he had to give. Unless Richard changed his mind.

The hostages continued to file past. The sun had risen to burn away the morning cool, and heat was rising in waves from the plain beyond the gate by the time the last man filed through. 'Today you will gain paradise,' John told him.

Richard came close behind the last hostage. The king was on horseback, followed by his lords. John stepped in front of his horse, forcing him to stop. 'Please, my lord. Do not do this.'

'It must be done.'

'If you make martyrs of the garrison, the Saracens will never surrender. This slaughter will only inspire them.'

'I think not, John. Who will garrison Saladin's cities now, knowing that death awaits them? The infidels will howl and cry and swear vengeance when they see their fellows die, but in their hearts, they will know fear.'

'You damn yourself, Your Grace.' John removed his mace and tossed it on the ground. 'I will serve you no more.'

Richard's expression blackened. 'You too swore an oath, priest, and I mean to hold you to it.' The king drew his sword and pointed to the mace. 'Pick it up, or you can join your heathen friends.'

John glared at the king and picked up his mace. Dying would be a grand gesture, but it would serve no purpose. Alive, he could help Joan and maybe stop Richard before he laid waste to the lands John loved. Dead, he was no good to anybody.

'Wise decision.' The king urged his horse forward but then reined in and looked back. 'I saw you speaking to the Saracens, John. What did you say?'

'The Muslims believe like us that those who are martyred in defence of the faith are sanctified. I told them that today they would gain paradise.'

'*Hmph*. They are infidels, John,' Richard said as he rode on through the gate. 'They will burn in hell.'

And you, Your Grace, will join them.

Numbers swam before his eyes as Yusuf squinted at a list of figures. He blinked. The numbers came into focus, but they still did not add up. 'We are twenty thousand dinars short of the full ransom.'

'If we tax the markets . . .' Imad ad-Din mused out loud.

'No. My people are tired after years of war. If I raise taxes not sanctioned by the Koran, there will be rebellions. I cannot fight my own people and the Franks.'

Yusuf's secretary spread his ink-stained hands. 'Then I do not know where to find more gold. The treasuries of Cairo, Damascus and Aleppo are empty. We have reduced your mamluks to quarter pay. If you squeeze any more from them, *they* will rebel.'

'Four emirs have left for home despite my orders to the contrary. Sell their lands to the highest bidder.'

'That will raise the coin we need, but you will create dangerous enemies, Malik.'

'Do it.'

Yusuf's eldest son, Al-Afdal, rushed into the tent. 'Father! Come quickly! The Franks have marched the hostages from Acre. I think they mean to execute them.'

Yusuf rose at once and hurried outside. 'My horse!' He turned to Al-Afdal. 'Gather the men and ride as soon as you are able!' Yusuf swung into the saddle and spurred for Acre. Fifty members of his khaskiya rode after him.

Yusuf had moved his camp further from the city to protect it against Frankish sorties and to block the path to the rich lands of the Jezreel Valley. It was a two-mile ride to Acre. He galloped along a dusty path, and the walls of the city slowly rose before him. He reined in atop the hill where his tent had once stood.

The hostages had been brought out of the city and lined up atop the old Frankish ramparts. The three thousand mamluks stretched the length of the barricade, from the Belus River to the sea. Behind each man stood a Frank with a sword in hand.

Yusuf looked behind him. He could see the dust thrown up by the mamluks riding from the camp. They were still more than a mile away. Too far. He turned towards Acre. The hostages had been pushed to their knees. They were chanting in unison, and their voices carried to Yusuf. They were reciting the first chapter of the Koran, which opened all Muslim prayer.

'. . . In the name of Allah, the Most Gracious, the Most Merciful. All praises to Allah, Lord of the Universe . . .'

The Franks raised their swords. Thousands of blades flashed in the sun.

'. . . The Most Gracious, the Most Merciful, sovereign of the day of judgement. You alone we worship, and You alone—'

The swords fell, and the chanting ceased. Sprays of crimson filled the air. A few mamluks lay screaming in agony. It took several more blows to kill them, and then there was silence, broken only by the harsh cries of the gulls wheeling overhead and the distant crash of the surf. Yusuf felt dizzy, and he gripped the pommel to stop himself sliding from the saddle. He heard approaching hoofbeats and straightened before turning to see Al-Afdal and his emirs, Qaraqush, Nu'man and Muhammad, arrive at the head of over a thousand men.

Al-Afdal rode up beside him. 'I cannot believe it,' Yusuf's son murmured.

'Signal the charge, Malik,' Nu'man urged. The short man brandished his battle-axe. 'I'll make those bastards pay!'

'No,' Yusuf told him.

Muhammad rode forward. His immaculately trimmed beard had gone silver since Yusuf first met him, and his soft hands had been hardened by years of war. 'Such an outrage cannot go unanswered, Malik!'

'Charging their fortifications will only cost more lives – ours, not theirs. I have seen enough of my men's blood spilled this morning. We will avenge our men, but when the time is right, not now.'

There were scowls and black looks. For a moment, Yusuf thought they might disobey his order. At last, Muhammad spoke.

'If you will not let us charge, then there are other Franks to be killed.'

Nu'man nodded. 'The prisoners.'

Yusuf grimaced. 'No. The Franks are savages, but we—'

'The prisoners!' Nu'man shouted. 'I will have blood!'

'No, wait!' Yusuf cried, but his words were lost among the shouts of his men.

'The prisoners! Kill the prisoners!'

Nu'man wheeled his horse about and galloped back towards camp, followed by the mamluks. Only Qaraqush, Al-Afdal and his khaskiya remained with Yusuf. He shook his head. 'More blood will not bring back our dead. It will only make the Franks less likely to surrender when we face them in battle.'

'A price worth paying, Malik,' Qaraqush said. 'Those were my men who were slaughtered. They deserve revenge.' He, too, rode for camp

Yusuf looked to Al-Afdal. 'They are only Franks, Father,' his son said. 'Whether we kill them now or later in war, dead is dead. You have told me so yourself.'

'I was wrong.'

Yusuf turned his horse to face Acre. When he had taken Jerusalem, he had thought it would be the beginning of an era of peace. Instead, it had only brought more bloodshed. It had brought Richard. Yusuf located Richard's flag, flying over a cluster of knights who had come out to watch the slaughter. He thought he spotted the king amongst them. Lionheart, they called him, but no lion was ever so savage. If this war were to end, then Richard must die.

Chapter 22

John's aching back woke him before sunrise. He sat up and felt another stab of pain. He had spent the last sixteen days in the saddle as the army crept south from Acre. The Saracens had harassed them constantly, shooting arrows into the column before peeling away. Their attacks forced the foot-soldiers to shuffle along in close formation. Richard was content to cover only a few miles a day. The army marched only in the morning before the day grew hot, and they stopped whenever they reached fresh water. Each afternoon, they set up a stockade before bedding down for the night.

John had not spent so much time in the saddle since he was a much younger man, and he was suffering for it. Sleeping on the hard ground had done nothing to help. He reached back to massage the tense muscles for a moment. Then he rose and went outside. The air was cool, which was a refreshing change from the past weeks. The autumn rains would come soon. The camp was silent and the tents around him barely visible in the dim light. As he made his way towards the river, the cicadas started up, filling the air with their song. The guard at the gate yawned as he waved John through.

John stripped off his caftan and waded into the stream just outside the stockade. He scooped up a double handful of the cold water. It was brackish this close to the sea, but still drinkable. On the far side of the stream, trees were appearing out of the darkness as the sky brightened. They were massive oaks, some of their canopies spreading so wide that two hundred men could have gathered beneath them. Yesterday, the army had marched through those woods, accompanied by the pungent odour of the acorns they ground to dust beneath their feet.

John dunked his head and came up shivering. He bathed every morning, even on cold days. It was a habit he had learned years ago in the household of Yusuf's father. John found his thoughts returning to that time more and more often. He had been a slave, yet those had been some of the sweetest years of his life. He had spent his days studying and teaching Yusuf to fight, and his nights with Zimat. Closing his eyes now, he could still see her long black hair, her dark eyes, her skin the golden colour of desert sands. She had asked him to take her away with him, and he had refused. He had spoken to her of duty and honour. He had been a fool.

He left the river and made his way back to camp. Yawning men were stumbling from the large barracks tents. They moved stiffly, sore after days of marching. John fetched his helmet and followed them to where the cooks stood over their huge caul-drons. He joined the line of men waiting to have tasteless boiled wheat ladled into their upturned helmets. John ate as he returned to his tent.

As secretary to the king, he had his own small tent and a servant to tend to his needs. The servant – a serious boy with a milky-white, pudgy face that had earned him the unflattering nickname Suet – had scrubbed John's mail and laid it out. John dressed in leather breeches, a padded jerkin, a long mail hauberk that fell to his knees and a mail coif to protect his head and neck. Suet helped him pull on a surcoat bearing Richard's three lions, and then handed him the round, open-faced helm, which was now cleaned. John buckled his mace at his side and stepped outside. Men were everywhere – pulling on armour, packing up the barracks tents, sharpening blades, taking down the barri-cade and loading the logs and other supplies aboard longboats to be rowed through the surf to the ships that mirrored the army's progress each day. John wove through the chaos to Richard's tent.

Each morning, the king met with the native lords to ask about the terrain ahead. John would have preferred to absent himself, but Richard had made it clear that if he did not attend, his loyalty would be called into question. So each day John went and stood tight-lipped. He would be damned if he was going to do anything more to help Richard.

Today, John was the first to arrive. Robert de Sablé came next. The Frenchman was a fleshy man with red cheeks and close-set eyes. He had served Richard for years, and as a reward, the king had installed him as Grand Master of the Temple. As such, de Sablé felt he had a place at the council of native lords. The Hospitaller Grand Master, Garnier of Nablus, scowled at Robert as he entered. There was no love lost between those two. Nablus had been raised in the Holy Land and thought Robert a fool. Balian and Guy came next. King Guy, John corrected himself. Before leaving Acre, Richard had declared him to be the king of Jerusalem, with Conrad as his heir. Conrad had taken his men back to Tyre in protest. That was another eight hundred men lost, including Reginald of Sidon, who had taken Conrad's side. The army, which had numbered nearly twenty-four thousand on the day that Acre fell, had been reduced to half that number. The Saracen army was still twenty thousand men strong.

Richard arrived last, as always. He spent the mornings with his men, breakfasting each day with a different set of common troops. The king's sunburnt face was finally starting to heal, and he was in good spirits, despite the hardships of the march. He grinned. 'What lies before us today, men?'

'We should reach Arsuf,' Nablus said in his high, reedy voice.

'What is the road like?'

'Open, Your Grace,' Balian said. 'No river crossings, no obstacles. The coastal plain is more than a mile wide.'

'A good place for Saladin to attack,' Nablus noted.

Richard nodded. 'We will march in close formation. De Sablé, you will ride in the vanguard with Hugh of Burgundy. I will march in the centre with King Guy. Nablus, you will command the rear. Our strength is in our discipline. If any man leaves the column without my order, I'll have his tongue. Is that understood?' The lords nodded. Richard ended each morning council with those words.

Balian caught up to John outside the tent. 'There will be a battle today, John. I can feel it.' He arched his back and it cracked. 'War is a young man's pursuit. I feel as if I've been on the rack.'

'I *have* been on the rack,' John replied. 'It is much worse.'

'*Hah*. I suppose it is.' Balian became suddenly serious and lowered his voice. 'Keep yourself alive, John, but do not strive too mightily to keep the Saracens from bashing in Richard's brains. He would have died at Acre were it not for you. We might all be better off if he had.'

John looked about and was relieved to see that none of Richard's knights were near by. He was glad to know he was not the only one who did not care for Richard, but he did not want to end his days swinging from a noose. 'Careful, Balian. Such words could get you killed. We will talk more of this later. God save you.'

John strode to where Suet held his horse, an even-tempered chestnut. He hauled himself into the saddle. The column was forming up along the coast, the foot-soldiers making a box around the cavalry. The ranks of sergeants were five rows deep on the landside. They were the men Richard liked to call pin-cushions, who were there to protect the knights' horses from the arrows of the Saracen skirmishers. At the fore and rear of the army, the ranks of foot-soldiers were fifty across and twenty men deep. Three divisions of cavalry, each four hundred strong, would ride at the centre of the box. Altogether, the column covered nearly half a mile.

John took his position with Richard and the English lords. As they set out, the sun was smouldering just above the hills to the east, transforming the sea into a swirling cauldron of gold and pink and red. The longboats were cutting through the waves, headed towards the twenty ships that carried the army's baggage. A cool sea breeze brought the tang of salty air and the cry of gulls. Wet sand crunched beneath the hooves of John's horse. As they rode, the coastal plain widened, the hills retreating inland until they were barely visible on the horizon. There was no sign of the Saracens. Then John heard it: the beat of distant drums, low and steady, like a pulse.

'They are late this morning,' Richard noted. 'Perhaps they grow tired of this game.'

The drums grew louder and were joined by the piercing wail of war horns. *Haa-room! Haa-room!* The foot-soldiers in the column nervously eyed the hills to the east. John saw a few of them take their shields from their backs, but there was still no sign of the enemy. The tide was coming in, the crashing surf competing with the beat of the drums. Above all the noise, the war horns continued to wail. *Haa-room! Haa-room!*

'There they are!' de Preaux called.

Young eyes. John squinted to the east but saw nothing. Richard had seen them though. 'Tighten ranks!' the king roared. 'Shields up!' The command was relayed forward and back down the line. The foot-soldiers unslung their shields from their backs and held them so that they overlapped, forming a wall around the outside of the formation. The pace slowed to a crawl and the column shrank to no more than a quarter-mile as the men tightened ranks.

They shuffled along in this formation for what seemed to be ages before John finally caught sight of the Saracen standards rising above the horizon. A black line of men appeared, rushing forward like flood water to fill the sandy coastal plain. There were thousands upon thousands of men formed in a crescent that stretched for more than a mile from tip to tip. Those were no mere skirmishers. Saladin was committing his infantry. Balian was right; the Saracens meant to do battle.

Richard was grinning. 'At last. I was beginning to fear Saladin had no taste for blood.' The king turned to his young cousin. 'Henry, ride forward and remind Hugh's Frenchmen to hold their place until my order. John, go and tell Nablus the same.'

John was happy to be away from Richard. He wheeled his mount and cantered down the line, his horse kicking up wet sand as he rode in the gap between the cavalry and infantry on the ocean side. The men of the rearguard had already turned around to march backwards so that their shields formed a wall protecting the army's back. Behind the shield wall came ranks of spearmen and then crossbowmen. John found Nablus riding just behind the crossbowmen.

'Grand Master,' he greeted him.

'John. Saladin means to test us today.' Nablus nodded towards the advancing Saracens. They were armoured in a mix of pale padded cotton and dark boiled leather. Spears rose above the enemy ranks.

'Richard bids you keep tight formation. Do not charge until his signal.'

'I know my duty.'

'I did not doubt it. God keep you, Nablus.'

'And you, John.'

By the time he returned to Richard's side, the Saracen infantry were only a hundred yards off. John spied mostly black Nubians and tanned Egyptians amongst their ranks. A horn sounded and was joined by the beat of drums, the wail of bagpipes and the war cries of thousands of men. The enemy charged as one, and the ground rumbled under the pounding of their feet.

John took his long, kite-shaped shield from his saddle and thrust his left arm through the leather straps. The enemy was only fifty yards away. Now forty . . . The archers on the seaward side of the Frankish line let fly, and their shafts arced over the column to fall amongst the Saracens. The effect was no more than swatting at a cloud of gnats. A few Saracens fell, but the rest charged on. When the front ranks of the enemy were only twenty yards away, they stopped and hurled their spears. Most clattered off the wall of shields, but there were scattered cries of pain as a few struck home. The Frankish foot-soldiers wore mostly leather or padded cotton armour, which provided poor protection if anything got past their shields. Holes appeared in the ranks as men collapsed. They were carried to the coast, where longboats waited to take them out to the ships. Fresh men stepped out to take their places.

'They are sticking it to the pincushions!' Richard roared merrily.

The front ranks of the Saracens peeled back, and more men stepped forward to hurl their spears. They aimed higher this time, sending the javelins over the ranks of the infantry. One of the spears hurtled straight towards John. He blocked it, and the force of the impact set his shield quivering and left his arm numb. The onslaught continued as the column crept up the coast. Rank after rank of Saracens ran forward to hurl their spears before peeling back. The Christian arrows took their toll, leaving dozens of the enemy dead or injured on the field, but the Christian losses were worse. Finally, the last of the Saracen infantry cast their spears. As they peeled back, light cavalry galloped forward, shooting arrows as they rode. The air filled with the hiss of deadly shafts. Most were absorbed by the wall of foot-soldiers, but a few fell amongst the cavalry. One hit John in the chest. He snapped the shaft off. At this distance, the blow had been too weak to penetrate the padded vest beneath his mail, but it would leave a bruise all the same. Another arrow lodged in the leather of his saddle. The Saracens were trying to take out the knight's horses. De Preaux's mount was struck in the neck, and the beast stumbled and fell, taking the young knight with it. De Preaux's leg was pinned beneath the dying beast, but he finally managed to pull free. He cut the horse's throat and limped after Richard. He would have to go on foot until a fresh mount was brought for him.

The Saracen cavalry had wheeled away long before they reached the range of the Frankish spears. Another wave of mounted archers followed, and another after that. The air was constantly filled with arrows. The men on the outside of the Frankish line stayed for only a moment before retreating inward, while fresh men stepped out to take their place. The sun rose above them, and John was soon sweating beneath his mail. And still the column shuffled forward, leaving the bodies of the dead behind on the plain.

By noon, the foot-soldiers along the line did indeed look like pincushions, with arrows protruding here and there from their padded armour. John had half a dozen arrowheads lodged in his mail. A chance arrow had caught him in the left calf just below the knee, and his boot was slowly filling with blood. He was lucky to still have his horse. They had lost well over a hundred mounts, forcing many of the knights to go on foot. They grumbled and cursed as they stumbled on in their heavy armour. Richard rode grim-faced, clutching his sword.

And they had been spared the worst. The Saracens had focused their attack on the rearguard. John glanced back. The air was so thick with arrows that it looked as if the heavens had begun to rain down death. Thousands of mounted mamluks swarmed around the lines. A few had begun to dismount to take better aim, and to deadly effect. Richard had been forced to reinforce the rearguard with men from the rest of the column.

'Arsuf at last!'

John turned to see Guy pointing ahead. He could just make out the city, squatting on the coast a little over a mile away. Even from this distance, John could see that the walls had been toppled to prevent the Franks from using Arsuf as a stronghold.

'And none too soon,' Richard said, wiping sweat from his

forehead. He turned in the saddle at the sound of shouting from the rear of the army. 'By the devil's hairy balls, what now?'

Exhausted by the constant onslaught and the long march backwards, the rearguard had begun to lag behind. Gaps opened up in the shields of the line connecting it to the rest of the army. The Saracens had been waiting for just such an opportunity. Hundreds of mamluks in mail, spears in hand, galloped forward and burst through the gaps. The ranks of foot-soldiers opened further. For a moment, John thought the line was breaking, but they were only parting to let the knights through. Nablus thundered through the gap at the head of his knights. The Saracens who had dismounted to shoot were cut down. The rest fled, Nablus and his knights close on their heels. But even as they drove the enemy back across the plain, more Saracens were slipping into the space they had left behind.

'Curse the fool!' Richard growled. 'He leaves me no choice. Signal the charge!'

John took his mace from his belt as de Preaux sounded his horn. Its call was answered by horns all along the column. The line of foot-soldiers on the landward side divided to the left and right. Richard raised his sword and with a roar charged through. John put his spurs to his horse and galloped after the king.

The mamluks melted away before them, riding in headlong flight across the plain. The few Saracens who stood their ground were trampled or impaled on lances. Ahead, Richard was grinning fiercely as he drove his sword into the back of a mamluk fleeing on foot. John looked beyond him to the distant hills, where the enemy was headed. He caught the flash of sun off steel. There it was again. He knew what he was seeing. The Saracens had fled too easily. They were laying a trap. John had to tell Richard. It was his duty. Instead, he reined in. To hell with duty. To hell with Richard. The rest of the knights charged on to their doom.

Guy flashed past him. 'Richard!' he was shouting as he spurred his horse after the king. 'Richard! We must stop! Stop!'

★

Yusuf sat in the saddle and watched as the Frankish knights thundered across the plain, driving his men before them. The mamluks and Bedouin and Turkmen skirmishers were racing towards the hills, keeping just close enough to ensure that the Franks followed. Yusuf nodded in satisfaction. 'They have taken the bait, Saqr. It is time we withdrew. Give the signal.'

Saqr blew a long blast on his horn, and other horns answered. Yusuf turned his horse and spurred to a canter. His khaskiya, five hundred strong, came after him. The hills loomed before Yusuf, and then he was amongst them, cantering along a twisting path between two high slopes. He rounded a corner and reined to a halt. Two hundred of his spearmen waited just ahead in ranks ten deep. Archers crouched high on the slopes to either side. Once the Franks rode into the trap, more spearmen would cut off their escape.

Yusuf turned his horse on to a trail that zigzagged up the slope to his left. Az-Zahir waited atop the hill. Yusuf had given him charge of the ambushes.

'All is ready?' he asked his son.

'It will be a slaughter, Father.'

From the hilltop, Yusuf had a good view of the coastal plain. His men were nearing the hills now, and the Frankish knights were still in pursuit. Beyond them, the field was littered with hundreds of dead, mostly his men. Along the coast, the Christian foot-soldiers were continuing into Arsuf. Yusuf looked back to the retreat. The first of his men had reached the hills. He saw a dozen mamluks gallop past on the trail at the base of the hill. The spearmen opened ranks to let them pass through. Four Frankish knights had followed the mamluks. They rounded the corner and charged straight on to the spearmen's lances. Their horses fell, and the knights were cut down.

More mamluks were entering the hills to Yusuf's left and right, with a handful of Franks in pursuit. The main body of knights was galloping closer and closer. They were almost to the hills when a horn sounded. It blew again and again, and the Frankish charge stopped just short of the hills. The knights turned and cantered back towards Arsuf.

'*Ya Allah*!' Az-Zahir cursed. 'Why did they turn back?'

Yusuf thought he knew. John. His friend would have anticipated the ambushes. Once again, he had put his duty to the Franks ahead of his friendship with Yusuf. Damn him! Yusuf had needed this victory, and not just to stop Richard. Each night brought more desertions, and Al-Mashtub reported that the men of Al-Jazirah were still bitter that Yusuf had not let them attack at Acre when Richard murdered the garrison. A victory would have put an end to their grumbling. With defeat, it would only grow louder.

'Shall I order the men to give chase, Father?'

'No.' Perhaps Yusuf could turn this setback to his advantage. 'Have the army withdraw beyond the hills. I want no skirmishers out tomorrow during the Franks' march to Jaffa. Let them think they have driven us off with a great victory. Inshallah, it will make them careless, and then we will strike again.'

SEPTEMBER 1191: JAFFA

Yusuf pushed a leafy branch out of the way as he crept forward through a stand of trees. The thick undergrowth scratched against his leather breeches and tore at the dark caftan that covered his armour. He reached the edge of the woods and found Az-Zahir waiting. His son pointed across the coastal plain to where Jaffa sat, a quarter-mile distant. In the hazy light of early dawn, Yusuf could just make out the ruins of the fortress sitting high on a hill overlooking the city. His men had destroyed it and torn down the city wall before the Franks invested the town. Yusuf squinted and could see smoke against the pale sky. Campfires. The nobles had taken up residence in the city, but most of their men were camped in tents beyond the walls. They had yet to build a palisade. Why would they? They believed they had routed Yusuf's army.

Yusuf turned to his son. Az-Zahir had command of Yusuf's scouts. He had been watching the Franks ever since the battle of Arsuf, five days ago. 'You say you have seen men leaving the city?'

Az-Zahir nodded. 'Heading north to Acre.'

'How many?'

'Hundreds. Thousands maybe.'

'Are they going for supplies?'

'I think not. They take no wagons, and those who return are empty-handed. Something else draws them.'

Yusuf could guess what that was. Since the fall of Acre, Franks had been flooding into the city from overseas. The merchants, farmers and craftsmen who had fled after the fall of Jerusalem were returning. And with them came whores, eager to service the men of Richard's army.

'You have done well, my son. Stay here. Let me know at once if the Franks make ready to march.'

'Yes, Father.'

Yusuf made his way through the stand of trees to where a dozen members of his khaskiya waited with his horse. He cantered back to his camp, which was hidden beyond the hills two miles from Jaffa. He had ordered his emirs to gather when he left that morning, and he found them crowded into his tent. Qaraqush, his old companion-in-arms, stood beside Al-Mashtub, who leaned on a staff to spare his ruined knee. Al-Afdal stood with two of Yusuf's younger sons, who had joined the army after Arsuf. Mas'ud was now sixteen, and Yaqub, fourteen. Yusuf had hardly recognized them when they arrived. They had been children when last he saw them, and now they were young men, their sparse beards filled out with kohl. Muhammad and Nu'man stood with dozens of lesser emirs from the Al-Jazirah. Yusuf frowned. He had only asked for his closest advisors. The presence of these additional men boded ill.

He addressed his emirs curtly. 'Today, we march on Jaffa. The Franks think us defeated and their pride has made them careless. The city is but poorly defended. They have not built a proper palisade, and many of their men are gone to Acre. We will charge in crescent formation, cutting them off from all escape. Al-Afdal will command the right wing and Az-Zahir, the left. I will have charge of the centre. You all know your positions, and you know your duty. The eyes of Allah are upon us. Let us make this a day of glory in his name. Let us drive the Franks back into the sea from whence they came!'

There was a time – before Acre, before Arsuf – when such a speech would have been met with cheers. But today the emirs made not a sound. They shifted uncomfortably, unwilling to meet his gaze. Yusuf felt a twinge in his gut. Something was wrong.

It was Muhammad who finally spoke. 'Perhaps it would be better to wait a few days before we strike,' he suggested in his silky voice. 'The Franks will be more vulnerable on the march, once they have left Jaffa.'

'They will not leave until they have finished repairing the walls and the city is lost to us. And when they do march, they will do so ready to fight. I tell you that the time to attack is now. Jaffa is only weakly held.'

'Even in its ruined state, the citadel will not be easy to take,' Muhammad countered. 'The Franks will take shelter there, and we will find ourselves entangled in another siege, as at Acre. I need not remind you how that ended.'

'Jaffa is not Acre. The Franks have only half as many men. The wall is in ruins. And this time, we have the element of surprise.'

'I wonder why are you are eager to attack,' Nu'man said in his rumbling baritone, 'when you refused to strike the infidel outside Acre, after they massacred our men.' Several emirs grunted their agreement. The pain in Yusuf's gut sharpened.

'If you want vengeance,' he responded, 'then you can have it now.'

'How can we know this is not a trap?' Nu'man demanded. 'This Lionheart is a clever man. He bested us at Acre. He anticipated our ruse at Arsuf. Surely he would not leave his men defenceless.'

'He is clever but arrogant. He thinks us defeated and has let down his guard. The city is ours for the taking!' No one spoke. His men's eyes were fixed on the carpeted ground. Yusuf felt anger rising within him, pushing aside the pain in his gut. His fists clenched. 'Has Richard so unmanned you that you fear to face him? I am your king! Have you forgotten your duty?'

'We have done our duty and more, Malik,' Nu'man replied. 'We have travelled far from our lands. I have not seen my wife or my children in more than two years. All that time, I have been at your side. My men have fought your battles. They have suffered hunger and cold.'

'Perhaps if we were paid the gold we are owed——' Muhammad started.

Yusuf's jaw clenched. It was all he could do not to strike Muhammad. The fate of the kingdom was at stake, and Muhammad spoke of gold like some merchant. 'The Franks carry with them the gold they took from Acre. You will have your coin when they are defeated.'

'If they are defeated,' Muhammad countered. 'Pay us now if you wish me by your side in today's battle. My men are done fighting for promises.' The other emirs of Al-Jazirah added their assent.

Muhammad was a lost cause. He had always been more of a courtier than a warrior. Yusuf turned to Nu'man. 'We have fought side by side many times, friend. I have saved your life, and you, mine. You would rebel against me?'

'I am no rebel, Malik. I would fight for you even now. But my men will not.'

Yusuf's hand went to his sword. 'Then go!' he shouted. 'Go! Leave my tent before I have your heads!' The emirs hurried out, but Qaraqush remained behind. 'I should have them all executed,' Yusuf muttered.

'Your emirs are not to blame, Malik. Nu'man spoke true: the men have no heart for a fight. They fear the Lionheart.'

'What sort of king am I, when I cannot command my own men?' Yusuf went to a table to pour a glass of water, but then flung it to the ground. 'Curse them all! We could have won!'

'What will you do, Malik?'

Yusuf rubbed his beard — more grey than black now — and could feel the sharp angles of his cheekbones. He felt every one of his fifty-three years. He wanted nothing more than to return to Damascus, to spend his days with Shamsa. But that was not to be. He forced himself to stand straight.

'Qaraqush, you will send men to destroy Ramlah, Lydda and Latrun. Take what crops are ripe from the fields and burn the rest. I will ride for Ascalon to tear down its walls. If I cannot stop Richard, then I will leave him nothing to conquer.'

Chapter 23

Black smoke roiled up from the base of the wall of Ascalon, stinging Yusuf's eyes and making him wrinkle his nose. His horse whinnied and tossed its head, and he tightened his grip on the reins. His men were burning the wooden supports that held up this last stretch of wall. To either side, the wall had already come down. Beyond the piles of rubble, a cloud of dark smoke hung over the city. Yusuf's men had set fire to it that morning. The last stretch of wall began to shake and then collapsed with a roar like thunder, causing Yusuf's horse to shy. He patted its neck, pulling a fold of his keffiyeh over his face as the cloud of smoke and dust thrown up by the collapse rolled forward to engulf him.

Beside him, Qaraqush coughed and spat. 'That's it.' The grizzled mamluk's voice was sombre. 'When we took Ascalon four years ago, I saw to the reinforcement of those walls. I never dreamt I'd be the one to tear them down.'

'It had to be done.' Yusuf's words were for him as much as for Qaraqush. The destruction of the city left him feeling queasy. Or perhaps it was the acrid smell of smoke that had turned his stomach. 'Richard will not be able to use Ascalon as a base for an attack on Egypt. That is all that matters.'

He rode away, his horse's hooves kicking up clouds of ash as he crossed a field of burnt crops. Beyond the field, he came to the impromptu market that had sprung up. The people of

Ascalon were selling their possessions before fleeing south to Gaza or inland to Hebron or Jerusalem. They glared as they stepped aside to let him pass. Yusuf did not blame them for their anger. He had destroyed their homes and turned them into refugees; poor refugees, for the most part. They would be lucky to get a fraction of what their belongings were worth. Yusuf saw a glass merchant selling cups that would normally fetch a dirham each for only one copper. Another man was practically giving away dark wood furniture inlaid with ivory and mother of pearl. The largest crowd had gathered around the horse market. 'Four hundred dinars,' the horse merchant cried as he auctioned off a bony old nag. 'Four hundred and fifty. Five hundred dinars!' The horse in question would not have brought fifty dinars three weeks ago, but the people of Ascalon were desperate for pack animals to carry their possessions. Yusuf came upon a field of red tents, where young women were selling the only thing they had: themselves. He spurred his horse to a canter and left the market behind.

His brother Selim was waiting inside his tent with letters in hand. Yusuf frowned. Of late, each letter brought only bad news. He had been avoiding Imad ad-Din, which was no doubt why his secretary had sent Selim with the day's post. Yusuf had a sudden desire to turn, mount his horse and ride away. Instead, he lowered himself on to his camp-stool with a sigh.

'What news, Brother?'

'Your son Az-Zahir writes from Ramlah. The city has been burned.' Selim flipped through several more letters. 'Al-Mashtub reports the same from Lydda. He has moved on to burn Latrun.'

Each name was like a punch to the gut. It was his duty to protect these towns, and he had ordered their destruction. But Egypt was safe. That was what mattered. 'We will leave tomorrow to protect the road to Jerusalem. Anything else?'

'This is why I came.' Selim produced a longer letter, written in a graceful hand. 'The Caliph writes.'

Yusuf had sent letter after letter requesting aid from the caliph in Baghdad. He searched Selim's face, trying to anticipate whether the news was good or bad. 'Is he sending men? Gold?'

'He writes of our nephew. Ubadah has laid siege to Akhlat. The city's ruler has called on the Artuqids to support him and has written to the Caliph, who has promised to intervene on his behalf. The Caliph says that if you do not curb Ubadah, then there will be war.'

Yusuf massaged his temples. He could not afford to become embroiled in a war in the east, or to anger the caliph. The men from Al-Jazirah were already on the verge of rebellion. If the caliph denounced him, then they would mutiny. And that would be just the beginning. He would find himself facing down uprising in his own kingdom. He shook his head. 'I sent Ubadah east hoping that time away would cool his passions.'

'You did all you could for the boy, Brother, but he has always been impetuous. If you wish, I will ride east. I will deal with Ubadah as I did with our cousin, Nasir ad-Din.'

Yusuf knew it was what he should do. It was, no doubt, what the Lionheart would have done. But he was not Richard, and Ubadah was no more to blame in this than he himself was. Perhaps if Yusuf had not lied to Ubadah, things would have been different. 'No, Brother. I'll not murder my own nephew.'

'The Saladin I knew—'

'I said no!' Yusuf continued in a softer tone. 'I have seen my reflection, Brother. Richard showed it to me at Acre, and I did not like what I saw.'

'Yes, Brother.'

'Go now. I will write to Ubadah myself.'

'God curse the craven bastard!' Richard roared as he threw his cup of wine across the tent. The contents splashed all over the white robes of Bishop Walter. 'Poisoned wells and burnt fields; this is not war, it is cowardice!' Richard glared about the tent as if daring his lords to contradict him. John was tempted to tell him that Richard's Norman ancestors had behaved little differently when they subdued England, but he held his tongue. He could not afford to anger Richard. Not today. Their army had shrunk with each passing day as men deserted to Jaffa or Acre. They were losing the war despite not having lost a battle. Perhaps Richard would listen now. Perhaps John could save the Holy Land before it was completely ruined.

The king poured another cup of wine. He drained it and wiped his mouth with the back of his hand. 'Saladin will not stop me. We do not have the supplies to reach Egypt, but the land of the Nile is not why I came to the Holy Land. Blanchemains, you will set the men to rebuilding the wall of Ascalon.'

'Forgive me for asking, but to what end, Your Grace? The city has been burned. There is nothing here to defend.'

'There is Jerusalem. I mean to take it and hold it. Ascalon must be strong to protect the Kingdom from invasion from Egypt. Now go.' Richard went to refill his cup.

John remained behind as the other lords trooped out. 'I would speak with you, Your Grace.'

Richard's brow furrowed. 'I have little patience for talk today. Do not waste your words, priest.'

'You must make peace with Saladin.'

Richard's eyes widened. He lowered his cup and began to laugh, softly at first, but then so loudly that his whole body shook. 'Thank you, John,' he gasped when he had recovered. 'Thank you. I needed a good laugh.'

'It was no jest, Your Grace.'

Richard's good humour was gone in an instant. 'Then you must be mad. Why should I make peace with a man who flees before me, who has yet to defeat me in battle?'

'You have not lost, it is true, but what have you won? You are lord over burnt fields and ruined cities.'

'Cities can be rebuilt.'

'And who will people them? The men in these lands are Muslim and Syrian Christian. They have more in common with one another than they do with you. They will betray you at the first chance.'

'Why should they? The Kingdom of Jerusalem stood for a hundred years before I arrived. The people served its kings well enough. They will serve again, and the Kingdom will stand a hundred years more after I am gone.'

'Only if you make peace, my lord. Think of what will happen if you take the Holy City. Your force is made up of pilgrims. They will pray at the altars and then they will return home. Your army will melt away, but the Saracens will remain. We must make peace with them if you wish to keep the lands you have conquered.'

'I swore a vow to retake Jerusalem, John. I will not be forsworn.'

'I do not ask you to halt your campaign, Your Grace. But you must think now to what will come after Jerusalem. Let me go to Saladin. I will speak with him on your behalf. I will make certain that we keep what you have gained.'

'That is not enough. I want Jerusalem, and all the lands west of the Jordan, as it was before. And we must have the True Cross.'

'And if I secure all of that?'

'Then you are a miracle worker, John.' Richard scratched his beard while he thought. He nodded. 'Go and work your miracle. Talk will cost us nothing. Take Humphrey of Toron with you. He is well known to the Saracens. Craft a peace if you can. Perhaps Saladin will be fool enough to give it to you.'

OCTOBER 1191: RAMLAH

'Conrad believes there can be peace between you and him.'

Yusuf studied the man before him. Reginald of Sidon had arrived at his camp in Ramlah two days before. Yusuf had made him wait before seeing him. The old Frankish lord was completely bald. He had ruddy cheeks and liver spots marked his forehead. He claimed to speak on behalf of Conrad, who styled himself the true king of Jerusalem.

'Conrad defied me at Tyre,' Yusuf said. 'He fought for more than a year at the siege of Acre. Now one of my most implacable foes seeks peace. What does he want in return?'

'Only what is his due. Richard has given the crown to Guy, but none of the barons support him. The throne is rightly Conrad's.'

'I am a Muslim. It is not for me to make Christian kings.'

'No, but with Conrad's help, you can drive off Richard. And with Richard gone, there will be no one to support Guy.'

'Conrad's help? His men will fight beside mine?'

Reginald nodded. 'He will help you retake Acre. In return, you will grant him Sidon and Beirut, along with Tyre. The rest of the Holy Land is yours.'

'Tyre, Sidon and Beirut. That is a high price.'

'It is a just price to help rid you of the Lionheart.'

As Yusuf sat back to consider this, Saqr stepped into the tent. He came to Yusuf and whispered in his ear. 'More envoys, Malik. From Richard.'

'Who?'

'Humphrey of Toron and John of Tatewic.'

'Selim will meet with Humphrey. Have John shown to a tent, somewhere private.' Yusuf turned back to Reginald. 'I will think on what you have said. Conrad will have my answer soon.'

Yusuf stood, and Reginald did likewise. The Frankish lord bowed and was shown out by a pair of guards. Yusuf poured himself a glass of water and went to stand before a table covered with a map of Palestine. The towns now held by the Franks were marked in red. Tripoli, Antioch, Tyre, Acre, Caesarea, Arsuf, Jaffa, Ascalon. He had lost almost the entire coast. Richard would turn inland now. Where would the king's conquest end? Jerusalem? Damascus even?

Yusuf found Saqr waiting for him outside his tent. 'Take me to John.'

'This way, Malik.'

Saqr led the way to a small tent near by. 'Wait outside,' Yusuf told him. 'Make certain we are not overheard.' He entered to find John seated cross-legged on the carpeted floor and sipping from a cup of water. He rose at once. He was wearing mail, with a surcoat bearing Richard's arms. He bowed.

'As-salaamu 'alaykum, Yusuf. Thank you for seeing me.'

'This meeting did not happen. You will let your king know that I did not dignify his emissaries by meeting with them.'

'I understand.'

They studied one another for a moment. John's sandy hair had continued to silver, but he looked as strong as ever. Yusuf gestured to the lions on his surcoat. 'What does your king wish to tell me?'

'He seeks peace.'

Yusuf's eyebrows arched. 'The Lionheart wishes for peace? Forgive me if I do not believe you, John.'

'You know me, Yusuf. I would not lie to you. This war does no one any good. Our armies are bleeding one another to death, but it is the common people who suffer most of all. Thousands have lost their homes, and where will they go? The land is utterly ruined. Famine will soon be upon us. We need peace, both of us.'

'If you had wanted peace, then you would have let Richard ride into my trap at Arsuf. Your king would be dead or on a boat for England, and my kingdom would be at peace.'

'It is not I who turned Richard back, Yusuf.'

'*Hmph.*' Yusuf did not believe it. He knew John too well. 'What of your honour?'

'There are more important things than honour, friend.'

'Such as?'

'Peace.'

'Peace is hard-bought after so much blood.'

'But not impossible. There are three points at issue: Jerusalem, the land, and the Cross. Jerusalem is holy to us, and Richard has sworn to take it. He will not give up that quest so long as he lives. As for the land, he asks for nothing that was not already ours: the territory between the coast and the Jordan. The True Cross is only a piece of wood to you, but to us it has great importance. Return it, give us Jerusalem, and withdraw across the Jordan, and you will have peace.'

Yusuf's forehead creased. At length, the corner of his mouth twitched in the beginnings of a smile. 'You are jesting, John.'

'Those are Richard's terms.'

'Those are not terms; they are insults. Jerusalem is ours as much as it is yours, as sacred to us as it is to you. You say Richard will fight for Jerusalem unto the death. Tell your king that he will find us no less willing to sacrifice our lives for the city. Richard has no claim to the lands west of the Jordan. They were ours first. Your ancestors only took them because we were divided and weak. We are strong now. If Richard wants those lands, then let him try to take them. As for the True Cross, I am well aware of its importance to your faith. It will not be surrendered except in exchange for something of equal value.'

'I told Richard that you would respond thus.'

'Then you must have also told him that there can be no peace between us.'

'If you reject peace, he will march on Jerusalem.'

'Let him come.'

'You are a brave man, Yusuf. I know that. But you are not a fool. You have not beaten Richard yet. You do not know him as I do. He is cruel and fickle, but he is clever, too, and a warrior unlike any I have known. Even you.'

'I know him well enough, John. I know that he will only wipe his arse with any treaty I make with him. He gave his word at Acre, and afterwards he slaughtered my men. I would as soon try to make peace with a lion as with the Lionheart.'

'He is savage, yes, but what has he done that you would not

do? You poisoned the waters at Acre. Thousands of men died shitting themselves as a result. You slaughtered the Templar and Hospitaller prisoners after Hattin. Your killed your Frankish prisoners at Acre.'

Yusuf scowled and rubbed his forehead with his palm. 'Acre was not my doing. As to the others, I had no choice. I fought for Allah. I did what I did in his name.'

'Richard also fights for God.'

'I am no Richard!' Yusuf snapped.

'Then make peace. It is the innocent who will suffer if you do not, Yusuf. Your people cannot eat revenge. They cannot eat victory. How many lives are you willing to sacrifice in the name of Allah?'

There was a fire in Yusuf's belly. John did not know the worst of it. Yusuf had sacrificed those closest to him: his father, Asimat, Al-Salih and Turan. Even those he spared, he could not save. His message to Ubadah had arrived too late. 'Your son is dead,' he murmured.

John blinked in shock. His face went pale and he was silent for a long time. 'How?' he finally managed. 'When?'

'I received the news three days ago. He took an arrow through the eye while doing battle outside Akhlat . . .' Yusuf's voice trailed off. He should never have sent Ubadah away. His nephew had died hating him. Yusuf was tired of war, tired of death. He looked up, his brown eyes meeting John's blue ones. 'I want peace as much as you, friend. But how? I'll not turn over to Richard all that I have fought for these many years.'

'I would never ask that. If you listen to me, there might be a way for both sides to have what they wish.'

'How?'

'A marriage: your brother Selim and Richard's sister, Joan of Sicily. They would live in Jerusalem and divide the Kingdom between them. The current Frankish possessions would be in her hands, and the Muslim possessions in his. Their marriage would craft a peace that lasted. Their children would be kings of Franks and Saracens alike. They would unite the Holy Land for all time.'

Yusuf had never even considered such a thing. The Franks were the enemy, to be fought and defeated. Yet what John said made sense. 'And this Joan will agree? She will marry a Muslim?'

'She will.'

'And Richard?'

'If it means a permanent peace and the freedom of Franks to settle in Jerusalem, then yes. I am sure of it.' John touched his arm. 'It is what we dreamed of long ago, Yusuf. There does not have to be war between our peoples. We can make this a land of peace and plenty, where all are welcome.'

Peace. Could it really be so easy? Yusuf prayed that it was so. 'Very well.' He embraced John and kissed him on both cheeks. 'Very well! Tell your king that I agree.'

NOVEMBER 1191: ASCALON

The sun was sinking into the Mediterranean when John spied Ascalon on the horizon. 'There she is.'

Humphrey nodded. They had talked very little during the two-day journey from Ramlah, where Yusuf's army had been camped. Humphrey was in a grim mood. His week of meetings with Selim had yielded no compromise. He believed his mission had been a failure. John and Yusuf had agreed to keep their plan secret. Yusuf was unsure of how his men would react. John had the same fears regarding Humphrey. The lord of Toron had been raised in the Holy Land, and though he spoke fluent Arabic, he would never view the Saracens as anything other than the enemy. He would not understand. John would speak to Richard first. If the king approved of his plan, then Humphrey would learn soon enough.

As they neared the city, John saw hundreds of men at work along the wall. Most were clearing away rubble and stacking the fallen stones. It was backbreaking work. In the areas they had cleared, stonemasons were rebuilding the wall. John spotted Blanchemains standing in the shade of a canvas and shouting orders. Humphrey guided his horse towards the king's lord high steward.

'How goes it, Leicester?' Humphrey asked.

Blanchemains wiped sweat from his brow. 'Rebuilding the wall is devilish work. Hundreds of men have deserted to Acre. Richard had to go there himself to bring them back. He returned in a foul mood. I hope you bring good news to cheer him.'

'Where is the King?' John asked.

'In the city. He has taken up residence in the church rectory. You should find it easily enough. It is one of the few buildings still standing.'

John and Humphrey rode through a gap in the wall. The streets of Ascalon were empty. Only a few stone buildings still stood amongst the wreckage of charred beams and ash. The church loomed over it all. It was in the Roman style, with a colonnaded front framed by twin towers. One of the guards under the colonnade took their horses, and another led them into the dim interior. They passed through the nave and out through the south transept to what had been the rectory before Richard took over. The king's quarters were upstairs. The door was closed and guarded by two knights, including Henry de Ferriers, the young man that John had fought on his arrival in London. Henry looked down his nose at John.

'The King is occupied.'

'We have urgent business,' John replied.

'He asked not to be disturbed.' Henry gestured to a bench along the wall. 'You can wait if you wish.'

They sat. A window on the wall opposite looked out over the sea. John watched the sun disappear into the water and the sky turn black as ink before the door to Richard's room finally opened. A plump young woman stepped out. She looked to be a native Christian, with curly dark hair and skin the brown of tanned leather. She lowered her gaze and hurried away down the stairs. Richard came after her, tying a silk robe about him. He noticed Humphrey and John. 'High time the two of you returned. Come.'

The room they entered was dominated by a table spread with maps and a bed large enough to sleep five. Richard went to a smaller table by the window and poured himself a glass of wine. 'What does Saladin say to my terms?'

'I met with his brother, Your Grace,' Humphrey said. 'Your offer upset him. He rejected it.'

'*Hmph*. Your negotiations have at least bought us time. The wall is well underway.'

John stepped forward. 'I have something more to report, my lord.' Humphrey's eyes widened at this.

'Speak,' Richard told him.

'I would prefer to speak with you alone, Your Grace.'

Richard nodded. 'Humphrey, leave us.' The king waited until the door had closed. 'Out with it, John.'

'Saladin is willing to make peace.'

Richard choked on his wine. 'What?' he spluttered. 'He has accepted my terms?'

'The True Cross will be returned, Jerusalem will be Christian, and the lands west of the Jordan will be under a Christian queen.'

'I cannot believe it. You are a miracle worker!' Richard's brow creased. 'A queen, you said? What of Guy? What have you done, priest?'

'I have crafted a peace as you commanded. Saladin's brother, Saif ad-Din, will marry your sister, and together they will rule as king and queen. Jerusalem will be open to Christians and Muslims alike. Those parts of the Kingdom currently in our power will be ruled by Joan, the rest—'

Richard slammed his glass of wine down on the table so forcefully that it shattered and wine spilled over the maps, staining the Holy Land red as if with blood. 'Are you mad, John?

Joan cannot marry an infidel. I will not sell her to some desert savage!'

'Speak to her, Your Grace. I believe she will accept the marriage willingly.'

Richard shook his head. 'My sister married to a Saracen,' he grumbled. He went to pour a new glass of wine.

'The marriage will win you everything you seek, my lord. Jerusalem will be in Christian hands.'

'Christian and Muslim.'

'That is the only way it can be held. This is their land, Your Grace. There will always be more Saracens than Christians. Even if you conquer Jerusalem, it will be lost again someday. This marriage will secure it for all time.'

'*Hmph.*' Richard sipped more wine. 'We would have to get the Pope's blessing. That will take three months at least. In the meantime, I can march on Jerusalem, and if I do not take it . . .' His eyes took on a far-away look. Finally, he turned to John. 'Go to my sister. She is in Ascalon, in a home not far from here. If she agrees to this marriage, then I will send a messenger to the Pope. With his approval, Joan will marry this infidel.'

'Yes, Your Grace.' John bowed and left. That had gone better than he could have hoped. For the first time, John dared to hope his plan might actually work. One of the guards outside the church showed him to the home where Joan was staying. It was a stone building and had thus survived the fire, but the door was new and black soot streaked the walls in the entryway. A maid led John to Joan's chambers. The queen was reading at a window.

She set her book aside when she saw him. 'Leave us,' she told her maid. When the door had closed, Joan fixed him with an appraising gaze. 'What brings you to me, father? I did not think to see you again.'

'I bring good news, my lady. I have found you a husband amongst the Saracens.'

Joan's eyes widened, and her mouth hung open in shock. 'Who?'

'Saif ad-Din, the brother of Saladin. He is a good man, kind and honest. You and he will rule from Jerusalem as king and queen.'

'And what does my brother say of this marriage?'

'He approves. If you are willing, then all that is needed is the Pope's blessing.'

'So I am to be a queen again.' Joan grinned, her eyes crinkling at the corners. For the first time since John had met her, she looked like the young woman she was. She stood and embraced him. 'You have my thanks.' She kissed him on each cheek.

John could feel himself flushing. 'I only did my duty, my lady,' he said gruffly.

'You did what my own family would not. They treated me like a prized mare to be sold for profit. You are more of a brother to me than Richard, more of a father than Henry.'

Her words made John think of Ubadah. John had abandoned the boy as a child. His own son had hated him. Now he was dead. What sort of a father had he been? 'I am glad to have been of service,' he murmured.

Joan did not notice his sombre tone. 'I will not forget what you have done,' she said brightly. 'When I am queen, you will have an honoured place at my court.'

Chapter 24

John rode with his head down. Rain pattered off the hood of his cloak and dripped through the fabric to wet his hair and trickle down his back. He rode past foot-soldiers marching under heavy packs through ankle-deep mud. Hills rose on either side, and the water ran in rivulets down their slopes. John looked ahead. They were nearly to the village of Beit Nuba, which sat only twelve miles from Jerusalem, but all he could see was a curtain of rain.

His horse lurched suddenly as it slipped in the mud, and it scrambled for a footing. John felt himself falling backwards and grabbed for the stallion's mane. He just managed to stay in the saddle, and the horse recovered.

'Careful, priest!' Richard called as he cantered up alongside. The king wore armour but no helmet, and his long, reddish-blond hair had been matted by the rain. 'If this rain keeps up, I'll need another miracle from you to dry things out.'

Richard moved on before John could respond. The king stopped here and there to jest with the men or shout encouragement. The men responded in kind. They were in good spirits despite the cold rain, for the goal that had brought them from all over Europe was within their reach. Richard had not been content to wait for the Pope's reply regarding Joan's marriage. 'Peace is well and good,' he had told John, 'but I'll try my hand at victory, first.' He had moved the army to Ramlah at the end of November. Now, after more than a month spent gathering supplies and men, they were on the road to Jerusalem. John had never been much inclined towards prayer, even after he became a priest, but he was praying now. He knew what had happened the last time the Franks took Jerusalem, and he knew Richard. He prayed that God would spare the city. It was as close to a home as any place he knew.

'Hellfire!'

The shout came from John's left. He looked and saw a sergeant sitting in the mud, an arrow protruding from his shoulder. Something buzzed just beyond John's head. He pushed back his hood. He could hear arrows hissing all around him now. One embedded in the pommel of his saddle. Bright blue feathers decorated the end of the shaft.

John took his mace from his belt. 'Form up, men! Shields out!'

Richard came galloping back down the line. 'Tighten ranks! Get those shields up before they make pincushions of you all!' he roared as he passed.

The foot-soldiers quickly unslung their shields from their backs and closed ranks, forming a moving wall on either side of the cavalry. John found himself riding beside Humphrey and Guy.

An arrow struck Guy in the chest. 'Strewth!' he cursed as he snapped off the shaft. 'I told Richard not to march in winter. Nothing but mud and rain.'

John peered to either side. The slopes were still lost in the rain. There was no sign of the enemy. Richard galloped up the line once more and reined in near them. He looked like a porcupine, with more than a dozen arrows protruding from his armour. His surcoat and horse were spattered with mud. Yet he was grinning fiercely. 'They think to make target practice of us, but we will give those sons of whores a taste of our steel. At the sound of my horn, the infantry will part and the knights will charge the hills.'

'But Your Grace—!' Guy protested. It was no use. Richard was already galloping away. 'He acts as if I must jump at his every command. I am a king, too.'

Humphrey was squinting as he tried to see through the curtain of rain. 'How are we supposed to charge an enemy that we cannot see?'

Guy nodded. 'We will become lost in those hills. This is madness, I tell you.'

'Better that than sit here and let them feather our arses,' John replied.

The horn sounded, its wailing call muffled by the rain. All down the line, the infantry split, opening up gaps for the knights to ride through. John tightened his grip on his mace and dug his spurs into his horse. '*Yalla!*' he cried as he galloped out past the foot-soldiers. He could hear other knights charging after him. Their horses' hooves did not thunder; they squelched and splattered through the mud. John's mount reached the slope and began to struggle up it. The beast was knee deep in mud. John could see nothing ahead but rain and more mud. The next moment, shapes emerged: men with bows. One of them drew back and aimed straight at him. The archer let fly from no more than ten yards away. John felt a blow, as if he had been punched in the breast. The arrowhead cut through his mail and the padded vest beneath to lodge in the left side of his chest. Gritting his teeth against the pain, he raised his mace. He was on the archer before he could nock another arrow. John's mace caught him on the top of the head, crushing his helmet. John was past before he saw the man fall. He swung at another Saracen. The archer had raised his bow in a vain effort to protect himself. John's mace splintered it and went on to make a bloody mess of the man's face.

John reined to a halt atop the slope. Most of the Saracens were fleeing now, slipping and sliding as they sprinted down the far side of the hill. To his right, John saw Humphrey laying about with his sword. Guy came up alongside him and hacked down an archer. John caught a flash of movement out of the corner of his eye and turned his horse just in time to avoid a blow. The Saracen's blade missed him and glanced off his horse's flank. The beast whinnied and bolted down the far slope. The pain in his chest forgotten, John struggled to stay in the saddle. Then his horse lost its footing and fell, throwing him. He landed on his back and began to slide down the slick slope. On the way down, he took the legs out from under one fleeing archer, and then another. All three men careered on together in a tangle of arms and legs, before coming to a stop just short of where the Saracen horses waited. John tried to get to his feet but slipped and went to one knee just before a sword sliced over his head. He slammed his mace into his attacker's knee. The Saracen screamed as he crumpled to the ground.

John stood and spun just in time to turn aside a knife thrust from the other Saracen. He swung backhanded, his mace crunching into the man's face and nearly ripping off his jaw. John heard a splash behind him and spun again. It was a knight riding past on horseback. There was no one left to fight. The Saracen horses were gone. They had all fled. A horn began to sound, calling the Christians back to the column.

There was no sign of John's horse. He slogged back up the hill, slipping and sliding in the mud. He soon had mud in his boots, even in his mouth, and by the time he reached the top of the hill again, he was covered from head to toe. He slid down the far side and arrived just in time to join the end of the column. He trudged into Beit Nuba along with the sergeants. The town consisted of no more than two dozen homes surrounding a small keep. Richard sat on horseback, greeting the men as they straggled in. There were splashes of bright blood mixed with the mud on the king's surcoat.

'Well done, men!' he shouted to the passing sergeants. 'We routed the bastards, sent them running to Jerusalem with their tails between their legs. John! Praise God! Guy said he saw you fall.'

'I did.'

'God spared you, priest. He looks after his own. The tents are up. Go inside and get some warm food inside you. You'll need your strength; we're on to Jerusalem as soon as this cursed rain ends!'

JANUARY 1192: JERUSALEM

Yusuf stood above the Jaffa Gate and watched as his men rode through below him. The rain had slackened during the night and was now falling in a fine mist. A chill had settled over Jerusalem. He could see his men's breath fogging the air. Their armour was spattered with dark mud and dried blood. Some clutched injuries. They rode in silence, their heads hanging.

'Malik,' Al-Afdal called as he approached along the wall. Yusuf's son was covered in black mud. There was a thin cut on his left cheek.

'What happened?' Yusuf demanded. 'I sent you to harass the Christians and slow their march, not to engage in battle.'

'Richard surprised us. The Franks broke formation and their knights charged. It was raining heavily, and we did not see them until they were nearly on us. I – forgive me, Father.'

'The fault is mine, Al-Afdal. I should have led the men myself. See that the injured are cared for, and give the men a double portion of their rations.'

'Yes, Father.' Al-Afdal bit his lip before continuing. 'There is talk amongst your emirs. Some of them feel the battle for Jerusalem is already lost. They – they plan to leave the city this very night.'

Yusuf gripped the stone battlement. *Damn them*! Where did they think they would go? If Jerusalem fell, then Damascus would be next, then Aleppo. 'Have the emirs gather in the palace,' he told Al-Afdal. 'All of them. Then see to your men.'

Al-Afdal bowed and moved away.

'And my son,' Yusuf called after him. 'See that your cheek is tended to.'

'Yes, Father.'

Yusuf turned back to watch his men. The last of them were riding through the gate. 'Allah give me strength,' he whispered. There was no response. There never was. He looked up to the grey sky. Was Allah punishing him for the crimes he had committed, the people he had killed?

He lowered his gaze. There was no use dwelling on such thoughts. The past was past. He must focus on what he could do here and now. To either side of the gate, thousands of men were at work in the ditch that ringed Jerusalem, digging with picks and shovels to deepen it. It was brutally hard work in the cold and rain. Yusuf was using Frankish slaves and prisoners. Above them, mamluks were hanging leather hides and bales of hay from the wall to dampen the impact of siege engines. Yusuf had other men in the fields around the city, blocking up or poisoning the wells for miles around. He thought of what Al-Afdal had told him. It would all be for naught if his men deserted him. The common people were already fleeing – a steady stream of refugees heading out the eastern gate. Those who remained were busy boarding up their windows and doors. From his room in the palace, Yusuf could hear the sound of hammers day and night.

Yusuf had hoped that peace might spare the city, but he was starting to believe that John's plan was only a mirage. Richard had consented; but the weeks had slipped by as the Lionheart prepared his campaign, and no answer had come from Rome. And now it was most likely too late. If Jerusalem fell, it would not matter what response the Pope gave. Yusuf should have accepted Conrad's offer of an alliance.

'Malik.' It was Saqr. 'The emirs have gathered in the palace.'

The palace was only a short walk south from the Jaffa Gate. It had been built by the Frankish kings in the Frankish style. The walls were thick, the windows topped with rounded arches.

But some eastern touches had been adopted. Shallow pools of water sat at the centre of the many courtyards, which were ringed with colonnaded walkways. Not for the first time, Yusuf reflected how strange it was to be walking the halls of his enemies. He had first come to this palace as a hostage to King Amalric. Now he ruled here as king. But for how much longer?

Nearly a hundred emirs were waiting for him in the barrel-vaulted audience chamber. They fell silent as he entered. Yusuf strode through their ranks and turned to face them. He searched their faces. There were his sons: Al-Afdal and Az-Zahir, and the younger ones, Ishaq, Mas'ud and Yaqub. Beside them stood Qaraqush, Al-Mashtub and Saqr. Yusuf had known them since they were young men. Qaraqush's beard was grizzled now, and he was bald. Al-Mashtub had never completely recovered from the fighting at Acre. He would walk with a limp for the rest of his life. Even Saqr, who Yusuf still thought of as a boy, now had a trace of grey in his beard. Yusuf recognized other faces, too. There were men who had fought for his uncle, Shirkuh. There were men of Egypt, Aleppo and Al-Jazirah. Many of them bore scars from their many battles at his side. Yusuf looked from man to man, meeting their eyes. Some held his gaze; others looked away. Yusuf said nothing. He let the silence do its work, let the men who thought to betray him stew in their guilt. That was a trick he had learned from his father. Some of the men began to shift uncomfortably.

Finally, Yusuf spoke. He started softly, so that the men in the back had to lean in to hear. 'When I was a boy, my father told me the story of Jerusalem's fall. After the Franks breached the wall, the city's defenders fled. They left the people behind to suffer. The Franks spared no one; not women, not children, not old men. The streets ran with blood. The alleyways echoed with the screams of the women they violated. I swore that I would avenge their suffering, that I would retake Jerusalem.

'I kept my oath. The city is ours once more. And once more, the Franks are at our gates. Today, you are the defenders of

Islam. Only you can save this city. Only you can protect our people. If you fail, then the streets will run red once more, and not just in Jerusalem but also in Damascus, then Aleppo, Cairo, perhaps even in Baghdad. Our enemies will roll up our lands as if they were rolling up a scroll.' Yusuf paused to let his words take effect. When he spoke again, his voice was firmer.

'That will not happen! I know you. You are more than my men. You are my brothers. You fought at my side when we retook Jerusalem, when we swept through the Franks' Kingdom like a scythe through a field of wheat. You stood firm outside the walls of Acre. And you will stand firm here in Jerusalem.' His voice was growing louder, filling the hall. 'Allah has set this test for us. The lion roars at our gates. This is our greatest battle. This is the line that we cannot let the enemy cross. Will you stand up to defend Islam? To defend our people? Will you fight beside me, my men? My brothers?'

Silence. Yet Yusuf's words had had their effect. The men who had met his gaze before now stood straighter. Many of those who had looked away now had their eyes fixed squarely on the floor. It was Al-Mashtub who finally spoke. 'My lord, you call us your brothers,' the huge mamluk rumbled. 'You honour us, for in truth, we are but your servants and your slaves. You have made us mighty and rich. Before you, we had little more than our necks. They are in your hands. By Allah, I will fight beside you until I die. I know every man here feels the same.'

'Aye! Till the death,' Qaraqush echoed.

There was a murmur of agreement. His speech had won over some of them and would no doubt shame others into staying, but it would not win them all. Yusuf took careful note of those who seemed less than enthusiastic. There were more of them than he would have liked, including some powerful emirs, such as Muhammad. He would need to keep them under close watch.

'You are true warriors,' he said. 'I expected no less from you.

We will stand together and die together, if needs be. And tonight we will feast together to celebrate the bond that unites us. You will be my guests at the palace, and afterwards, you will all stay here, with me.'

'But Malik—' Muhammad began.

'I insist. Until this evening, men.'

As the emirs filed out, Yusuf called for Qaraqush to stay behind. The thick-necked mamluk came to him. 'A powerful speech, Malik.'

'But still only words. I want you to seal the city gates. No one is to leave. Take charge of this yourself, and use only our most trusted men.'

'Of course, Malik.' Qaraqush bowed and left.

Yusuf went in the other direction. He had done all he could. The rest was in the hands of Allah. He would go to Al-Aqsa to pray.

Crack! John blinked awake just as his tent collapsed on top of him. He could hear the wind howling outside. It had snapped his tent pole in half. John was not surprised. Dozens of other tents had already suffered the same fate. He struggled out from under the heavy canvas and into the driving rain. No, not rain. Snow. The fat flakes stung his face, and he shivered. He had slept in his armour, with his cloak wrapped around him, but everything was long since soaked. Richard had decided to wait for the storm to stop before moving on to Jerusalem, but it had yet to let up. John's feet and hands had gone numb with cold the first night they had arrived in Beit Nuba, five days ago. The shallow wound in his chest had become inflamed, making him feverish. That only made the cold worse.

John pulled his damp cloak more tightly about him as he examined the wreckage of his tent. There would be no fixing it so long as this wind lasted. He looked to the sky. The clouds that hung low overhead were lightening. Dawn had broken, such as it was. That meant the cooks would already be at work.

John slogged through ankle-deep mud to the cooks' tents. The endless rain had ruined the stores of biscuit and grain that they had brought, but the men had not gone hungry. A cook handed him a chunk of charred horsemeat. The knights' mounts were dying from cold and lack of feed, but at least they kept the men's bellies full.

John took his meal towards the fort, where he joined a dozen other men eating in the lee of the wall. No one acknowledged him. His fellows were hunched glumly over their breakfasts. The man next to him had blue lips and was shivering so violently that he had difficulty bringing his meat to his mouth. He looked like he might not survive the day. None of them would last much longer if this madness did not end. Someone had to talk sense to Richard.

John finished his breakfast and trudged through the mud to one of the squat houses in the village. Inside, more than twenty nobles were packed into the tiny space, which smelt little better than a latrine. Still, it was dry and warm. These men were the lucky ones. John spotted Balian and stepped over the bodies of sleeping men as he made his way to him. There was snot crusted on Balian's nose and lip, and he was snoring loudly. John shook him awake. 'I would speak with you,' he whispered. 'About Richard.'

Balian nodded. 'Something must be done,' he said as he sat up and picked sleep from his eyes.

'Who else of the great lords feels the same?'

'Humphrey. And Hugh of Burgundy, the French commander. That one hates Richard.'

'Fetch them and meet me at the wall of the fort.'

The cold seemed even sharper when John stepped outside. He returned to the lee of the wall and paced back and forth, stomping his feet in a futile attempt to restore some warmth to them. Balian finally appeared. He was followed by two men. Humphrey's fat cheeks had thinned and there were dark circles under his eyes. Hugh looked far from well. His face was flushed with fever and he was sweating despite the cold. He had taken an arrow to his ankle during the battle of Arsuf, and the wound had festered.

'Thank you for coming.' John spoke loudly to be heard over the screaming wind. 'I am going to speak to Richard. Someone must turn him from this madness.'

Balian nodded. 'We should never have marched in winter. At this rate, Saladin will destroy us without a battle.'

'I am only a priest,' John said. 'Richard will not listen to me alone, but he cannot ignore your counsel. Will you join me?'

'Anything to escape this cursed cold,' Hugh muttered.

The other men nodded.

The guards at the fort gate waved them through. The keep was a simple, two-storey building of white limestone. Richard's chamber was on the second floor. They found the king alone. He was sitting before a roaring fire, a goblet of wine in hand. He gestured for them to enter.

'Your Grace,' John began. 'We would have a word with you.'

Richard scowled. 'You wish to tell me to retreat. I will not do it.'

John exchanged a glance with the other lords. 'I beg you to reconsider,' Hugh urged. 'We cannot take the city, Richard, not in this weather.'

'We can, and we will! The prophet in Sicily foretold that I would not lose a battle in the Holy Land. You were there, John. Tell them.'

'You may not lose a battle, my lord, but you are losing your army nonetheless. Over half the horses are dead, and when the last of them are gone, what will the men eat? Many have deserted already. When the food runs out, they will leave en masse. We must fall back. You cannot fight the rain and snow.'

'I swore to take Jerusalem.'

'It will not happen,' Balian said. 'Not now.'

Richard's brow furrowed and his fist clenched around the

goblet. He hurled it at Balian, who ducked. Wine splashed across John's face and the goblet clattered off the wall. Richard pushed himself up from his chair. 'You are cowards, all of you!' he roared. 'Leave if you wish. Run back to Acre. I will stay here.'

Hugh met his gaze without flinching. 'Then you will die here. Alone.'

'So be it.' Richard turned to stare into the fire.

'There is another way to take the city,' John suggested. 'Peace, Your Grace. We still await the Pope's response regarding Joan's marriage.'

Richard snorted. 'Do not play the fool, John. I agreed to your scheme only to weaken our enemy's resolve and to keep Saladin from allying with Conrad. My sister will never marry a Saracen. And if we turn back now, the advantage will lie with Saladin. He will piss on your precious marriage. Go, all of you. Leave me.'

'The blind fool,' Humphrey grumbled as the lords headed for the door.

John stayed behind. 'You are not the only one whose life will be lost if you stay, Your Grace. Your men will die with you. You will have sacrificed their lives for nothing.'

'I told you to leave,' the king muttered. He went to the window and threw the shutters open. Wet snow swirled inside to melt on the stone floor. 'When will this cursed storm end?' Richard looked to John. 'I fight for God, priest. Why does He thwart me?'

Because your God is not the only one in this fight, John wished to say. Instead, he said, 'You have won great victories, Your Grace. You took Acre, Jaffa and Ascalon. You have saved the Kingdom. God made that possible.'

'And now it seems He is done with me.' Richard shivered and closed the shutters. 'I am not the blind fool that Humphrey thinks me, John. There are French and English, Italians and Germans, Hospitallers and Templars in my army. Jerusalem is all that keeps them from happily slitting one another's throats. With that goal gone, my army will disintegrate. I cannot retreat.'

'If you stay, they will abandon you all the same. Or they will die. You must fall back. Your crusade is over, Your Grace.'

Richard's shoulders slumped. It was the first time John had ever seen him look defeated. 'I am stubborn, John, and sometimes a fool. But I am not a stubborn fool. I'll not throw away the lives of my men. We will fall back to Ascalon.'

'O Allah forgive me; have mercy on me,' Yusuf murmured as he knelt beneath the dome of the Al-Aqsa mosque. He prostrated himself and then sat back on his heels. 'Greeting to you, O Prophet, and the mercy and blessing of Allah. Peace be unto us, and unto the righteous servants of Allah . . .'

The words spilled out with hardly a thought. Yusuf had years of prayers to make up. He had missed them while on the march or while fighting. He could hardly remember a time when he was not at war. He had spent years in the saddle, far from his family. He had done horrible things, all in the name of Allah.

'I bear witness that there is none worthy of worship except Allah, and I bear witness that Muhammad is His servant and messenger.' Yusuf looked to his left. 'Peace be upon you.' He looked right and repeated the phrase. The sound of footsteps, soft on the carpeted floor, came to him as he stood to begin another round of prayer. He turned. It was Az-Zahir.

'Father!' Yusuf's son was grinning. 'A thousand pardons, but I have important news. The Franks are retreating!'

Yusuf bowed his head. Allah had heard his prayers. 'Alhamdulillah.'

'It is a great victory, Father.'

'It is Allah's victory. His storm drove them away.'

'Your emirs are eager to give chase.'

Five days ago, they had been prepared to desert him. Now

they longed to fight. Yusuf shook his head. 'The roads are impassable, and the cold and wet will slacken our bowstrings. Let the storm chase our enemy to the coast. We have held Jerusalem. Soon enough, we will drive the Lionheart back across the sea, his tail between his legs.'

Chapter 25

As John strode through the camp outside Ascalon, he passed a troop of thirty or so men marching north on foot. Hundreds left every day. They were headed for Jaffa, or perhaps Acre. Nothing was being done to stop them. At the edge of the tents, John came upon half a dozen men of Aquitaine trading insults with some English archers. A punch was thrown, and in the blink of an eye a brawl began. More men came running to join. John gave the fisticuffs a wide berth. A week ago, he had tried to stop a fight and had got a black eye for his pains. The English lords only laughed when he told them. 'They are men,' de Preaux had replied. 'They fight.' The lords were blind, too busy hunting and fucking whores to see the truth: Richard's army was falling apart, as he had predicted. The fights were growing nasty. Rifts were appearing in the ranks. A few more months of this, and there would be open war, as there already was in the north where Conrad had joined forces with the Frenchman Hugh of Burgundy to lay siege to Guy in Acre.

John left the brawl behind and crossed the burnt fields, where Syrian Christians were busy ploughing the ash back into the soil. The city wall loomed up ahead. The reconstruction was half completed. That was the one thing that had been accomplished in the two and a half months since the retreat from Jerusalem. John nodded to the guards as he passed through one of the rebuilt gates. The Syrian Christians had begun to filter back into the city, which was alive with the sounds of saws and hammers. To his right, men were busy clearing a site – separating nails, roofing tiles and other pieces that could be salvaged from the rubble. At the centre of town, there was a thriving market in such products. Everywhere, new homes were springing up from the ashes. Some belonged to native Christians; others to nobles who had moved to the city. Ahead, men crowded around an impromptu market in the middle of the street. Men-at-arms were selling goods from a caravan they had raided the day before. John shouldered through the crowd and turned down a narrow side street. He stopped before Joan's home and knocked.

A maidservant answered the door. 'I wish to see your lady,' John told her. 'I have important news.'

Without a word, the maidservant motioned him inside and led the way to Joan's room. The floor and walls were bare. Two trunks sat open on the floor. As John entered, Joan took a robe from the pile of clothes on her bed and folded it before placing it in one of the trunks. She looked up at him and gave a half-smile. 'John, I am pleased to see you.'

He gestured to the trunks. 'What is this?'

'My dear brother is shipping me back to England until he finds a husband for me.'

'Then you already know?'

'I knew before you did. Richard's messenger has returned, and the Pope has forbidden my marriage to Saif ad-Din. But you have my thanks for coming to tell me yourself.'

'It was the least I could do. I am sorry, my lady.'

'You tried to help me, John. That is more than can be said for the rest of Richard's knights.'

'I truly thought I could end this war once and for all.' John shook his head. 'I was a fool. Richard never intended for you to marry Saif ad-Din.'

'My brother is a man of blood, John. Peace comes hard for him, but it will come.'

'Saladin has sent emissaries, but Richard refuses to see them.'

'He will. He must. We have had news from England. Our brother John has made a mess of things. He has driven out the chancellor William Longchamp and taken rule upon himself. There are rumours that he means to ally himself with King Philip and move against Richard's lands in France.'

'If Richard leaves now, there will be civil war between Guy and Conrad's men. Saladin will strike, and this time he will crush us once and for all. The Christians will be driven out.' *And me with them, back to miserable England.*

'Then something must be done. Richard must end their conflict.'

'He has hardly left his chamber since we returned from Beit Nuba. He speaks to no one, not even his closest advisors.'

Joan tapped her index finger against her teeth as she considered this. 'Even as a child, Richard could never stomach defeat. I remember one time when our older brother Henry bested him in a joust. Richard kept to his room for days. He refused to even eat. He has not changed. His failure to take Jerusalem has wounded his pride, and he sulks like a spoilt child. When he was a boy, our mother Eleanor would simply slap him and tell him to behave like a man. Now, it is up to you to rouse him. Take matters into your own hands. If Richard will not make peace, then you must do it.'

John's brow knit. 'I am no king.'

'Nor need you be. Whoever holds the King's seal may speak in his name.'

'But that is treason.'

'What better way to capture my brother's attention?'

John nodded. 'You have my thanks, Lady Joan. I wish you Godspeed on your journey.'

She crossed the room and kissed him gently on the lips. 'Thank you, John of Tatewic, and farewell.'

★

Barons of the Kingdom,

A house divided against itself cannot stand, yet the Kingdom of Jerusalem is divided as never before. French have turned against English, Pisans against Genoese, men of Acre against men of Tyre. Some look to Guy as their king, while others hail Conrad. And when they meet in combat, as at Acre, they fight Saladin's battles for him.

John set the quill aside and massaged his cramping hand. He had already written this same letter six times. He glanced at the heavily embroidered bag of blue velvet beside him on the floor of his tent. The ease with which he had taken it had surprised him. The keeper of the seal, Lord de Ferriers, was staying in a newly built home not far from where Joan lived. He had been out hunting when John arrived. A thin young servant with a blond beard as wispy as peach fuzz had answered the door. John told him that he was on urgent business of the king and had shouldered his way inside. A short search of de Ferrier's chamber had turned up the seal.

John took a silver box from the velvet bag. He undid the latch and opened it. The seal sat inside, nestled on a bed of silk. It was a two-sided silver mould with both sides depicting Richard seated on his throne, a sword in one hand and an orb in the other. To either side of Richard's head was a crescent, and above each crescent, a star emanating six wavy rays. When John had finished his letters to the great lords of the Kingdom, he would pour hot wax into the mould to produce a series of seals. When he affixed them to the letters with ribbons, his words would become those of the king. He took up the quill again.

We must end this strife. I, Richard, called Lionheart, King of England by the grace of God, Duke of Normandy, Aquitaine and Gascony, Lord of Cyprus and Count of Anjou, Maine and Nantes, summon you and your vassal lords to the Haute Cour,

to be held two weeks hence in Acre, on the fifth day of April.
There we will—

'What is the meaning of this?'

Richard stood in the entrance to John's tent. The king was red-faced and held a sword in his hand. John had expected nothing less. He calmly set down his quill and put his lap desk to one side. The letter he had been writing floated off the desk to land at Richard's feet. John rose and bowed. 'Your Grace.'

'Spare me your courtesies, priest. They will not save you.' Richard pointed his sword at the seal. 'What are you doing with that?'

'Serving Your Grace.'

'By stealing from me? By forging decrees in my name?'

John met the king's eyes without flinching. 'Yes.'

Richard speared the letter John had been writing with his sword. He took it from the blade and began to read. The king's forehead creased so deeply that his eyebrows touched. 'What is this council of yours meant to do?' he demanded.

'Choose a king.'

'We have a king: Guy.'

'A king who is little loved by the native barons. A king you appointed. By tradition, the barons have named their own king. At the Haute Cour, they will decide once and for all between Guy and Conrad.'

'This cannot be. Guy is my man. On Cyprus, I promised him a crown.'

'The crown you gave him is tearing the Kingdom apart. Hugh and Conrad are besieging Guy in Acre. Worse still, there are rumours that Conrad will soon sign a treaty with Saladin. A treaty aimed against you, Your Grace. Meanwhile, your army is disintegrating. You have less than five thousand men. You cannot defeat Saladin with so few. Peace is your only option, and we cannot have peace without a true king. If you leave

Guy to rule without the barons' consent, the Kingdom will not survive a year.'

Richard crumpled the letter in his fist. 'You go too far, John. This is treason. I am your king.'

'Then act the part, Your Grace. Stop sulking in your chambers.'

Richard turned a darker shade of crimson. He took a step forward. For a moment, John thought the king would cut him down, but instead, Richard punched him with his free hand, catching John in the jaw and sending him reeling into the wall of the tent. John grabbed at the fabric to steady himself. Richard's mouth was open, and his chest heaving. It took John a moment to realize that the king was laughing silently. His laughter grew in volume until Richard was roaring.

'By God, it feels good to hit someone! You are right, John. I have spent too long drowning in my cups. Call your council. We will settle this matter once and for all, and then I will have my army back.' Richard stood straighter. 'This crusade is not over, John. Far from it. I only need one great victory to break the Saracens. I need only kill Saladin and Jerusalem will be mine.'

MARCH 1192: RAMLAH

'Conrad will be king,' Yusuf said.

Reginald lowered his wine glass. 'He will be pleased to hear it, Malik.'

They were dining alone in Yusuf's tent. A week ago, he had sent an envoy to Tyre, beckoning Reginald here. Yusuf had given up on peace with Richard. After the Lionheart's retreat, he had thought the king would be eager to agree to terms, but Yusuf's envoys had been sent away unheard. If Richard would not make peace, then Yusuf would crush him, even if that meant making an ally of his former enemy, Conrad.

'I agree to the terms you suggested the last time we met,' Yusuf said. 'Conrad will help me reclaim Acre. I will grant him and his heirs Tyre, Sidon and Beirut, to rule as their kingdom forever.'

'And if Richard or Guy lays siege to Tyre?'

'Then I will march to relieve the city. In return, I expect Conrad to supply troops for my battles.'

'It will be done.' Reginald raised his glass. 'To the alliance between our peoples.'

Yusuf held up a glass of water. 'To the defeat of the Lionheart.'

Both men drained their glasses. Reginald took a piece of flat-bread and used it to scoop from a dish of tender chicken cooked with eggs, onions, carrots and pounded almonds, and spiced with cinnamon, coriander and cumin. He chewed for a moment and then sighed in contentment. 'I am always glad to be a guest in your tent, Saladin.'

The tharidah *was* quite good tonight. Yusuf would need to remember to reward the cook.

'I will be frank with you, Malik,' Reginald continued. 'This alliance could not have come at a better time. Richard is march-ing north for Acre.' Yusuf nodded. His scouts kept him apprised of the English king's movements. 'There is talk of a council to settle the dispute between Conrad and Guy, but Conrad fears that Richard is moving against him. He has retired to Tyre.'

'Then you must take our treaty to him with all haste. Once it has been sealed, he will march south on Acre and I will take my army north to strike Richard from behind. Together, we will crush the Lionheart.'

APRIL 1192: ACRE

John stood behind the English lords in the shadows along the wall. The council chamber looked much as it had the first time he had come to it, forty-four years ago, when he was little more than a boy. Thick columns ran in two rows down the length of the hall, with blazing lamps affixed to them. Now, as then, the hall was filled to bursting. Balian of Ibelin, Reginald of Sidon and Humphrey of Toron were all present, along with dozens of their liegemen. In addition, there were the Grand Masters of the Hospital and the Temple, the French under Hugh of Burgundy, and representatives of the Pisans, Venetians, Genoese and Provençals. The new patriarch, Rodolfo – his seat now in Acre instead of Jerusalem – stood in gold-embroidered robes, surrounded by priests. Guy and his men stood near by. Only Conrad had not come.

The doors at the far end of the hall swung open and all heads turned that way. Richard entered, his boots sounding loud on the stone floor. The king had set aside his armour for the occasion. He wore a closely fitted tunic of scarlet silk, and over it, a rose-coloured vest ornamented with rows of solid silver crescents. A thin circlet of gold sat atop his head. He crossed the hall to the dais where the King of Jerusalem traditionally sat and turned to face the court.

'Lords of the Kingdom, friends and allies, brothers in arms!' Richard's deep, booming voice reached every corner of the hall. 'I welcome you all to Acre and to this meeting of the Haute Cour. Only nine months ago, we all stood together outside these walls, fighting shoulder to shoulder as brothers against the infidel Saracens. In those bloody battles, my life was saved more than once by men who now stand here. I know that I am not alone. Each man before me now owes his life to men of other countries, other lords. Yet I have come to Acre to find you at one another's throats. The time has come to put an end to our squabbling.'

John found himself nodding along to the king's words. He was once more surprised by Richard's eloquence. The king might be a bloody-minded fool, but he had a tongue of silver.

'When our ancestors first came to the Holy Land, nearly one hundred years ago,' Richard continued, 'they elected their first king by common consent. From that time on, each King of Jerusalem was named by the Haute Cour. Your King Baldwin broke from this tradition by calling on the kings of England and France to decide his successor. It was by his authority that I named Guy of Lusignan king. Guy is a brave man, an honest and righteous man, whose actions have shown his worthiness for the crown. He led the siege at Acre, holding firm against tremendous odds. He joined in the conquest of Cyprus. He fought bravely at Arsuf.'

'He lost us the Kingdom at Hattin!' someone shouted from the crowd.

Richard scowled. 'And won it back at Acre! Guy is a worthy man. Conrad – I will let his actions speak for him. He has insulted all of you by not deigning to grace us with his presence today. If the choice were mine, I know the man I would choose. But my word alone is not enough. It is for this Haute Cour to select a king, as they have by tradition. So today, we will decide – Conrad or Guy – and that choice will be honoured by all: French and English, Pisans and Venetians, supporters of Conrad and supporters of Guy. Any who oppose the rightful king – myself included – will be declared traitors and outlaws, and will be driven from this land.'

Richard paused for a moment to let the threat sink in. 'Now we will choose. Who favours Guy of Lusignan?'

A smattering of men led by Guy's vassals and Richard's English lords shouted 'Aye!' Richard's brow creased at the less than enthusiastic response, but he forged on. 'And who favours Conrad of Montferrat?'

'Of Jerusalem!' someone shouted.

'Aye, of Jerusalem!'

A swell of voices rose in favour of Conrad. The acclamation quickly resolved into a chant: 'Conrad of Jerusalem! Conrad of Jerusalem!'

Richard had flushed red with anger. 'So be it!' he growled and stormed from the hall. Guy fell in beside him, and John pushed through the crowd to follow. He caught up with them in the courtyard outside the hall.

'You promised me the crown!' Guy complained.

'I know what I promised,' Richard retorted between gritted teeth.

'Conrad cannot be king! He has been conducting secret negotiations with Saladin. The man is a traitor!'

Richard turned to John. 'This is your doing, priest!'

'You have what you wanted, Your Grace,' John replied. 'The civil war is at an end. The barons are united behind their king.'

'*I* am their king!' Guy protested.

'Not any more.'

Guy pointed an accusing finger in John's face. 'You have been against me from the first, priest.'

'No. I have been for the Kingdom.' John knocked Guy's arm aside, and Guy's hand fell to the dagger at his belt.

'Enough squabbling!' Richard roared. He took a deep breath. 'I will set this right. You will be king again, Guy.'

'But the barons have spoken, Your Grace,' John reminded him.

'Guy will be king of Cyprus. The island is mine by right of conquest. I need no council to dispose of it.'

Guy bowed. 'Thank you, Your Grace. You are most generous.'

Richard nodded and strode from the court, leaving Guy behind, still bowing. John hurried after the king. 'What of Conrad? Will you support him?'

'No. I do not trust him.'

'But you have given your word not to oppose the king.'

'Then I shall have to find another king, shan't I?'

APRIL 1192: RAMLAH

Thwack! *Thwack*! Yusuf watched as the axes dug into the trunk of the old oak, sending wood chips flying. The two mamluks were alternating blows. *Thwack, thwack! Thwack, thwack!* The pile of woodchips on the forest floor grew steadily, until finally, with a creak that grew into a rumbling crash, the tree fell. The leaves had hardly stopped shaking when men swarmed over it, cutting away branches and dragging the wood away.

'The branches will provide wood for catapults and siege towers,' Az-Zahir said. Yusuf had placed him in charge of building siege engines. It was work that his clever son was well suited for. 'The trunk will become a battering ram.'

'Well done, my son. Keep me apprised of your progress.'

Yusuf urged his horse forward. He rode out from the shade of the massive, spreading oaks and on to a grassy field dotted with tents. He had moved his army north in preparation for the attack on Acre. They were camped two miles inland from Caesarea. South of the tents, a cloud of dust hovered over two dozen men playing polo. Yusuf nodded in satisfaction. Games meant that the men were in good spirits. After months of falling back before the Lionheart, it was good to be on the offensive again.

As Yusuf neared his tent, Al-Afdal cantered up. 'Reginald of Sidon has returned, Malik!'

'Excellent! Have him shown to my tent.'

Yusuf entered and poured himself a glass of water. He was sipping from it when Reginald stepped inside. Yusuf greeted him with a smile. 'Welcome, friend! You have made good time.' The smile fell from his lips as he took in Reginald's grim expression. 'What has happened? Has Conrad signed the treaty?'

'No, Malik. Conrad is dead.'

'Dead?'

'Hashashin.' Reginald spat. 'Conrad had gone to dine with the Bishop of Beauvais. On his way home, two men disguised in monks' robes approached him. One gave him a letter while the other stabbed him. Conrad managed to flee to a church, but they chased him down and killed him there.'

Yusuf shook his head in disbelief. Once again, his plans were crumbling to dust. 'Do you know who sent them?'

'The Hashashin both died fighting, but I suspect Richard. The barons had named Conrad king. Richard made no secret of his anger at the result. Conrad's death was very convenient for him.'

'Who will be king now?'

'Richard's cousin, young Henry of Champagne, was proclaimed king by the people of Tyre. Rumour has it that Richard distributed money so that they would declare for him. Regardless, the barons have agreed. Henry is to rule. He will marry Baldwin's sister Isabella before the month is out, though she is pregnant with Conrad's child.'

Yusuf grimaced in disgust. 'Has he no decency?'

'Men have done worse things for a throne, though I understand that Henry refuses to actually be crowned king. He has declared himself Lord of Jerusalem.'

'A wise man. Of late, Frankish kings do not last long in the Holy Land.'

Reginald grunted in agreement.

Yusuf placed his hand on his heart and bowed slightly. 'Thank you, Reginald. You did not have to come to tell me this.'

'I only wish I brought happier news.'

'You can stay, if you wish. I will find you a place in my household.'

'No, Malik. My place is in Tyre with my family.'

'Very well, but I insist that you stay the night. My men will show you on your way on the morrow.'

'You are too kind, Malik.' Reginald bowed and was shown out by the guards.

When Yusuf was alone, he went to stand before a table where a map of Palestine was spread out. Carved figures of men on horseback — pale pine for his allies and dark cherry for his enemies — represented the positions of the various armies: the bulk of Richard's men in Ascalon; Hugh of Burgundy in Acre, along with the Genoese and Pisan forces; his own men in Ramlah; Conrad's men in Tyre. Yusuf angrily swept the figurine representing Conrad's men from the table, and replaced it with a dark figurine. He heard the tent flap part and turned to see Al-Afdal enter.

'Do you have the treaty, Father?' he asked eagerly. 'Will we march on Acre?'

'There will be no treaty, my son. Tomorrow, we withdraw to Ramlah, to defend Jerusalem again.'

Chapter 26

Richard slammed his fist down on the table. 'We must strike again!'

His declaration was met with silence by the lords around the table. Balian frowned, while Hugh of Burgundy shifted uncomfortably as he leaned on his crutch. The new king, Henry of Champagne, bit his lip. The Pisan and Genoese envoys appeared to be carefully studying the map on the table. John looked away, out of the window. Beyond the rooftops of Jaffa, he noticed a dozen men heading north along the coast. They were no doubt marching for Acre, where they would take a ship for home.

'Well?' Richard demanded. 'Have you all lost your tongues?'

'I have my tongue,' Hugh replied. The French commander was flushed. Fever had burned away his belly, leaving him painfully thin. He had never fully recovered from the arrow he took in his ankle at Arsuf. After the first attempt on Jerusalem, the doctors had wanted to take his foot, but he had refused. Corruption had set in, and now he looked likely to lose his whole leg, if not his life. 'It is your wits that I fear have been lost.'

'You'll not long keep your tongue if you speak to me thus,' Richard growled. 'I am king—'

'Of England,' Hugh finished. 'And I am a Frenchman. I'll not follow you blindly, and I'll not throw away the lives of my men. We have already tried for Jerusalem twice, and twice we have failed.'

A murmur of assent went around the table. The army had returned from Beit Nuba only three days before. This time, it had not been the cold and wet that had stopped them, but rather the heat. Yusuf had poisoned or filled all the wells within miles of Jerusalem. Richard had sent men to fetch water from beyond Ramlah, but half of them fell prey to Muslim raiding parties. Those who returned could not possibly bring enough water for horses and men alike. Richard had favoured the horses. After a month, the men were mad with thirst. Hundreds deserted. John's lips had become blistered, and he suffered from piercing headaches and dizzy spells. When the horses began to die, too, they had withdrawn to Jaffa.

'It is true. We have not taken Jerusalem,' Richard acknowledged. 'But nor have we been defeated. We need only crush our enemy in the field! If we kill Saladin, his army will collapse, and the Holy Land will spread its legs for us.'

'And how do you plan to kill Saladin?' Balian asked. 'He knows our armies are disintegrating. He need only wait to achieve victory. Why would he be fool enough to meet us in battle?'

'Because our failure to take Jerusalem has served at least one purpose: it has made the Saracens over-confident. If they see an easy prize, they will reach out to take it. And we will strike!'

'Then you will do so without the French,' Hugh said.

'You would abandon your brothers-in-arms? Is it your life you fear for, Hugh, or have the Saracens so cowed your spirit that you dare not raise your sword against them?'

Hugh's lips pressed together in a thin line. When he spoke, his voice was cold. 'My lords and I fought beside you at Acre and Arsuf. None can question our bravery. But we have also frozen on the road to Jerusalem in the winter, and have burned there in the summer. We have had enough.'

'Go, then. There will be more glory for those who do follow me.'

'Glory? *Hah*. If you keep at this mad quest, you will find only death.' Hugh limped from the room, his crutch tapping loudly on the stone floor.

Richard let him go and then looked around the table. 'If you also fear death, go. Follow Hugh. As for me, I am not afraid to give my life in the service of God.' He paused to meet each man's eyes. 'Who will fight beside me?'

Again, there was silence. Richard's knuckles went white where he gripped the edge of the table. Just when it seemed no one would respond, Henry cleared his throat. 'The men of the Kingdom will join you, Richard.'

'But my lord!' Balian protested.

'You were born and raised in the Holy Land, Balian,' Henry said. 'Will you not fight for it?'

'Of course, but—'

Richard cut him short. 'You have my thanks, Henry. Who else?'

The Templar and Hospitaller Grand Masters reluctantly gave their support. The Pisan envoy agreed to provide two thousand crossbowmen, for a fee.

'It is settled then,' Richard declared. 'Go now and prepare your men to march. We leave for Acre tomorrow, where we will gather our forces.'

The men trooped out. John remained behind.

'Speak, John,' Richard said as he went to a side table to pour himself a cup of wine.

'This is not the time to think of conquest, Your Grace. The men are dispirited. Thousands have already taken ship to return home, and now we have lost the French, too. You must turn your mind to peace.'

'Peace is all you ever talk of, priest,' Richard grumbled. 'I begin to think Guy was right. You love the infidels overmuch.'

'I only speak the truth, Your Grace. You must make peace

before you leave the Holy Land. With every failed assault on Jerusalem, the terms of that peace grow worse for us.'

'That is why I need a victory, John. God is on our side. The Saracens cannot defeat me.'

'Yet still you have lost.' Richard's brow furrowed at this, but John pushed on regardless. 'A wise king must know when to fight and when to put aside his sword. Make peace, Your Grace.'

Richard sat at the table and took a long drink of wine. He wiped his mouth with the back of his hand. 'Go. This talk of peace sickens me. I have no patience for cowards.'

John's jaw set. 'I am no coward, but to attack again and again in the face of defeat is not bravery. It is madness.'

'It is madness to insult one's king, John.' Richard's voice was soft, and all the more dangerous for that. 'I could have you beheaded for less.' He let the threat hang in the air. 'But no. No doubt the heat has addled your wits. When I depart, you will stay in Jaffa to recover.'

John would have been happy to be rid of Richard, but he feared what the Lionheart might do without his restraining influence. 'My place is at your side, Your Grace.'

'Your place is wherever I decide. You will stay.'

The sword slashed towards John's face. He knocked it aside with his shield and swung his mace, but his opponent leaned back out of the way. John attempted to attack backhanded, but the sudden change of direction of the mace caused a sharp pain in his shoulder. ''Sblood!'

His sparring partner stepped back and removed his helm, revealing curly red hair. Rand was a young man-at-arms. The men called him Quickfingers because he had once been caught cheating at cards. He had paid for that with the little finger of his left hand. Rand was one of the hundred men that Richard had left behind to garrison the citadel of Jaffa. A hundred was hardly enough. John had asked for more, but Richard refused.

Rand's face wore a look of concern. 'Are you well, father?'

'It is nothing.' John raised his mace and winced as the pain returned.

'We will spar again later,' Rand suggested. 'I must see to my duties.' The young man hurried off.

'If you fear for my old bones, just say it,' John grumbled. All these young ones treated him as if he had one foot in the grave. John removed his helm and wiped the sweat from his forehead. Training against younger men was hard, but he had had little else to occupy his time in the two weeks since Richard left for Acre. He massaged his aching shoulder. He needed a hot bath.

He changed out of his armour in his quarters in the citadel and went into the city. He paid three coppers to the stooped old man at the bathhouse door. Inside, he left his clothes in a cubby and pulled on a thin cotton bathing tunic. The rays of sunshine that lit the warm room were visible in the roiling steam that filled the air. Three other men sat in the hot waters. None looked up as John sank into the bath with a sigh of relief.

He worked his shoulder until he could lift his arm without pain and then sat back and closed his eyes. His mind drifted. He thought of his first time in a bathhouse. It had been the day he arrived in the Holy Land. He had gone in the women's entrance. They had shrieked at him in a tongue he did not understand, and John had feared they might castrate him. He thought of Yusuf's sister Zimat, whom he had loved, and then of Reynald, the man he had hated above all others. They were both gone now. He thought of Yusuf. When the two had met, Yusuf had been a skinny, bookish boy, who dreamed he would someday be king. John thought of Richard, the king he now served. The thought made him frown.

Shouting from the streets intruded on his thoughts, and John opened his eyes. The other men were leaving the bath. John followed them to the changing room. The shouting was growing louder. He dressed quickly and stepped outside. 'What is happening?' he asked the old man at the door. The man shrugged.

All along the street, men and women were stepping out of their homes. 'Saladin!' a young boy shouted as he sprinted past John. 'Saladin is here!'

The words were no sooner out of his mouth than the people rushed back into their homes, only to emerge a moment later carrying their most valuable possessions. John joined the crowd hurrying towards the shelter of the citadel. He entered and climbed atop the wall. Quickfingers was there, along with most of the garrison. Without a word, the young soldier pointed to the east. An army was approaching under a cloud of dust. Their column of mounted men stretched to the horizon.

John squinted at the flag that flew over the head of the army. It bore Yusuf's eagle. He quickly scanned the rest of the column. 'At least seven thousand men.'

Quickfingers nodded. 'We cannot hold against so many. What do we do?'

'Send a rider north to Acre. And get as many of the people inside as you can. Put the men on the walls. I will speak with Saladin.'

Yusuf rode into Jaffa with his emirs and personal guard trailing behind. He heard distant shouts of pain and terror. Those would be the men who had waited too long to seek shelter in the citadel. He rode past home after home with their doors kicked in – some doors sagged on their hinges while the wood had splintered around the lock on others. Further up the street, a mamluk stepped out of a house with a heavy bag over his shoulder. The man behind him carried an armful of silks.

The town had put up no resistance. Most of the occupants had fled to the citadel long before Yusuf had arrived. They had taken their most valuable possessions, but more than enough had been left behind to make his men happy. It had been a long time since they had taken any plunder. His men needed this victory. Yusuf needed it more. When he heard that Richard had left Jaffa almost undefended, he had struck at once. Perhaps the city's fall would finally convince the Lionheart to make peace.

As he reached the square at the heart of town, Yusuf heard a woman's screams coming from an alleyway to his left. He frowned. He had ordered his troops to spare all the women and Muslim men when they took the town. He turned to Qaraqush. 'Put an end to that.'

'Yes, Malik.'

Yusuf rode into the long shadow cast by the citadel, which stood on a tall hill near the coast. The flag of the Kingdom of Jerusalem flew from its keep, alongside the three lions of Richard. He could see men lining the walls. He estimated their numbers at less than five hundred, and that no doubt included citizens from the town, dragooned into standing there with sticks in hand to make the citadel look better defended than it actually was. Five hundred men or one hundred, it hardly mattered. They did not have enough men to resist for long. Nor, it seemed, did they intend to. The citadel gate opened and a man in mail rode out under a white flag.

Yusuf reined to a halt. Al-Afdal came up beside him. His son smirked. 'Shall I bring you the fool's head?'

'He comes under a flag of truce. I will speak with him.'

'You mean to negotiate?' Al-Afdal asked incredulously. 'We should slaughter them, Father. Kill them all, as they murdered our men at Acre.'

Yusuf sighed. 'Have you learned nothing, my son? Acre was Richard's greatest mistake. We have suffered defeat after defeat since then, yet the desire for vengeance has held our army together when there was nothing else. The massacre at Acre is the only reason Richard has not taken Jerusalem. I will not make the same mistake. If we want the Lionheart gone, we must seek peace, not vengeance.'

Al-Afdal frowned. 'As you say, Father.'

The Frank with the white flag was drawing closer. Yusuf squinted. Then his eyes widened in recognition. He urged his mount forward. 'John!'

'As-salaamu 'alaykum, friend,' John replied as his horse came alongside Yusuf's.

'What are you doing here?'

'Richard left me behind. I have come to negotiate the citadel's surrender.'

'If you turn the citadel over to me, I will give your men and the people of Jaffa free passage to Acre.'

John looked about. The occasional scream still punctuated the morning air. At the edge of the square, a Christian in a blood-stained tunic stumbled past with four taunting mamluks at his heels. 'I trust your word, Yusuf, but your men's blood is up. I fear that if the people leave the citadel now, they will be slaughtered.'

Yusuf nodded. 'I will give my men five days to sack the city and have their sport. That will also give your people time to prepare their departure. On the fifth day, you will leave.'

John nodded. 'Thank you, Yusuf.'

'You need not thank me, John. Blood only begets more blood. The time has come for peace.'

Yusuf watched as a ship far out to sea made its way along the horizon, gliding along under the same gentle northerly wind that ruffled his hair. In the hazy morning sky, gulls floated on the breeze. The tide was at its lowest point and the surf was quiet. His horse shook its head, and the jingle of tack sounded loud in the morning calm. He heard the nickering of horses amongst the men behind him. Fifty members of his khaskiya waited there, along with the four hundred men who would take control of the citadel when the Franks left. There was a loud cawing to Yusuf's right, and he looked to see a crow settling on to one of the branches of a dead tree. The black bird seemed to look right at him. It cawed again.

'An ill omen,' Qaraqush muttered.

'You see ill omens in everything.'

'Of late, I am usually right.'

'It is just a bird,' Yusuf said, though in truth, he was ill at ease. Crows followed armies and always seemed to know when a battle was in the offing.

'The flags are coming down.' Al-Afdal pointed to the citadel. The three lions of Richard fluttered in the breeze as his standard was lowered. Next came the flag of Jerusalem – a gold cross, surrounded by four smaller crosses. Yusuf raised his voice. 'Prepare to ride, men!'

A horn sounded over his last words. *Aah-hoo! Aah-hoo!*

Qaraqush frowned. 'That did not come from the citadel.'

'There!' Saqr pointed out to sea.

More ships had appeared north of the city. There were ten of them. Yusuf squinted. No, fifteen – shallow-drafted longships, each packed with men. The closest were surging towards the shore, their oars beating at the waves. Over each boat flew a flag: three golden lions on a field of scarlet. Richard.

Yusuf turned to Saqr. 'Sound the call to arms. We will hold the light cavalry in reserve. Al-Afdal, you will lead the mamluks. No bows; close with sword and lance. We will ride them down before they reach the shore.'

'Yes, Malik!'

Al-Afdal galloped away as Saqr sounded his horn. Behind Yusuf, the camp sprang to life, men grabbing their weapons and running for their horses. As was his custom, Yusuf had ordered his men to pitch their tents in order of the line of battle, so that they could form up at a moment's notice. The Frankish ships were still well out to sea when the line formed, the mamluks in the fore with spears in hand. The four hundred men who were to have formed the citadel's garrison joined them, with the Bedouin and Turkmen cavalry gathered behind. Al-Afdal waved his sword overhead as he cantered down the line of mamluks. He turned back and stopped at the centre of the line. He shouted something, and the men roared back: '*For Islam! For Saladin!*' Four thousand strong, the mamluks headed north at a trot, riding for where the Frankish ships would come ashore.

'With me, men!' Yusuf called to the troops gathered around him. They rode after the mamluks at a slower pace, and the light cavalry fell in behind them. Yusuf counted twenty-four enemy ships now. At something like a hundred fighting men per ship, that meant approximately twenty-five hundred Franks against his more than seven thousand. Yusuf raised a fist and reined to a stop on the sandy dunes overlooking the beach.

Below them, the line of mamluks had accelerated to a gallop and was thundering across the sand. The first longship was nearing the shore, moving faster now as it surged forward on the waves, their crests foaming at its sides. The mamluks splashed into the water, their mount's hooves kicking up clouds of spray. Yusuf looked back to the ship. The men crowded in the prow did not hold swords or spears. Crossbows. Yusuf recognized the weapons just as they released a volley into the charging mamluks. The effect was devastating. Dozens of horses went down, and their riders were thrown under the waves. Frankish warriors poured from the ship, led by Richard himself. The king towered over the others. He set about him with his double-bladed battle-axe, cutting down the fallen mamluks as they rose from the sea.

More ships surged towards the coast, the crossbowmen in the prows releasing volleys of quarrels. Horses fell by the dozen. The beasts thrashed and kicked in the surf, reducing the advancing mamluk line to chaos. Spears in hand, the Frankish men-at-arms were vaulting from their ships into water, which came up to their waists. They were met by mamluks, many of them now on foot. The wind picked up, carrying to Yusuf the injured beasts' loud whinnies, the men's shouts of pain and anger and the ring of steel upon steel. He saw a spray of blood as a mamluk slashed through an enemy's throat.

'Selim!' Yusuf called. 'Lead in the light cavalry. Have them stop on the beach and shoot at the crossbowmen in the boats.'

Selim galloped away, and Yusuf turned back towards the fighting. He could not find Al-Afdal amidst the chaos. Richard was clearly visible, driving forward into a knot of half a dozen mamluks. The king's battle-axe flashed in the sun, and Yusuf saw an arm go flying. Another man had his head nearly cut off. Three of the mamluks fled, and the remaining man took a blow to the chest and disappeared beneath the waves.

'The bastard is brave,' Qaraqush noted.

'A brave fool. We outnumber them four to one.'

The Turkmen and Bedouin cavalry had reached the beach and began arcing arrows over the mamluks. Yusuf saw one of the crossbowmen take an arrow in the gut and tumble from his ship into the water. Several more were hit, and the rest took shelter. The hail of crossbow bolts slackened, allowing the mamluks to press forward. Their numbers soon began to tell. The Franks were pushed back into deeper water, first up to their waists, and then to their chests. Only Richard and two dozen of his knights remained in the shallower water. A hundred mamluks swarmed around them.

'For Christ! For the Kingdom!'

A loud cry came from Yusuf's left. He looked over to see that the citadel gates had opened, and two hundred Frankish spearmen were pouring out to strike his men in the flank. They cut into the light cavalry on the beach, spearing them from their horses. Yusuf's men began to panic. A few retreated, and then more and more fled. As the rain of arrows from the light cavalry ceased, the Frankish crossbowmen began to shoot once more. At the same time, the spearmen veered into the sea to strike the mamluks from behind. The Frankish men-at-arms led by Richard pushed forward again.

'Stand your ground, men!' Yusuf shouted. 'Stand your ground!'

'It is no use, Malik,' Qaraqush urged. 'They fear the Lionheart.'

'Then we must kill him. If we strike down Richard, the battle is ours.' Yusuf drew his sword and held it aloft. 'With me, men! For Islam!' He spurred his horse down from the dunes and on to the beach. His guard came close behind. They streamed past the fleeing Bedouin and Turkmen and splashed into the water, heading straight for Richard. A Frankish spearman lunged at him, and Yusuf knocked aside the spear point and slashed down. The Frank blocked the blow with his shield, but Saqr came close behind and finished him. Yusuf rode another spearman down from behind, and slashed across the face of a third Frank. His mount had slowed. The waves were crashing against its chest now. Richard was only ten yards away when Yusuf's horse whinnied and stumbled. Yusuf saw a crossbow quarrel protruding from the beast's neck, and then it fell.

Yusuf managed to get free of his stirrups just before he splashed under the waves. His helmet came off, and he slammed into the sandy sea floor. He opened his eyes, but quickly shut them; the briny water stung, and it was too churned up and murky for him to see. He began to rise when someone kneed him in the side of the head. He fell back to his knees. He stabbed up blindly and felt his sword strike home. Yusuf rose from the waves, blinking water from his eyes. A wide-eyed Frank with blood dribbling from the corners of his mouth was impaled on the end of his sword. A wave hit Yusuf in the chest. He stumbled backwards, and the Frank slid off his blade to disappear beneath the water.

Yusuf looked about, trying to locate Richard. There. The king had moved about twenty yards further away. He was hacking down a mamluk, while Saqr rode up behind him, unseen. Saqr brought his sword down hard; Richard moved at the last second, and the blade glanced off his conical helm. With a roar, the Lionheart spun and sank his axe into the neck of

Saqr's horse. A spray of blood spattered the king as he pulled his weapon free. The horse collapsed, and Saqr vanished beneath the waves. He came up swinging. Richard deflected the blow with his axe.

Yusuf waded towards the two men through waist-deep water. A Frank appeared from his left and lunged at his chest. Yusuf lurched sideways to avoid the blow and hacked down, catching the Frank on the wrist. The man fell to his knees, screaming and clutching his nearly severed sword hand. Ahead, Saqr and Richard were trading blows. Lean and compact, Saqr looked like a child next to the towering king, but he was quicker. He landed a blow against Richard's side, and red showed on the king's surcoat. Saqr pressed his attack and struck the king's left arm above the elbow. Richard grunted in pain, and his guard came down. Saqr slashed at the king's face, but the Lionheart brought his axe up, knocking Saqr's blade up above his head. Richard brought his axe back down in a vicious blow. The blade caught Saqr where the neck and shoulder meet. It sliced through flesh and bone, cutting him to the navel.

Yusuf's mouth stretched open in a scream, but he heard nothing. All sound had drained from the world, all but the pounding of blood in his ears. Richard turned towards him, and their eyes met. Yusuf raised his sword. He took a step towards the king, but someone came between them. Yusuf slashed angrily, but his sword was parried.

'Yusuf!'

He swung again, and again his blade was knocked aside.

'Yusuf!'

This time, the shout penetrated the fog of anger that had enveloped him. Yusuf took a step back. 'John?' His friend was dressed in mail. John spread his hands in a gesture of peace and lowered his mace beneath the waves. 'Stand aside!' Yusuf shouted at him.

'I will not let you fight him.'

And I thought you were my friend. Yusuf's lips curled back in a snarl. He lunged, but John's mace rose from the water to deflect the blow. John took a step back and again lowered his weapon.

'I am not protecting him, Yusuf. I am protecting you.'

Yusuf swung again. This time, his sword caught in the grooves of the mace, and the two weapons locked together, bringing the two men close. They struggled against one another, but John was the stronger. Yusuf was shoved back just as a wave struck him. He lost his balance and went down beneath the water. He slashed beneath the waves and felt his sword make contact. He rose to see that John was clutching his right leg and struggling to stand. The water around him was turning crimson. A wave hit him, and John fell to his knees, so that his chin was just above the water. He dropped his mace.

'He will kill you, Yusuf, and if you fall, your army will scatter. There will be no peace. Richard will take Jerusalem, and the war between our people will never end. You must not fight him.'

Yusuf scowled. 'I am not afraid to die.'

'I know. You are the bravest man I have ever known. That is why you will retreat, because you do not fear the jeers of your enemy, because you know that the lives of your people matter more than glory, more even than your honour.'

Yusuf hesitated. Richard was still fifteen yards away. Man after man waded forward to try for the glory of striking down the king. Richard hacked off a mamluk's hand. He nearly cleaved a warrior's head from his body. He stove in the next man's helm.

'This is Richard's last chance, Yusuf,' John said. 'All you have to do is survive, and you will win.'

John was right. Richard was younger and stronger, and he fought with a ferocity that Yusuf could not match. If he faced the king, Yusuf would die in these waters. All he had fought for would be lost. He lowered his sword, and reached out to pull John to his feet.

John gripped his shoulder. 'I knew you were no Richard.'

'Thanks to you, friend.' Yusuf took a step back, then turned and moved toward the beach. 'Retreat!' he shouted. 'Fall back, men! Back!'

Chapter 27

Richard hacked up a gob of greenish-brown phlegm and spat it on the floor of his tent. It landed just beside John's foot. 'We will march!' the king declared, and then he was overcome with a fit of coughing that left him red-faced. 'I will not squander our victory at Jaffa.'

After driving off Yusuf's army, Richard had established his camp outside the citadel of Jaffa. The Saracens had attacked again five days later, and though Richard had only fifty-four knights and several hundred men-at-arms, his two thousand Pisan crossbowmen had made the difference. Volley after volley of crossbow bolts had shredded the enemy charge and sent the Saracens running. The victory had inspired Richard, and here they were in Ramlah once more, on the road to Jerusalem. No one but Richard believed they could take the Holy City. It was a tribute to the king's hold on his men that they had marched at all. John and the other lords had spent the march urging him to turn back, but in vain. Now it looked as if camp fever might accomplish what their words could not. Richard had taken ill shortly after the battle in the waves, and his sickness had grown worse with each passing day.

'But my lord,' Blanchemains protested, 'you are too ill to ride.'

'I am well enough,' Richard grumbled and struggled up from his folding chair. He took a few steps and then leaned heavily on the tent post. His face had turned pale.

His doctor – a skeletal man in monk's robes, his nose peeling from sunburn – stepped forward. 'Please, Your Grace. I beg you to lie down. You must rest.'

'I will rest—' Richard blew bright yellow snot from his nose. 'I will rest when Jerusalem is in Christian hands once more.'

'You won a battle at Jaffa, Your Grace, not the war,' John cautioned. 'Saladin still lives. His army is intact. Jerusalem is as difficult a prize as ever.'

'And I am still the Lionheart! I tell you, I will have Jerusalem.'

'At what cost, Your Grace?' Bishop Walter put in. 'Is Jerusalem worth losing England? Worth losing Aquitaine? Longchamp writes that your brother John has claimed you are dead and that he has seized the throne for himself. And King Philip has taken advantage of your absence to take land in France. If we do not return soon, you will have no kingdom to go home to.'

'Fie!' Richard pushed off from the tent pole. 'Fie on all of you!' He stumbled from the tent, his court following. 'My horse!' he shouted. 'Bring my horse! Where is my armour?' The two young squires glanced at one another, and then looked to Blanchemains. 'What are you looking at him for?' Richard roared. 'I am your king. Bring my armour, dullards!'

The squires retrieved the king's padded vest, his mail hauberk and coif, mail leggings and mail mittens. As he dressed, Richard glared at his councillors, daring them to speak. He was breathing heavily by the time he pulled on his conical helmet.

'Your Grace—' John began.

Richard rounded on him. 'Peace? You wish me to make peace, yes? I will not have it, John. I will have Jerusalem!'

Richard went to where de Preaux held the reins of his horse. He pulled himself into the saddle and swayed for a moment before grabbing the pommel to steady himself. 'What are you standing there for?' he demanded. 'Break camp and form ranks!' He urged his horse forward. 'Break camp, men! We march for Jerusalem, to give the devil Saracens a taste of our steel! Break—'

Richard's eyes rolled back in his head. He tilted to the side and fell from the saddle to land with a crash. The doctor rushed to his side and felt his head and neck. He put his cheek close to the king's mouth. 'I do not believe he is injured, but he is grievously ill. He must rest.'

Blanchemains gestured to the men-at-arms who stood guard outside Richard's tent. 'Take the King inside.'

'What do we do now?' de Preaux asked as Richard was carried away.

'We make peace,' John said.

'Against the King's will?'

Blanchemains nodded. 'I am high steward. With the King ill, command falls to me, and I say this war is over. It has been over for some time.'

AUGUST 1192: ACRE

'Five years,' Humphrey said.

'Two years and eight months,' Selim replied.

They sat across the table from one another in the chancellery of the palace at Acre. John sat beside Humphrey, quill in hand. With Richard ill – drifting in and out of consciousness – peace negotiations had proceeded quickly. Now after two weeks, they had agreed to the treaty's major provisions. The Franks would keep most of what they held: the coastal strips from Jaffa to Caesarea and from Acre to Tyre, along with Antioch and Tripoli. Ascalon would be surrendered to Yusuf, on the condition that he tear down the walls and leave the city unfortified. Free travel would be allowed between the two kingdoms. The Franks would be able to make pilgrimage to Jerusalem. All that remained was to decide upon the length of the truce.

'Two years and eight months?' Humphrey raised an eyebrow. 'Eight months?'

John whispered to him. 'A peace of that length would expire in May, at the start of campaign season.'

Humphrey scowled. 'We make peace, and you are already planning for war, Selim.'

'My brother wants only peace,' Selim assured him. 'John, you know my people. After nearly driving the Franks from our lands, this peace will taste like defeat to them. But the prospect of revenge will sweeten the dish. It will win their acceptance of the treaty.'

'Two years and eight months is not long enough,' Humphrey said.

Selim rose and went to the window. 'What will you do once peace is made, Humphrey?'

Humphrey glared at him. This was a tactic that Selim employed frequently. Rather than butting heads over an issue, he would change the subject to something entirely different.

'I shall return to Aleppo,' Selim mused. 'Perhaps I shall retire from public life. I could spend my days with my family. Or perhaps become a holy man like you, John.'

John laughed. 'I am a priest, not a holy man. Four years, Selim.'

'Three years, eight months.'

Humphrey rubbed his chin. He nodded. 'Very well.'

John began to write down the details, his quill scratching on the parchment while Selim looked over his shoulder. Finally, he set the quill down. 'It is done.'

'Alhumdillah.'

'Our lords must still approve,' Humphrey cautioned.

'Saladin will agree.'

'As will King Henry,' John said. 'Richard—'

The king's name was still hanging in the air when the door opened. Blanchemains entered. There was an ugly bruise forming on the high steward's cheek. 'Richard is awake,' he declared. 'He wishes to speak with you, priest.'

It was a short walk to the king's chambers. As he approached, John could hear loud cursing from beyond the door. One of the guards outside nodded to him. 'God save you, father.' He pulled the door open.

As John stepped inside, he spotted a flash of metal flying towards him and jumped aside just before a goblet slammed into the door, which was swinging closed behind him.

'What have you done, priest?' Richard roared. The king was leaning on the table at the centre of the room. He wore only a thin linen bed tunic.

'The Lord High Steward—'

'I did not ask you about Blanchemains. What have you done?'

'I negotiated a peace, Your Grace.'

'Peace.' Richard spat as if he could not stomach the taste of the word. 'I swore to take Jerusalem. Would you make an oath-breaker of me, John? You can stuff you treaty up your arse. I'll not agree to it.'

'You have no choice, Your Grace.'

'What was that?'

'You have no choice, my lord.'

Richard moved surprisingly fast for someone who had been confined to bed only moments before. He rounded the table, crossed the room in four great strides and swung for John's head. John ducked the blow and slipped away. Richard was breathing heavily after his sudden exertion. John moved to put the table between them.

'Hugh of Burgundy died while you were ill, Your Grace. The French troops have left for France. Many of your men have gone as well. The rest only wait to make the pilgrimage to Jerusalem before departing.'

'It does not matter,' Richard said between breaths. He went to the table and slumped into a chair. 'King Henry will lend me the men of the Kingdom.'

'They were not enough to defend Jerusalem. They are not enough to retake it. You must make peace.'

'I am king, damn you!' Richard slammed his fist on to the table so hard that the flagon of wine at its centre jumped. 'Do not tell me what I must do!' He coughed and spat. 'You are bastards. All of you, bastards.'

'We only sought to serve you, Your Grace.'

'By betraying me?'

John's forehead creased. Richard's words were closer to the mark than the king knew. John had always been a man of honour, and it was his duty to serve Richard as best he could. Instead, he had prayed for the king's failure and done his part to assure it. But John had no regrets. Joan had been right: honour would neither save lives nor protect the innocent. John had done what was right, honour be damned.

'I only did what you should have done, Your Grace.'

Richard's voice became dangerously quiet, almost a whisper. 'You think you know my duty better than I, priest?'

'I know it.'

Richard stood, knocking his chair over, and John tensed, ready to fight if needs be. 'I promised you an earldom if you made peace on my terms, John. You failed. I shall have you cast in chains for our return to England.'

'I will not be returning to England, Your Grace.'

'You will go where I say! You are my man.'

'I am God's man.' John met Richard's blue eyes. 'And I thank God for that. You are a great warrior, but you have put your sword in the service of only you, not God. I will not serve you a moment longer. Not if my life depended on it, Your Grace.'

'I will have your head,' Richard growled.

'Then you will have no peace.'

Richard clenched the edge of the table. His face shaded purple with rage. 'Go, then. Go! Go before I kill you myself!'

'Your Grace.' John bowed. 'Godspeed on your journey.'

SEPTEMBER 1192: RAMLAH

Rain pattered off the roof of the pavilion. The men inside were huddled together uncomfortably close; the Franks on one side of the table where the treaty sat, the Saracens on the other. John had watched the pavilion's shadow slowly shrink away to almost nothing while the treaty was read in its entirety, first in French, then in Latin and finally in Arabic. He clenched his teeth as Imad ad-Din droned on. The leg John had injured at Arsuf was aching, and blood had started to seep through the bandages to wet his tunic.

Yusuf's secretary finally finished reading, and Henry stepped forward. As king of Jerusalem, he would be the first to take his oath. The other Frankish lords would give their oaths to him. 'I, Henry, Count of Champagne and Lord of Jerusalem, ruler of the Kingdom, in the presence of Balian of Ibelin, Humphrey of Toron and many other honourable men, both Christian and Muslim, swear that I will abide by the terms of this treaty . . .'

After John had left Richard, the king had continued to rage for a full day, but in the end, he had agreed to honour the terms of the treaty. He had little choice. He was desperately needed in England, and even though he still longed to fight, he had no army.

Henry was reaching the end of his oath. 'And if any of my lords do not observe the terms therein, then let their lands be forfeit. And if I or my successors do not observe this treaty, then let our word be counted for nothing, and our rule stripped from us. All this do I swear on this third day of September, in the eleven hundred and ninety-second year of Our Lord.'

Joscius, the archbishop of Tyre, whom Henry had named his chancellor, stepped forward with the king's seal. It was two-sided: one side showing the king seated on his throne; the other, the tower of David, the Church of the Holy Sepulchre and the Dome of the Rock. Two seals had been prepared in advance, one for each copy of the treaty. Joscius attached them to the treaties with ribbons that had been embedded in the wax.

Balian gave his oath next, followed by Humphrey of Toron and Reginald of Sidon. The Grand Masters of the Hospital and the Temple swore to uphold the treaty. Then it was the turn of the English lords: Blanchemains, Bishop Walter, de Preaux, de Ferriers and John.

'And what of Richard?' Selim asked after John had given his oath.

'The King recognizes the terms of the peace,' Blanchemains replied, 'but he will not give his oath, nor will he make pilgrimage to Jerusalem. He bid me deliver this promise: once the peace is over, he will return to take Jerusalem.'

Selim frowned. 'Those are words of war, not peace.'

'It is the King's actions that matter, not his words,' Balian assured him. 'More than half his men have already left for home. Richard himself will be on a ship before another month has passed.'

'If Richard will not swear, then nor shall Saladin. His men and I will take the oath in his name.'

Balian looked to Henry. The king nodded. 'Very well. Proceed.'

Selim cleared his throat. 'I swear by Allah that I will keep the peace and honour the terms of this treaty.' As he spoke, Imad ad-Din traced Selim's signature on the two copies of the treaty. Al-Afdal swore next, then Az-Zahir and Al-Mashtub. Imad ad-Din recorded their names. Qaraqush gave his oath last of all, after which there ensued an awkward silence in which the only sound was that of Imad ad-Din's quill scratching on the parchment. The secretary finished and set the quill aside.

There were no smiles, no exclamations of joy. The Saracens were no doubt thinking of how close they had come to driving the Franks from their lands once and for all. The Christians simply looked tired.

'It is done,' Selim declared at last. 'As a sign of friendship, Saladin wishes to invite you to a feast in his tent.'

'We would be honoured to attend,' Henry replied.

Selim led them further into the Saracen camp, to a tent large enough to hold more than a hundred men. A long, low table ran down its centre, with glasses of wine on one side and glasses of water on the other. The Franks took their places, with Henry at their centre, and the Saracens followed suit. John found a place near the end of the table. The space opposite Henry had been left open for Saladin. Selim raised his glass. 'My brother does not wish us to wait on him. Eat, drink!'

John took a sip of wine. There was a tap on his shoulder, and Az-Zahir leaned close to whisper in his ear. 'My father wishes to see you. Come.'

John followed him to a much smaller tent and Az-Zahir held the flap aside. John limped inside to find Yusuf seated cross-legged on the carpeted floor. He looked exhausted. There were dark circles under his eyes and his cheekbones protruded sharply from his face. His mouth was turned down at the ends, making him look melancholy. His robes hung like clothes on a scarecrow. He gestured to a cushion across from him. 'Sit, friend.' John lowered himself with care. 'Your wound pains you. I am sorry, John.'

'Do not be. I am old, Yusuf. If not my wound, it would be my back, or my shoulder.'

Yusuf nodded. 'I hardly eat any more, my gut troubles me so. Perhaps peace will cure my ills. I have not seen Damascus in years, nor Shamsa . . .' His voice trailed off and his eyes took on a far-away look, as if he were gazing at distant mountains. 'I do not know what I shall do now that peace has come. I have spent my life fighting the Franks. I knit my kingdom together with the hope of defeating them. What shall we hope for now? What will hold my people together?'

'You will.'

'But for how long? After I took Jerusalem, I dreamed of peace, of the flourishing kingdom I would build. Now that peace has come, I fear I shall not enjoy it long. I am weak, John. The fire in my belly burns without cease; it eats me up from the inside. It is Allah, punishing me for my crimes. I have done terrible things.'

'You are a king. You did what you must.'

Yusuf shook his head. 'I once believed that. Now, I am not so sure. I had Turan killed. Asimat, too, and Al-Salih . . . my own son, John.' Yusuf took a deep breath. 'I have not admitted that to anyone. I am a monster.'

'I killed my brother, Yusuf. If you are a monster, then so am I.'

'That was different.'

'We both have blood on our hands, but it is not our past that defines us. You tamed the Lionheart. You have brought peace to the Holy Land. You have opened Jerusalem to Franks and Muslims alike. This is how you will be judged.'

'Inshallah,' Yusuf murmured. 'But I did not call you here to speak of these things. I wished to thank you.'

'Thank me?'

'For saving my life again, amongst other things. You were right, John. You have always been right. For years, I thought of nothing but defeating the Franks. I thought victory would make me great, but it only made me cruel. My wars have ruined the country. The fields have gone unplanted. My subjects are beaten down and confused. The rich are reduced to hunger and the poor to destitution. I fought in the name of Allah, but I was not doing his work. My people do not need victory; they need peace.'

'I only reminded you of what you once taught me.'

'I could have used you by my side these many years, John. I have missed you.'

'And I, you. Though I served other kings, I was always your friend.'

'I know. What will you do now that war is ended? Will you return home to England?'

'There is nothing for me there. My home is here. I only joined Richard's crusade so that I could return. I wish to return to Damascus, if you will permit it.'

Yusuf smiled. 'Of course. You are welcome at my court.'

'Thank you, but I have had enough of kings and courts, my friend.'

'As have I.' Yusuf's smile faded and his face resumed its melancholy cast. 'If you will not accept a post, at least accept my coin, enough to settle you comfortably.'

'You do not have to—'

'I insist.'

John placed his hand over his heart and bowed at the waist. 'Shukran Allah.'

Yusuf nodded. 'I have many subjects, but few friends, John. You will visit me from time to time?'

'Of course.'

'Good.' Yusuf stood and extended a hand to help John to his feet. 'Now come. They will be missing us at the feast, and we have much to celebrate, you and I. Do you remember the first time you spoke to me of peace between our people?' John nodded. 'I called you a dreamer.' Yusuf laughed softly. 'Now, your dream has come true.'

'Our dream, friend.'

'Yes, our dream.' Yusuf put his arm around John, and together they limped from the tent.

After the peace, the Frankish crusaders made their pilgrimage to Jerusalem and then returned home. Richard refused to visit the Holy City, vowing to only set foot inside as a conqueror. He never did. He took ship in October and did not return. I do not know what became of him, though I have heard it told that during his journey to England, he was made a prisoner in Austria by the same Leopold on whose flag he once pissed.

Saladin settled in Damascus with his wife Shamsa at his side, and set himself to doing good works and making up the prayers and days of fasting that he had missed during his long years of war. Allah did not grant him long to enjoy the peace he had crafted. The fire in his belly grew hotter and hotter until it consumed him from within. He died on the twenty-ninth day of Muharram in the five hundred and eighty-ninth year of the Hijra – the fourth day of May in the year 1193. I was by his side at the end, along with Shamsa, Imad ad-Din, Ibn Jumay,

Qaraqush, Al-Mashtub and his son Al-Afdal. Shamsa also summoned Faridah, Saladin's first love, from her home in the city. She had become an old, wrinkled woman, but her hair was still fiery red. She held Shamsa while the sultan's wife wept.

All of Damascus was in tears. The people dressed in black sackcloth. When Saladin's body was marched around the city, their lamentations were so loud that it was said they could be heard in Jerusalem. I do not know the truth of this, but I know that no man better merited the tears of his people. Saladin was a righteous man, a mighty warrior, a great king. He united his people. He tamed the Lionheart. He retook Jerusalem and opened it to Franks, Saracens and Jews alike. Before he died, he brought peace to a land of war. I am but a poor man. I cannot build a church or endow a school of learning in honour of Saladin. This chronicle is my tribute to the truest friend I have ever known.

And here, I must put down my quill. This chronicle has taken the last ten years of my life. I am old, my hands crooked, and writing does not come as easy as it once did. Soon I will follow Saladin. He is no doubt in Paradise. Perhaps I shall see him there, if God lets me in. I have not lived a holy life. I was raised in England and came to these lands with blood on my head. Here, I have known love and pain and death. I have been called by many names and titles: Iain of Tatewic, John the Saxon, Canon, Archdeacon, Abbot, Priest, and finally, John of Damascus — Yahya al-Dimashqi. I have more than once made a mockery of the vows I took as a priest. But if my life has not been holy, if my actions have not always been honourable, I have always done as I thought best for the good of the Kingdom and its people. I pray that is enough.

The Chronicle of Yahya al-Dimashqi

Historical Note

E*agle*, the first book in the Saladin Trilogy, was a challenge to write because we know so little about Saladin's early years. The challenge of *Holy War* was precisely the opposite. The Battle of Hattin, the siege of Jerusalem and the Third Crusade are all momentous events, any of which could easily support a novel in its own right. Contemporary chroniclers and modern historians alike have spilled much ink describing them. The challenge of this book was thus what to leave out, and I had to make some painful decisions. I wish I could have kept the Battle of Jacob's Ford, mostly because it was the final battle of the constable Humphrey of Toron, a character of whom I have grown fond. In April 1179, Saladin sent a small army to reconnoitre the area around the ford, where Baldwin was building a castle. The Saracens surprised and routed a Christian army, which was only saved from total destruction by the valiant rearguard action of Humphrey, who later died from his wounds. I also left out Saladin's attack of the Kingdom in 1182, which featured an assault by land and sea on Beirut – the first time Saladin had combined his navy and army in that way. Most notably, I greatly streamlined Saladin's many Al-Jazirah campaigns, which present a long list of alliances made and broken and citadels taken and retaken. Rather than dwell on this complex back and forth, I wanted my story to drive more directly towards the spectacular events at Hattin.

At Hattin, I did my best to faithfully reconstruct a battle that, like most great conflicts of the Middle Ages, has remained stubbornly opaque. Most historians of the day were priests (on the Frankish side) or scribes and poets (on the Muslim side), and thus not overly familiar or concerned with the details of warfare. As a result, historians disagree on some of the most basic details, such as where exactly the Horns were, but what is clear is that the Frankish army made a number of tactical errors. They should never have left the springs at La Sephorie, and once on the march, they should not have made camp short of water. Once they did so, their fate was sealed. The Frankish army's greatest strength was its discipline. Terrible thirst destroyed that discipline, and as soon as the Frankish sergeants broke ranks, the battle was lost.

Hattin and the conquest of Jerusalem that swiftly followed were the high points of Saladin's rule. The clemency he showed at Jerusalem – in sharp contrast to the behaviour of the crusaders almost a hundred years earlier – won him plaudits even amongst his enemies. In my eyes, though, the true measure of Saladin's greatness is found not in his triumphs but in his stubborn resistance to King Richard. The Lionheart was a fascinating, complex man, and a worthy adversary for Saladin. His wars in France had already won him a reputation as a great warrior long before he took up the cross. I tried to capture what precisely made him great: his incredible personal valour and his ability to inspire men through both words and deed. But I did not want to ignore the dark side of Richard. He was a man who twice rebelled against his father and eventually hounded him to death. He used the threat of pogroms to squeeze money out of the English Jews for his crusade. He conducted war through rape and pillage. While such actions might be excused – the Middle Ages was, after all, a brutal time, when such things were common – his massacre of the prisoners at Acre upset even contemporary chroniclers. It was not just the scale of the slaughter that was decried, but the fact that Richard had given his word that the men would be spared. And as brilliant as he was on the battlefield, he seems to have been just as clumsy in his relations with his fellow rulers.

King Philip of France's siege craft, more than anything else, helped bring about the fall of Acre, but Richard seized the lion's share of the credit and in doing so, alienated his fellow king. His domineering attitude also drove off Conrad and the Germans. Richard never suffered defeat in the Holy Land, but neither did he achieve his goal of retaking Jerusalem. He had only himself to blame for that.

Against a lesser opponent, Richard might have succeeded. The first crusaders triumphed because in the face of their early victories, their enemies fell to squabbling amongst themselves. After the Lionheart's successes at Acre and Arsuf, there was the very real possibility that history would repeat itself. But when the men of Egypt, of Syria and of Al-Jazirah wished to go their separate ways, Saladin would not let them. His greatest achievement was holding a fractious army together. It was an achievement that Richard could not match.

Nonetheless, it took its toll on Saladin. This was a man who had devoted his life to defeating the Franks and driving them from Jerusalem, only to see a new enemy come from overseas in overwhelming numbers. He suffered from repeated illnesses, and his collapse outside Mosul, and again during the siege of Acre, is attested by contemporaries. Yet he could not retreat to his palaces to recover. Knowing that his troops would not fight without him, he was forced to stay in the field for years on end in order to beat back his enemies. Had Saladin faltered, even for a moment, it is more than likely Richard would have succeeded.

Saladin's legacy, therefore, is one of both great triumph and steadfastness in the face of adversity. He unified Egypt, Syria and Al-Jazirah, providing a model for a united Middle East. He turned the tide against the Franks, retook Jerusalem and left the Kingdom a shadow of its former glorious self. When England, France and the Holy Roman Empire brought their armies together against him, he fought them to a standstill. For all his military achievements, though, perhaps his greatest moment was one of compromise. In his peace with Richard, he made Jerusalem a city open to all. After a lifetime spent fighting the Franks, he nevertheless understood that the Holy Land had to be shared if there were ever to be peace. That is his greatest legacy of all.